PRAISE FOR
BEAUTIFUL CREATURES

An Instant **NEW YORK TIMES** Bestseller
An **AMAZON** #1 Teen Best Book of the Year
A **BORDERS** Original Voices Selection
An **INDIE NEXT LIST** Selection
A **WILLIAM C. MORRIS YA DEBUT AWARD** Finalist
A **NEW YORK PUBLIC LIBRARY** Book for the Teen Age

"In the Gothic tradition of Anne Rice. . . . Give this to fans of
Stephenie Meyer's *Twilight* or HBO's *True Blood* series."
— SCHOOL LIBRARY JOURNAL

"Gorgeously crafted, atmospheric, and original."
— MELISSA MARR, *New York Times* bestselling
author of **WICKED LOVELY**

"Smart, textured and romantic. . . . Ethan's wry narrative
voice will resonate with readers of John Green as well as
the hordes of supernatural-romance fans looking
for the next book to sink their teeth into."
— KIRKUS REVIEWS

"A lush Southern gothic."
— HOLLY BLACK, *New York Times* bestselling
author of **TITHE: A MODERN FAERIE TALE**

"[Readers] will be swept up by the haunting and detailed
atmosphere, the conventions and strictures of Southern life,
and a compelling and dimensional mythology."
— PUBLISHERS WEEKLY

"A hauntingly delicious dark fantasy."
— **CASSANDRA CLARE,** *New York Times* bestselling
author of **CITY OF BONES**

"This book has it all: a creepy setting, a deadly curse,
reincarnation, spells, witchcraft and voodoo, plus characters
that simply will not let the reader put the book down until
finished. . . . Who could ask for more? A sequel? Please!"
— **VOYA**

"Like a thick, hot Carolina summer, this story seeps
into you until it's all you can think about."
— **CARRIE RYAN,** *New York Times* bestselling
author of **THE FOREST OF HANDS AND TEETH**

"Otherworldly."
— **BOOKLIST**

"A multi-faceted Southern gothic saga that culminates
in a dramatic good-versus-evil showdown."
— **HORN BOOK GUIDE**

"Exactly the right blend of dark suspense and romance."
— **NEWARK STAR LEDGER**

"*Beautiful Creatures* is a page-turner that will keep
readers up until the wee hours of the morning."
— **DESERET NEWS**

BEAUTIFUL CREATURES

BY

KAMI GARCIA &
MARGARET STOHL

LITTLE, BROWN AND COMPANY
New York • Boston

Little, Brown and Company

Hachette Book Group
237 Park Avenue, New York, NY 10017
Visit our website at www.lb-teens.com

Little, Brown and Company is a division of Hachette Book Group, Inc.
The Little, Brown name and logo are trademarks of Hachette Book Group, Inc.

First Paperback Edition: September 2010
First published in hardcover in December 2009 by Little, Brown and Company

The characters and events portrayed in this book are fictitious. Any similarity to real
persons, living or dead, is coincidental and not intended by the authors. To the extent any
real names of individuals, locations, or organizations are included in the book, they are
used fictitiously and not intended to be taken otherwise.

STRENGTH TO LOVE and LETTER FROM BIRMINGHAM JAIL speeches by DR.
MARTIN LUTHER KING JR. copyright © 1963 by Dr. Martin Luther King Jr.; copyright
renewed © 1991 by Coretta Scott King. Reprinted by arrangement with the heirs to the estate
of Martin Luther King Jr., c/o Writers House New York, NY.

Library of Congress Cataloging-in-Publication Data

Garcia, Kami.
Beautiful creatures / by Kami Garcia and Margaret Stohl.—1st ed.
p. cm.
Summary: In a small South Carolina town, where it seems little has changed since the Civil
War, sixteen-year-old Ethan is powerfully drawn to Lena, a new classmate with whom he
shares a psychic connection and whose family hides a dark secret that may be revealed on
her sixteenth birthday.
ISBN 978-0-316-04267-3 (hc) / ISBN 978-0-316-07703-3 (pb)
[1. Supernatural—Fiction. 2. Psychic ability—Fiction. 3. Love—Fiction. 4. High
schools—Fiction. 5. Schools—Fiction. 6. Dreams—Ficition. 7. Recluses—Fiction.
8. South Carolina—Fiction. 9. South Carolina—History—Civil War, 1861–1865—
Fiction.] I. Stohl, Margaret, 1967– II. Title.
PZ7.G155627Bed 2010   [Fic]—dc22   2008051306

10 9 8 7 6 5 4 3 2 1
RRD-H
Book design by David Caplan
Printed in the United States of America

For
Nick & Stella
Emma, May & Kate
and
all our casters & outcasters, everywhere.
There are more of us than you think.

Darkness cannot drive out darkness;
only light can do that.
Hate cannot drive out hate;
only love can do that.

— MARTIN LUTHER KING JR.

The Middle of Nowhere

There were only two kinds of people in our town. "The stupid and the stuck," my father had affectionately classified our neighbors. "The ones who are bound to stay or too dumb to go. Everyone else finds a way out." There was no question which one he was, but I'd never had the courage to ask why. My father was a writer, and we lived in Gatlin, South Carolina, because the Wates always had, since my great-great-great-great-granddad, Ellis Wate, fought and died on the other side of the Santee River during the Civil War.

Only folks down here didn't call it the Civil War. Everyone under the age of sixty called it the War Between the States, while everyone over sixty called it the War of Northern Aggression, as if somehow the North had baited the South into war over a bad bale of cotton. Everyone, that is, except my family. We called it the Civil War.

1

Just another reason I couldn't wait to get out of here.

Gatlin wasn't like the small towns you saw in the movies, unless it was a movie from about fifty years ago. We were too far from Charleston to have a Starbucks or a McDonald's. All we had was a Dar-ee Keen, since the Gentrys were too cheap to buy all new letters when they bought the Dairy King. The library still had a card catalog, the high school still had chalkboards, and our community pool was Lake Moultrie, warm brown water and all. You could see a movie at the Cineplex about the same time it came out on DVD, but you had to hitch a ride over to Summerville, by the community college. The shops were on Main, the good houses were on River, and everyone else lived south of Route 9, where the pavement disintegrated into chunky concrete stubble— terrible for walking, but perfect for throwing at angry possums, the meanest animals alive. You never saw that in the movies.

Gatlin wasn't a complicated place; Gatlin was Gatlin. The neighbors kept watch from their porches in the unbearable heat, sweltering in plain sight. But there was no point. Nothing ever changed. Tomorrow would be the first day of school, my sophomore year at Stonewall Jackson High, and I already knew everything that was going to happen—where I would sit, who I would talk to, the jokes, the girls, who would park where.

There were no surprises in Gatlin County. We were pretty much the epicenter of the middle of nowhere.

At least, that's what I thought, when I closed my battered copy of *Slaughterhouse-Five*, clicked off my iPod, and turned out the light on the last night of summer.

Turns out, I couldn't have been more wrong.
There was a curse.
There was a girl.
And in the end, there was a grave.
I never even saw it coming.

Dream On

Falling.

I was free falling, tumbling through the air.

"Ethan!"

She called to me, and just the sound of her voice made my heart race.

"Help me!"

She was falling, too. I stretched out my arm, trying to catch her. I reached out, but all I caught was air. There was no ground beneath my feet, and I was clawing at mud. We touched fingertips and I saw green sparks in the darkness.

Then she slipped through my fingers, and all I could feel was loss.

Lemons and rosemary. I could smell her, even then.

But I couldn't catch her.

And I couldn't live without her.

I sat up with a jerk, trying to catch my breath.

"Ethan Wate! Wake up! I won't have you bein' late on the first day a school." I could hear Amma's voice calling from downstairs.

My eyes focused on a patch of dim light in the darkness. I could hear the distant drum of the rain against our old plantation shutters. It must be raining. It must be morning. I must be in my room.

My room was hot and damp, from the rain. Why was my window open?

My head was throbbing. I fell back down on the bed, and the dream receded as it always did. I was safe in my room, in our ancient house, in the same creaking mahogany bed where six generations of Wates had probably slept before me, where people didn't fall through black holes made of mud, and nothing ever actually happened.

I stared up at my plaster ceiling, painted the color of the sky to keep the carpenter bees from nesting. What was wrong with me?

I'd been having the dream for months now. Even though I couldn't remember all of it, the part I remembered was always the same. The girl was falling. I was falling. I had to hold on, but I couldn't. If I let go, something terrible would happen to her. But that's the thing. I couldn't let go. I couldn't lose her. It was like I was in love with her, even though I didn't know her. Kind of like love *before* first sight.

Which seemed crazy because she was just a girl in a dream. I didn't even know what she looked like. I had been having the dream for months, but in all that time I had never seen her face, or I couldn't remember it. All I knew was that I had the same sick feeling inside every time I lost her. She slipped through my fingers, and my stomach dropped right out of me—the way you feel when you're on a roller coaster and the car takes a big drop.

Butterflies in your stomach. That was such a crappy metaphor. More like killer bees.

Maybe I was losing it, or maybe I just needed a shower. My earphones were still around my neck, and when I glanced down at my iPod, I saw a song I didn't recognize.

Sixteen Moons.

What was that? I clicked on it. The melody was haunting. I couldn't place the voice, but I felt like I'd heard it before.

Sixteen moons, sixteen years
Sixteen of your deepest fears
Sixteen times you dreamed my tears
Falling, falling through the years . . .

It was moody, creepy—almost hypnotic.

"Ethan Lawson Wate!" I could hear Amma calling up over the music.

I switched it off and sat up in bed, yanking back the covers. My sheets felt like they were full of sand, but I knew better.

It was dirt. And my fingernails were caked with black mud, just like the last time I had the dream.

I crumpled up the sheet, pushing it down in the hamper under yesterday's sweaty practice jersey. I got in the shower and tried to forget about it as I scrubbed my hands, and the last black bits of my dream disappeared down the drain. If I didn't think about it, it wasn't happening. That was my approach to most things the past few months.

But not when it came to her. I couldn't help it. I always thought about her. I kept coming back to that same dream, even though I couldn't explain it. So that was my secret, all there was to tell. I was sixteen years old, I was falling in love with a girl who didn't exist, and I was slowly losing my mind.

No matter how hard I scrubbed, I couldn't get my heart to stop pounding. And over the smell of the Ivory soap and the Stop & Shop shampoo, I could still smell it. Just barely, but I knew it was there.

Lemons and rosemary.

I came downstairs to the reassuring sameness of everything. At the breakfast table, Amma slid the same old blue and white china plate—Dragonware, my mom had called it—of fried eggs, bacon, buttered toast, and grits in front of me. Amma was our housekeeper, more like my grandmother, except she was smarter and more ornery than my real grandmother. Amma had practically raised me, and she felt it was her personal mission to grow me another foot or so, even though I was already 6'2". This morning I was strangely starving, like I hadn't eaten in a week. I shoveled an egg and two pieces of bacon off my plate, feeling better already. I grinned at her with my mouth full.

"Don't hold out on me, Amma. It's the first day of school." She slammed a giant glass of OJ and a bigger one of milk—whole milk, the only kind we drink around here—in front of me.

"We out of chocolate milk?" I drank chocolate milk the way some people drank Coke or coffee. Even in the morning, I was always looking for my next sugar fix.

7

"A. C. C. L. I. M. A. T. E." Amma had a crossword for everything, the bigger the better, and liked to use them. The way she spelled the words out on you letter by letter, it felt like she was paddling you in the head, every time. "As in, get used to it. And don't you think about settin' one foot out that door till you drink the milk I gave you."

"Yes, ma'am."

"I see you dressed up." I hadn't. I was wearing jeans and a faded T-shirt, like I did most days. They all said different things; today it was *Harley Davidson*. And the same black Chuck Taylors I'd had going on three years now.

"I thought you were gonna cut that hair." She said it like a scolding, but I recognized it for what it really was: plain old affection.

"When did I say that?"

"Don't you know the eyes are the windows to the soul?"

"Maybe I don't want anyone to have a window into mine."

Amma punished me with another plate of bacon. She was barely five feet tall and probably even older than the Dragonware, though every birthday she insisted she was turning fifty-three. But Amma was anything but a mild-mannered old lady. She was the absolute authority in my house.

"Well, don't think you're goin' out in this weather with wet hair. I don't like how this storm feels. Like somethin' bad's been kicked up into the wind, and there's no stoppin' a day like that. It has a will a its own."

I rolled my eyes. Amma had her own way of thinking about things. When she was in one of these moods, my mom used to call it going dark—religion and superstition all mixed up, like it can only be in the South. When Amma went dark, it was just

8

better to stay out of her way. Just like it was better to leave her charms on the windowsills and the dolls she made in the drawers where she put them.

I scooped up another forkful of egg and finished the breakfast of champions—eggs, freezer jam, and bacon, all smashed into a toast sandwich. As I shoved it into my mouth, I glanced down the hallway out of habit. My dad's study door was already shut. My dad wrote at night and slept on the old sofa in his study all day. It had been like that since my mom died last April. He might as well be a vampire; that's what my Aunt Caroline had said after she stayed with us that spring. I had probably missed my chance to see him until tomorrow. There was no opening that door once it was closed.

I heard a honk from the street. Link. I grabbed my ratty black backpack and ran out the door into the rain. It could have been seven at night as easily as seven in the morning, that's how dark the sky was. The weather had been weird for a few days now.

Link's car, the Beater, was in the street, motor sputtering, music blasting. I'd ridden to school with Link every day since kindergarten, when we became best friends after he gave me half his Twinkie on the bus. I only found out later it had fallen on the floor. Even though we had both gotten our licenses this summer, Link was the one with the car, if you could call it that.

At least the Beater's engine was drowning out the storm.

Amma stood on the porch, her arms crossed disapprovingly. "Don't you play that loud music here, Wesley Jefferson Lincoln. Don't think I won't call your mamma and tell her what you were doin' in the basement all summer when you were nine years old."

9

Link winced. Not many people called him by his real name, except his mother and Amma. "Yes, ma'am." The screen door slammed. He laughed, spinning his tires on the wet asphalt as we pulled away from the curb. Like we were making a getaway, which was pretty much how he always drove. Except we never got away.

"What did you do in my basement when you were nine years old?"

"What didn't I do in your basement when I was nine years old?" Link turned down the music, which was good, because it was terrible and he was about to ask me how I liked it, like he did every day. The tragedy of his band, Who Shot Lincoln, was that none of them could actually play an instrument or sing. But all he could talk about was playing the drums and moving to New York after graduation and record deals that would probably never happen. And by probably, I mean he was more likely to sink a three-pointer, blindfolded and drunk, from the parking lot of the gym.

Link wasn't about to go to college, but he still had one up on me. He knew what he wanted to do, even if it was a long shot. All I had was a whole shoebox full of college brochures I couldn't show my dad. I didn't care which colleges they were, as long as they were at least a thousand miles from Gatlin.

I didn't want to end up like my dad, living in the same house, in the same small town I'd grown up in, with the same people who had never dreamed their way out of here.

—☙

On either side of us, dripping old Victorians lined the street, almost the same as the day they were built over a hundred years ago. My street was called Cotton Bend because these old houses used to back up to miles and miles of plantation cotton fields. Now they just backed up to Route 9, which was about the only thing that had changed around here.

I grabbed a stale doughnut from the box on the floor of the car. "Did you upload a weird song onto my iPod last night?"

"What song? What do you think a this one?" Link turned up his latest demo track.

"I think it needs work. Like all your other songs." It was the same thing I said every day, more or less.

"Yeah, well, your face will need some work after I give you a good beatin'." It was the same thing he said every day, more or less.

I flipped through my playlist. "The song, I think it was called something like *Sixteen Moons*."

"Don't know what you're talkin' about." It wasn't there. The song was gone, but I had just listened to it this morning. And I knew I hadn't imagined it because it was still stuck in my head.

"If you wanna hear a song, I'll play you a new one." Link looked down to cue the track.

"Hey, man, keep your eyes on the road."

But he didn't look up, and out of the corner of my eye, I saw a strange car pass in front of us. . . .

For a second, the sounds of the road and the rain and Link dissolved into silence, and it was like everything was moving in slow motion. I couldn't drag my eyes away from the car. It was just a feeling, not anything I could describe. And then it slid past us, turning the other way.

I didn't recognize the car. I had never seen it before. You can't imagine how impossible that is, because I knew every single car in town. There were no tourists this time of year. They wouldn't take the chance during hurricane season.

This car was long and black, like a hearse. Actually, I was pretty sure it was a hearse.

Maybe it was an omen. Maybe this year was going to be worse than I thought.

"Here it is. 'Black Bandanna.' This song's gonna make me a star."

By the time he looked up, the car was gone.

⊰ 9.02 ⊱

New Girl

Eight streets. That's how far we had to go to get from Cotton Bend to Jackson High. Turns out I could relive my entire life, going up and down eight streets, and eight streets were just enough to put a strange black hearse out of your mind. Maybe that's why I didn't mention it to Link.

We passed the Stop & Shop, otherwise known as the Stop & Steal. It was the only grocery store in town, and the closest thing we had to a 7-Eleven. So every time you were hanging out with your friends out front, you had to hope you weren't going to run into someone's mom shopping for dinner, or worse, Amma.

I noticed the familiar Grand Prix parked out front. "Uh-oh. Fatty's camped out already." He was sitting in the driver's seat, reading *The Stars and Stripes*.

"Maybe he didn't see us." Link was watching the rearview mirror, tense.

"Maybe we're screwed."

Fatty was Stonewall Jackson High School's truant officer, as well as a proud member of the Gatlin police force. His girlfriend, Amanda, worked at the Stop & Steal, and Fatty was parked out front most mornings, waiting for the baked goods to be delivered. Which was pretty inconvenient if you were always late, like Link and me.

You couldn't go to Jackson High without knowing Fatty's routine as well as your own class schedule. Today, Fatty waved us on, without even looking up from the sports section. He was giving us a pass.

"Sports section and a sticky bun. Know what that means."

"We've got five minutes."

We rolled the Beater into the school parking lot in neutral, hoping to slink past the attendance office unnoticed. But it was still pouring outside, so by the time we got into the building, we were soaked and our sneakers were squeaking so loud we might as well have just stopped in there anyway.

"Ethan Wate! Wesley Lincoln!"

We stood dripping in the office, waiting for our detention slips.

"Late for the first day a school. Your mamma is goin' to have a few choice words for you, Mr. Lincoln. And don't you look so smug, Mr. Wate. Amma's gonna tan your hide."

Miss Hester was right. Amma would know I'd shown up late about five minutes from now, if she didn't already. That's what it was like around here. My mom used to say Carlton Eaton, the postmaster, read any letter that looked half-interesting. He didn't even bother to seal them back up anymore. It's not like there was any actual news. Every house had its secrets, but everyone on the street knew them. Even that was no secret.

"Miss Hester, I was just drivin' slow, on account a the rain." Link tried to turn on the charm. Miss Hester pulled down her glasses a little and looked back at Link, uncharmed. The little chain that held her glasses around her neck swung back and forth.

"I don't have time to chat with you boys right now. I'm busy fillin' out your detention slips, which is where you'll be spendin' this afternoon," she said, as she handed each of us our blue slip.

She was busy all right. You could smell the nail polish before we even turned the corner. Welcome back.

In Gatlin, the first day of school never really changes. The teachers, who all knew you from church, decided if you were stupid or smart by the time you were in kindergarten. I was smart because my parents were professors. Link was stupid, because he crunched up the pages of the Good Book during Scripture Chase, and threw up once during the Christmas pageant. Because I was smart, I got good grades on my papers; because Link was stupid, he got bad ones. I guess nobody bothered to read them. Sometimes I wrote random stuff in the middle of my essays, just to see if my teachers would say anything. No one ever did.

Unfortunately, the same principle didn't apply to multiple-choice tests. In first-period English, I discovered my seven-hundred-year-old teacher, whose name really was Mrs. English, had expected us to read *To Kill a Mockingbird* over the summer,

15

so I flunked the first quiz. Great. I had read the book about two years ago. It was one of my mom's favorites, but that was a while ago and I was fuzzy on the details.

A little-known fact about me: I read all the time. Books were the one thing that got me out of Gatlin, even if it was only for a little while. I had a map on my wall, and every time I read about a place I wanted to go, I marked it on the map. New York was *Catcher in the Rye*. *Into the Wild* got me to Alaska. When I read *On the Road*, I added Chicago, Denver, L.A., and Mexico City. Kerouac could get you pretty much everywhere. Every few months, I drew a line to connect the marks. A thin green line I'd follow on a road trip, the summer before college, if I ever got out of this town. I kept the map and the reading thing to myself. Around here, books and basketball didn't mix.

Chemistry wasn't much better. Mr. Hollenback doomed me to be lab partners with Ethan-Hating Emily, also known as Emily Asher, who had despised me ever since the formal last year, when I made the mistake of wearing my Chuck Taylors with my tux and letting my dad drive us in the rusty Volvo. The one broken window that permanently wouldn't roll up had destroyed her perfectly curled blond prom-hair, and by the time we got to the gym she looked like Marie Antoinette with bedhead. Emily didn't speak to me for the rest of the night and sent Savannah Snow to dump me three steps from the punch bowl. That was pretty much the end of that.

It was a never-ending source of amusement for the guys, who kept expecting us to get back together. The thing they didn't know was, I wasn't into girls like Emily. She was pretty, but that was it. And looking at her didn't make up for having to listen to what came out of her mouth. I wanted someone different, someone I could talk to about something other than parties and getting crowned at winter formal. A girl who was smart, or funny, or at least a decent lab partner.

Maybe a girl like that was the real dream, but a dream was still better than a nightmare. Even if the nightmare was wearing a cheerleading skirt.

I survived chemistry, but my day only got worse from there. Apparently, I was taking U.S. History again this year, which was the only history taught at Jackson, making the name redundant. I would be spending my second consecutive year studying the "War of Northern Aggression" with Mr. Lee, no relation. But as we all knew, in spirit Mr. Lee and the famous Confederate general were one and the same. Mr. Lee was one of the few teachers who actually hated me. Last year, on a dare from Link, I had written a paper called "The War of Southern Aggression," and Mr. Lee had given me a D. Guess the teachers actually did read the papers sometimes, after all.

I found a seat in the back next to Link, who was busy copying notes from whatever class he had slept through before this one. But he stopped writing as soon as I sat down. "Dude, did you hear?"

"Hear what?"

"There's a new girl at Jackson."

"There are a ton of new girls, a whole freshman class of them, moron."

"I'm not talkin' about the freshmen. There's a new girl in *our* class." At any other high school, a new girl in the sophomore class wouldn't be news. But this was Jackson, and we hadn't had a new girl in school since third grade, when Kelly Wix moved in with her grandparents after her dad was arrested for running a gambling operation out of their basement in Lake City.

"Who is she?"

"Don't know. I've got civics second period with all the band geeks, and they didn't know anythin' except she plays the violin, or somethin'. Wonder if she's hot." Link had a one-track mind, like most guys. The difference was, Link's track led directly to his mouth.

"So she's a band geek?"

"No. A musician. Maybe she shares my love a classical music."

"Classical music?" The only classical music Link had ever heard was in the dentist's office.

"You know, the classics. Pink Floyd. Black Sabbath. The Stones." I started laughing.

"Mr. Lincoln. Mr. Wate. I'm sorry to interrupt your conversation, but I'd like to get started if it's a'right with you boys." Mr. Lee's tone was just as sarcastic as last year, and his greasy comb-over and pit stains just as bad. He passed out copies of the same syllabus he had probably been using for ten years. Participating in an actual Civil War reenactment would be required. Of course it would. I could just borrow a uniform from one of my relatives who participated in reenactments for fun on the weekends. Lucky me.

After the bell rang, Link and I hung out in the hall by our lockers, hoping to get a look at the new girl. To hear him talk, she was already his future soul mate and band mate and probably a few other kinds of mates I didn't even want to hear about. But the only thing we got a look at was too much of Charlotte Chase in a jean skirt two sizes too small. Which meant we weren't going to find out anything until lunch, because our next class was ASL, American Sign Language, and it was strictly no talking allowed. No one was good enough at signing to even spell "new girl," especially since ASL was the one class we had in common with the rest of the Jackson basketball team.

I'd been on the team since eighth grade, when I grew six inches in one summer and ended up at least a head taller than everyone else in my class. Besides, you had to do something normal when both of your parents were professors. It turned out I was good at basketball. I always seemed to know where the players on the other team were going to pass the ball, and it gave me a place to sit in the cafeteria every day. At Jackson, that was worth something.

Today that seat was worth even more because Shawn Bishop, our point guard, had actually seen the new girl. Link asked the only question that mattered to any of them. "So, is she hot?"

"Pretty hot."

"Savannah Snow hot?"

As if on cue, Savannah—the standard by which all other girls at Jackson were measured—walked into the cafeteria, arm in arm with Ethan-Hating Emily, and we all watched because Savannah was 5'8" worth of the most perfect legs you've ever seen. Emily and Savannah were almost one person, even when they weren't in their cheerleading uniforms. Blond hair, fake tans, flip-flops, and jean skirts so short they could pass for belts. Savannah was the legs, but Emily was the one all the guys tried to get a look at in her bikini top, at the lake in the summer. They never seemed to have any books, just tiny metallic bags tucked under one arm, with barely enough room for a cell phone, for the few occasions when Emily actually stopped texting.

Their differences boiled down to their respective positions on

19

the cheer squad. Savannah was the captain, and a base: one of the girls who held up two more tiers of cheerleaders in the Wildcats' famous pyramid. Emily was a flyer, the girl at the top of the pyramid, the one thrown five or six feet into the air to complete a flip or some other crazy cheer stunt that could easily result in a broken neck. Emily would risk anything to stay on top of that pyramid. Savannah didn't need to. When Emily got tossed, the pyramid went on fine without her. When Savannah moved an inch, the whole thing came tumbling down.

Ethan-Hating Emily noticed us staring and scowled at me. The guys laughed. Emory Watkins clapped a hand on my back. "In like sin, Wate. You know Emily, the more she glares, the more she cares."

I didn't want to think about Emily today. I wanted to think about the opposite of Emily. Ever since Link had brought it up in history, it had stuck with me. The new girl. The possibility of someone different, from somewhere different. Maybe someone with a bigger life than ours, and, I guess, mine.

Maybe even someone I'd dreamed about. I knew it was a fantasy, but I wanted to believe it.

"So did y'all hear about the new girl?" Savannah sat down on Earl Petty's lap. Earl was our team captain and Savannah's on-again, off-again boyfriend. Right now, they were on. He rubbed his hands over her orangey-colored legs, just high enough so you didn't know where to look.

"Shawn was just fillin' us in. Says she's hot. You gonna put her on the squad?" Link grabbed a couple of Tater Tots off my tray.

"Hardly. You should see what she's wearin'." Strike One.

"And how pale she is." Strike Two. You could never be too thin or too tan, as far as Savannah was concerned.

Emily sat down next to Emory, leaning over the table just a little too much. "Did he tell you *who* she is?"

"What do you mean?"

Emily paused for dramatic effect.

"She's Old Man Ravenwood's niece."

She didn't need the pause for this one. It was like she had sucked the air right out of the room. A couple of the guys started laughing. They thought she was kidding, but I could tell she wasn't.

Strike Three. She was out. So far out, I couldn't even picture her anymore. The possibility of my dream girl showing up disappeared before I could even imagine our first date. I was doomed to three more years of Emily Ashers.

Macon Melchizedek Ravenwood was the town shut-in. Let's just say, I remembered enough of *To Kill a Mockingbird* to know Old Man Ravenwood made Boo Radley look like a social butterfly. He lived in a run-down old house, on Gatlin's oldest and most infamous plantation, and I don't think anyone in town had seen him since before I was born, maybe longer.

"Are you serious?" asked Link.

"Totally. Carlton Eaton told my mom yesterday when he brought by our mail."

Savannah nodded. "My mamma heard the same thing. She moved in with Old Man Ravenwood a couple a days ago, from Virginia, or Maryland, I don't remember."

They all kept talking about her, her clothes and her hair and her uncle and what a freak she probably was. That's the thing I hated most about Gatlin. The way everyone had something to say about everything you said or did or, in this case, wore. I just stared at the noodles on my tray, swimming in runny orange liquid that didn't look much like cheese.

Two years, eight months, and counting. I had to get out of this town.

_____⟨⟩

After school, the gym was being used for cheerleading tryouts. The rain had finally let up, so basketball practice was on the outside court, with its cracked concrete and bent rims and puddles of water from the morning rain. You had to be careful not to hit the fissure that ran down the middle like the Grand Canyon. Aside from that, you could almost see the whole parking lot from the court, and watch most of the prime social action of Jackson High while you warmed up.

Today I had the hot hand. I was seven-for-seven from the free throw line, but so was Earl, matching me shot for shot.

Swish. Eight. It seemed like I could just look at the net, and the ball would sail through. Some days were like that.

Swish. Nine. Earl was annoyed. I could tell by the way he was bouncing the ball harder and harder every time I made a shot. He was our other center. Our unspoken agreement was: I let him be in charge, and he didn't hassle me if I didn't feel like hanging out at the Stop & Steal every day after practice. There were only so many ways you could talk about the same girls and so many Slim Jims you could eat.

Swish. Ten. I couldn't miss. Maybe it was just genetics. Maybe it was something else. I hadn't figured it out, but since my mom died, I had stopped trying. It was a wonder I made it to practice at all.

Swish. Eleven. Earl grunted behind me, bouncing the ball even harder. I tried not to smile and looked over to the parking lot as I took the next shot. I saw a tangle of long black hair, behind the wheel of a long black car.

A hearse. I froze.

Then, she turned, and through the open window, I could see a girl looking in my direction. At least, I thought I could. The basketball hit the rim, and bounced off toward the fence. Behind me, I heard the familiar sound.

Swish. Twelve. Earl Petty could relax.

As the car pulled away, I looked down the court. The rest of the guys were standing there, like they'd just seen a ghost.

"Was that—?"

Billy Watts, our forward, nodded, holding onto the chain-link fence with one hand. "Old Man Ravenwood's niece."

Shawn tossed the ball at him. "Yep. Just like they said. Drivin' his hearse."

Emory shook his head. "She's hot all right. What a waste."

They went back to playing ball, but by the time Earl took his next shot, it had started to rain again. Thirty seconds later, we were caught in a downpour, the heaviest rain we'd seen all day. I stood there, letting the rain hammer down on me. My wet hair hung in my eyes, blocking out the rest of the school, the team.

The bad omen wasn't just a hearse. It was a girl.

For a few minutes, I had let myself hope. That maybe this year wouldn't be just like every other year, that something would change. That I would have someone to talk to, someone who really got me.

But all I had was a good day on the court, and that had never been enough.

A Hole in the Sky

Fried chicken, mashed potatoes and gravy, string beans, and biscuits—all sitting angry and cold and congealed on the stove where Amma had left them. Usually, she kept my dinner warm for me until I got home from practice, but not today. I was in a lot of trouble. Amma was furious, sitting at the table eating Red Hots, and scratching away at the *New York Times* crossword. My dad secretly subscribed to the Sunday edition, because the ones in *The Stars and Stripes* had too many spelling mistakes, and the ones in *Reader's Digest* were too short. I don't know how he got it past Carlton Eaton, who would've made sure the whole town knew we were too good for *The Stars and Stripes*, but there was nothing my dad wouldn't do for Amma.

She slid the plate in my direction, looking at me without looking at me. I shoveled cold mashed potatoes and chicken into my mouth. There was nothing Amma hated like food left on your plate. I tried to keep my distance from the point of her special black # 2 pencil, used only for her crosswords, kept so sharp it could actually draw blood. Tonight it might.

I listened to the steady patter of rain on the roof. There wasn't another sound in the room. Amma rapped her pencil on the table.

"Nine letters. Confinement or pain exacted for wrongdoin'." She shot me another look. I shoveled a spoonful of potatoes into my mouth. I knew what was coming. Nine across.

"C. A. S. T. I. G. A. T. E. As in, punish. As in, if you can't get yourself to school on time, you won't be leavin' this house."

I wondered who had called to tell her I was late, or more likely who hadn't called. She sharpened her pencil, even though it was already sharp, grinding it into her old automatic sharpener on the counter. She was still pointedly Not Looking at me, which was even worse than staring me right in the eye.

I walked over to where she was grinding and put my arm around her, giving her a good squeeze. "Come on, Amma. Don't be mad. It was pouring this morning. You wouldn't want us speeding in the rain, would you?"

She raised an eyebrow, but her expression softened. "Well, it looks like it'll be rainin' from now until the day after you cut that hair, so you better figure out a way to get yourself to school before that bell rings."

"Yes, ma'am." I gave her one last squeeze and went back to my cold potatoes. "You'll never believe what happened today. We got a new girl in our class." I don't know why I said it. I guess it was still on my mind.

"You think I don't know about Lena Duchannes?" I choked on my biscuit. Lena Duchannes. Pronounced, in the South, to rhyme with rain. The way Amma rolled it out, you would have thought the word had an extra syllable. Du-kay-yane.

"Is that her name? Lena?"

Amma pushed a glass of chocolate milk in my direction. "Yes and no and it's none a your business. You shouldn't be messin' with things you don't know anything about, Ethan Wate."

Amma always spoke in riddles, and she never gave you anything more than that. I hadn't been to her house in Wader's Creek since I was a kid, but I knew most of the people in town had. Amma was the most respected tarot card reader within a hundred miles of Gatlin, just like her mother before her and her grandmother before her. Six generations of card readers. Gatlin was full of God-fearing Baptists, Methodists, and Pentecostals, but they couldn't resist the lure of the cards, the possibility of changing the course of their own destiny. Because that's what they believed a powerful reader could do. And Amma was nothing if not a force to be reckoned with.

Sometimes I'd find one of her homemade charms in my sock drawer or hanging above the door of my father's study. I had only asked what they were for once. My dad teased Amma whenever he found one, but I noticed that he never took any of them down. "Better safe than sorry." I guess he meant safe from Amma, who could make you plenty sorry.

"Did you hear anything else about her?"

"You watch yourself. One day you're gonna pick a hole in the sky and the universe is gonna fall right through. Then we'll all be in a fix."

My father shuffled into the kitchen in his pajamas. He poured himself a cup of coffee and took a box of Shredded Wheat out of the pantry. I could see the yellow wax earplugs still stuck in his ears. The Shredded Wheat meant he was about to start his day. The earplugs meant it hadn't really started yet.

I leaned over and whispered to Amma, "What did you hear?"

She yanked my plate away and took it to the sink. She rinsed some bones that looked like pork shoulder, which was weird since we'd had chicken tonight, and put them on a plate. "That's none a your concern. What I'd like to know is why you're so interested."

I shrugged. "I'm not, really. Just curious."

"You know what they say about curiosity." She stuck a fork in my piece of buttermilk pie. Then she shot me the Look, and was gone.

Even my father noticed the kitchen door swinging in her wake, and pulled an earplug out of one ear. "How was school?"

"Fine."

"What did you do to Amma?"

"I was late for school."

He studied my face. I studied his.

"Number 2?"

I nodded.

"Sharp?"

"Started out sharp and then she sharpened it." I sighed. My dad almost smiled, which was rare. I felt a surge of relief, maybe even accomplishment.

"Know how many times I sat at this old table while she pulled a pencil on me when I was a kid?" he asked, though it wasn't really a question. The table, nicked and flecked with paint and glue and marker from all the Wates leading up to me, was one of the oldest things in the house.

I smiled. My dad picked up his cereal bowl and waved his

spoon in my direction. Amma had raised my father, a fact I'd been reminded of every time I even thought about sassing her when I was a kid.

"M. Y. R. I. A. D." He spelled out the word as he dumped his bowl into the sink. "P. L. E. T. H. O. R. A. As in, more than you, Ethan Wate."

As he stepped into the kitchen light, the half-smile faded to a quarter, and then it was gone. He looked even worse than usual. The shadows on his face were darker, and you could see the bones under his skin. His face was a pallid green from never leaving the house. He looked a little bit like a living corpse, as he had for months now. It was hard to remember that he was the same person who used to sit with me for hours on the shores of Lake Moultrie, eating chicken salad sandwiches and teaching me how to cast a fishing line. "Back and forth. Ten and two. Ten and two. Like the hands of a clock." The last five months had been hard for him. He had really loved my mother. But so had I.

My dad picked up his coffee and started to shuffle back toward his study. It was time to face facts. Maybe Macon Ravenwood wasn't the only town shut-in. I didn't think our town was big enough for two Boo Radleys. But this was the closest thing to a conversation we'd had in months, and I didn't want him to go.

"How's the book coming?" I blurted out. Stay and talk to me. That's what I meant.

He looked surprised, then shrugged. "It's coming. Still got a lot of work to do." He couldn't. That's what he meant.

"Macon Ravenwood's niece just moved to town." I said the words just as he put his earplug back in. Out of sync, our usual timing. Come to think of it, that had been my timing with most people lately.

My dad pulled out the earplug, sighed, and pulled out the other. "What?" He was already walking back to his study. The meter on our conversation was running out.

"Macon Ravenwood, what do you know about him?"

"Same as everyone else, I guess. He's a recluse. He hasn't left Ravenwood Manor in years, as far as I know." He pushed open the study door and stepped over the threshold, but I didn't follow him. I just stood in the doorway.

I never set foot in there. Once, just once, when I was seven years old, my dad had caught me reading his novel before he had finished revising it. His study was a dark, frightening place. There was a painting that he always kept covered with a sheet over the threadbare Victorian sofa. I knew never to ask what was underneath the sheet. Past the sofa, close to the window, my father's desk was carved mahogany, another antique that had been handed down along with our house, from generation to generation. And books, old leather-bound books that were so heavy they rested on a huge wooden stand when they were open. Those were the things that kept us bound to Gatlin, and bound to Wate's Landing, just as they had bound my ancestors for more than a hundred years.

On the desk was his manuscript. It had been sitting there, in an open cardboard box, and I just had to know what was in it. My dad wrote gothic horror, so there wasn't much he wrote that was okay for a seven-year-old to read. But every house in Gatlin was full of secrets, just like the South itself, and my house was no exception, even back then.

My dad had found me, curled up on the couch in his study, pages spread all around me like a bottle rocket had exploded in the box. I didn't know enough to cover my tracks, something I learned pretty quickly after that. I just remember him yelling at me, and my mom coming out to find me crying in the old magnolia tree in our backyard. "Some things are private, Ethan. Even for grown-ups."

I had just wanted to know. That had always been my problem. Even now. I wanted to know why my dad never came out of his study. I wanted to know why we couldn't leave this worthless old house just because a million Wates had lived here before us, especially now that my mom was gone.

But not tonight. Tonight I just wanted to remember chicken salad sandwiches and ten and two and a time when my dad ate his Shredded Wheat in the kitchen, joking around with me. I fell asleep remembering.

Before the bell even rang the next day, Lena Duchannes was all everyone at Jackson could talk about. Somehow between storms and power outages, Loretta Snow and Eugenie Asher, Savannah's and Emily's mothers, had managed to get supper on the table and call just about everyone in town to let them know that crazy Macon Ravenwood's "relation" was driving around Gatlin in his hearse, which they were sure he used to transport dead bodies in when no one was watching. From there it just got wilder.

There are two things you can always count on in Gatlin. One, you can be different, even crazy, as long as you come out of the house every now and then, so folks don't think you're an axe murderer. Two, if there's a story to tell, you can be sure there'll be someone to tell it. A new girl in town, moving into the Haunted Mansion with the town shut-in, that's a story, probably the biggest story to hit Gatlin since my mom's accident. So I don't know why I was surprised when everyone was talking about her—everyone except the guys. They had business to attend to first.

"So, what've we got, Em?" Link slammed his locker door.

"Countin' cheerleadin' tryouts, looks like four 8's, three 7's, and a handful a 4's." Emory didn't bother to count the freshman girls he rated below a four.

I slammed my locker door. "This is news? Aren't these the same girls we see at the Dar-ee Keen every Saturday?"

Emory smiled, and clapped his hand on my shoulder. "But they're in the game now, Wate." He looked at the girls in the hall. "And I'm ready to play." Emory was mostly all talk. Last year, when we were freshmen, all we heard about were the hot seniors he thought he was going to hook up with now that he'd made JV. Em was as delusional as Link, but not as harmless. He had a mean streak; all the Watkinses did.

Shawn shook his head. "Like pickin' peaches off the vine."

"Peaches grow on trees." I was already annoyed, maybe because I'd met up with the guys at the Stop & Steal magazine stand before school and been subjected to this same conversation while Earl flipped through issues of the only thing he ever read—magazines featuring girls in bikinis, lying across the hoods of cars.

Shawn looked at me, confused. "What are you talkin' about?"

I don't know why I even bothered. It was a stupid conversation, the same way it was stupid that all the guys had to meet up before school on Wednesday mornings. It was something I'd come to think of as roll call. A few things were expected if you were on the team. You sat together in the lunchroom. You went to Savannah Snow's parties, asked a cheerleader to the winter formal, hung out at Lake Moultrie on the last day of school. You could bail on almost anything else, if you showed up for roll call. Only it was getting harder and harder for me to show up, and I didn't know why.

I still hadn't come up with the answer when I saw her.

Even if I hadn't seen her, I'd have known she was there because the hallway, which was usually crammed with people rushing to their lockers and trying to make it to class before the second bell, cleared out in a matter of seconds. Everyone actually stepped aside when she came down the hall. Like she was a rock star.

Or a leper.

But all I could see was a beautiful girl in a long gray dress, under a white track jacket with the word *Munich* sewn on it, and beat-up black Converse peeking out underneath. A girl who wore a long silver chain around her neck, with tons of stuff dangling from it—a plastic ring from a bubblegum machine, a safety pin, and a bunch of other junk I was too far away to see. A girl who didn't look like she belonged in Gatlin. I couldn't take my eyes off her.

Macon Ravenwood's niece. What was wrong with me?

She tucked her dark curls behind her ear, black nail polish catching the fluorescent light. Her hands were covered with black ink, like she had written on them. She walked down the hall as if we were invisible. She had the greenest eyes I'd ever seen, so green they could've been considered some new color altogether.

"Yeah, she's hot," said Billy.

I knew what they were thinking. For a second, they were thinking about dumping their girlfriends for the chance to hit on her. For a second, she was a possibility.

Earl gave her the once-over, then slammed his locker door. "If you ignore the fact that she's a freak."

There was something about the way he said it, or more like, the reason he said it. She was a freak because she wasn't from Gatlin, because she wasn't scrambling to make it onto the cheer squad, because she hadn't given him a second look, or even a first. On any other day, I would've ignored him and kept my mouth shut, but today I didn't feel like shutting up.

"So she's automatically a freak, why? Because she doesn't have on the uniform, blond hair and a short skirt?"

Earl's face was easy to read. This was one of those times when I was supposed to follow his lead, and I wasn't holding up my end of our unspoken agreement. "Because she's a Ravenwood."

The message was clear. Hot, but don't even think about it. She wasn't a possibility anymore. Still, that didn't keep them from looking, and they were all looking. The hallway, and everyone in it, had locked in on her as if she was a deer caught in the crosshairs.

But she just kept walking, her necklace jingling around her neck.

Minutes later, I stood in the doorway of my English class. There she was. Lena Duchannes. The new girl, who would still be called that fifty years from now, if she wasn't still called Old

Man Ravenwood's niece, handing a pink transfer slip to Mrs. English, who squinted to read it.

"They messed up my schedule and I didn't have an English class," she was saying. "I had U.S. History for two periods, and I already took U.S. History at my old school." She sounded frustrated, and I tried not to smile. She'd never had U.S. History, not the way Mr. Lee taught it.

"Of course. Take any open seat." Mrs. English handed her a copy of *To Kill a Mockingbird*. The book looked like it had never been opened, which it probably hadn't since they'd made it into a movie.

The new girl looked up and caught me watching her. I looked away, but it was too late. I tried not to smile, but I was embarrassed, and that only made me smile more. She didn't seem to notice.

"That's okay, I brought my own." She pulled out a copy of the book, hardback, with a tree etched on the cover. It looked really old and worn, like she had read it more than once. "It's one of my favorite books." She just said it, like it wasn't weird. Now I was staring.

I felt a steamroller plow into my back, and Emily pushed through the doorway as if I wasn't standing there, which was her way of saying hello and expecting me to follow her to the back of the room, where our friends were sitting.

The new girl sat down in an empty seat in the first row, in the No Man's Land in front of Mrs. English's desk. Wrong move. Everybody knew not to sit there. Mrs. English had one glass eye, and the terrible hearing you get if your family runs the only shooting range in the county. If you sat anywhere else but right in front of her desk, she couldn't see you and she wouldn't call on you. Lena was going to have to answer questions for the whole class.

Emily looked amused and went out of her way to walk past her seat, kicking over Lena's bag, sending her books sliding across the aisle.

"Whoops." Emily bent down, picking up a battered spiral notebook that was one tear away from losing its cover. She held it up like it was a dead mouse. "Lena Duchannes. Is that your name? I thought it was Ravenwood."

Lena looked up, slowly. "Can I have my book?"

Emily flipped through the pages, as if she didn't hear her. "Is this your journal? Are you a writer? That's *so* great."

Lena reached out her hand. "Please."

Emily snapped the book shut, and held it away from her. "Can I just borrow this for a minute? I'd love to read somethin' you wrote."

"I'd like it back now. Please." Lena stood up. Things were going to get interesting. Old Man Ravenwood's niece was about to dig herself into the kind of hole there was no climbing back out of; nobody had a memory like Emily.

"First you'd have to be able to read." I grabbed the journal out of Emily's hand and handed it back to Lena.

Then I sat down in the desk next to her, right there in No Man's Land. Good-Eye Side. Emily looked at me in disbelief. I don't know why I did it. I was just as shocked as she was. I'd never sat in the front of any class in my life. The bell rang before Emily could say anything, but it didn't matter; I knew I'd pay for it later. Lena opened her notebook and ignored both of us.

"Can we get started, people?" Mrs. English looked up from her desk.

Emily slunk to her usual seat in the back, far enough from the front that she wouldn't have to answer any questions the whole year, and today, far enough from Old Man Ravenwood's niece. And now, far enough from me. Which felt kind of liberating, even if I had to analyze Jem and Scout's relationship for fifty minutes without having read the chapter.

When the bell rang, I turned to Lena. I don't know what I thought I was going to say. Maybe I was expecting her to thank me. But she didn't say anything as she shoved her books back into her bag.

156. It wasn't a word she had written on the back of her hand. It was a number.

Lena Duchannes didn't speak to me again, not that day, not that week. But that didn't stop me from thinking about her, or seeing her practically everywhere I tried not to look. It wasn't just her that was bothering me, not exactly. It wasn't about how she looked, which was pretty, even though she was always wearing the wrong clothes and those beat-up sneakers. It wasn't about what she said in class—usually something no one else would've thought of, and if they had, something they wouldn't have dared to say. It wasn't that she was different from all the other girls at Jackson. That was obvious.

It was that she made me realize how much I was just like the rest of them, even if I wanted to pretend I wasn't.

It had been raining all day, and I was sitting in ceramics, otherwise known as AGA, "a guaranteed A," since the class was graded on effort. I had signed up for ceramics last spring because I had to fulfill my arts requirement, and I was desperate to stay out of band, which was practicing noisily downstairs, conducted by the crazily skinny, overly enthusiastic Miss Spider. Savannah sat down next to me. I was the only guy in the class, and since I was a guy, I had no idea what I was supposed to do next.

"Today is all about experimentation. You aren't being graded on this. Feel the clay. Free your mind. And ignore the music from downstairs." Mrs. Abernathy winced as the band butchered what sounded like "Dixie."

"Dig deep. Feel your way to your soul."

I flipped on the potter's wheel and stared at the clay as it started to spin in front of me. I sighed. This was almost as bad as band. Then, as the room quieted and the hum of the potter's wheels drowned out the chatter of the back rows, the music from downstairs shifted. I heard a violin, or maybe one of those bigger violins, a viola, I think. It was beautiful and sad at the same time, and it was unsettling. There was more talent in the raw voice of the music than Miss Spider had ever had the pleasure of conducting. I looked around; no one else seemed to notice the music. The sound crawled right under my skin.

I recognized the melody, and within seconds I could hear the words in my mind, as clearly as if I was listening to my iPod. But this time, the words had changed.

> *Sixteen moons, sixteen years*
> *Sound of thunder in your ears*
> *Sixteen miles before she nears*
> *Sixteen seeks what sixteen fears. . . .*

As I stared at the spinning clay in front of me, the lump became a blur. The harder I focused on it, the more the room dissolved around it, until the clay seemed to be spinning the classroom, the table, my chair along with it. As if we were all tied together in this whirlwind of constant motion, set to the rhythm of the melody from the music room. The room was disappearing around me. Slowly, I reached out a hand and dragged one fingertip along the clay.

Then a flash, and the whirling room dissolved into another image—

I was falling.

We were falling.

I was back in the dream. I saw her hand. I saw my hand grabbing at hers, my fingers digging into her skin, her wrist, in a desperate attempt to hold on. But she was slipping; I could feel it, her fingers pulling through my hand.

"Don't let go!"

I wanted to help her, to hold on. More than I had ever wanted anything. And then, she fell through my fingers. . . .

"Ethan, what are you doin'?" Mrs. Abernathy sounded concerned.

I opened my eyes, and tried to focus, to bring myself back. I'd been having the dreams since my mom died, but this was the first time I'd had one during the day. I stared at my gray, muddy hand, caked with drying clay. The clay on the potter's wheel held the perfect imprint of a hand, like I had just flattened whatever I was working on. I looked at it more closely. The hand wasn't mine, it was too small. It was a girl's.

It was hers.

I looked under my nails, where I could see the clay I had clawed from her wrist.

"Ethan, you could at least try to make somethin'." Mrs. Abernathy put her hand on my shoulder, and I jumped. Outside the classroom window, I heard the rumble of thunder.

"But Mrs. Abernathy, I think Ethan's soul is communicatin' with him." Savannah giggled, leaning over to get a good look. "I think it's tellin' you to get a manicure, Ethan."

The girls around me started to laugh. I mashed the handprint with my fist, turning it back into a lump of gray nothing. I stood up, wiping my hands on my jeans as the bell rang. I grabbed my backpack and sprinted out of the room, slipping in my wet high-tops when I turned the corner and almost tripping over my untied laces as I ran down the two flights of stairs that stood between the music room and me. I had to know if I had imagined it.

I pushed open the double doors of the music room with both hands. The stage was empty. The class was filing past me. I was going the wrong way, heading downstream when everyone else was going up. I took a deep breath, but knew what I would smell before I smelled it.

Lemons and rosemary.

Down on the stage, Miss Spider was picking up sheet music, scattered along the folding chairs she used for the sorry Jackson orchestra. I called down to her, "Excuse me, ma'am. Who was just playing that—that song?"

She smiled in my direction. "We have a wonderful new addition to our strings section. A viola. She's just moved into town—"

No. It couldn't be. Not her.

I turned and ran before she could say the name.

39

When the eighth-period bell rang, Link was waiting for me in front of the locker room. He raked his hand through his spiky hair and straightened out his faded Black Sabbath T-shirt.

"Link. I need your keys, man."

"What about practice?"

"I can't make it. There's something I've gotta do."

"Dude, what are you talkin' about?"

"I just need your keys." I had to get out of there. I was having the dreams, hearing the song, and now blacking out in the middle of class, if that's even what you'd call it. I didn't know what was going on with me, but I knew it was bad.

If my mom was still alive, I probably would've told her everything. She was like that, I could tell her anything. But she was gone, and my dad was holed up in his study all the time, and Amma would be sprinkling salt all over my room for a month if I told her.

I was on my own.

Link held out his keys. "Coach is gonna kill you."

"I know."

"And Amma's gonna find out."

"I know."

"And she's gonna kick your butt all the way to the County Line." His hand wavered as I grabbed the keys. "Don't be stupid."

I turned and bolted. Too late.

⊰ 9.11 ⊱

Collision

By the time I got to the car, I was soaking wet. The storm had been building all week. There was a weather advisory on every radio station I could get any reception from, which wasn't saying much considering the Beater only got three stations, all AM. The clouds were totally black, and since it was hurricane season, that wasn't something to be taken lightly. But it didn't matter. I needed to clear my head and figure out what was going on, even if I had no idea where I was going.

I had to turn on the headlights to even drive out of the parking lot. I couldn't see more than three feet in front of the car. It wasn't a day to be driving. Lightning sliced through the dark sky ahead of me. I counted, as Amma had taught me years ago—one, two, three. Thunder cracked, which meant the storm wasn't far off—three miles according to Amma's calculations.

I pulled up at the stoplight by Jackson, one of only three in town. I had no idea what to do. The rain jackhammered down on the Beater. The radio was reduced to static, but I heard something. I cranked the volume and the song flooded through the crappy speakers.

Sixteen Moons.

The song that had disappeared from my playlist. The song no one else seemed to hear. The song Lena Duchannes had been playing on the viola. The song that was driving me crazy.

The light turned green and the Beater lurched into drive. I was on my way, and I had absolutely no idea where I was going.

Lightning ripped across the sky. I counted—one, two. The storm was getting closer. I flipped on the windshield wipers. It was no use. I couldn't even see halfway down the block. Lightning flashed. I counted—one. Thunder rumbled above the roof of the Beater, and the rain turned horizontal. The windshield rattled as if it could give way at any second, which, considering the condition of the Beater, it could have.

I wasn't chasing the storm. The storm was chasing me, and it had found me. I could barely keep the wheels on the slick road, and the Beater started to fishtail, skating erratically back and forth between the two lanes of Route 9.

I couldn't see a thing. I slammed on the brakes, spinning out into the darkness. The headlights flickered, for barely a second, and a pair of huge green eyes stared back at me from the middle of the road. At first I thought it was a deer, but I was wrong.

There was someone in the road!

I pulled on the wheel with both hands, as hard as I could. My body slammed against the side of the door.

Her hand was outstretched. I closed my eyes for the impact, but it never came.

The Beater jerked to a stop, not more than three feet away. The headlights made a pale circle of light in the rain, reflecting off one of those cheap plastic rain ponchos you can buy for three dollars at the drugstore. It was a girl. Slowly, she pulled the hood off her head, letting the rain run down her face. Green eyes, black hair.

Lena Duchannes.

I couldn't breathe. I knew she had green eyes; I'd seen them before. But tonight they looked different—different from any eyes I had ever seen. They were huge and unnaturally green, an electric green, like the lightning from the storm. Standing in the rain like that, she almost didn't look human.

I stumbled out of the Beater into the rain, leaving the engine running and the door open. Neither one of us said a word, standing in the middle of Route 9 in the kind of downpour you only saw during a hurricane or a nor'easter. Adrenaline was pumping through my veins and my muscles were tense, as if my body was still waiting for the crash.

Lena's hair whipped in the wind around her, dripping with rain. I took a step toward her, and it hit me. Wet lemons. Wet rosemary. All at once, the dream started coming back to me, like waves crashing over my head. Only this time, when she slipped through my fingers—I could see her face.

Green eyes and black hair. I remembered. It was her. She was standing right in front of me.

I had to know for sure. I grabbed her wrist. There they were: the tiny moon-shaped scratches, right where my fingers had reached for her wrist in the dream. When I touched her, electricity ran through my body. Lightning struck the tree not ten feet from where we were standing, splitting the trunk neatly in half. It began to smolder.

"Are you crazy? Or just a terrible driver?" She backed away from me, her green eyes flashing—with anger? With something.

"It's you."

"What were you trying to do, kill me?"

"You're real." The words felt strange in my mouth, like it was full of cotton.

"A real corpse, almost. Thanks to you."

"I'm not crazy. I thought I was, but I'm not. It's you. You're standing right in front of me."

"Not for long." She turned her back on me and started up the road. This wasn't going the way I had imagined it.

I ran to catch up with her. "You're the one who just appeared out of nowhere and ran out into the middle of the highway."

She waved her arm dramatically like she was waving away more than just the idea. For the first time, I saw the long black car in the shadows. The hearse, with its hood up. "Hello? I was looking for someone to help me, genius. My uncle's car died. You could have just driven by. You didn't have to try to run me down."

"It was you in the dreams. And the song. The weird song on my iPod."

She whirled around. "What dreams? What song? Are you drunk, or is this some kind of joke?"

"I know it's you. You have the marks on your wrist."

She turned her hand over and looked down, confused. "These? I have a dog. Get over it."

But I knew I wasn't wrong. I could see the face from my dream so clearly now. Was it possible she didn't know?

She pulled up her hood and began the long walk to Ravenwood in the pouring rain. I caught up with her. "Here's a hint. Next time, don't get out of your car in the middle of the road during a storm. Call 911."

She didn't stop walking. "I wasn't about to call the police. I'm not even supposed to be driving. I only have a learner's permit. Anyway, my cell is dead." Clearly she wasn't from around here. The only way you'd get pulled over in this town was if you were driving on the wrong side of the road.

The storm was picking up. I had to shout over the howl of the rain. "Just let me give you a ride home. You shouldn't be out here."

"No thanks. I'll wait for the next guy who almost runs me down."

"There isn't gonna be another guy. It could be hours before anyone else comes by."

She started walking again. "No problem. I'll walk."

I couldn't let her wander around alone in the pouring rain. My mom had raised me better than that. "I can't let you walk home in this weather." As if on cue, thunder rolled over our heads. Her hood blew off. "I'll drive like my grandma. I'll drive like your grandma."

"You wouldn't say that if you knew my gramma." The wind was picking up. Now she was shouting, too.

"Come on."

"What?"

"The car. Get in. With me."

She looked at me, and for a second I wasn't sure if she was

going to give in. "I guess it's safer than walking. With you on the road, anyway."

The Beater was drenched. Link would lose it when he saw it. The storm sounded different once we were in the car, both louder and quieter. I could hear the rain pounding the roof, but it was nearly drowned out by the sound of my heart beating and my teeth chattering. I pushed the car into drive. I was so aware of Lena sitting next to me, just inches away in the passenger seat. I snuck a look.

Even though she was a pain, she was beautiful. Her green eyes were enormous. I couldn't figure out why they looked so different tonight. She had the longest eyelashes I had ever seen, and her skin was pale, made even paler by the contrast of her wild black hair. She had a tiny, light brown birthmark on her cheekbone just below her left eye, shaped sort of like a crescent moon. She didn't look like anybody at Jackson. She didn't look like anybody I'd ever seen.

She pulled the wet poncho over her head. Her black T-shirt and jeans clung to her like she'd fallen in a swimming pool. Her gray vest dripped a steady stream of water onto the pleather seat. "You're s-staring."

I looked away, out the windshield, anywhere but at her. "You should probably take that off. It'll only make you colder."

I could see her fumbling with the delicate silver buttons on the vest, unable to control the shaking in her hands. I reached forward, and she froze. Like I would've dared touch her again. "I'll turn up the heat."

She went back to the buttons. "Th-thanks."

I could see her hands—more ink, now smeared from the rain. I could just make out a few numbers. Maybe a one or a seven, a five, a two. 152. What was that about?

I glanced in the backseat for the old army blanket Link usually kept back there. Instead there was a ratty sleeping bag, probably from the last time Link got in trouble at home and had to sleep in his car. It smelled like old campfire smoke and basement mold. I handed it to her.

"Mmmm. That's better." She closed her eyes. I could feel her ease into the warmth of the heater, and I relaxed, just watching her. The chattering of her teeth slowed. After that, we drove in silence. The only sound was the storm, and the wheels rolling and spraying through the lake the road had become. She traced shapes on the foggy window with her finger. I tried to keep my eyes on the road, tried to remember the rest of the dream—some detail, one thing that would prove to her that she was, I don't know, her, and that I was me.

But the harder I tried, the more it all seemed to fade away, into the rain and the highway and the passing acres and acres of tobacco fields, littered with dated farm equipment and rotting old barns. We reached the outskirts of town, and I could see the fork in the road up ahead. If you took a left, toward my house, you'd hit River, where all the restored antebellum houses lined the Santee. It was also the way out of town. When we came to the fork in the road, I automatically started to turn left, out of habit. The only thing to the right was Ravenwood Plantation, and no one ever went there.

"No, wait. Go right here," she said.

"Oh, yeah. Sorry." I felt sick. We climbed the hill up toward

Ravenwood Manor, the great house. I had been so wrapped up in who she was, I had forgotten *who* she was. The girl I'd been dreaming about for months, the girl I couldn't stop thinking about, was Macon Ravenwood's niece. And I was driving her home to the Haunted Mansion—that's what we called it.

That's what I had called it.

She looked down at her hands. I wasn't the only one who knew she was living in the Haunted Mansion. I wondered what she'd heard in the halls. If she knew what everyone was saying about her. The uncomfortable look on her face said she did. I don't know why, but I couldn't stand seeing her like that. I tried to think of something to say to break the silence. "So why did you move in with your uncle? Usually people are trying to get out of Gatlin; no one really moves here."

I heard the relief in her voice. "I've lived all over. New Orleans, Savannah, the Florida Keys, Virginia for a few months. I even lived in Barbados for a while."

I noticed she didn't answer the question, but I couldn't help thinking about how much I would've killed to live in one of those places, even for a summer. "Where are your parents?"

"They're dead."

I felt my chest tighten. "Sorry."

"It's okay. They died when I was two. I don't even remember them. I've lived with lots of my relatives, mainly my gramma. She had to take a trip for a few months. That's why I'm staying with my uncle."

"My mom died, too. Car accident." I had no idea why I said that. I spent most of my time trying not to talk about it.

"I'm sorry."

I didn't say it was okay. I had a feeling she was the kind of girl who knew it wasn't.

We stopped in front of a weather-beaten black wrought-iron gate. In front of me, on the rising hill, barely visible through the blanket of fog, stood the dilapidated remains of Gatlin's oldest and most notorious plantation house, Ravenwood Manor. I'd never been this close to it before. I turned off the motor. Now the storm had faded into a kind of soft, steady drizzle. "Looks like the lightning's gone."

"I'm sure there's more where that came from."

"Maybe. But not tonight."

She looked at me, almost curiously. "No. I think we're done for tonight." Her eyes looked different. They had faded back to a less intense shade of green, and they were smaller somehow—not small, but more normal looking.

I started to open my door, to walk her up to the house.

"No, don't." She looked embarrassed. "My uncle's kind of shy." That was an understatement.

My door was half open. Her door was half open. We were both getting even wetter, but we just sat there without saying anything. I knew what I wanted to say, but I also knew I couldn't say it. I didn't know why I was sitting here, soaking wet, in front of Ravenwood Manor. Nothing was making any sense, but I knew one thing. Once I drove back down the hill and turned back onto Route 9, everything would change back. Everything would make sense again. Wouldn't it?

She spoke first. "Thanks, I guess."

"For not running you down?"

She smiled. "Yeah, that. And the ride."

I stared at her smiling at me, almost like we were friends, which was impossible. I started to feel claustrophobic, like I had to get out of there. "It was nothing. I mean, it's cool. Don't worry about it." I flipped up the hood of my basketball sweatshirt, the way Emory did when one of the girls he'd blown off tried to talk to him in the hall.

She looked at me, shaking her head, and tossed the sleeping bag at me, a little too hard. The smile was gone. "Whatever. I'll see you around." She turned her back on me, slipped through the gates and ran up the steep, muddy drive toward the house. I slammed the door.

The sleeping bag lay on the seat. I picked it up to throw it into the back. It still had the moldy campfire smell, but now it also smelled faintly of lemons and rosemary. I closed my eyes. When I opened them, she was already halfway up the driveway.

I rolled down my window. "She has a glass eye."

Lena looked back at me. "What?"

I shouted, the rain dripping down the inside of the car door. "Mrs. English. You have to sit on her other side, or she'll make you talk."

She smiled as the rain rolled down her face. "Maybe I like to talk." She turned back to Ravenwood and ran up the steps to the veranda.

I shifted the car into reverse and drove back down to the fork in the road, so I could turn the way I usually turned, and take the road I had taken my whole life. Until today. I saw something shining from the crack in the seat. A silver button.

I shoved it into my pocket, and wondered what I'd dream about tonight.

Broken Glass

Nothing.

It was a long, dreamless sleep, the first I'd had in a long time.

When I woke up, the window was closed. No mud in my bed, no mysterious songs on my iPod. I checked twice. Even my shower just smelled like soap.

I lay in my bed, looking up at my blue ceiling, thinking about green eyes and black hair. Old Man Ravenwood's niece. Lena Duchannes, it rhymes with rain.

How far off could a guy be?

When Link pulled up, I was waiting at the curb. I climbed in and my sneakers sank into the wet carpet, which made the Beater smell even worse than usual. Link shook his head.

"I'm sorry, man. I'll try to dry it out after school."

"Whatever. Just do me a favor and get off the crazy train,

or everyone'll be talkin' about you instead a Old Man Raven-wood's niece."

For a second, I considered keeping it to myself, but I had to tell someone. "I saw her."

"Who?"

"Lena Duchannes."

He looked blank.

"Old Man Ravenwood's niece."

By the time we pulled up in the parking lot, I had told Link the whole story. Well, maybe not the whole story. Even best friends have their limits. And I can't say that he believed all of it, but then again, who would? I was still having a hard time believing it myself. But even if he wasn't clear on the details, as we walked up to join the guys, he was clear about one thing. Damage control.

"It's not like anything happened. You drove her home."

"Nothing happened? Were you even listening? I've been dreaming about her for months and she turns out to be—"

Link cut me off. "You didn't hook up or anything. You didn't go in the Haunted Mansion, right? And you never saw, you know . . . him?" Even Link couldn't bring himself to say his name. It was one thing to hang out with a beautiful girl, in any situation. It was another thing to hang out with Old Man Ravenwood.

I shook my head. "No, but—"

"I know, I know. You're screwed up. I'm just sayin', keep it to yourself, dude. All this is on a strictly need-to-know basis. As in, nobody else needs to know." I knew that was going to be hard. I didn't know it was going to be impossible.

♦ ♦ ♦

When I pushed open the door to English, I was still thinking about everything—about her, the nothing that had happened. Lena Duchannes.

Maybe it was the way she wore that crazy necklace with all the junk on it, as if every single thing she touched could matter or did matter to her. Maybe it was the way she wore those beat-up sneakers whether she was wearing jeans or a dress, like she could take off running, any minute. When I looked at her, I was farther away from Gatlin than I'd ever been. Maybe it was that.

I guess when I started thinking, I stopped walking, and I felt someone bump into me. Only it wasn't a steamroller this time, more like a tsunami. We collided, hard. The second we touched, the ceiling light shorted out over us, and a shower of sparks rained down on our heads.

I ducked. She didn't.

"Are you trying to kill me for the second time in two days, Ethan?" The room went dead quiet.

"What?" I could barely get the word out.

"I said, are you trying to kill me again?"

"I didn't know you were there."

"That's what you said last night."

Last night. The two little words that could forever change your life at Jackson. Even though there were plenty of lights still working, you would've thought there was a spotlight on us, to go with our live audience. I could feel my face going red.

"Sorry. I mean—hi," I mumbled, sounding like an idiot. She looked amused, but kept walking. She slung her book bag on the same desk she had been sitting at all week, right in front of Mrs. English. Good-Eye Side.

I'd learned my lesson. There was no telling Lena Duchannes where she could or couldn't sit. No matter what you thought about the Ravenwoods, you had to give her that. I slid into the seat next to her, smack in the middle of No Man's Land. Like I had all week. Only this time she was talking to me, and somehow that made everything different. Not bad-different, just terrifying.

She started to smile, but caught herself. I tried to think of something interesting to say, or at least not stupid. But before I came up with anything, Emily sat down on the other side of me, with Eden Westerly and Charlotte Chase flanking her on either side. Six rows closer than usual. Not even sitting on the Good-Eye Side was going to help me today.

Mrs. English looked up from her desk, suspicious.

"Hey, Ethan." Eden turned back to me, and smiled, like I was in on their little game. "How's it goin'?"

I wasn't surprised to see Eden following Emily's lead. Eden was just another one of the pretty girls who wasn't quite pretty enough to be Savannah. Eden was strictly second string, on the cheer squad and in life. Not a base, not a flyer, sometimes she didn't even get on the mat. Eden never gave up trying to do something to make that leap, though. Her thing was to be different, except for, I guess, the part about being different. Nobody was different at Jackson.

"We didn't want ya to have to sit up here all by yourself." Charlotte giggled. If Eden was second string, Charlotte was third. Charlotte was one thing no self-respecting Jackson cheerleader should ever be, a little chunky. She had never quite lost her baby fat, and even though she was on a perpetual diet she just couldn't shed those last ten pounds. It wasn't her fault; she was always trying. Ate the pie and left the crust. Double the biscuits and half the gravy.

"Can this book get any more borin'?" Emily didn't even look my way. This was a territorial dispute. She might have dumped me, but she certainly didn't want to see Old Man Ravenwood's niece anywhere near me. "Like I wanna read about a town fulla people who are completely mental. We've got enough a that around here."

Abby Porter, who usually sat on the Good-Eye Side, sat down next to Lena and gave her a weak smile. Lena smiled back and looked as if she was going to say something friendly, when Emily shot Abby a look that made it clear that the famed Southern hospitality did not apply to Lena. Defying Emily Asher was an act of social suicide. Abby pulled out her Student Council folder and buried her nose in it, avoiding Lena. Message received.

Emily turned to Lena and expertly shot her a look that managed to work its way from the very top of Lena's un-highlighted hair, past her un-tanned face, down to the tips of her un-pinked fingernails. Eden and Charlotte swung around in their chairs to face Emily, as if Lena didn't exist. The girl freeze-out—today it was negative fifteen.

Lena opened her tattered spiral notebook and started to write. Emily got out her phone and began to text. I looked back down at my notebook, slipping my Silver Surfer comic between the pages, which was a lot harder to do in the front row.

"All right, ladies and gentleman, since it looks like the rest of the lights will be staying on, you're out of luck. I hope everyone did the reading last night." Mrs. English was scribbling madly on the chalkboard. "Let's take a minute to discuss social conflict in a small-town setting."

Someone should have told Mrs. English. Halfway through class, we had more than social conflict in a small-town setting. Emily was coordinating a full-scale attack.

"Who knows why Atticus is willing to defend Tom Robinson, in the face of small-mindedness and racism?"

"I bet Lena Ravenwood knows," Eden said, smiling innocently at Mrs. English. Lena looked down into the lines of her notebook, but didn't say a word.

"Shut up," I whispered, a little too loudly. "You know that's not her name."

"It may as well be. She's livin' with that freak," Charlotte said.

"Watch what you say. I hear they're, like, a couple." Emily was pulling out the big guns.

"That's enough." Mrs. English turned her good eye on us, and we all shut up.

Lena shifted her weight; her chair scraped loudly against the floor. I leaned forward in mine, trying to become a wall between Lena and Emily's minions like I could physically deflect their comments.

You can't.

What? I sat up, startled. I looked around, but no one was talking to me; no one was talking at all. I looked at Lena. She was still half-hidden in her notebook. Great. It wasn't enough to dream real girls and hear imaginary songs. Now I had to hear voices, too.

The whole Lena thing was really getting to me. I guess I felt responsible, in a way. Emily, and the rest of them, wouldn't hate her so much if it wasn't for me.

They would.

There it was again, a voice so quiet I could barely hear it. It was like it was coming from the back of my head.

Eden, Charlotte, and Emily kept firing away, and Lena didn't even blink, like she could just block them out as long as she kept writing in that notebook of hers.

"Harper Lee seems to be saying that you can't really get to know someone until you take a walk in his shoes. What do you make of that? Anyone?"

Harper Lee never lived in Gatlin.

I looked around, stifling a laugh. Emily looked at me like I was nuts.

Lena raised her hand. "I think it means you have to give people a chance. Before you automatically skip to the hating part. Don't you think so, Emily?" She looked at Emily and smiled.

"You little freak," Emily hissed under her breath.

You have no idea.

I stared more closely at Lena. She had given up on the notebook; now she was writing on her hand in black ink. I didn't have to see it to know what it was. Another number. 151. I wondered what it meant, and why it couldn't go in the notebook. I buried my head back in *Silver Surfer*.

"Let's talk about Boo Radley. What would lead you to believe he is leaving gifts for the Finch children?"

"He's just like Old Man Ravenwood. He's probably tryin' to lure those kids into his house so he can kill them," Emily whispered, loud enough for Lena to hear, but quiet enough to keep Mrs. English from hearing. "Then he can put their bodies in his hearse and take them out to the middle a nowhere and bury them."

Shut up.

I heard the voice in my head again, and something else. It was a creaking sound. Faint.

"And he has that crazy name like Boo Radley. What is it again?"

"You're right, it's that creepy Bible name nobody uses anymore."

I stiffened. I knew they were talking about Old Man Ravenwood, but they were also talking about Lena. "Emily, why don't you give it a rest," I shot back.

She narrowed her eyes. "He's a freak. They all are and everyone knows it."

I said shut up.

The creaking was getting louder and started to sound more like splintering. I looked around. What was that noise? Even weirder, it didn't seem like anyone else heard it—like the voice.

Lena was staring straight ahead, but her jaw was clenched and she was unnaturally focused on one point in the front of the room, like she couldn't see anything but that spot. The room felt like it was getting smaller, closing in.

I heard Lena's chair drag across the floor again. She got out of her seat, heading toward the bookcase under the window, on the side of the room. Most likely pretending to sharpen her pencil so she could escape the inescapable, Jackson's judge and jury. The sharpener began to grind.

"Melchizedek, that's it."

Stop it.

I could still hear the grinding.

"My grandmamma says that's an evil name."

Stop it stop it stop it.

"Suits him, too."

ENOUGH!

Now the voice was so loud, I grabbed my ears. The grinding stopped. Glass went flying, splintering into the air, as the window shattered out of nowhere—the window right across from our row in the classroom, right next to where Lena stood, sharpening her pencil. Right next to Charlotte, Eden, Emily, and me. They screamed and dove out of their seats. That's when I realized what that creaking sound had been. Pressure. Tiny cracks in the glass, spreading out like fingers, until the window collapsed inward like it had been pulled by a thread.

It was chaos. The girls were screaming. Everyone in the class was scrambling out of their seats. Even I jumped.

"Don't panic. Is everyone all right?" Mrs. English said, trying to regain control.

I turned toward the pencil sharpener. I wanted to make sure Lena was okay. She wasn't. She was standing by the broken window, surrounded by glass, looking panic-stricken. Her face was even paler than usual, her eyes even bigger and greener. Like last night in the rain. But they looked different. They looked frightened. She didn't seem so brave anymore.

She held out her hands. One was cut and bleeding. Red drops splattered on the linoleum floor.

I didn't mean it—

Did she shatter the glass? Or had the glass shattered and cut her?

"Lena—"

She bolted out of the room, before I could ask her if she was all right.

"Did you see that? She broke the window! She hit it with somethin' when she walked over there!"

"She punched clean through the glass. I saw it with my own eyes!"

"Then how come she's not gushin' blood?"

"What are you, CSI? She tried to kill us."

"I'm callin' my daddy right now. She's crazy, just like her uncle!"

They sounded like a pack of angry alley cats, shouting over each other. Mrs. English tried to restore order, but that was asking the impossible. "Everyone calm down. There's no reason to panic. Accidents happen. It was probably nothing that can't be explained by an old window and the wind."

But no one believed it could be explained by an old window and the wind. More like an old man's niece and a lightning storm. The green-eyed storm that just rolled into town. Hurricane Lena.

One thing was for sure. The weather had changed, all right. Gatlin had never seen a storm like this.

And she probably didn't even know it was raining.

Greenbrier

D*on't.*

I could hear her voice in my head. At least I thought I could.

It's not worth it, Ethan.

It was.

That's when I pushed back my chair and ran down the hallway after her. I knew what I'd done. I had taken sides. I was in a different kind of trouble now, but I didn't care.

It wasn't just Lena. She wasn't the first. I'd watched them do it, my whole life. They'd done it to Allison Birch when her eczema got so bad nobody would sit near her at the lunch table, and poor Scooter Richman because he played the worst trombone in the history of the Jackson Symphony Orchestra.

While I'd never picked up a marker and written *LOSER* across a locker myself, I had stood by and watched, plenty of times. Either way, it had always bothered me. Just never enough to walk out of the room.

But somebody had to do something. A whole school couldn't just take down one person like that. A whole town couldn't just take down one family. Except, of course, they could, because they had been doing it forever. Maybe that's why Macon Ravenwood hadn't left his house since before I was born.

I knew what I was doing.

You don't. You think you do, but you don't.

She was there in my head again, as if she'd always been there.

I knew what I'd be facing the next day, but none of that mattered to me. All I cared about was finding her. And I couldn't have told you just then if it was for her, or for me. Either way, I didn't have a choice.

I stopped at the bio lab, out of breath. Link took one look at me and tossed me his keys, shaking his head without even asking. I caught them and kept running. I was pretty sure I knew where to find her. If I was right, she had gone where anyone would go. It's where I would have gone.

She had gone home. Even if home was Ravenwood, and she had gone home to Gatlin's own Boo Radley.

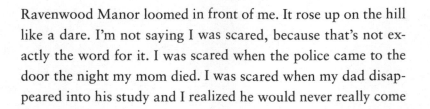

Ravenwood Manor loomed in front of me. It rose up on the hill like a dare. I'm not saying I was scared, because that's not exactly the word for it. I was scared when the police came to the door the night my mom died. I was scared when my dad disappeared into his study and I realized he would never really come back out. I was scared when I was a kid and Amma went dark, when I figured out the little dolls she made weren't toys.

I wasn't scared of Ravenwood, even if it turned out to be as creepy as it looked. The unexplained was sort of a given in the South; every town has a haunted house, and if you asked most folks, at least a third of them would swear they'd seen a ghost or two in their lifetime. Besides, I lived with Amma, whose beliefs included painting our shutters haint blue to keep the spirits out, and whose charms were made from pouches of horsehair and dirt. So I was used to unusual. But Old Man Ravenwood, that was something else.

I walked up to the gate and hesitantly laid my hand on the mangled iron. The gate creaked open. And then, nothing happened. No lightning, no combustion, no storms. I don't know what I was expecting, but if I had learned anything about Lena by now, it was to expect the unexpected, and to proceed with caution.

If anyone had told me a month ago that I would ever walk past those gates, up that hill, and set foot anywhere on the grounds of Ravenwood, I would've said they were crazy. In a town like Gatlin, where you can see everything coming, I wouldn't have seen this. Last time, I had only made it as far as the gates. The closer I got, the easier it was to see that everything was falling apart. The great house, Ravenwood Manor, looked just like the stereotypical Southern plantation that people from up North would expect to see after all those years of watching movies like *Gone with the Wind*.

Ravenwood Manor was still that impressive, at least in scale. Flanked by palmetto and cypress trees, it looked like it could have been the kind of place where people sat on the porch drinking mint juleps and playing cards all day, if it wasn't falling apart. If it wasn't Ravenwood.

It was a Greek Revival, which was unusual for Gatlin. Our town was full of Federal-style plantation houses, which made Ravenwood stand out even more like the sore thumb it was. Huge white Doric pillars, paint peeling from years of neglect, supported a roof that sloped too sharply to one side, giving the impression that the house was leaning over like an arthritic old woman. The covered porch was splintered and falling away from the house, threatening to collapse if you dared set so much as a foot on it. Thick ivy grew so densely over the exterior walls that in some places it was impossible to see the windows underneath. As if the grounds had swallowed up the house itself, trying to take it back down into the very dirt it had been built upon.

There was an overlapping lintel, the part of the beam that lies over the door of some really old buildings. I could see some sort of carving in the lintel. Symbols. They looked like circles and crescents, maybe the phases of the moon. I took a tentative step onto a groaning stair so I could get a closer look. I knew something about lintels. My mom had been a Civil War historian, and she had pointed them out to me on our countless pilgrimages to every historical site within a day's drive of Gatlin. She said they were really common in old houses and castles, in places like England and Scotland. Which is where some of the people from around here were from, well, before they were from around here.

I had never seen one with symbols carved into it before, only words. These were more like hieroglyphs, surrounding what looked like a single word, in a language I didn't recognize. It had probably meant something to the generations of Ravenwoods who lived here before this place was falling apart.

I took a breath and vaulted up the rest of the porch steps, two at a time. Figured I increased my odds of not falling through them by fifty percent if I only landed on half of them. I reached for the brass ring suspended from a lion's mouth that served as a knocker, and I knocked. I knocked again, and again. She wasn't home. I had been wrong, after all.

But then I heard it, the familiar melody. *Sixteen Moons.* She was here somewhere.

I pushed down on the calcified iron of the door handle. It groaned, and I heard a bolt responding on the other side of the door. I prepared myself for the sight of Macon Ravenwood, who nobody had seen in town, not in my lifetime anyway. But the door didn't open.

I looked up at the lintel, and something told me to try. I mean, what was the worst that could happen—the door wouldn't open? Instinctively, I reached up and touched the central carving above my head. The crescent moon. When I pressed on it, I could feel the wood giving way under my finger. It was some kind of trigger.

The door swung open without so much as a sound. I stepped past the threshold. There was no going back now.

Light flooded through the windows, which seemed impossible considering the windows on the outside of the house were completely covered with vines and debris. Yet, inside it was light, bright, and brand new. There was no antique period furniture or oil paintings of the Ravenwoods who came before Old Man Ravenwood, no antebellum heirlooms. This place looked more like a page out of a furniture catalog. Overstuffed couches and chairs and glass-topped tables, stacked with coffee table books.

It was all so suburban, so new. I almost expected to see the delivery truck still parked outside.

"Lena?"

The circular staircase looked like it belonged in a loft; it seemed to keep winding upward, far above the second-floor landing. I couldn't see the top.

"Mr. Ravenwood?" I could hear my own voice echo against the high ceiling. There was nobody here. At least, nobody interested in talking to me. I heard a noise behind me, and jumped, nearly tripping over some kind of suede chair.

It was a jet-black dog, or maybe a wolf. Some kind of scary house pet, because it wore a heavy leather collar with a dangling silver moon that jingled when it moved. It was staring right at me like it was plotting its next move. There was something odd about its eyes. They were too round, too human-looking.

The wolf-dog growled at me and bared its teeth. The growl became loud and shrill, more like a scream. I did what anyone would do.

I ran.

I stumbled down the stairs before my eyes had even adjusted to the light. I kept running, down the gravel path, away from Ravenwood Manor, away from the frightening house pet and the strange symbols and the creepy door, and back into the safe, dim light of the real afternoon. The path wound on and on, snaking through unkempt fields and groves of uncultivated trees, wild with brambles and bushes. I didn't care where it led, as long as it was away.

I stopped and bent over, hands on knees, my chest exploding. My legs were rubber. When I looked up, I saw a crumbling rock wall in front of me. I could barely make out the tops of the trees beyond the wall.

I smelled something familiar. Lemon trees. She was here.

I told you not to come.

I know.

We were having a conversation, except we weren't. But just like in class, I could hear her in my head, as if she was standing next to me whispering in my ear.

I felt myself moving toward her. There was a walled garden, maybe even a secret garden, like something out of a book my mother would have read growing up in Savannah. This place must have been really old. The stone wall was worn away in places and completely broken in others. When I pushed through the curtain of vines that hid the old, rotting wooden archway, I could just barely hear the sound of someone crying. I looked through the trees and the bushes, but I still couldn't see her.

"Lena?" Nobody answered. My voice sounded strange, as if it wasn't mine, echoing off the stone walls that surrounded the little grove. I grabbed the bush closest to me and ripped off a branch. Rosemary. Of course. And in the tree above my head, there it was: a strangely perfect, smooth, yellow lemon.

"It's Ethan." As the muffled sounds of sobbing grew, I knew I was coming closer.

"Go away, I told you." She sounded like she had a cold; she had probably been crying since she left school.

"I know. I heard you." It was true, and I couldn't explain it. I stepped carefully around the wild rosemary, stumbling through the overgrown roots.

"Really?" She sounded interested, momentarily distracted.

"Really." It was like the dreams. I could hear her voice, except she was here, crying in an overgrown garden in the middle of nowhere, instead of falling through my arms.

I parted a large tangle of branches. There she was, curled up in the tall grasses, staring up at the blue sky. She had one arm tossed over her head, and another clutching at the grass, as if she thought she would fly away if she let go. Her gray dress lay in a puddle around her. Her face was streaked with tears.

"Then why didn't you?"

"What?"

"Go away?"

"I wanted to make sure you were okay." I sat down next to her. The ground was surprisingly hard. I ran my hand underneath me and discovered I was sitting on a smooth slab of flat stone, hidden by the muddy overgrowth.

Just as I lay back, she sat up. I sat up, and she flopped back down. Awkward. That was my every move, when it came to her.

Now we were both lying down, staring up at the blue sky. It was turning gray, the color of the Gatlin sky during hurricane season.

"They all hate me."

"Not all of them. Not me. Not Link, my best friend."

Silence.

"You don't even know me. Give it time; you'll probably hate me, too."

"I almost ran you down, remember? I have to be nice to you, so you don't have me arrested."

It was a lame joke. But there it was, the smallest smile I have possibly ever seen in my life. "It's right up at the top of my list. I'll report you to that fat guy who sits in front of the supermarket all day." She looked back up at the sky. I watched her.

"Give them a chance. They're not all bad. I mean, they are, right now. They're just jealous. You know that, right?"

"Yeah, sure."

"They are." I looked at her, through the tall grass. "I am."

She shook her head. "Then you're crazy. There's nothing to be jealous of, unless you're really into eating lunch alone."

"You've lived all over."

She looked blank. "So? You've probably gotten to go to the same school and live in the same house your whole life."

"I have, that's the problem."

"Trust me, it's not a problem. I know about problems."

"You've gone places, seen things. I'd kill to do that."

"Yeah, all by myself. You have a best friend. I have a dog."

"But you're not scared of anyone. You act the way you want and say whatever you want. Everyone else around here is scared to be themselves."

Lena picked at the black polish on her index finger. "Sometimes I wish I could act like everyone else, but I can't change who I am. I've tried. But I never wear the right clothes or say the right thing, and something always goes wrong. I just wish I could be myself and still have friends who noticed whether I'm in school or not."

"Believe me, they notice. At least, they did today." She almost laughed—almost. "I mean, in a good way." I looked away.

I notice.

What?

Whether you're in school or not.

"Then I guess you are crazy." But when she said the words, it sounded like she was smiling.

Looking at her, it didn't seem to matter anymore if I had a

lunch table to sit at or not. I couldn't explain it, but she was, this was, bigger than that. I couldn't sit by and watch them try to take her down. Not her.

"You know, it's always like this." She was talking to the sky. A cloud floated into the darkening gray-blue.

"Cloudy?"

"At school, for me." She held up her hand and waved it. The cloud seemed to swirl in the direction her hand was moving. She wiped her eyes with her sleeve.

"It's not like I really care if they like me. I just don't want them to automatically hate me." Now the cloud was a circle.

"Those idiots? In a few months, Emily will get a new car and Savannah will get a new crown and Eden will dye her hair a new color and Charlotte will get, I don't know, a baby or a tattoo or something, and this will all be ancient history." I was lying, and she knew it. Lena waved her hand again. Now the cloud looked more like a slightly dented circle, and then maybe a moon.

"I know they're idiots. Of course they're idiots. All that dyed blond hair and those stupid little matching metallic bags."

"Exactly. They're stupid. Who cares?"

"I care. They bother me. And that's why I'm stupid. That makes me exponentially more stupid than stupid. I'm stupid to the power of stupid." She waved her hand. The moon blew away.

"That's the stupidest thing I've ever heard." I looked at her out of the corner of my eye. She tried not to smile. We both just lay there for a minute.

"You know what's stupid? I have books under my bed." I just said it, like it was something I said all the time.

"What?"

"Novels. Tolstoy. Salinger. Vonnegut. And I read them. You know, because I want to."

She rolled over, propping her head on her elbow. "Yeah? What do your jock buddies think of that?"

"Let's just say I keep it to myself and stick to my jump shot."

"Yeah, well. At school, I noticed you stick to comics." She tried to sound casual. "*Silver Surfer.* I saw you reading it. Right before everything happened."

You noticed?

I might have noticed.

I didn't know if we were speaking, or if I was just imagining the whole thing, except I wasn't that crazy—yet.

She changed the subject, or more accurately, she changed it back. "I read, too. Poetry mostly."

I could imagine her stretched out on her bed reading a poem, although I had trouble imagining that bed in Ravenwood Manor. "Yeah? I've read that guy, Bukowski." Which was true, if two poems counted.

"I have all his books."

I knew she didn't want to talk about what had happened, but I couldn't take it anymore. I had to know. "Are you going to tell me?"

"Tell you what?"

"What happened back there?"

There was a long silence. She sat up and pulled at the grass around her. She flopped around on her stomach and looked me in the eye. She was only a few inches away from my face. I lay there, frozen, trying to focus on what she was saying. "I really don't know. Things like that just happen to me, sometimes. I can't control it."

"Like the dreams." I watched her face, looking for even a flicker of recognition.

"Like the dreams." She said it without thinking, then flinched and looked at me, stricken. I had been right all along.

"You remember the dreams."

She hid her face in her hands.

I sat up. "I knew it was you, and you knew it was me. You knew what I was talking about the whole time." I pulled her hands away from her face, and the current buzzed up my arm.

You're the girl.

"Why didn't you say something last night?"

I didn't want you to know.

She wouldn't look at me.

"Why?" The word sounded loud, in the quiet of the garden. And when she looked at me, her face was pale, and she looked different. Frightened. Her eyes were like the sea before a storm on the Carolina coast.

"I didn't expect you to be here, Ethan. I thought they were just dreams. I didn't know you were a real person."

"But once you knew it was me, why didn't you say anything?"

"My life is complicated. And I didn't want you—I don't want anyone to get mixed up in it." I had no idea what she was talking about. I was still touching her hand; I was so aware of it. I could feel the rough stone beneath us, and I grabbed for the edge of it, supporting myself. Only my hand closed around something small and round, stuck to the edge of the stone. A beetle, or maybe a rock. It came off from the stone into my hand.

Then the shock hit. I felt Lena's hand tighten around mine.

What's happening, Ethan?

I don't know.

Everything around me changed, and it was like I was somewhere else. I was in the garden, but not in the garden. And the smell of lemons changed, into the smell of smoke—

It was midnight, but the sky was on fire. The flames reached into the sky, pushing forth massive fists of smoke, swallowing everything in their path. Even the moon. The ground had turned to swamp. Burned ashen ground that had been drenched by the rains that preceded the fire. If only it had rained today. Genevieve choked back the smoke that burned her throat so badly it hurt to breathe. Mud clung to the bottom of her skirts, causing her to stumble every few feet on the voluminous folds of fabric, but she forced herself to keep moving.

It was the end of the world. Of her world.

And she could hear the screams, mixed with gunshots and the unrelenting roar of the flames. She could hear the soldiers shouting orders of murder.

"Burn down those houses. Let the Rebels feel the weight of their defeat. Burn it all!"

And one by one, Union soldiers had lit the great houses of the plantations ablaze, with their own kerosene-laden bed sheets and curtains. One by one, Genevieve watched the homes of her neighbors, of her friends and family, surrender to the flames. And in the worst of circumstances, many of those friends and relatives surrendered as well, eaten alive by the flames in the very homes where they were born.

That's why she was running, into the smoke, toward the fire—right into the mouth of the beast. She had to get to Greenbrier before the soldiers. And she didn't have much time. The soldiers were methodical, working their way down the Santee burning the houses one by one. They had already burned Blackwell; Dove's Crossing would be next, then Greenbrier and Ravenwood. General Sherman and his army had started the burning campaign hundreds of miles before they reached Gatlin. They had burned Columbia to the ground, and continued marching east, burning everything in their path. When they reached the outskirts of Gatlin the Confederate flag was still waving, the second wind they needed.

It was the smell that told her she was too late. Lemons. The tart smell of lemons mixed with ash. They were burning the lemon trees.

Genevieve's mother loved lemons. So when her father had visited a plantation in Georgia when she was a girl, he had brought her mother two lemon trees. Everyone said they wouldn't grow, that the cold South Carolina winter nights would kill them. But Genevieve's mother didn't listen. She planted those trees right in front of the cotton field, tending them herself. On those cold winter nights, she had covered the trees with wool blankets and piled dirt along the edges to keep the moisture out. And those trees grew. They grew so well that over the years, Genevieve's father had bought her twenty-eight more trees. Some of the other ladies in town asked their husbands for lemon trees, and a few of them even got a tree or two. But none of them could figure out how to keep their trees alive. The trees only seemed to flourish at Greenbrier, at her mother's hand.

Nothing had ever been able to kill those trees. Until today.

"What just happened?" I felt Lena pull her hand away from mine, and opened my eyes. She was shaking. I looked down and opened my hand to reveal the object I had inadvertently grabbed from under the stone.

"I think it had something to do with this." My hand had been curled around a battered old cameo, black and oval, with a woman's face etched in ivory and mother of pearl. The work on the face of it was intricate with detail. On the side, I noticed a small bump. "Look. I think it's a locket."

I pushed on the spring, and the cameo front opened to reveal a tiny inscription. "It just says GREENBRIER. And a date."

She sat up. "What's Greenbrier?"

"This must be it. This isn't Ravenwood. It's Greenbrier. The next plantation over."

"And that vision, the fires, did you see it, too?"

I nodded. It was almost too horrible to talk about. "This has to be Greenbrier, what's left of it, anyway."

"Let me see the locket." I handed it to her carefully. It looked like something that had survived a lot—maybe even the fire from the vision. She turned it over in her hands. "FEBRUARY 11TH, 1865." She dropped the locket, turning pale.

"What's wrong?"

She stared down at it in the grass. "February eleventh is my birthday."

"So it's a coincidence. An early birthday present."

"Nothing in my life is a coincidence."

I picked up the locket and flipped it over. On the back were two sets of engraved initials. "ECW & GKD. This locket must have belonged to one of them." I paused. "That's weird. My initials are ELW."

"My birthday, your initials. Don't you think that's a little more than weird?" Maybe she was right. Still—

"We should try it again, so we can find out." It was like an itch that had to be scratched.

"I don't know. It could be dangerous. It really felt like we were there. My eyes are still burning from the smoke." She was right. We hadn't left the garden, but it had felt like we had been right there in the middle of the fires. I could feel the smoke in my lungs, but it didn't matter. I had to know.

I held out the locket, and my hand. "Come on, aren't you braver than that?" It was a dare. She rolled her eyes, but reached toward it all the same. Her fingers brushed against mine, and I felt the warmth of her hand spreading into mine. Electric goosebumps. I don't know any other way to describe it.

I closed my eyes and waited—nothing. I opened my eyes. "Maybe we just imagined it. Maybe it's just out of batteries."

Lena looked at me like I was Earl Petty in Algebra, the second time around. "Maybe you can't tell something like that what to do, or when to do it." She got up and brushed herself off. "I've gotta go."

She paused, looking down at me. "You know, you're not what I expected." She turned her back on me and began to weave her way through the lemon trees, to the outer edge of the garden.

"Wait!" I called after her, but she kept going. I tried to catch up with her, stumbling back over the roots.

When she reached the last lemon tree, she stopped. "Don't."

"Don't what?"

She wouldn't look at me. "Just leave me alone, while everything's still okay."

"I don't understand what you're talking about. Seriously. And I'm trying, here."

"Forget it."

"You think you're the only complicated person in the world?"

"No. But—it's sort of my specialty." She turned to go. I hesitated, and put my hand on her shoulder. It was warm from the fading sun. I could feel the bone beneath her shirt, and in that moment she seemed like a fragile thing, like in the dreams. Which was weird, because when she was facing me, all I could think of was how unbreakable she seemed. Maybe it had something to do with those eyes.

We stood like that for a moment, until finally she gave in and turned toward me. I tried again. "Look. There's something going on here. The dreams, the song, the smell, and now the locket. It's like we're supposed to be friends."

"Did you just say, the smell?" She looked horrified. "In the same sentence as friends?"

"Technically, I think it was a different sentence."

She stared at my hand, and I took it off her shoulder. But I couldn't let it go. I looked right into her eyes, really looked, maybe for the first time. The green abyss looked like it went somewhere so far away I could never reach it, not in a whole lifetime. I wondered what Amma's "eyes are the windows to the soul" theory would make of that.

It's too late, Lena. You're already my friend.

I can't be.

We're in this together.

Please. You have to trust me. We're not.

77

She broke her eyes away from me, leaning her head back against the lemon tree. She looked miserable. "I know you're not like the rest of them. But there are things you can't understand about me. I don't know why we connect the way we do. I don't know why we have the same dreams, any more than you."

"But I want to know what's going on—"

"I turn sixteen in five months." She held up her hand, inked with a number as usual. 151. "A hundred and fifty-one days." Her birthday. The changing number written on her hand. She was counting down to her birthday.

"You don't know what that means, Ethan. You don't know anything. I may not even be here after that."

"You're here now."

She looked past me, up toward Ravenwood. When she finally spoke, she wasn't looking at me. "You like that poet, Bukowski?"

"Yeah," I answered, confused.

"Don't try."

"I don't understand."

"That's what it says, on Bukowski's grave." She disappeared through the stone wall and was gone. Five months. I had no idea what she was talking about, but I recognized the feeling in my gut.

Panic.

By the time I made it through the door in the wall, she had vanished as if she was never there, leaving only the wafting breeze of lemons and rosemary behind her. Funny thing was, the more she ran, the more determined I was to follow.

Don't try.

I was pretty sure my grave would say something different.

⊰ 9.12 ⊱

The Sisters

The kitchen table was still set when I got home, lucky for me, because Amma would have killed me if I'd missed dinner. What I hadn't considered was the phone tree that had been activated the minute I walked out of English class. No less than half the town must have called Amma by the time I got home.

"Ethan Wate? Is that you? Because if it is, you are in for a world a trouble."

I heard a familiar banging sound. Things were worse than I thought. I ducked under the doorway and into the kitchen. Amma was standing at the counter in her industrial denim tool apron, which had fourteen pockets for nails and could hold up to four power tools. She was holding her Chinese cleaver, the counter piled high with carrots, cabbage, and other vegetables I couldn't identify. Spring rolls required more chopping than any other recipe in Amma's blue plastic box. If she was making spring rolls, it only meant one thing, and it wasn't just that she liked Chinese food.

I tried to come up with an acceptable explanation, but I had nothing.

"Coach called this afternoon, and Mrs. English, and Principal Harper, and Link's mamma, and half the ladies from the DAR. And you know how I hate talkin' to those women. Evil as sin, every one a them."

Gatlin was full of ladies' auxiliaries, but the DAR was the mother of them all. True to its name, the Daughters of the American Revolution, you had to prove you were related to an actual patriot from the American Revolution to be eligible for membership. Being a member apparently entitled you to tell your River Street neighbors what colors to paint their houses and generally boss, pester, and judge everyone in town. Unless you were Amma. That I'd like to see.

"They all said the same thing. That you ran out a school, in the middle a class, chasin' after that Duchannes girl." Another carrot rolled across the cutting board.

"I know, Amma, but—"

The cabbage split in half. "So I said, 'No, my boy wouldn't leave school without permission and skip practice. There must be some mistake. Must be some other boy disrepectin' his teacher and sullyin' his family name. Can't be a boy I raised, livin' in this house.'" Green onions flew across the counter.

I'd committed the worst of crimes, embarrassing her. Worst of all, in the eyes of Mrs. Lincoln and the women of the DAR, her sworn enemies.

"What do you have to say for yourself? What would make

you run out a school like your tail was on fire? And I *don't* wanna hear it was some girl."

I took a deep breath. What could I say? I had been dreaming about some mystery girl for months, who showed up in town and just happened to be Macon Ravenwood's niece? That, in addition to terrifying dreams about this girl, I had a vision of some other woman, who I definitely didn't know, who lived during the Civil War?

Yeah, that would get me out of trouble, around the same time the sun exploded and the solar system died.

"It's not what you think. The kids in our class were giving Lena a hard time, teasing her about her uncle, saying he hauls dead bodies around in his hearse, and she got really upset and ran out of class."

"I'm waitin' for the part that explains what any a this has to do with you."

"Aren't you the one always telling me to 'walk in the steps of our Lord?' Don't you think He'd want me to stick up for someone who was being picked on?" Now I'd done it. I could see it in her eyes.

"Don't you dare use the Word a the Lord to justify breakin' the rules at school, or I swear I will go outside and get a switch and burn some sense into your backside. I don't care how old you are. You hear me?" Amma had never hit me with anything in my life, although she had chased me with a switch a few times to make a point. But this wasn't the moment to bring that up.

The situation was quickly going from bad to worse; I needed a distraction. The locket was still burning a hole in my back pocket. Amma loved mysteries. She had taught me to read when

I was four using crime novels and the crossword over her shoulder. I was the only kid in kindergarten who could read *examination* on the blackboard because it looked so much like *medical examiner*. As for mysteries, the locket was a good one. I'd just leave out the part about touching it and seeing a Civil War vision.

"You're right, Amma. I'm sorry. I shouldn't have left school. I was just trying to make sure Lena was okay. A window broke in the classroom right behind her, and she was bleeding. I just went to her house to see if she was all right."

"You were up at that house?"

"Yeah, but she was outside. Her uncle is really shy, I guess."

"You don't need to tell me about Macon Ravenwood, like you know anything I don't already know." The Look.

"H. E. B. E. T. U. D. I. N. O. U. S."

"What?"

"As in, you don't have a lick a sense, Ethan Wate."

I fished the locket out of my pocket and walked over to where she was still standing by the stove. "We were out back, behind the house, and we found something," I said, opening my hand so she could take a look. "It has an inscription inside."

The expression on Amma's face stopped me cold. She looked like something had knocked the wind right out of her.

"Amma, are you okay?" I reached for her elbow, to steady her in case she was about to faint. But she pulled her arm away before I could touch her, like she'd burned her hand on the handle of a pot.

"Where did you get that?" Her voice was a whisper.

"We found it in the dirt, at Ravenwood."

"You didn't find that at Ravenwood Plantation."

"What are you talking about? Do you know who it belonged to?"

"Stand right here. Don't you move," she instructed, rushing out of the kitchen.

But I ignored her, following her to her room. It had always looked more like an apothecary than a bedroom, with a low white single bed tucked beneath rows of shelves. On the shelves were neatly stacked newspapers—Amma never threw away a finished crossword—and Mason jars full of her stock ingredients for making charms. Some were her old standards: salt, colored stones, herbs. Then there were more unusual collections, like a jar of roots and another of abandoned bird nests. The top shelf was just bottles of dirt. She was acting weird, even for Amma. I was only a couple of steps behind her, but she was already tearing through her drawers by the time I got there.

"Amma, what are you—"

"Didn't I tell you to stay in the kitchen? Don't you bring *that* thing in here!" she shrieked, when I took a step forward.

"What are you so upset about?" She stuffed a few things I couldn't get a look at into her tool apron, and rushed back out of the room. I caught up with her back in the kitchen. "Amma, what's the matter?"

"Take this." She handed me a threadbare handkerchief, careful not to let her hand touch mine. "Now you wrap that thing up in here. Right now, right this second."

This was beyond going dark. She was totally losing it.

"Amma—"

"Do as I say, Ethan." She never called me by my first name without my last.

Once the locket was safely wrapped in the handkerchief, she calmed down a little bit. She rifled through the lower pockets of her apron, removing a small leather bag and a vial of powder. I knew enough to recognize the makings of one of her charms when I saw them. Her hand shook slightly as she poured some of the dark powder into the leather pouch. "Did you wrap it up tight?"

"Yeah," I said, expecting her to correct me for answering her so informally.

"You sure?"

"Yes."

"Now you put it in here." The leather pouch was warm and smooth in my hand. "Go on now."

I dropped the offending locket into the pouch.

"Tie this around it," she instructed, handing me a piece of what looked like ordinary twine, although I knew nothing Amma used for her charms was ever ordinary, or what it seemed. "Now you take it back there, where you found it, and you bury it. Take it there straightaway."

"Amma, what's going on?" She took a few steps forward and grabbed my chin, pushing the hair out of my eyes. For the first time since I pulled the locket out of my pocket, she looked me in the eye. We stayed that way for what seemed like the longest minute of my life. Her expression was an unfamiliar one, uncertain.

"You're not ready," she whispered, releasing her hand.

"Not ready for what?"

"Do as I say. Take that bag back to where you found it and bury it. Then you come right home. I don't want you messin' with that girl anymore, you hear me?"

She had said all she planned to say, maybe more. But I'd never know because if there was one thing Amma was better at than reading cards or solving a crossword, it was keeping secrets.

—◠

"Ethan Wate, you up?"

What time was it? Nine-thirty. Saturday. I should have been up by now, but I was exhausted. Last night I'd spent two hours wandering around, so Amma would believe I had gone back to Greenbrier to bury the locket.

I climbed out of bed and stumbled across the room, tripping on a box of stale Oreos. My room was always a mess, crammed with so much stuff my dad said it was a fire hazard and one day I was going to burn the whole house down, not that he'd been in here in a while. Aside from my map, the walls and ceiling were plastered with posters of places I hoped I'd get to see one day— Athens, Barcelona, Moscow, even Alaska. The room was lined with stacks of shoeboxes, some three or four feet high. Although the stacks looked random, I could tell you the location of every box—from the white Adidas box with my lighter collection from my eighth grade pyro phase, to the green New Balance box with the shell casings and a torn piece of flag I found at Fort Sumter with my mom.

And the one I was looking for, the yellow Nike box, with the locket that had sent Amma off the deep end. I opened the box and pulled out the smooth leather pouch. Hiding it had seemed like a good idea last night, but I put it back in my pocket, just in case.

Amma shouted up the stairs again. "Get on down here or you're gonna be late."

"I'll be down in a minute."

Every Saturday, I spent half the day with the three oldest women in Gatlin, my great-aunts Mercy, Prudence, and Grace. Everyone in town called them the Sisters, like they were a single entity, which in a way they were. Each of them was about a hundred years old, and even they couldn't remember who was the oldest. All three of them had been married multiple times, but they'd outlived all their husbands and moved into Aunt Grace's house together. And they were even crazier than they were old.

When I was about twelve, my mom started dropping me off there on Saturdays to help out, and I had been going there ever since. The worst part was, I had to take them to church on Saturdays. The Sisters were Southern Baptist, and they went to church on Saturdays and Sundays, and most other days, too.

But today was different. I was out of bed and into the shower before Amma could call me a third time. I couldn't wait to get over there. The Sisters knew just about everyone who had ever lived in Gatlin; they should, since between the three of them, they had been related to half the town by marriage, at one time or another. After the vision, it was obvious the *G* in *GKD* stood for Genevieve. But if there was anyone who would know what the rest of the initials stood for, it would be the three oldest women in town.

When I opened the top drawer of my dresser to grab some socks, I noticed a little doll that looked like a sock monkey holding a tiny bag of salt and a blue stone, one of Amma's charms. She made them to ward off evil spirits or bad luck, even a cold. She put one over the door of my dad's study when he started working on Sundays instead of going to church. Even though my dad never paid much attention when he was there, Amma said the Good Lord still gave you credit for showing up. A couple of months later, my dad bought her a kitchen witch on the Internet and hung it over the stove. Amma was so angry she served him cold grits and burnt coffee for a week.

Usually, I didn't give it much thought when I found one of Amma's little gifts. But there was something about the locket. Something she didn't want me to find out.

There was only one word to describe the scene when I arrived at the Sisters' house. Chaos. Aunt Mercy answered the door, hair still in rollers.

"Thank goodness you're here, Ethan. We have an E-mergency on our hands," she said, pronouncing the "E" as if it was a word all by itself. Half the time I couldn't understand them at all, their accents were so thick and their grammar so bad. But that's the way it was in Gatlin; you could tell how old someone was by the way they spoke.

"Ma'am?"

"Harlon James's been injured, and I'm not convinced he ain't about ta pass over." She whispered the last two words like God Himself might be listening, and she was afraid to give Him any ideas. Harlon James was Aunt Prudence's Yorkshire terrier, named after her most recent late husband.

"What happened?"

"I'll tell you what happened," Aunt Prudence said, appearing out of nowhere with a first aid kit in her hand. "Grace tried ta kill poor Harlon James, and he is barely hangin' on."

"I did not try ta kill him," Aunt Grace shrieked from the kitchen. "Don't you tell tales, Prudence Jane. It was an accident!"

"Ethan, you call Dean Wilks, and tell him we have an E-mergency," Aunt Prudence instructed, pulling a capsule of smelling salts and two extra-large Band-Aids out of the first aid kit.

"We're losin' him!" Harlon James was lying on the kitchen floor, looking traumatized but nowhere close to death. His back leg was tucked up underneath him, and it dragged behind him when he tried to get up. "Grace, the Lord as my witness, if Harlon James dies . . ."

"He's not going to die, Aunt Prue. I think his leg is broken. What happened?"

"Grace tried ta beat him ta death with a broom."

"That's not true. I told you, I wasn't wearing my spectacles and he looked just like a wharf rat runnin' through the kitchen."

"How would you know what a wharf rat looks like? You've never been ta a wharf in all your life."

So I drove the Sisters, who were completely hysterical, and Harlon James, who probably wished he was dead, to Dean Wilks' place in their 1964 Cadillac. Dean Wilks ran the feed store, but he was the closest thing to a vet in town. Luckily, Harlon James had only suffered a broken leg, so Dean Wilks was up to the task.

By the time we got back to the house, I was wondering if I wasn't the crazy one for thinking I'd be able to get any information out of the Sisters. Thelma's car was in the driveway. My dad had hired Thelma to keep an eye on the Sisters after Aunt Grace almost burned their house down ten years ago, when she put a

lemon meringue pie in the oven and left it in there all afternoon
when they were at church.

"Where you girls been?" Thelma called from the kitchen.

They bumped into each other trying to push their way into
the kitchen to tell Thelma about their misadventure. I slumped
into one of the mismatched kitchen chairs next to Aunt Grace,
who looked depressed about being the villain of the story again.
I pulled the locket out of my pocket, holding the chain in the
handkerchief, and spun it around a few times.

"Whatcha got there, handsome?" Thelma asked, pinching
some snuff out of the can on the windowsill and tucking into
her bottom lip, which looked even weirder than it sounded,
since Thelma was kind of dainty and resembled Dolly Parton.

"It's just a locket I found out by Ravenwood Plantation."

"Ravenwood? What the devil were you doin' out there?"

"My friend's staying there."

"You mean Lena Duchannes?" Aunt Mercy asked. Of course
she knew, the whole town knew. This was Gatlin.

"Yes, ma'am. We're in the same class at school." I had their
attention. "We found this locket in the garden behind the
great house. We don't know who it belonged to, but it looks
really old."

"That's not Macon Ravenwood's property. That's part a
Greenbrier," Aunt Prue said, sounding sure of herself.

"Let me get a look at that," Aunt Mercy said, taking her
glasses out of the pocket of her housecoat.

I handed her the locket, still wrapped in the handkerchief. "It
has an inscription."

"I can't read that. Grace, can you make that out?" she asked,
handing the locket to Aunt Grace.

89

"I don't see nothin' at all," Aunt Grace said, squinting hard.

"There are two sets of initials, right here," I said, pointing to the grooves in the metal, "ECW and GKD. And if you flip that disc over, there's a date. February 11, 1865."

"That date seems real familiar," Aunt Prudence said. "Mercy, what happened on that date?"

"Weren't you married on that date, Grace?"

"1865, not 1965," Aunt Grace corrected. Their hearing wasn't much better than their vision. "February 11, 1865 . . ."

"That was the year the Fed'rals almost burned Gatlin ta the ground," Aunt Grace said. "Our great-granddaddy lost everything in that fire. Don't you remember that story, girls? Gen'ral Sherman and the Union army marched clean through the South, burnin' everything in their path, includin' Gatlin. They called it the Great Burnin'. At least part a every plantation in Gatlin was destroyed, except Ravenwood. My granddaddy used ta say Abraham Ravenwood musta made a deal with the Devil that night."

"What do you mean?"

"It was the only way that place coulda been left standin'. The Fed'rals burned every plantation along the river, one at a time, till they got ta Ravenwood. They just marched on past, like it wasn't there at all."

"The way Granddaddy told it, that wasn't the only thing strange 'bout that night," Aunt Prue said, feeding Harlon James a piece of bacon. "Abraham had a brother, lived there with him, and he just up and disappeared that night. Nobody ever saw him again."

"That doesn't seem that strange. Maybe he was killed by the Union soldiers, or trapped in one of those burning houses," I said.

Aunt Grace raised an eyebrow. "Or maybe it was somethin' else. They never did find a body." I realized people had been talking about the Ravenwoods for generations; it didn't start with Macon Ravenwood. I wondered what else the Sisters knew.

"What about Macon Ravenwood? What do you know about him?"

"That boy never did have a chance on account a bein' E-legitimate." In Gatlin, being illegitimate was like being a communist or an atheist. "His daddy, Silas, met Macon's mamma after his first wife left him. She was a pretty girl, from New Orleans, I think. Anyhow, not long after, Macon and his brother were born. But Silas never did marry her, and then she up and left, too."

Aunt Prue interrupted, "Grace Ann, you don't know how ta tell a story. Silas Ravenwood was an E-centric, and as mean as the day is long. And there were strange things goin' on at that house. The lights were on all night long, and every now and again a man in a tall black hat was seen wanderin' 'round up there."

"And the wolf. Tell him about the wolf." I didn't need them to tell me about that dog, or whatever it was. I'd seen it myself. But it couldn't be the same animal. Dogs, even wolves, didn't live that long.

"There was a wolf up at the house. Silas kept it like it was a pet!" Aunt Mercy shook her head.

"But those boys, they moved back and forth between Silas and their mamma, and when they were with him, Silas treated them somethin' awful. Beat on 'em all the time and barely let 'em outta his sight. He wouldn't even let 'em go ta school."

"Maybe that's why Macon Ravenwood never leaves his house," I said.

Aunt Mercy waved her hand in the air, as if that was the silliest thing she'd ever heard. "He leaves his house. I've seen him a mess a times over at the DAR buildin', right after supper time." Sure she had.

That was the thing about the Sisters; half the time they had a firm grasp on reality, but that was only half the time. I had never heard of anyone seeing Macon Ravenwood, so I doubted he was hanging around the DAR looking at paint chips and chatting up Mrs. Lincoln.

Aunt Grace scrutinized the locket more carefully, holding it up to the light. "I can tell you one thing. This here handkerchief belonged ta Sulla Treadeau, Sulla the Prophet they called her, on account a folks said she could see the future in the cards."

"Tarot cards?" I asked.

"What other kind a cards are there?"

"Well, there are playin' cards, and greetin' cards, and place cards for parties . . ." Aunt Mercy rambled.

"How do you know the handkerchief belonged to her?"

"Her initials are embroidered right here on the edge, and you see that there?" she asked, pointing to a tiny bird embroidered under the initials. "That there was her mark."

"Her mark?"

"Most readers had a mark back then. They'd mark their decks ta make sure nobody switched their cards. A reader is only as good as her deck. I know that much," Thelma said, spitting into a small urn in the corner of the room with the precision of a marksman.

Treadeau. That was Amma's last name.

"Was she related to Amma?"

"Of course she was. She was Amma's great-great-grand-mamma."

"What about the initials on the locket? ECW and GKD? Do you know anything about them?" It was a long shot. I couldn't remember the last time the Sisters had ever had a moment of clarity that lasted this long.

"Are you teasin' an old woman, Ethan Wate?"

"No ma'am."

"ECW. Ethan Carter Wate. He was your great-great-great-uncle, or was it your great-great-great-great-uncle?"

"You've never been any good with arithmetic," Aunt Prudence interrupted.

"Anyhow, he was your great-great-great-great-granddaddy Ellis' brother."

"Ellis Wate's brother was named Lawson, not Ethan. That's how I got my middle name."

"Ellis Wate had two brothers, Ethan and Lawson. You were named for both of 'em. Ethan Lawson Wate." I tried to picture my family tree. I had seen it enough times. And if there's one thing a Southerner knows, it's their family tree. There was no Ethan Carter Wate on the framed copy hanging in our dining room. I had obviously overestimated Aunt Grace's lucidity.

I must have looked unconvinced because a second later, Aunt Prue was up and out of her chair. "I have the Wate Family Tree in my genealogy book. I keep track a the whole lineage for the Sisters a the Confed'racy."

The Sisters of the Confederacy, the lesser cousin of the DAR, but equally horrifying, was some kind of sewing circle holdover from the War. These days, members spent most of their time

93

tracking their Civil War roots for documentaries and miniseries like *The Blue and the Gray.*

"Here it is." Aunt Prue shuffled back into the kitchen carrying a huge leather-bound scrapbook, with yellowed pieces of paper and old photographs sticking out from the edges. She flipped through the pages, dropping scraps of paper and old newspaper clippings all over the floor.

"Will you look at that . . . Burton Free, my third husband. Wasn't he just the handsomest a all my husbands?" she asked, holding up the cracked photograph for the rest of us.

"Prudence Jane, keep lookin'. This boy is testin' our memory." Aunt Grace was noticeably agitated.

"It's right here, after the Statham Tree."

I stared at the names I knew so well from the family tree in my dining room at home.

There was the name, the name missing from the family tree at Wate's Landing—Ethan Carter Wate. Why would the Sisters have a different version of my family tree? It was obvious which tree was the real one. I was holding the proof in my hand, wrapped in the handkerchief of a hundred-and-fifty-year-old prophet.

"Why isn't he on my family tree?"

"Most family trees in the South are fulla lies, but I'm surprised he made it onta any copy a the Wate Family Tree," Aunt Grace said, shutting the book and sending a cloud of dust into the air.

"It's only on account a my excellent record keepin' that he's even on this one." Aunt Prue smiled proudly, showing off both sets of her dentures.

I had to get them to focus. "Why wouldn't he make it on the family tree, Aunt Prue?"

"On account a him bein' a deserter."

WATE FAMILY TREE

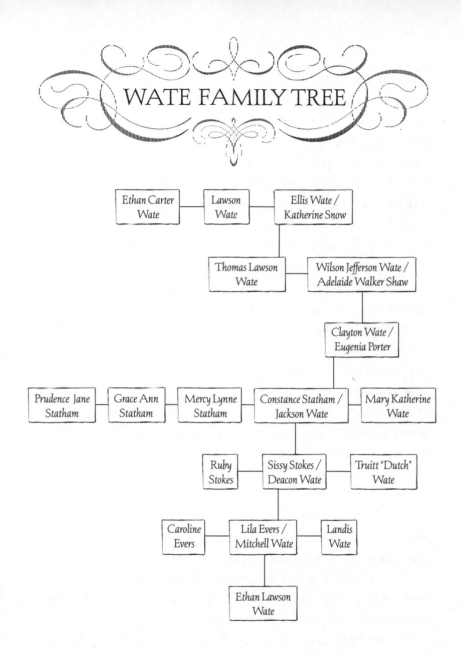

Ethan Carter Wate — Lawson Wate — Ellis Wate / Katherine Snow

Thomas Lawson Wate — Wilson Jefferson Wate / Adelaide Walker Shaw

Clayton Wate / Eugenia Porter

Prudence Jane Statham — Grace Ann Statham — Mercy Lynne Statham — Constance Statham / Jackson Wate — Mary Katherine Wate

Ruby Stokes — Sissy Stokes / Deacon Wate — Truitt "Dutch" Wate

Caroline Evers — Lila Evers / Mitchell Wate — Landis Wate

Ethan Lawson Wate

I wasn't following. "What do you mean, a deserter?"

"Lord, what do they teach you young'uns in that fancy high school a yours?" Aunt Grace was busy picking all the pretzels out of the Chex Mix.

"Deserters. The Confederates who ran out on Gen'ral Lee durin' the War." I must have looked confused because Aunt Prue felt compelled to elaborate. "There were two kinds a Confederate soldiers durin' the War. The ones who supported the cause of Confed'racy and the ones whose families made them enlist." Aunt Prue stood up and walked toward the counter, pacing back and forth like a real history teacher delivering a lecture.

"By 1865, Lee's army was beaten, starvin', and outnumbered. Some say the Rebels were losin' faith, so they up and left. Deserted their regiments. Ethan Carter Wate was one of 'em. He was a deserter." All three of them lowered their heads as if the shame was just too much for them.

"So you're telling me he was erased from the family tree because he didn't want to starve to death, fighting a losing war for the wrong side?"

"That's one way a lookin' at it, I suppose."

"That's the stupidest thing I've ever heard."

Aunt Grace jumped up out of her chair, as much as any ninety-something-year-old woman can jump. "Don't you sass us, Ethan. That tree was changed long before we were born."

"I'm sorry, ma'am." She smoothed her skirt and sat back down. "Why would my parents name me after some great-great-great-uncle who shamed the family?"

"Well, your mamma and daddy had their own ideas 'bout all that, what with all those books they read about the War. You know they've always been liberal. Who knows what they were thinkin'? You'd have ta ask your daddy." Like there was any chance he would tell me. But knowing my parents' sensibilities, my mom had probably been proud of Ethan Carter Wate. I was pretty proud, too. I ran my hand over the faded brown page of Aunt Prue's scrapbook.

"What about the initials GKD? I think the G might stand for Genevieve," I said, already knowing it did.

"GKD. Didn't you date a boy with the initials GD once, Mercy?"

"I can't recollect. Do you remember a GD, Grace?"

"GD . . . GD? No, I can't say as I do." I'd lost them.

"Oh my goodness. Look here at the time, girls. It's time for church," Aunt Mercy said.

Aunt Grace motioned toward the garage door. "Ethan, you be a good boy and pull the Cadillac around, ya hear. We just have ta put on our faces."

I drove them four blocks to the afternoon service, at the Evangelical Missionary Baptist Church, and pushed Aunt Mercy's wheelchair up the gravel driveway. This took longer than actually driving to the church because every two or three feet the chair would sink into the gravel and I'd have to wiggle it from side to side to free it, nearly tipping it and dumping my great-aunt into the dirt. By the time the preacher took the third testimony from an old lady who swore Jesus had saved her rosebushes from Japanese beetles or her quilting hand from arthritis, I was zoning out. I flipped the locket through my fingers, inside the pocket of my jeans. Why did it show us that vision? Why did it suddenly stop working?

Ethan. Stop. You don't know what you're doing.

Lena was in my head again.

Put it away!

The room started to disappear around me and I could feel Lena's fingers grasping mine, as if she was there beside me—

Nothing could have prepared Genevieve for the sight of Greenbrier burning. The flames licked up its sides, eating away at the lattice and swallowing the veranda. Soldiers carried antiques and paintings out of the house, looting like common thieves. Where was everyone? Were they hiding in the woods like she was? Leaves crackled. She sensed someone behind her, but before she could turn around a muddy hand clamped over her mouth. She grabbed the person's wrist with both hands, trying to break their hold.

"Genevieve, it's me." The hand loosened its grip.

"What are you doin' here? Are you all right?" Genevieve threw her arms around the soldier, dressed in what was left of his once proud gray Confederate uniform.

"I am, darlin'," Ethan said, but she knew he was lying.

"I thought you might be . . ."

Genevieve had only heard from Ethan in letters for the better part of the last two years, since he had enlisted, and she hadn't received a letter since the Battle at Wilderness. Genevieve knew that many of the men who had followed Lee into that battle had never marched back out of Virginia. She had resigned herself to die a spinster. She had been so sure she had lost Ethan. It was almost unimaginable that he was alive, standing here, on this night.

"Where is the rest a your regiment?"

"The last I saw, they were outside a Summit."

"What do you mean, the last you saw? Are they all dead?"

"I don't know. When I left, they were still alive."

"I don't understand."

"I deserted, Genevieve. I couldn't fight one more day for somethin' I didn't believe in. Not after what I've seen. Most a the boys fightin' with me didn't even realize what this war is about—that they're just spillin' their blood over cotton."

Ethan took her cold hands in his, rough with cuts. "I understand if you can't marry me now. I don't have any money and now I don't have any honor."

"I don't care if you have any money, Ethan Carter Wate. You are the most honorable man I've ever known. And I don't care if my daddy thinks our differences are too great to overcome. He's wrong. You're home now and we're gonna get married."

Genevieve clung to him, afraid he might disappear into thin air if she let go. The smell brought her back to the moment. The rancid smell of lemons burning, of their lives burning. "We have to head for the river. That's where Mamma would go. She'd head south toward Aunt Marguerite's place." But Ethan never had time to answer. Someone was coming. Branches were cracking like someone was thrashing through the brush.

"Get behind me," Ethan ordered, pushing Genevieve behind him with one arm and grabbing his rifle with the other. The brush parted and Ivy, Greenbrier's cook, stumbled into view. She was still in her nightgown, black with smoke. She screamed at the sight of the uniform, too frightened to notice it was gray, not blue.

"Ivy, are you all right?" Genevieve rushed forward to catch the old woman, who was already starting to fall.

"Miss Genevieve, what in the world are you doin' out here?"

"I was tryin' to get to Greenbrier. To warn y'all."

"It's too late for that, child, and it wouldn't a done no good. Those Blue Birds broke down the doors and walked right into the house, like it was their own. They gave the place the once-over to see what they wanted to take, and then they just started settin' fires." It was almost impossible to understand her. She was hysterical, and every few seconds she was wracked with a fit of coughing, choking on both the smoke and her tears.

"In all my life I never seen the likes a devils like that. Burnin' a house with women in it. Every one a them will have to answer to God Almighty Himself in the hereafter." Ivy's voice faltered.

It took a moment for Ivy's words to register.

"What do you mean burnin' a house with women in it?"

"I'm so sorry, child."

Genevieve felt her legs buckle beneath her. She knelt in the mud, the rain running down her face, mixing

with her tears. Her mother, her sister, Greenbrier—they
were all gone.

Genevieve looked up at the sky.

"God's the one who's goin' to have to answer to me."

It pulled us out as fast as it had sucked us in. I was staring at the preacher again, and Lena was gone. I could feel her slip away.

Lena?

She didn't answer. I sat in the church in a cold sweat, sandwiched between Aunt Mercy and Aunt Grace, who were fishing in their purses for change for the collection basket.

Burning a house with women in it, a house lined with lemon trees. A house where I'd bet Genevieve had lost her locket. A locket engraved with the day Lena was born, but over a hundred years before. No wonder Lena didn't want to see the visions. I was starting to agree with her.

There were no coincidences.

⊰ 9.14 ⊱

The Real Boo Radley

Sunday night, I reread *The Catcher in the Rye* until I felt tired enough to fall asleep. Only I never got tired enough. And I couldn't read, because reading didn't feel the same. I couldn't disappear into the character of Holden Caulfield, because I couldn't get lost in the story, not the way you need to be, to become somebody else.

I wasn't alone in my head. It was full of lockets, and fires, and voices. People I didn't know, and visions I didn't understand.

And something else. I put the book down and slid my hands behind my head.

Lena? You're there, aren't you?

I stared up at the blue ceiling.

It's no use. I know you're there. Here. Whatever.

I waited, until I heard it. Her voice, unfolding like a tiny, bright memory in the darkest, furthest corner of my mind.

No. Not exactly.

You are. You have been, all night.

Ethan, I'm sleeping. I mean, I was.

I smiled to myself.

No you weren't. You were listening.

I was not.

Just admit it, you were.

Guys. You think everything is about you. Maybe I just like that book.

Can you just drop in whenever you want, now?

There was a long pause.

Not usually, but tonight it just sort of happened. I still don't understand how it works.

Maybe we can ask someone.

Like who?

I don't know. Guess we'll have to figure it out on our own. Just like everything else.

Another pause. I tried not to wonder if the "we" spooked her, in case she could hear me. Maybe it was that, or maybe it was the other thing; she didn't want me to find out anything, if it had to do with her.

Don't try.

I smiled, and felt my eyes closing. I could barely keep them open.

I'm trying.

I turned out the light.

Good night, Lena.

Good night, Ethan.

I hoped she couldn't read all my thoughts.

Basketball. I was definitely going to have to spend more time thinking about basketball. And as I thought about the playbook in my mind, I felt my eyes closing, myself sinking, losing control. . . .

—⌒꙳

Drowning.

I was drowning.

Thrashing in the green water, waves crashing over my head. My feet kicked for the muddy bottom of a river, maybe the Santee, but there was nothing. I could see some kind of light, skimming the river, but I couldn't get to the surface.

I was going down.

"It's my birthday, Ethan. It's happening."

I reached out. She grabbed at my hand, and I twisted to catch it, but she drifted away, and I couldn't hold on anymore. I tried to scream as I watched her pale little hand drift down toward the darkness, but my mouth filled with water and I couldn't make a sound. I could feel myself choking. I was starting to black out.

"I tried to warn you. You have to let me go!"

I sat up in bed. My T-shirt was soaking wet. My pillow was wet. My hair was wet. And my room was sticky and humid. I guessed I'd left the window open again.

"Ethan Wate! Are you listenin' to me? You better get yourself down here yesterday, or you won't be havin' breakfast again this week."

I was in my seat just as three eggs over-easy slid onto my plate of biscuits and gravy. "Good morning, Amma."

She turned her back to me without so much as a look. "Now you know there's nothin' good about it. Don't spit down my back and tell me it's rainin'." She was still aggravated with me, but I wasn't sure if it was because I had walked out of class or brought the locket home. Probably both. I couldn't blame her, though; I didn't usually get in trouble at school. This was all new territory.

"Amma, I'm sorry about leaving class on Friday. It's not gonna happen again. Everything'll be back to normal."

Her face softened, just a little, and she sat down across from me. "Don't think so. We all make our choices, and those choices have consequences. I expect you'll have some hell to pay for yours when you get to school. Maybe you'll start listenin' to me now. Stay away from that Lena Duchannes, and that house."

It wasn't like Amma to side with everyone else in town, considering that was usually the wrong side of things. I could tell she was worried by the way she kept stirring her coffee, long after the milk had disappeared. Amma always worried about me and I loved her for it, but something felt different since I showed her the locket. I walked around the table and gave her a hug. She smelled like pencil lead and Red Hots, like always.

She shook her head, muttering, "Don't want to hear about any green eyes and black hair. It's fixin' to come up a bad cloud today, so you be careful."

Amma wasn't just going dark. Today she was going pitch-black. I could feel it coming up a bad cloud, myself.

Link pulled up in the Beater blasting some terrible tunes, as usual. He turned down the music when I slid into the seat, which was always a bad sign.

"We got trubs."

"I know."

"Jackson's got itself a regular lynch mob this mornin'."

"What'd you hear?"

"Been goin' on since Friday night. I heard my mom talkin', and I tried to call you. Where were you, anyway?"

"I was pretending to bury a hexed locket over at Greenbrier, so Amma would let me back in the house."

Link laughed. He was used to talk about hexes and charms and the evil eye, where Amma was concerned. "At least she's not makin' you wear that stinkin' bag a onion mess around your neck. That was nasty."

"It was garlic. For my mom's funeral."

"It was nasty."

The thing about Link was, we'd been friends since the day he gave me that Twinkie on the bus, and after that he didn't care much what I said or did. Even back then, you knew who your friends were. That's what Gatlin was like. Everything had already happened, ten years ago. For our parents, everything had already happened twenty or thirty years ago. And for the town itself, it seemed like nothing had happened for more than a hundred years. Nothing of consequence, that is.

I had a feeling that was all about to change.

My mom would have said it was time. If there was one thing my mom liked, it was change. Unlike Link's mom. Mrs. Lincoln was a rage-aholic, on a mission, with a network—a dangerous combination. When we were in the eighth grade, Mrs. Lincoln ripped the cable box out of the wall because she found Link watching a Harry Potter movie, a series she had campaigned to ban from the Gatlin County Library because she thought it promoted witchcraft. Luckily, Link managed to sneak over to Earl Petty's house to watch MTV, or Who Shot Lincoln would never have become Jackson High's premier—and by premier, I mean only—rock band.

I never understood Mrs. Lincoln. When my mom was alive, she would roll her eyes and say, "Link may be your best friend, but don't expect me to join the DAR and start wearing a hoop skirt for reenactments." Then we'd both crack up, imagining my mom, who walked miles of muddy battlefields looking for old shell casings, who cut her own hair with garden scissors, as a member of the DAR, organizing bake sales and telling everyone how to decorate their houses.

Mrs. Lincoln was easy to picture in the DAR. She was the Recording Secretary, and even I knew that. She was on the Board with Savannah Snow's and Emily Asher's mothers, while my mom spent most of her time holed up in the library looking at microfiche.

Had spent.

Link was still talking and soon I'd heard enough to start listening. "My mom, Emily's mom, Savannah's . . . they've been burnin' up the phone lines, last couple a nights. Overheard my mom talkin' about the window breakin' in English and how she heard Old Man Ravenwood's niece had blood on her hands."

He swerved around the corner, without even taking a breath. "And about how your girlfriend just got outta a mental institution in Virginia, and how she's an orphan, and has bi-schizo-manic somethin'."

"She's not my girlfriend. We're just friends," I said automatically.

"Shut up. You're so whipped I should buy you a saddle." Which he would've said about any girl I talked to, talked about, or even looked at in the hall.

"She's not. Nothing's happened. We just hang out."

"You're so full a crap, you could pass for a toilet. You like her, Wate. Admit it." Link wasn't big on subtleties, and I don't think he could imagine hanging out with a girl for any reason other than maybe she played lead guitar, except for the obvious ones.

"I'm not saying I don't like her. We're just friends." Which was the truth, actually, whether or not I wanted it to be. But that was a different question. Either way, I must have smiled a little. Wrong move.

Link pretended to vomit into his lap and swerved, narrowly missing a truck. But he was just messing around. Link didn't care who I liked, as long as it gave him something to hassle me about. "Well? Is it true? Did she?"

"Did she what?"

"You know. Fall outta the crazy tree and hit every branch on the way down?"

"A window broke, that's all that happened. It's not a mystery."

"Mrs. Asher's sayin' she punched it out, or threw somethin' at it."

"That's funny, seeing how Mrs. Asher isn't in my English class, last time I checked."

"Yeah well, my mom isn't either, but she told me she was comin' by school today."

"Great. Save her a seat at our lunch table."

"Maybe she's done this at all her schools, and that's why she was in some kinda institution." Link was serious, which meant he'd overheard a whole lot of something since the window incident.

For a second, I remembered what Lena had said about her life. Complicated. Maybe this was one of those complications, or just one of the twenty-six thousand other things she couldn't talk about. What if all the Emily Ashers of the world were right? What if I had taken the wrong side, after all?

"Be careful, man. Could be she's got her own place over in Nutsville."

"If you really believe that, you're an idiot."

We pulled into the school parking lot without speaking. I was annoyed, even though I knew Link was just trying to look out for me. But I couldn't help it. Everything felt different today. I got out and slammed the car door.

Link called after me. "I'm worried about you, dude. You've been actin' crazy."

"What, are you and me a couple now? Maybe you should spend a little more time worrying about why you can't even get a girl to talk to you, crazy or not."

He got out of the car and looked up at the administration building. "Either way, maybe you better tell your 'friend,' whatever that means, to be careful today. Look."

Mrs. Lincoln and Mrs. Asher were talking to Principal Harper on the front steps. Emily was huddled next to her mother, trying to look pathetic. Mrs. Lincoln was lecturing Principal

Harper, who was nodding as if he was memorizing every word. Principal Harper may have been the one running Jackson High, but he knew who ran the town. He was looking at two of them.

When Link's mom finished, Emily dove into a particularly animated version of the window-shattering incident. Mrs. Lincoln reached out and put her hand on Emily's shoulder, sympathetic. Principal Harper just shook his head.

It was a bad cloud day, all right.

—

Lena was sitting in the hearse, writing in her beat-up notebook. The engine was idling. I knocked on the window and she jumped. She looked back toward the administration building. She had seen the mothers, too.

I motioned for her to open the door, but she shook her head. I walked around to the passenger side. The doors were locked, but she wasn't going to get rid of me that easily. I sat down on the hood of her car and dropped my backpack on the gravel next to me. I wasn't going anywhere.

What are you doing?

Waiting.

It's gonna be a long wait.

I've got time.

She stared at me through the windshield. I heard the doors unlock. "Did anyone ever tell you that you're crazy?" She walked around to where I was sitting on the hood, her arms folded, like Amma ready to scold.

"Not as crazy as you, I hear."

She had her hair tied back with a silky black scarf that had conspicuously bright pink cherry blossoms scattered across it. I could imagine her staring at herself in the mirror, feeling like she was going to her own funeral, and tying it on to cheer herself up. A long black, I don't know, a cross between a T-shirt and a dress, hung over her jeans and black Converse. She frowned and looked over at the administration building. The mothers were probably sitting in Principal Harper's office right now.

"Can you hear them?"

She shook her head. "It's not like I can read people's minds, Ethan."

"You can read mine."

"Not really."

"What about last night?"

"I told you, I don't know why it happens. We just seem to— connect." Even the word seemed hard for her to say this morning. She wouldn't look me in the eye. "It's never been like this with anyone before."

I wanted to tell her I knew how she felt. I wanted to tell her when we were together like that in our minds, even if our bodies were a million miles away, I felt closer to her than I'd ever felt to anyone.

I couldn't. I couldn't even think it. I thought about the basketball playbook, the cafeteria menu, the green pea-soup-colored hallway I was about to walk down. Anything else. Instead, I cocked my head to the side. "Yeah. Girls say that to me all the time." Idiot. The more nervous I got, the worse my jokes were.

She smiled, a wobbly, crooked smile. "Don't try to cheer me up. It's not going to work." But it was.

111

I looked back at the front steps. "If you want to know what they're saying, I can tell you."

She looked at me, skeptically.

"How?"

"This is Gatlin. There's nothing even close to a secret here."

"How bad is it?" She looked away. "Do they think I'm crazy?"

"Pretty much."

"A danger to the school?"

"Probably. We don't take kindly to strangers around here. And it doesn't get much stranger than Macon Ravenwood, no offense." I smiled at her.

The first bell rang. She grabbed my sleeve, anxious. "Last night. I had a dream. Did you—"

I nodded. She didn't have to say it. I knew she had been there in the dream with me. "Even had wet hair."

"Me, too." She held out her arm. There was a mark on her wrist, where I had tried to hold on. Before she had sunk down into the darkness. I hoped she hadn't seen that part. Judging from her face, I was pretty sure she had. "I'm sorry, Lena."

"It's not your fault."

"I wish I knew why the dreams are so real."

"I tried to warn you. You should stay away from me."

"Whatever. I'll consider myself warned." Somehow I knew I couldn't do that—stay away from her. Even though I was about to walk into school and face a huge load of crap, I didn't care. It felt good to have someone I could talk to, without editing everything I said. And I could talk to Lena; at Greenbrier it felt like I could've sat there in the weeds and talked to her for days. Longer. As long as she was there to talk to.

"What is it about your birthday? Why did you say you might not be here after that?"

She quickly changed the subject. "What about the locket? Did you see what I saw? The burning? The other vision?"

"Yeah. I was sitting in the middle of church and almost fell out of the pew. But I found out some things from the Sisters. The initials ECW, they stand for Ethan Carter Wate. He was my great-great-great-great-uncle, and my three crazy aunts say I was named after him."

"Then why didn't you recognize the initials on the locket?"

"That's the strange part. I'd never heard of him, and he's conveniently missing from the family tree at my house."

"What about GKD? It's Genevieve, right?"

"They didn't seem to know, but it has to be. She's the one in the visions, and the D must stand for Duchannes. I was gonna ask Amma, but when I showed her the locket her eyes almost fell out of her head. Like it was triple hexed, soaked in a bucket of voodoo, and wrapped in a curse for good measure. And my dad's study is off-limits, where he keeps all my mom's old books about Gatlin and the War." I was rambling. "You could talk to your uncle."

"My uncle won't know anything. Where's the locket now?"

"In my pocket, wrapped in a pouch full of powder Amma dumped all over it when she saw it. She thinks I took it back to Greenbrier and buried it."

"She must hate me."

"No more than any of my girl, you know, friends. I mean, friends who are girls." I couldn't believe how stupid I sounded. "I think we'd better get to class before we get in even more trouble."

113

"Actually, I was thinking about going home. I know I'm going to have to deal with them eventually, but I'd like to live in denial for one more day."

"Won't you get in trouble?"

She laughed. "With my uncle, the infamous Macon Ravenwood, who thinks school is a waste of time and the good citizens of Gatlin are to be avoided at all costs? He'll be thrilled."

"Then why do you even go?" I was pretty sure Link would never show up at school again if his mom wasn't chasing him out the door every morning.

She twisted one of the charms on her necklace, a seven-pointed star. "I guess I thought it would be different here. Maybe I could make some friends, join the newspaper or something. I don't know."

"Our newspaper? *The Jackson Stonewaller?*"

"I tried to join the newspaper at my old school, but they said all the staff positions were filled, even though they never had enough writers to get the paper out on time." She looked away, embarrassed. "I should get going."

I opened the door for her. "I think you should talk to your uncle about the locket. He might know more than you think."

"Trust me, he doesn't." I slammed the door. As much as I wanted her to stay, a part of me was relieved she was going home. I was going to have enough to deal with today.

"Do you want me to turn that in for you?" I pointed at the notebook lying on the passenger seat.

"No, it's not homework." She flipped open the glove compartment and shoved the notebook inside. "It's nothing." Nothing she was going to tell me about, anyway.

"You'd better go before Fatty starts scouting the lot." She

started the car before I could say anything else, and waved as she pulled away from the curb.

I heard a bark. I turned to see the enormous black dog from Ravenwood, only a few feet away, and who it was barking at.

Mrs. Lincoln smiled at me. The dog growled, the hair along its back standing on end. Mrs. Lincoln looked down at it with such revulsion, you would've thought she was looking at Macon Ravenwood himself. In a fight, I wasn't sure which one of them would come out on top.

"Wild dogs carry rabies. Someone should notify the county."

Yeah, someone.

"Yes, ma'am."

"Who was that I just saw drivin' off in that strange black car? You seemed to be havin' quite a conversation." She already knew the answer. It wasn't a question. It was an accusation.

"Ma'am."

"Speakin' a strange, Principal Harper was just tellin' me he's plannin' on offerin' that Ravenwood girl an occupational transfer. She can take her pick, any school in three counties. As long as it's not Jackson."

I didn't say anything. I didn't even look at her.

"It's our responsibility, Ethan. Principal Harper's, mine— every parent in Gatlin's. We have to be sure to keep the young people in this town outta harm's way. And away from the wrong sorta people." Which meant anyone who wasn't like her.

She reached out her hand and touched me on the shoulder, just as she had done to Emily, not ten minutes ago. "I'm sure you understand my meanin'. After all, you're one of us. Your daddy was born here and your mamma was buried here. You belong here. Not *everyone* does."

I stared back at her. She was in her van before I could say another word.

This time, Mrs. Lincoln was after more than burning a few books.

———

Once I got to class, the day became abnormally normal, weirdly normal. I didn't see any more parents, though I suspected they were there loitering around the office. At lunch, I ate three bowls of chocolate pudding with the guys, as usual, though it was clear what and who we weren't talking about. Even the sight of Emily madly texting all through English and chemistry seemed like some kind of reassuring universal truth. Except for the feeling that I knew what, or rather who, she was texting about. Like I said, abnormally normal.

Until Link dropped me off after basketball practice and I decided to do something completely insane.

Amma was standing on the front porch—a sure sign of trouble. "Did you see her?" I should've expected this.

"She wasn't in school today." Technically that was true.

"Maybe that's for the best. Trouble follows that girl around like Macon Ravenwood's dog. I don't want it followin' you into this house."

"I'm going to take a shower. Will dinner be ready soon? Link and I have a project to do tonight." I called from the stairs, trying to sound normal.

"Project? What kinda project?"

"History."

"Where are you goin' and when are you fixin' to get back?"

I let the bathroom door slam before I answered that one. I had a plan, but I needed a story, and it had to be good.

Ten minutes later, sitting at the kitchen table, I had it. It wasn't airtight, but it was the best I could do without a little time. Now I just had to pull it off. I wasn't the best liar, and Amma was no fool. "Link is picking me up after dinner and we're gonna be at the library until it closes. I think it's sometime around nine or ten." I glopped Carolina Gold onto my pulled pork. Carolina Gold, a sticky mess of mustard barbeque sauce, was the one thing Gatlin County was famous for that had nothing to do with the Civil War.

"The library?"

Lying to Amma always made me nervous, so I tried not to do it that often. And tonight I was really feeling it, mostly in my stomach. The last thing I wanted to do was eat three plates of pulled pork, but I had no choice. She knew exactly how much I could put away. Two plates, and I would rouse suspicion. One plate, and she would send me to my room with a thermometer and ginger ale. I nodded and set to work clearing my second plate.

"You haven't set foot in the library since . . ."

"I know." Since my mom died.

The library was home away from home to my mom, and my family. We had spent every Sunday afternoon there since I was a little boy, wandering around the stacks, pulling out every book with a picture of a pirate ship, a knight, a soldier, or an astronaut. My mom used to say, "This is my church, Ethan. This is how we keep the Sabbath holy in our family."

The Gatlin County head librarian, Marian Ashcroft, was my mom's oldest friend, the second smartest historian in Gatlin next to my mom, and until last year, her research partner. They had been grad students together at Duke, and when Marian finished her PhD in African-American studies, she followed my mom down to Gatlin to finish their first book together. They were halfway through their fifth book before the accident.

I hadn't set foot in the library since then, and I still wasn't ready. But I also knew there was no way Amma would stop me from going there. She wouldn't even call to check up on me. Marian Ashcroft was family. And Amma, who had loved my mom as much as Marian did, respected nothing more than family.

"Well, you mind your manners and don't raise your voice. You know what your mamma used to say. Any book is a Good Book, and wherever they keep the Good Book safe is also the House a the Lord." Like I said, my mom would have never made it in the DAR.

Link honked. He was giving me a ride on his way to band practice. I fled the kitchen, feeling so guilty I had to fight the impulse to fling myself into Amma's arms and confess everything, like I was six years old again and had eaten all the dry Jell-O mix out of the pantry. Maybe Amma was right. Maybe I had picked a hole in the sky and the universe was all about to fall in on me.

———

As I stepped up to the door of Ravenwood, my hand tightened around the glossy blue folder, my excuse for showing up at Lena's house uninvited. I was dropping by to give her the English assignment she'd missed today—that's what I planned to say, anyway. It had sounded convincing, in my head, when I was standing on my own porch. But now that I was on the porch at Ravenwood, I wasn't so sure.

I wasn't usually the kind of guy who would do something like this, but it was obvious there was no way Lena was ever going to invite me over on her own. And I had a feeling her uncle could help us, that he might know something.

Or maybe it was the other thing. I wanted to see her. It had been a long, dull day at Jackson without Hurricane Lena, and I was starting to wonder how I ever got through eight periods without all the trouble she caused me. Without all the trouble she made me want to cause myself.

I could see light flooding from the vine-covered windows. I heard the sounds of music in the background, old Savannah songs, from that Georgian songwriter my mom had loved. *"In the cool cool cool of the evening . . ."*

I heard barking from the other side of the door before I even knocked, and within seconds the door swung open. Lena was standing there in her bare feet, and she looked different—dressed up, in a black dress with little birds embroidered on it, like she was going out to have dinner at a fancy restaurant. I looked more like I was headed to the Dar-ee Keen in my holey Atari T-shirt and jeans. She stepped out onto the veranda, pulling the door shut behind her. "Ethan, what are you doing here?"

I held up the folder, lamely. "I brought your homework."

"I can't believe you just showed up here. I told you my uncle doesn't like strangers." She was already pushing me down the stairs. "You have to go. Now."

"I just thought we could talk to him."

119

Behind us, I heard the awkward clearing of a throat. I looked up to see Macon Ravenwood's dog, and beyond him, Macon Ravenwood himself. I tried not to look surprised, but I'm pretty sure it gave me away when I almost jumped out of my skin.

"Well, that's one I don't hear often. And I do hate to disappoint, as I am nothing if not a Southern gentleman." He spoke in a measured Southern drawl, but with perfect enunciation. "It's a pleasure to finally meet you, Mr. Wate."

I couldn't believe I was standing in front of him. The mysterious Macon Ravenwood. Only, I really had been expecting Boo Radley—some guy trudging around the house in overalls, mumbling in some kind of monosyllabic language like a Neanderthal, maybe even drooling a bit around the edges of his mouth.

This was no Boo Radley. This was more of an Atticus Finch.

Macon Ravenwood was dressed impeccably, as if it was, I don't know, 1942. His crisp white dress shirt was fastened with old-fashioned silver studs, instead of buttons. His black dinner jacket was spotless, perfectly creased. His eyes were dark and gleaming; they looked almost black. They were clouded over, tinted, like the glass of the hearse windows Lena drove around town. There was no seeing into those eyes, no reflection. They stood out from his pale face, which was as white as snow, white as marble, white as, well, you'd expect from the town shut-in. His hair was salt and pepper, gray near his face, as black as Lena's on the top.

He could have been some kind of American movie star, from before they invented Technicolor, or maybe royalty, from some small country nobody had ever heard of around here. But Macon Ravenwood, he was from these parts. That was the confusing thing. Old Man Ravenwood was the boogeyman of Gatlin, a story I'd heard since kindergarten. Only now he seemed like he belonged here less than I did.

He snapped shut the book he was holding, never taking his eyes off me. He was looking at me, but it was almost like he was looking through me, searching for something. Maybe the guy had x-ray vision. Given the past week, anything was possible.

My heart was beating so loudly I was sure he could hear it. Macon Ravenwood had me rattled and he knew it. Neither one of us smiled. His dog stood tense and rigid at his side, as if waiting for the command to attack.

"Where are my manners? Do come in, Mr. Wate. We were just about to sit down to dinner. You simply must join us. Dinner is always quite the affair, here at Ravenwood."

I looked at Lena, hoping for some direction.

Tell him you don't want to stay.

Trust me, I don't.

"No, that's okay, sir. I don't want to intrude. I just wanted to drop off Lena's homework." I held the shiny blue folder up for the second time.

"Nonsense, you must stay. We'll enjoy a few Cubans in the conservatory after dinner, or are you more of a Cigarillo man? Unless, of course, you're uncomfortable coming in, in which case, I completely understand." I couldn't tell if he was joking.

Lena slipped her arm around his waist, and I could see his face change instantly. Like the sun breaking through the clouds on a gray day. "Uncle M, don't tease Ethan. He's the only friend I have here, and if you scare him away I'll have to go live with Aunt Del, and then you'll have no one left to torture."

"I'll still have Boo." The dog looked up at Macon, quizzically.

"I'll take him with me. It's me he follows around town, not you."

I had to ask. "Boo? Is the dog's name Boo Radley?"

Macon cracked the smallest of smiles. "Better him than me." He threw back his head and laughed, which startled me, since there was no way I could have imagined his features composing themselves into even so much as a smile. He flung open the door behind him. "Really, Mr. Wate, please join us. I so love company, and it's been ages since Ravenwood has had the pleasure of hosting a guest from our own delicious little Gatlin County."

Lena smiled awkwardly, "Don't be a snob, Uncle M. It's not their fault you never speak to any of them."

"And it's not my fault that I have a penchant for good breeding, reasonable intelligence, and passable personal hygiene, not necessarily in that order."

"Ignore him. He's in a mood." Lena looked apologetic.

"Let me guess. Does it have something to do with Principal Harper?"

Lena nodded. "The school called. While the incident is being *investigated*, I'm on probation." She rolled her eyes. "One more 'infraction' and they'll suspend me."

Macon laughed dismissively, as if we were talking about something completely inconsequential. "Probation? How amusing. Probation would imply a source of authority." He pushed us both into the hall in front of him. "An overweight high school principal who barely finished college, and a pack of angry housewives with pedigrees that couldn't rival Boo Radley's, hardly qualify."

I stepped over the threshold and stopped dead in my tracks. The entry hall was soaring and grand, not the suburban model home I had stepped into just days ago. A monstrously huge oil painting, a portrait of a terrifyingly beautiful woman with glowing gold eyes, hung over the stairs, which weren't contemporary anymore, but a classic flying staircase seemingly supported only by the air itself. Scarlett O'Hara could have swept down them in a hoop skirt and she wouldn't have looked a bit out of place. Tiered crystal chandeliers were dripping from the ceiling. The hall was thick with clusters of antique Victorian furniture, small groupings of intricately embroidered chairs, marble tabletops, and graceful ferns. A candle glowed from every surface. Tall, shuttered doors were thrown open; the breeze carried the scent of gardenias, which were arranged in tall silver vases, artfully placed on the tabletops.

For a second, I almost thought I was back in one of the visions, except the locket was safely wrapped in the handkerchief in my pocket. I knew, because I checked. And that creepy dog was watching me from the stairs.

But it didn't make sense. Ravenwood had transformed into something entirely different since the last time I was there. It looked impossible, like I had stepped back in history. Even if it wasn't real, I wished my mom could have seen it. She would have loved this place. Only now it felt real, and I knew this was the way the great house looked, most of the time. It felt like Lena, like the walled garden, like Greenbrier.

Why didn't it look like this before?

What are you talking about?

I think you know.

Macon walked in front of us. We turned a corner, into what was the cozy sitting room, last week. Now it was a grand ballroom, with a long claw-footed table set for three, as if he was expecting me.

The piano continued to play itself in the corner. I guessed it was one of those mechanical ones. The scene was eerie, as if the room should have been full of the tinkling of glasses, and laughter. Ravenwood was throwing the party of the year, but I was the only guest.

Macon was still talking. Everything he said echoed off of the giant frescoed walls and vaulted, carved ceilings. "I suppose I am a snob. I loathe towns. I loathe townspeople. They have small minds and giant backsides. Which is to say, what they lack in interiors they make up in posteriors. They're junk food. Fatty, but ultimately, terribly unsatisfying." He smiled, but it wasn't a friendly smile.

"So why don't you just move?" I felt a surge of annoyance that brought me back to reality, whatever reality I was currently in. It was one thing for me to make fun of Gatlin. It was different coming from Macon Ravenwood. It came from a different place.

"Don't be absurd. Ravenwood is my home, not Gatlin." He spat out the word like it was toxic. "When I pass on from the binds of this life, I will have to find someone to care for Ravenwood in my place, since I have no children. It's always been my great and terrible purpose, to keep Ravenwood alive. I like to think of myself as the curator of a living museum."

"Don't be so dramatic, Uncle M."

"Don't be so diplomatic, Lena. Why you want to interact with those unenlightened townsfolk, I'll never understand."

The guy has a point.

Are you saying you don't want me to come to school?

No—I just meant—

Macon looked at me. "Present company excluded, of course."

The more he spoke, the more curious I was. Who knew that

124

Old Man Ravenwood would be the third-smartest person in town, after my mom and Marian Ashcroft? Or maybe the fourth, depending on if my father ever showed his face again.

I tried to see the name of the book Macon was holding. "What is that, Shakespeare?"

"Betty Crocker, a fascinating woman. I was trying to recall what it was that the local town constituents considered an evening meal. I was in the mood for a regional recipe this evening. I decided on pulled pork." More pulled pork. I felt sick just thinking about it.

Macon pulled out Lena's chair with a flourish. "Speaking of hospitality, Lena, your cousins are coming out for the Gathering Days. Let's remember to tell House and Kitchen we will be five more."

Lena looked irritated. "I will tell the kitchen *staff* and the house *keepers*, if that's what you mean, Uncle M."

"What are the Gathering Days?"

"My family is so weird. The Gathering is just an old harvest festival, like an early Thanksgiving. Just forget about it." I never knew anyone visited Ravenwood, family or otherwise. I'd never seen a single car take that turn at the fork in the road.

Macon seemed amused. "As you wish. Speaking of Kitchen, I am absolutely ravenous. I'll go see what she has whipped up for us." Even as he spoke, I could hear the pots and pans banging in some faraway room off the ballroom.

"Don't go overboard, Uncle M. Please."

I watched Macon Ravenwood disappear through a salon, and then he was gone. I could still hear the clip of his dress shoes on the polished floors. This house was ridiculous. It made the White House look like a backwoods shack.

"Lena, what's going on?"

"What do you mean?"

"How did he know to set a place for me?"

"He must have done it when he saw us on the porch."

"What about this place? I was in your house, the day we found the locket. It didn't look anything like this."

Tell me. You can trust me.

She played with the hem of her dress. Stubborn. "My uncle is into antiques. The house changes all the time. Does it really matter?"

Whatever was going on, she wasn't going to tell me about it right now. "Okay, then. Do you mind if I look around?" She frowned, but didn't say anything. I got up from the table, and walked over to the next salon. It was set up like a small study, with settees, a fireplace, and a few small writing tables. Boo Radley was lying in front of the fire. He started to growl the moment I set foot in the room.

"Nice doggy." He growled louder. I backed up out of the room. He stopped growling and put his head down on the hearth.

Lying on the nearest writing table was a package, wrapped in brown paper and tied with a string. I picked it up. Boo Radley began to growl again. It was stamped *Gatlin County Library*. I knew the stamp. My mom had gotten hundreds of packages like this one. Only Marian Ashcroft would bother to wrap a book like that.

"You have an interest in libraries, Mr. Wate? Do you know Marian Ashcroft?" Macon appeared next to me, taking the parcel out of my hand and eyeing it with delight.

"Yes, sir. Marian, Dr. Ashcroft, she was my mom's best friend. They worked together."

Macon's eyes flickered, a momentary brightness, then nothing. It passed. "Of course. How incredibly dull-witted of me. Ethan Wate. I knew your mother."

I froze. How could Macon Ravenwood have known my mother?

A strange expression passed over his face, like he was recalling something he'd forgotten. "Only through her work, of course. I've read everything she's ever written. In fact, if you look closely at the footnotes for *Plantations & Plantings: A Garden Divided*, you will see that several of the primary sources for their study came from my personal collection. Your mother was brilliant, a great loss."

I managed a smile. "Thanks."

"I'd be honored to show you my library, naturally. It would be a great pleasure to share my collection with the only son of Lila Evers."

I looked at him, struck by the sound of my mother's name coming out of Macon Ravenwood's mouth. "Wate. Lila Evers Wate."

He smiled more broadly. "Of course. But first things first. I believe, from Kitchen's general lack of din, that dinner has been served." He patted my shoulder, and we walked back into the grand ballroom.

Lena was waiting for us at the table, lighting a candle that had blown out in the evening breeze. The table was covered with an elaborate feast, though I couldn't imagine how it had gotten there. I hadn't seen a single person in the house, aside from the three of us. Now there was a new house, a wolf-dog, and all this. And I had expected Macon Ravenwood to be the weirdest part of the evening.

There was enough food to feed the DAR, every church in town, and the basketball team, combined. Only it wasn't the kind of food that had ever been served in Gatlin. There was something that looked like a whole roast pig, with an apple stuck in its mouth. A standing rib roast, with little paper puffs on the top of each rib, sat next to a mangled-looking goose covered with chestnuts. There were bowls of gravies and sauces and creams, rolls and breads, collards and beets and spreads that I couldn't name. And of course, pulled pork sandwiches, which looked particularly out of place among the other dishes. I looked at Lena, feeling sick at the thought of how much I'd have to eat to be polite.

"Uncle M. This is too much." Boo, curled around the legs of Lena's chair, thumped his tail in anticipation.

"Nonsense. This is a celebration. You've made a friend. Kitchen will be offended."

Lena looked at me anxiously, like she was afraid I was going to get up to use the bathroom and bolt. I shrugged, and began to load my plate. Maybe Amma would let me skip breakfast tomorrow.

By the time Macon was pouring his third glass of scotch, it seemed like a good time to bring up the locket. Come to think of it, I had seen him load up his plate with food, but I hadn't seen him eat a thing. It seemed to disappear off his plate, with only the smallest bite or two. Maybe Boo Radley was the luckiest dog in town.

I folded up my napkin. "Do you mind, sir, if I ask you something? Since you seem to know so much about history, and, well, I can't really ask my mom."

What are you doing?

I'm just asking a question.

He doesn't know anything.

Lena, we have to try.

"Of course." Macon took a sip from his glass.

I reached into my pocket and pulled the locket out of the pouch Amma had given me, careful to keep it wrapped in the handkerchief. All the candles went out. The lights dimmed and then spluttered out. Even the music of the piano died.

Ethan, what are you doing?

I didn't do anything.

I heard Macon's voice in the darkness. "What is that in your hand, son?"

"It's a locket, sir."

"Do you mind very much if you put it back in your pocket?" His voice was calm, but I knew that he wasn't. I could tell he was taking great efforts to compose himself. His glib manner was gone. His voice had an edge, a sense of urgency he was trying very hard to disguise.

I crammed the locket back into the pouch and stuffed it in my pocket. At the other end of the table, Macon touched his fingers to the candelabra. One by one, the candles on the table came back to light. The entire feast had disappeared.

In the candlelight, Macon looked sinister. He was also quiet for the first time since I'd met him, as if he was weighing his options on an invisible scale that somehow held our fate in the balance. It was time to go. Lena was right, this was a bad idea. Maybe there was a reason Macon Ravenwood never left his house.

"I'm sorry, sir. I didn't know that would happen. My house-keeper, Amma, acted like the—like it, was really powerful when

I showed it to her. But when Lena and I found it, nothing bad happened."

Don't tell him anything else. Don't mention the visions.

I won't. I just wanted to find out if I was right about Genevieve.

She didn't have to worry; I didn't want to tell Macon Ravenwood anything. I just wanted to get out of there. I started to get up. "I think I should be getting home, sir. It's getting late."

"Would you mind describing the locket to me?" It was more of an order than a request. I didn't say a word.

It was Lena who finally spoke. "It's old and battered, with a cameo on the front. We found it at Greenbrier."

Macon twisted his silver ring, agitated. "You should have told me you went to Greenbrier. That's not part of Ravenwood. I can't keep you safe there."

"I was safe there. I could feel it." Safe from what? This was more than a little overprotective.

"You weren't. It's beyond the boundaries. It can't be controlled, not by anyone. There is a lot you don't know. And he—" Macon gestured to me at the other end of the table. "He knows nothing. He can't protect you. You shouldn't have brought him into this."

I spoke up. I had to. He was talking about me like I wasn't even there. "This is about me, too, sir. There were initials on the back of the locket. ECW. ECW was Ethan Carter Wate, my great-great-great-great-uncle. And the other initials are GKD, and we're pretty sure the D stands for Duchannes."

Ethan, stop.

But I couldn't. "There's no reason to keep anything from us

130

because whatever it is that's happening, it's happening to both of us. And like it or not, it seems to be happening right now." A vase of gardenias went flying across the room and crashed into the wall. This was the Macon Ravenwood we'd all been telling stories about since we were kids.

"You have no idea what you are talking about, young man." He stared me right in the eye, with a dark intensity that made the hair on the back of my neck stand on end. He was having trouble keeping it together now. I had pushed him too far. Boo Radley rose and paced behind Macon like he was stalking prey, his eyes hauntingly round and familiar.

Don't say anything else.

His eyes narrowed. The movie star glamour was gone, replaced with something much darker. I wanted to run, but I was rooted to the ground. Paralyzed.

I was wrong about Ravenwood Manor, and Macon Ravenwood. I was afraid of both of them.

When he finally spoke, it was as if he was speaking to himself. "Five months. Do you know what lengths I will go to, to keep her safe for five months? What it will cost me? How it will drain me, perhaps, destroy me?" Without a word, Lena moved next to him, and laid her hand on his shoulder. And then, the storm in his eyes passed as quickly as it had come, and he regained his composure.

"Amma sounds like a wise woman. I would consider taking her advice. I would return that item to the place where you found it. Please do not bring it into my home again." Macon stood up and threw his napkin on the table. "I think our little library visit will have to wait, don't you? Lena, can you see to it that your friend finds his way home? It was, of course, an extraordinary evening. Most illuminating. Please do come again, Mr. Wate."

And then the room was dark, and he was gone.

I couldn't get out of the house fast enough. I wanted to get away from Lena's creepy uncle and his freak show of a house. What the hell had just happened? Lena rushed me to the door, like she was afraid of what might happen if she didn't get me out of there. But as we passed through the main hall, I noticed something I hadn't before.

The locket. The woman with the haunting gold eyes in the oil painting was wearing the locket. I grabbed Lena's arm. She saw it and froze.

It wasn't there before.

What do you mean?

That painting has been hanging there since I was a child. I've walked by it a thousand times. She was never wearing a locket.

A Fork in the Road

We barely spoke as we drove back to my house. I didn't know what to say, and Lena just looked grateful I wasn't saying it. She let me drive, which was good because I needed something to distract me until my pulse slowed back down. We passed my street, but I didn't care. I wasn't ready to go home. I didn't know what was going on with Lena, or her house, or her uncle, but she was going to tell me.

"You passed your street." It was the first thing she'd said since we left Ravenwood.

"I know."

"You think my uncle is crazy, like everyone else. Just say it. Old Man Ravenwood." Her voice was bitter. "I need to get home."

I didn't say a word as we circled the General's Green, the round patch of faded grass that encircled just about the only thing in Gatlin that ever made it into the guidebooks—the General, a statue of Civil War General Jubal A. Early. The General stood his ground, just as he always had, which now struck me as sort of wrong. Everything had changed; everything kept changing. I was different, seeing things and feeling things and doing things that even a week ago would have seemed impossible. It felt like the General should have changed, too.

I turned down Dove Street and pulled the hearse over alongside the curb, right under the sign that said WELCOME TO GATLIN, HOME OF THE SOUTH'S MOST UNIQUE HISTORIC PLANTATION HOMES AND THE WORLD'S BEST BUTTERMILK PIE. I wasn't sure about the pie, but the rest was true.

"What are you doing?"

I turned the car off. "We need to talk."

"I don't park with guys." It was a joke, but I could hear it in her voice. She was petrified.

"Start talking."

"About what?"

"You're kidding, right?" I was trying not to shout.

She pulled at her necklace, twisting the tab from a soda can. "I don't know what you want me to say."

"How about explaining what just happened back there."

She stared out the window, into the darkness. "He was angry. Sometimes he loses his temper."

"Loses his temper? You mean hurls things across the room without touching them and lights candles without matches?"

"Ethan, I'm sorry." Her voice was quiet.

But mine wasn't. The more she avoided my questions, the angrier it made me. "I don't want you to be sorry. I want you tell me what's going on."

"With what?"

"With your uncle and his weird house, that he somehow managed to redecorate within a couple of days. With the food that appears and disappears. With all that talk about boundaries and protecting you. Pick one."

She shook her head. "I can't talk about it. And you wouldn't understand, anyway."

"How do you know if you don't give me a chance?"

"My family is different from other families. Trust me, you can't handle it."

"What's that supposed to mean?"

"Face it, Ethan. You say you're not like the rest of them, but you are. You want me to be different, but just a little. Not really different."

"You know what? You're as crazy as your uncle."

"You came to my house without being invited, and now you're angry because you didn't like what you saw."

I didn't answer. I couldn't see out the windows, and I couldn't think clearly, either.

"And you're angry because you're afraid. You all are. Deep down, you're all the same." Lena sounded tired now, like she had already given up.

"No." I looked at her. "You're afraid."

She laughed, bitterly. "Yeah, right. The things I'm afraid of, you couldn't even imagine."

"You're afraid to trust me."

She didn't say anything.

"You're afraid to get to know someone well enough to notice whether or not they show up for school."

She dragged her finger through the fog on her window. It made a shaky line, like a zigzag.

"You're afraid to stick around and see what happens."

The zigzag turned into what looked like a bolt of lightning.

"You're not from here. You're right. And you're not just a little different."

She was still staring out the window, at nothing, because you still couldn't see out of it. But I could see her. I could see everything. "You're incredibly, absolutely, extremely, supremely, unbelievably different." I touched her arm, with just my fingertips, and immediately I felt the warmth of electricity. "I know because deep down, I think I am, too. So tell me. Please. Different how?"

"I don't want to tell you."

A tear dripped down her cheek. I caught it with my finger, and it burned. "Why not?"

"Because this could be my last chance to be a normal girl, even if it is in Gatlin. Because you're my only friend here. Because if I tell you, you won't believe me. Or worse, you will." She opened her eyes, and looked into mine. "Either way, you're never going to want to talk to me again."

There was a rap on the window, and we both jumped. A flashlight shone through the fogged-in glass. I dropped my hand and rolled down the window, swearing under my breath.

"Kids get lost on your way home?" Fatty. He was grinning like he'd stumbled across two doughnuts on the side of the road.

"No, sir. We're on our way home right now."

"This isn't your car, Mr. Wate."

"No, sir."

He shined his flashlight over at Lena, lingering for a long time. "Then move on, and get home. Don't want to keep Amma waitin'."

"Yes, sir." I turned the key in the ignition. When I looked in the rearview mirror, I could see his girlfriend, Amanda, in the front seat of his police cruiser, giggling.

I slammed the car door. I could see Lena through the driver's window now, as she idled in front of my house. "See you tomorrow."

"Sure."

But I knew we wouldn't see each other tomorrow. I knew if she drove down my street that was it. It was a path, just like the fork in the road leading to Ravenwood or to Gatlin. You had to pick one. If she didn't pick this one, now, the hearse would keep on going the other way at the fork, passing me by. Just as it had the morning I first saw it.

If she didn't pick me.

You couldn't take two roads. And once you were on one, there was no going back. I heard the motor grind into drive, but kept walking up to my door. The hearse pulled away.

She didn't pick me.

I was lying on my bed, facing the window. The moonlight was streaming in, which was annoying, because it kept me from falling asleep when all I wanted was for this day to end.

Ethan. The voice was so soft I almost couldn't hear it.

I looked at the window. It was locked, I had made sure of it.

Ethan. Come on.

I closed my eyes. The latch on my window rattled.

Let me in.

The wooden shutters banged open. I would say it was the wind, but of course there wasn't even a breeze. I climbed out of bed and looked outside.

Lena was standing on my front lawn in her pajamas. The neighbors would have a field day, and Amma would have a heart attack. "You come down or I'm coming up."

A heart attack, and then a stroke.

We sat out on the front step. I was in my jeans, because I didn't sleep in pajamas, and if Amma had walked out and found me with a girl in my boxers, I would've been buried under the back lawn by morning.

Lena leaned back against the step, looking up at the white paint peeling off the porch. "I almost turned around at the end of your street, but I was too scared to do it." In the moonlight, I could see her pajamas were green and purple and sort of Chinese.

"Then by the time I got home, I was too scared not to do it." She was picking at the nail polish on her bare feet, which was how I knew she had something to say. "I don't really know how to do this. I've never had to say it before, so I don't know how it will all come out."

I rubbed my messy hair with one hand. "Whatever it is, you can tell me. I know what it's like to have a crazy family."

"You think you know crazy. You have no idea."

She took a deep breath. Whatever she was about to say, it was hard for her. I could see her struggling to find the words. "The people in my family, and me, we have powers. We can do

138

things that regular people can't do. We're born that way, we can't help it. We are what we are."

It took me a second to understand what she was talking about, or at least what I thought she was talking about.

Magic.

Where was Amma when I needed her?

I was afraid to ask, but I had to know. "And what, exactly, are you?" It sounded so crazy that I almost couldn't say the words.

"Casters," she said quietly.

"Casters?"

She nodded.

"Like, spell casters?"

She nodded again.

I stared at her. Maybe she was crazy. "Like, witches?"

"Ethan. Don't be ridiculous."

I exhaled, momentarily relieved. Of course, I was an idiot. What was I thinking?

"That's such a stupid word, really. It's like saying jocks. Or geeks. It's just a dumb stereotype."

My stomach lurched. Part of me wanted to bolt up the steps, lock the door, and hide in my bed. But then another part of me, a bigger part, wanted to stay. Because hadn't a part of me known all along? I may not have known what she was, but I had known there was something about her, something bigger than just that junky necklace and those old Chucks. What was I expecting, from someone who could bring on a downpour? Who could talk to me without even being in the room? Who could control the way the clouds floated in the sky? Who could fling open the shutters to my room from my front yard?

"Can you come up with a better name?"

"There's not one word that describes all the people in my family. Is there one word that describes everyone in yours?"

I wanted to break the tension, to pretend she was just like any other girl. To convince myself that this could be okay. "Yeah. Lunatics."

"We're Casters. That's the broadest definition. We all have powers. We're gifted, just like some families are smart, and others are rich, or beautiful, or athletic."

I knew what the next question was, but I didn't want to ask it. I already knew she could break a window just by thinking about it. I didn't know if I was ready to find out what else she could shatter.

Anyway, it was starting to feel like we were talking about just another crazy Southern family, like the Sisters. The Ravenwoods had been around as long as any family in Gatlin. Why should they be any less crazy? Or at least that's what I tried to tell myself.

Lena took the silence as a bad sign. "I knew I shouldn't have said anything. I told you to leave me alone. Now you probably think I'm a freak."

"I think you're *talented*."

"You think my house is weird. You already admitted that."

"So you redecorated, a lot." I was trying to hold it together. I was trying to keep her smiling. I knew what it must have cost her to tell me the truth. I couldn't run out on her now. I turned around and pointed to the lit study above the azalea bushes, hidden behind thick wooden shutters. "Look. See that window over there? That's my dad's study. He works all night and sleeps all day. Since my mom died, he hasn't left the house. He won't even show me what he's writing."

"That's so romantic," she said quietly.

"No, it's crazy. But nobody talks about it, because there's nobody left to talk to. Except Amma, who hides magic charms in my room and screams at me for bringing old jewelry into the house."

I could tell she was almost smiling. "Maybe you are a freak."

"I'm a freak, you're a freak. Your house makes rooms disappear, my house makes people disappear. Your shut-in uncle is nuts and my shut-in dad is a lunatic, so I don't know what you think makes us so different."

Lena smiled, relieved. "I'm trying to find a way to see that as a compliment."

"It is." I looked at her smiling in the moonlight, a real smile. There was something about the way she looked just at that moment. I imagined leaning in a little farther and kissing her. I pushed myself away, up one step higher than she was.

"Are you okay?"

"Yeah, I'm fine. Just tired." But I wasn't.

We stayed like that, just talking on the steps, for hours. I lay on the step above; she lay on the step below. We watched the dark night sky, then the dark morning sky, until we could hear the birds.

By the time the hearse finally pulled away, the sun was starting to rise. I watched Boo Radley lope slowly home after it. At the rate he was going, it would be sunset before that dog got home. Sometimes I wondered why he bothered.

Stupid dog.

I put my hand on the brass doorknob of my own door, but I almost couldn't bring myself to open it. Everything was upside down, and nothing inside could change that. My mind was scrambled, all stirred up like a big frying pan of Amma's eggs, the way my insides had felt like for days now.

T. I. M. O. R. O. U. S. That's what Amma would call me. Eight across, as in another name for a coward. I was scared. I'd told Lena it was no big deal that she and her family—were what? Witches? Casters? And not the ten and two kind my dad had taught me about.

Yeah, no big deal.

I was a big liar. I bet even that stupid dog could sense that.

The Last Three Rows

You know that expression, "It hit me like a ton of bricks"? It's true. The minute she turned the car around and ended up on my doorstep in her purple pajamas, that's how I felt about Lena.

I knew it was coming. I just didn't know it would feel like this.

Since then, there were two places I wanted to be: with Lena, or alone, so I could try to hammer it all out in my mind. I didn't have the words for what we were. She wasn't my girlfriend; we weren't even dating. Up until last week, she wouldn't even admit we were friends. I had no idea how she felt about me, and it wasn't like I could send Savannah over to find out. I didn't want to risk whatever we had, whatever it was. So why did I think about her every second? Why was I so much happier the minute I saw her? I felt like maybe I knew the answer, but how could I be sure? I didn't know, and I didn't have any way to find out.

Guys don't talk about stuff like that. We just lie under the pile of bricks.

"So what are you writing?"

She closed the spiral notebook she seemed to carry around everywhere. The basketball team had no practice on Wednesdays, so Lena and I were sitting in the garden at Greenbrier, which I'd sort of come to think of as our special place, though that's not something I would ever admit, not even to her. It was where we found the locket. It was a place we could hang out without everyone staring and whispering. We were supposed to be studying, but Lena was writing in her notebook, and I'd read the same paragraph about the internal structure of atoms nine times now. Our shoulders were touching, but we were facing different directions. I was sprawled in the fading sun; she sat under the growing shadow of a moss-covered oak. "Nothing special. I'm just writing."

"It's okay, you don't have to tell me." I tried not to sound disappointed.

"It's just . . . it's stupid."

"So tell me anyway."

For a minute she didn't say anything, scribbling on the rubber rim of her shoe with her black pen. "I just write poems sometimes. I've been doing it since I was a kid. I know it's weird."

"I don't think it's weird. My mom was a writer. My dad's a writer." I could feel her smiling, even though I wasn't looking at her. "Okay, that's a bad example, because my dad is really weird, but you can't blame that on the writing."

I waited to see if she was going to just hand me the notebook and ask me to read one. No such luck. "Maybe I can read one sometime."

"Doubtful." I heard the notebook open again and her pen moving across the page. I stared at my chemistry book, rehearsing the phrase I'd gone over a hundred times in my head. We were alone. The sun was slipping away; she was writing poetry. If I was going to do it, now was the time.

"So, do you want to, you know, hang out?" I tried to sound casual.

"Isn't that what we're doing?"

I chewed on the end of an old plastic spoon I had found in my backpack, probably from a pudding cup. "Yeah. No. I mean, do you want to, I don't know, go somewhere?"

"Now?" She took a bite out of an open granola bar, and swung her legs around so she was next to me, holding it out toward me. I shook my head.

"Not now. Friday, or something. We could see a movie." I stuck the spoon in my chemistry book, closing it.

"That's gross." She made a face, and turned the page.

"What do you mean?" I could feel my face turning red. *I was only talking about a movie.* *You idiot.*

She pointed at my dirty spoon bookmark. "I meant that."

I smiled, relieved. "Yeah. Bad habit I picked up from my mom."

"She had a thing for cutlery?"

"No, books. She would have maybe twenty going at a time, lying all over our house—on the kitchen table, by her bed, the bathroom, our car, her bags, a little stack at the edge of each stair. And she'd use anything she could find for a bookmark. My missing sock, an apple core, her reading glasses, another book, a fork."

"A dirty old spoon?"

"Exactly."

"Bet that drove Amma crazy."

"It drove her nuts. No, wait for it—she was—" I dug deep. "P. E. R. T. U. R. B. E. D."

"Nine down?" She laughed.

"Probably."

"This was my mom's." She held out one of the charms suspended from the long silver chain she never seemed to take off. It was a tiny gold bird. "It's a raven."

"For Ravenwood?"

"No. Ravens are the most powerful birds in the Caster world. Legend has it that they can draw energy into themselves and release it in other forms. Sometimes they're even feared because of their power." I watched as she let go of the raven and it fell back into place between a disc with strange writing etched into it and a black glass bead.

"You've got a lot of charms."

She tucked a strand of hair behind her ear and looked down at the necklace. "They aren't really charms, just things that mean something to me." She held out the tab of the soda can. "This is from the first can of orange soda I ever drank, sitting on the porch of our house in Savannah. My gramma bought it for me when I came home from school crying because no one put anything in my valentine shoebox at school."

"That's cute."

"If by cute you mean tragic."

"I mean, that you kept it."

"I keep everything."

"What's this one?" I pointed to the black bead.

"My Aunt Twyla gave it to me. They're made from these rocks in a really remote area of Barbados. She said it would bring me luck."

"It's a cool necklace." I could see how much it meant to her, the way she held each thing on it so carefully.

"I know it just looks like a bunch of junk. But I've never lived anywhere very long. I've never had the same house, or the same room for more than a few years, and sometimes I feel like the little pieces of me on this chain are all I have."

I sighed and pulled a blade of grass. "Wish I'd lived in one of those places."

"But you have roots here. A best friend you've had your whole life, a house with a bedroom that's always been yours. You probably even have one of those doorjambs with your height written on it." I did.

You do, don't you?

I nudged her with my shoulder. "I can measure you on my doorjamb if you want. You can be immortalized for all time at Wate's Landing." She smiled into her notebook and pushed her shoulder against mine. From the corner of my eye, I could see the afternoon sunlight hitting one side of her face, a single page of her notebook, the curling edge of her black hair, the tip of one black Converse.

About the movies. Friday works.

Then she slid her granola bar into the middle of her notebook, and closed it.

The toes of our ratty black sneakers touched.

The more I thought about Friday night, the more nervous I got. It wasn't a date, not officially—I knew that. But that was part of the problem. I wanted it to be. What do you do when you realize you might have feelings for a girl who will barely admit to being your friend? A girl whose uncle kicked you out of their house, and who isn't all that welcome in yours, either? A girl who almost everyone you know hates? A girl who shares your dreams, but maybe not your feelings?

I had no idea, which is why I didn't do anything. But it didn't stop me from thinking about Lena, and almost driving by her house on Thursday night—if her house wasn't outside of town, if I had my own car. If her uncle wasn't Macon Ravenwood. Those were the "ifs" that kept me from making a fool of myself.

Every day was like a day out of someone else's life. Nothing had ever happened to me, and now everything was happening to me—and by everything, I really meant Lena. An hour was both faster and slower. I felt like I had sucked the air out of a giant balloon, like my brain wasn't getting enough oxygen. Clouds were more interesting, the lunchroom less disgusting, music sounded better, the same old jokes were funnier, and Jackson went from being a clump of grayish-green industrial buildings to a map of times and places where I might run into her. I found myself smiling for no reason, keeping my earphones in and replaying our conversations in my head, just so I could listen to them again. I had seen this kind of thing before.

I had just never felt it.

By Friday night, I had been in a great mood all day, which meant I'd done worse than everyone in class, and better than everyone at practice. I had to put all that energy somewhere. Even Coach noticed, and kept me late to talk. "Keep it up, Wate, an' you just might get yourself scouted next year."

Link gave me a ride to Summerville after practice. The guys were planning on catching a movie, too, which I probably should have considered since the Cineplex only had one screen. But it was too late for that, and I was past the point of caring.

When we pulled up in the Beater, Lena was standing outside in the darkness, in front of the brightly lit theater. She was wearing a purple T-shirt, with a skinny black dress over it that made you remember how much of a girl she was, and trashed black boots that made you forget.

Inside the door, aside from the usual crowd of Summerville Community College students, the cheer squad was assembled in formation, hanging out in the lobby arcade with guys from the team. My mood started to evaporate.

"Hi."

"You're late. I got the tickets." Lena's eyes were unreadable in the darkness. I followed her inside. We were off to a great start.

"Wate! Get over here!" Emory's voice boomed over the arcade and the crowd and the eighties music playing in the lobby.

"Wate, you got a date?" Now Billy was riding me. Earl didn't say anything, but only because Earl hardly ever said anything.

Lena ignored them. She rubbed her head, walking ahead of me like she didn't want to look at me.

"It's called a life." I shouted back over the crowd. I would hear about this on Monday. I caught up to Lena. "Hey, sorry about that."

She whirled around to look at me. "This isn't going to work if you're the kind of person who doesn't want to watch the previews."

I waited for you.

I grinned. "Previews and credits, and the dancing popcorn guy."

She looked past me, back to my friends, or at least, the people who had historically functioned that way.

Ignore them.

"Butter or no butter?" She was annoyed. I had been late, and she had faced the Jackson High social stockade alone. Now it was my turn.

"Butter," I confessed, knowing this would be the wrong answer. Lena made a face.

"But I'll trade you butter for extra salt," I said. Her eyes looked past me, then back. I could hear Emily's laughter getting closer. I didn't care.

Say the word and we'll go, Lena.

"No butter, salt, tossed with Milk Duds. You'll like it," she said, her shoulders relaxing just a little.

I already like it.

The squad and the guys walked past us. Emily made a point of not looking at me, while Savannah stepped around Lena like she was infected with some kind of airborne virus. I could just imagine what they would tell their mothers when they got home.

I grabbed Lena's hand. A current ran through my body, but this time, it wasn't the shock I had felt that night in the rain. It

150

was more like a confusion of the senses. Like being hit by a wave at the beach and climbing under an electric blanket on a rainy night, all at the same time. I let it wash over me. Savannah noticed and elbowed Emily.

You don't have to do this.

I squeezed her hand.

Do what?

"Hey, kids. Did you see the guys?" Link tapped me on the shoulder, carrying a monster-size buttered popcorn and a giant blue slush.

The Cineplex was showing some kind of murder mystery, which Amma would have liked, given her penchant for mysteries and dead bodies. Link had gone to sit up front with the guys, scoping the aisles for college girls on his way. Not because he didn't want to sit with Lena, but because he assumed we wanted to be alone. We did—at least, I did.

"Where do you want to sit? Up close, in the middle?" I waited for her to decide.

"Back here." I followed her down the aisle of the last row.

Hooking up was the main reason kids from Gatlin went to the Cineplex, considering any movie showing there was already on DVD. But it was the only reason you sat in the last three rows. The Cineplex, the water tower, and in the summer, the lake. Aside from that, there were a few bathrooms and basements, but not many other options. I knew we wouldn't be doing any hooking up, but even if it was like that between us I wouldn't have brought her here to do it. Lena wasn't just some girl you took to the last three rows of the Cineplex. She was more than that.

Still, it was her choice, and I knew why she chose it. You couldn't get farther away from Emily Asher than the last row.

Maybe I should have warned her. Before the opening credits, people were already starting to go at it. We both stared at the popcorn, since there was nowhere else safe to look.

Why didn't you say anything?

I didn't know.

Liar.

I'll be a perfect gentleman. Honest.

I pushed it all to the back of my mind, thinking about anything, the weather, basketball, and reached into the popcorn tub. Lena reached in at the same time, and our hands touched for a second, sending a chill up my arm, hot and cold all mixed up together. Pick 'n' Roll. Picket Fences. Down the Lane. There were only so many plays in the Jackson basketball playbook. This was going to be harder than I thought.

The movie was terrible. Ten minutes in, I already knew the ending.

"He did it," I whispered.

"What?"

"That guy. He's the murderer. I don't know who he kills, but he did it." That was the other reason Link didn't want to sit by me: I always knew the ending at the beginning and I couldn't keep it to myself. It was my version of doing the crossword. It was the reason I was so good at video games, carnival games, checkers with my dad. I could figure things out, right from the first move.

"How do you know?"

"I just do."

How does this end?

I knew what she meant. But for the first time, I just didn't know the answer.

Happy. Very, very happy.

Liar. Now hand over the Milk Duds.

She pushed her hand into the pocket of my sweatshirt, looking for them. Only it was the wrong side, and instead she found the last thing she was expecting. There it was, the little pouch, the hard lump that we both knew was the locket. Lena sat up with a start, pulling it out and holding it up like it was some kind of dead mouse. "Why are you still carrying that around in your pocket?"

"Shh." We were annoying the people around us, which was funny considering they weren't even watching the movie.

"I can't leave it in the house. Amma thinks I buried it."

"Maybe you should have."

"It doesn't matter, the thing has a mind of its own. It almost never works. You've seen it every time it has."

"Can you shut up?" The couple in front of us came up for air. Lena jumped, dropping the locket. We both grabbed for it. I saw the handkerchief falling off, as if it were in slow motion. I could barely see the white square in the dark. The big screen twisted into an inconsequential spark of light, and we could already smell the smoke—

Burning a house with women in it.

It couldn't be true. Mamma. Evangeline. Genevieve's mind was racing. Maybe it wasn't too late. She broke into a run, ignoring the ragged claws of the bushes urging her to go back and Ethan and Ivy's voices calling

153

after her. The bushes opened up, and there were two Federals in front of what was left of the house Genevieve's grandfather had built. Two Federals pouring a tray full of silver into a government-issue rucksack. Genevieve was a rush of black billowing fabric catching the gusts kicked up by the fire.

"What the—"

"Grab her, Emmett," the first teenage boy called to the other.

Genevieve was taking the stairs two at a time, choking on the gales of smoke pouring from the opening where the front door had been. She was out of her mind. Mamma. Evangeline. Her lungs were raw. She felt herself falling. Was it the smoke? Was she going to faint? No, it was something else. A hand on her wrist, pulling her down.

"Where do you think you're going, girl?"

"Let me go!" she screamed, her voice raw from the smoke. Her back hit the stairs one by one as he dragged her, a blur of navy and gold. Her head hit next. Heat, then something wet dripping down the collar of her dress. Dizziness and confusion mixed with desperation.

A gunshot. The sound was so loud it brought her back, cutting through the darkness. The hand gripping her wrist relaxed. She tried to will her eyes to focus.

Two more shots rang out.

Lord, please spare Mamma and Evangeline. *But in the end, it was too much to ask, or maybe it had been the wrong question. Because when she heard the sound of the third body drop, her eyes refocused long enough*

to see Ethan's gray wool jacket sprayed with blood.
Shot by the very soldiers he had refused to fight against
anymore.

And the smell of blood mixed with gunpowder and
burning lemons.

The credits were rolling, and the lights were coming up. Lena's eyes were still closed, and she was lying back in her seat. Her hair was messed up, and neither one of us could catch our breath.

"Lena? You okay?"

She opened her eyes, and pushed up the armrest between us. Without a word, she rested her head on my shoulder. I could feel her shaking so hard she couldn't even speak.

I know. I was there, too.

We were still sitting like that when Link and the rest of them walked by. Link winked at me and held out his fist as he passed, like he was going to tap it against mine the way he did after I made a tough shot on the court.

But he had it wrong, they all did. We may have been in the last row, but we hadn't been hooking up. I could smell the blood and the gunshots were still ringing in my ears.

We had just watched a man die.

ᵈ 10.09 ᵇ

Gathering Days

After the Cineplex, it didn't take long. Word got out that Old Man Ravenwood's niece was hanging out with Ethan Wate. If I wasn't *Ethan Wate Whose Mamma Died Just Last Year*, the talk might have spread with more speed, or more cruelty. Even the guys on the team had something to say. It just took them longer than usual to say it, because I hadn't given them a chance.

For a guy who couldn't survive without three lunches, I'd been skipping half of them since the Cineplex—at least, skipping them with the team. But there were only so many days I could get by on half a sandwich on the bleachers, and there were only so many places to hide.

Because really, you couldn't hide. Jackson High was just a smaller version of Gatlin; there was nowhere to go. My disappearing act hadn't gone unnoticed with the guys. Like

I said, you had to show up for roll call, and if you let a girl get in the way of that, especially a girl who wasn't on the approved list—meaning, approved by Savannah and Emily—things got complicated.

When the girl was a Ravenwood, which is what Lena would always be to them, things were pretty much impossible.

I had to man up. It was time to take on the lunchroom. It didn't matter that we weren't even really a couple. At Jackson, you might as well have parked behind the water tower if you were eating lunch together. Everyone always assumed the worst, more like, the most. The first time Lena and I walked into the lunchroom together, she almost turned around and walked back out. I had to grab the strap on her bag.

Don't be crazy. It's just lunch.

"I think I forgot something in my locker." She turned, but I kept holding on to the strap.

Friends eat lunch together.

They don't. We don't. I mean, not in here.

I picked up two orange plastic lunch trays. "Tray?" I pushed the tray in front of her and shoved a shiny triangle of pizza on it.

We do now. Chicken.

You don't think I've tried this before?

You haven't tried it with me. I thought you wanted things to be different than they were at your old school.

Lena looked around the room doubtfully. She took a deep breath and dropped a plate of carrots and celery onto my tray.

You eat those, and I'll sit anywhere you want.

I looked at the carrots, then out at the lunchroom. The guys were already hanging out at our table.

Anywhere?

If this was a movie, we would've sat down at the table with the guys, and they would've learned some kind of valuable lesson, like not to judge people by the way they look, or that being different was okay. And Lena would've learned that all jocks weren't stupid and shallow. It always seemed to work in movies, but this wasn't a movie. This was Gatlin, which severely limited what could happen. Link caught my eye as I turned toward the table, and started shaking his head, as in, no way, man. Lena was a few steps behind me, ready to bolt. I was beginning to see how this was going to play out, and let's just say no one was going to be learning any valuable lessons. I almost turned around, when Earl looked at me.

That one look said it all. It said if you bring her over here, you're done.

Lena must have seen it too, because when I turned back to her, she was gone.

———ᘓ

That day after practice, Earl was nominated to have a talk with me, which was pretty funny, since talking had never really been his thing. He sat down on the bench in front of my gym locker. I could tell it was a plan because he was alone, and Earl Petty was almost never alone. He didn't waste any time. "Don't do it, Wate."

"I'm not doing anything." I didn't look up from my locker.

"Be cool. This isn't you."

"Yeah? What if it is?" I pulled on my Transformers T-shirt.

"The guys don't like it. Go down this road, no goin' back."

If Lena hadn't disappeared in the cafeteria, Earl would've known I didn't care what they thought. I hadn't cared for a while now. I slammed my locker door, and he left before I could tell him what I thought about him and his dead end of a road.

I had a feeling it was my last warning. I didn't blame Earl. For once, I agreed with him. The guys were going down one road, and I was going down another. Who could argue with that?

Still, Link refused to desert me. And I went to practice; people even passed me the ball. I was playing better than I ever had, no matter what they said, or more often didn't say, in the locker room. When I was around the guys, I tried not to let on that my universe had split in half, that even the sky looked different to me now, that I didn't care if we got to the state finals. Lena was in the back of my mind, no matter where I was or who I was with.

Not that I mentioned that at practice, or today, after practice, when Link and I hit the Stop & Steal to refuel on the way home. The rest of the guys were there, too, and I was trying to act like part of the team, for Link's sake. My mouth was full of powdered doughnuts, which I almost choked on when I stepped through the sliding doors.

There she was. The second-prettiest girl I had ever seen.

She was probably a little older than I was because, though she looked vaguely familiar, she had never been at Jackson when I was there. I was sure of that. She was the kind of girl a guy would remember. She was blasting some music I had never heard, and lounging at the wheel of her convertible black-and-white

Mini Cooper, which was parked haphazardly across two spaces in the parking lot. She didn't seem to notice the lines, or she didn't care. She was sucking on a lollipop like a cigarette, her pouty red lips made even redder by the cherry-colored stain.

She looked us over, and turned up the music. In a split second, two legs came flying over the side of the door, and she was standing in front of us, still sucking on the lollipop. "Frank Zappa. 'Drowning Witch.' A little before your time, boys." She walked closer, slowly, as if she was giving us time to check her out, which I admit, we were.

She had long blond hair, with a thick pink stripe sweeping down one side of her face, past her choppy bangs. She was wearing giant black sunglasses and a short black pleated skirt, like some kind of Goth cheerleader. Her cut-off white tank was so thin, you could see half of some kind of black bra, and most of everything else. And there was plenty to see. Black motorcycle boots, a belly ring, and a tattoo. It was black and tribal looking and surrounded her belly button, but I couldn't tell from here what it was, and I was trying not to stare.

"Ethan? Ethan Wate?"

I stopped in my tracks. Half the basketball team collided into me.

"No way." Shawn was as surprised as I was when my name came out of her mouth. He was the kind of guy who had game.

"Hot." Link just stared, with his mouth open. "TDB hot." Third Degree Burns. The highest compliment Link could pay a girl, even higher than Savannah Snow hot.

"Looks like trouble."

"Hot girls *are* trouble. That's the whole point."

She walked right up to me, sucking on her lollipop. "Which one of you lucky boys is Ethan Wate?" Link shoved me forward.

"Ethan!" She flung her arms around my neck. Her hands felt surprisingly cold, like she'd been holding a bag of ice. I shivered and backed away.

"Do I know you?"

"Not a bit. I'm Ridley, Lena's cousin. But don't I wish you'd met me first—"

At the mention of Lena, the guys shot me some weird looks, and reluctantly drifted off toward their cars. In the wake of my talk with Earl, we had come to a mutual understanding about Lena, the only kind guys ever come to. Meaning, I hadn't brought it up, and they hadn't brought it up, and between us, we somehow all agreed to go on like this indefinitely. Don't ask, don't tell. Which wasn't going to be much longer, especially if Lena's odd relatives started showing up in town.

"Cousin?"

Had Lena mentioned a Ridley?

"For the holidays? Aunt Del? Rhymes with hell? Ring a bell?" She was right; Macon had brought it up at dinner.

I grinned, relieved, except my stomach was still wrenched into a massive knot, so I must not have been that relieved. "Right. Sorry, I forgot. The cousins."

"Honey, you're lookin' at *the* Cousin. The rest are just children my mother happened to have after me." Ridley hopped back in the Mini Cooper. And when I say that, I mean, she literally hopped over the side of the car and landed in the driver seat of the Mini. I wasn't joking about the cheerleader thing. The girl had some powerful legs.

I could see Link still staring as he stood next to the Beater.

Ridley patted the seat next to her. "Hop in, Boyfriend, we're gonna be late."

"I'm not . . . I mean, we're not—"

"You really are cute. Now get in. You don't want us to be late, do you?"

"Late for what?"

"Family dinner. The High Holidays. The Gathering. Why do you think they sent me all the way out here into Gat-dung to find you?"

"I don't know. Lena never invited me."

"Well, let's just say there's no keeping Aunt Del from checking out the first guy Lena's ever brought home. So you've been summoned, and since Lena's busy with dinner and Macon's still, you know, 'sleeping,' I drew the short straw."

"She didn't bring me home. I just went by one night to drop off her homework."

Ridley opened the car door from the inside. "Get in, Short Straw."

"Lena would've called me if she wanted me to come." Somehow I knew I was going to get in even as I was saying it. I hesitated.

"Are you always like this? Or are you flirting with me? Because if you're playing hard to get, just tell me now and we'll go park at the swamp and get it on already."

I got in the car. "Fine. Let's go."

She reached over and pushed the hair out of my eyes with her cold hand. "You've got nice eyes, Boyfriend. You shouldn't keep them all covered up."

♦ ♦ ♦

By the time we got to Ravenwood, I didn't know what had happened. She kept playing music I'd never heard, and I started to talk, and I just kept talking, until I had told her things I had never told anyone, except Lena. I can't really explain it. It was like I had lost control of my mouth.

I told her about my mom, about how she died, even though I almost never talked about it with anyone. I told her about Amma, about how she read cards, and about how she was like my mom now that I didn't have one, except for the charms and dolls and her generally disagreeable nature. I told her about Link, and his mom, and how she had changed lately and spent all her time trying to convince everyone that Lena was just as crazy as Macon Ravenwood, and a danger to every student at Jackson.

I told her about my dad, about how he was holed up in his study, with his books and some secret painting I was never allowed to see, and how I felt like I needed to protect him, even though it was from something that had already happened.

I told her about Lena, about how we'd met in the rain, how we had seemed to know each other before we'd even met, and about the messed-up scene with the window.

It almost felt like she was sucking it all out of me, like she sucked on that sticky red lollipop, the one she kept licking as she drove. It took all the strength I had to not tell her about the locket, and the dreams. Maybe the fact that she was Lena's cousin just made everything a little easier between us. Maybe it was something else.

Just as I was starting to wonder, we pulled up at Ravenwood Manor, and she flipped off the radio. The sun had set, the lollipop was gone, and I had finally shut up. When had that happened?

Ridley leaned in toward me, close. I could see my face reflected in her sunglasses. I breathed her in. She smelled sweet and sort of damp, nothing like Lena, but still familiar somehow. "You don't need to be worried, Short Straw."

"Yeah, why not?"

"You're the real deal." She smiled at me, and her eyes flashed. Behind the glasses, I could see a gold glint, like goldfish swimming in a dark pond. They were hypnotic, even through her shades. Maybe that's why she wore them. Then the glasses went dark, and she messed up my hair. "Too bad she'll probably never see you again once you meet the rest of us. Our family is just a little wack." She got out of the car, and I followed her.

"More wack than you?"

"Infinitely."

Great.

She put her cold hand on my arm, once again, when we got to the bottom step of the house. "And, Boyfriend. When Lena blows you off, which she will in about five months, give me a call. You'll know how to find me." She looped her arm through mine, suddenly strangely formal. "May I?"

I gestured with my free hand. "Sure. After you." As we walked up the stairs, they groaned under our combined weight. I pulled Ridley up to the front door, still not quite sure if the stairs were going to support us or not.

I knocked, but there was no response. I reached up and felt for the moon. The door swung open, slowly—

Ridley seemed tentative. And as we crossed the threshold, I could almost feel the house settle, as if the climate inside had changed, almost imperceptibly.

"Hello, Mother."

A round woman, bustling to lay gourds and golden leaves along the mantel, startled and dropped a small white pumpkin. It exploded onto the ground. She grabbed onto the mantel to steady herself. She looked odd, like she was wearing a dress from a hundred years ago. "Julia! I mean Ridley. What are you doing here? I must be confused. I thought, I thought . . ."

I knew something was wrong. This didn't seem like your average mother-daughter hello.

"Jules? Is that you?" A younger version of Ridley, maybe ten, came walking into the front hall with Boo Radley, who was now wearing a sparkly blue cape over his back. Dressing up the family wolf, as if nothing unusual was going on. Everything about the girl was like light; she had blond hair and radiant blue eyes, as if they had little flecks of the sky on a sunny afternoon in them. The girl smiled, and then frowned. "They said you'd gone away."

Boo started to growl.

Ridley opened her arms, waiting for the little girl to rush into them, but the girl didn't move. So Ridley held her hands out and uncurled each one. A red lollipop appeared in the first and, not to be outdone, a little gray mouse wearing a sparkly blue cape that matched Boo's sniffed the air in her other hand—like a cheap carnival trick.

The little girl stepped forward, tentatively, as if her sister had the power to pull her across the room, without so much as a touch, like the moon and the tides. I had felt it myself.

When Ridley spoke, her voice was thick and husky like honey. "Come now, Ryan. Mamma was just pulling your tail to see if it squeaked. I haven't gone anywhere. Not really. Would your favorite big sister ever leave you?"

Ryan grinned and ran toward Ridley, jumping up, as if she was about to leap into her open arms. Boo barked. For a moment, Ryan hung suspended in mid-air, like one of those cartoon characters that accidentally jumps of a cliff and just hangs there for a few seconds, before they fall. Then, she fell, hitting the floor abruptly, as if she had smacked into an invisible wall. The lights inside the house grew brighter, all at once, as if the house was a stage, and the lighting was changing to signal the end of an act. In the light, Ridley's features cast harsh shadows.

The light changed things. Ridley held a hand up to her eyes, calling out to the house. "Oh please, Uncle Macon. Is that really necessary?"

Boo leaped forward, positioning himself between Ryan and Ridley. Growling, the dog pressed closer and closer, the hair on his back standing on end, making him look even more like a wolf. Apparently Ridley's charms were lost on Boo.

Ridley looped her arm back through mine tightly, and laugh-growled, or something like that. It wasn't a friendly sound. I tried to keep it together, but my throat felt like it was stuffed with wet socks.

Keeping one hand on my arm, she raised her other hand over her head and threw it up toward the ceiling. "Well, if you're going to be rude." Every light in the house went dark. The whole house seemed to short out.

Macon's voice calmly floated down from the top of the dim shadows. "Ridley, my dear, what a surprise. We weren't expecting you."

Not expecting her? What was he talking about?

"I wouldn't miss the Gathering for anything in the world,

and look, I brought a guest. Or, I guess you could say, I'm his guest."

Macon walked down the staircase, without taking his eyes off Ridley. I was watching two lions circle each other, and I was standing in the middle. Ridley had played me, and I had gone along with it, like a sucker, like the red sucker she was sucking on right now.

"I don't think that's the best idea. I'm sure you're expected elsewhere."

She pulled the lollipop out of her mouth with a pop. "Like I said, I wouldn't miss this for the world. Besides, you wouldn't want me to drive Ethan *all* the way home. What ever would we talk about?"

I wanted to suggest we leave, but I couldn't get the words out. Everyone just stood there in the main hall, staring at each other. Ridley leaned against one of the pillars.

Macon broke the silence. "Why don't you show Ethan to the dining room? I'm sure you remember where it is."

"But Macon—" The woman I guessed was Aunt Del looked panicked, and again, confused, like she didn't quite know what was going on.

"It's all right, Delphine." I could see in Macon's face he was working things out, jumping from step to step, ahead of the step we were all on. Without knowing what I had stumbled into, it was actually comforting to know he was there.

The last place I wanted to go was the dining room. I wanted to bolt out of there, but I couldn't make it happen. Ridley wouldn't let go of my arm, and as long as she was touching me, I felt like I was on autopilot. She led me into the formal dining room where I had offended Macon the first time. I looked at Ridley, clinging to my arm. This offense was far worse.

The room was lit by hundreds of tiny black votive candles, and strands of black glass beads hung from the chandelier. There was an enormous wreath, made entirely of black feathers, on the door leading into the kitchen. The table was set with silver and pearl-white plates, which were actually made of pearl, for all I knew.

The kitchen door swung open. Lena backed through the door, carrying a huge silver tray, piled high with exotic-looking fruits that definitely were not from South Carolina. She wore a fitted black floor-length jacket, cinched at her waist. It looked strangely timeless, like nothing I had ever seen in this county, or even this century, but when I looked down, I noticed she was wearing her Converse. She looked even more beautiful than when I had come over for dinner . . . when? A few weeks ago?

My mind felt cloudy, like I was half asleep. I took a deep breath, but all I could smell was Ridley, a musky smell mixed with something way too sweet, like syrup bubbling on the stove. It was strong and suffocating.

"We're almost ready. Just a few more—" Lena froze, the door still in mid-swing. She looked like she had seen a ghost, or something much worse. I wasn't sure if it was just the sight of Ridley, or the two of us standing there arm in arm.

"Well, hello, Cuz. Long time no see." Ridley advanced a few steps, dragging me along next to her. "Aren't you going to give me a kiss?"

The tray Lena was carrying crashed to the floor. "What are you doing here?" Lena's voice was barely a whisper.

"Why, I came to see my favorite cousin of course, and I brought a date."

"I'm not your date," I said lamely, barely choking the words out, still glued to her arm. She pulled a cigarette from the pack tucked in her boot and lit it, all with her free hand.

"Ridley, please do not smoke in the house," Macon said, and the cigarette instantly went out. Ridley laughed and flicked it into a bowl of something that looked like mashed potatoes, but probably wasn't.

"Uncle Macon. You always were such a stickler for the house *rules*."

"The rules were set long ago, Ridley. There's nothing you or I can do to change them now."

They stared at each other. Macon gestured, and a chair pulled itself away from the table. "Why don't we all have a seat? Lena, can you let Kitchen know we will be two more for dinner?"

Lena just stood there, seething. "She can't stay."

"It's all right. Nothing can harm you here," Macon assured her. But Lena didn't look scared. She looked furious.

Ridley smiled. "You sure about that?"

"Dinner is ready, and you know how Kitchen feels about serving cold food." Macon walked into the dining room. Everyone filed in after him, even though he had barely spoken loud enough for the four of us in the room to hear him.

Boo led the way, lumbering in with Ryan. Aunt Del followed, on the arm of a gray-haired man about my dad's age. He was dressed like he was right out of one of the books in my mom's study, with knee-high boots, a frilly shirt, and a weird opera cape. The two of them looked like an exhibit from a Smithsonian museum.

An older girl entered the room. She looked a lot like Ridley, except she had on more clothing and she didn't look so dangerous. She had long, straight blond hair with a neater version of Ridley's choppy bangs. She looked like the kind of girl you'd see carrying a stack of books on a fancy old college campus up North like Yale or Harvard. The girl locked eyes with Ridley, like she could see Ridley's eyes through the dark shades she was still wearing.

"Ethan, I'd like to introduce you to my older sister, Annabel. Oh, I'm sorry, I mean Reece." Who doesn't know their own sister's name?

Reece smiled and spoke slowly as if she was choosing her words carefully. "What are you doin' here, Ridley? I thought you had another engagement tonight."

"Plans change."

"So do families." Reece reached out her hand and waved it in front of Ridley's face, just a simple flourish, like a magician waving his hand over a top hat. I flinched; I don't know what I was thinking, but for a second I thought Ridley might disappear. Or more preferably, I might.

But she didn't disappear, and this time, it was Ridley who flinched and looked away, like it was physically painful to look Reece in the eye.

Reece peered into Ridley's face, as if it were a mirror. "Interestin'. Why is it, Rid, when I look in your eyes all I can see are *hers*? You two are as thick as thieves, aren't you?"

"You're babbling again, *Sis*."

Reece closed her eyes, concentrating. Ridley squirmed like a pinned butterfly. Reece fluttered her hand again, and for a moment, Ridley's face dissolved into the murky image of another woman. The woman's face was somehow familiar, only I couldn't remember why.

Macon clapped his hand down heavily on Ridley's shoulder. It was the only time I'd seen anyone touch her, except me. Ridley winced, and I could feel a twinge of pain shooting from her hand, down my arm. Macon Ravenwood was clearly not a man to be taken lightly. "Now. Like it or not, the Gathering has commenced. I won't have anyone ruining the High Holidays, not under my roof. Ridley has been, as she so helpfully clarified, *invited* to join us. Nothing more needs to be said. Please, everyone have a seat."

Lena sat down, her eyes locked on the two of us.

Aunt Del looked even more worried than when we had first arrived. The man in the opera cape patted her hand reassuringly. A tall guy about my age in black jeans, a faded black T-shirt, and scuffed motorcycle boots wandered in looking bored.

Ridley handled the introductions. "You've already met my mother. And this is my father, Barclay Kent, and my brother, Larkin."

"It's nice to meet you, Ethan." Barclay stepped forward as if to shake my hand, but when he noticed Ridley's hand on my arm, he stepped back. Larkin drew his arm around my shoulder, only when I looked over his arm had become a snake, flickering its tongue in and out of its mouth.

"Larkin!" Barclay hissed. The snake became Larkin's arm again in an instant.

"Jeez. Just tryin' to lift the mood around here. You're all such a bunch a whiners." Larkin's eyes flickered yellow, slitted. Snake eyes.

"Larkin, I said that was enough." His father gave him the

kind of look only a father can give a son who's always disappointing him. Larkin's eyes changed back to green.

Macon took a seat at the head of the table. "Why don't we all sit down? Kitchen has prepared one of her finest holiday meals. Lena and I have been subjected to the clatter for days." Everyone took their seats at the enormous rectangular claw-foot table. It was dark wood, almost black, and there were intricate designs, like vines, carved into the legs. Huge black candles flickered in the center of the table.

"Sit over here by me, Short Straw." Ridley led me to an empty chair, across from the silver bird holding Lena's place card, as if I had a choice.

I tried to make eye contact with Lena, but her eyes were fixed on Ridley. And they were fierce. I just hoped Ridley was the only one her anger was directed at.

The table was overflowing with food, even more than the last time I was here; every time I looked at the table there was more. A crown roast, filet tied with rosemary, and more exotic dishes I'd never seen before. A large bird stuffed with dressing and pears, resting on peacock feathers arranged to resemble a live bird's open tail. I was hoping it wasn't an actual peacock, but considering the tail feathers, I was pretty sure it was. And sparkling candies, I think, shaped exactly like real seahorses.

But no one was eating, no one except Ridley. She seemed to be enjoying herself. "I just love sugar horses." She popped two of the tiny golden seahorses into her mouth.

Aunt Del coughed a few times, pouring a glass of black liquid, the consistency of wine, into her glass from the decanter on the table.

Ridley looked at Lena across the table. "So, Cuz, any big

172

plans for your birthday?" Ridley dipped her fingers into a dark brown sauce in the gravy boat next to the bird I hoped wasn't a peacock, and licked it off her fingers suggestively.

"We're not discussing Lena's birthday tonight," Macon warned.

Ridley was enjoying the tension. She popped another seahorse into her mouth. "Why not?"

Lena's eyes were wild. "You don't need to worry about *my* birthday. You won't be invited."

"*You* certainly should. Worry, I mean. It's such an *important* birthday, after all." Ridley laughed. Lena's hair started to curl and uncurl itself as if there was a wind in the room. There wasn't.

"Ridley, I said that's enough." Macon was losing his patience. I recognized his tone as the same one he'd had after I took the locket out of my pocket, during my first visit.

"Why are you taking her side, Uncle M? I spent just as much time with you as Lena did, growing up. How did she suddenly become your favorite?" For a moment, she almost sounded hurt.

"You know it has nothing to do with favorites. You have been Claimed. It's out of my hands."

Claimed? By what? What was he talking about? The suffocating haze around me was getting thicker. I couldn't be sure I was hearing everything correctly.

"But you and I are the same." She was pleading with Macon, like a spoiled child.

The table began to shake almost imperceptibly, the black liquid in the wine glasses gently sloshing from side to side. Then I heard a rhythmic tapping on the roof. Rain.

Lena was gripping the edge of the table, her knuckles white. "You are NOT the same," she hissed.

I felt Ridley's body stiffen against my arm, which she was still wrapped around like a snake. "You think you are so much better than me, Lena . . . is it? You don't even know your real name. You don't even realize this relationship of yours is doomed. Just wait until you're Claimed and you find out how things really work." She laughed, a sinister, painful sort of sound. "You have no idea if we are the same or not. In a few months, you could end up exactly like me."

Lena looked at me, panicked. The table began to shake harder, the plates rattling against the wood. There was a crackle of lightning outside, and rain began pouring down the windows like tears. "Shut up!"

"Tell him, Lena. Don't you think Short Straw here deserves to know everything? That you have no idea if you're Light or Dark? That you have no choice?"

Lena leapt to her feet, knocking her chair over behind her. "I said, shut up!"

Ridley was relaxed again, enjoying herself. "Tell him how we lived together, in the same room, like sisters, that I was exactly like you a year ago and now . . ."

Macon stood at the head of the table, gripping it with both hands. His pale face seemed even whiter than usual. "Ridley, that's enough! I will Cast you out of this house if you say another word."

"You can't Cast me out, Uncle. You aren't strong enough for that."

"Don't overestimate your skills. No Dark Caster on Earth is powerful enough to enter Ravenwood on their own. I Bound the place myself. We all did."

Dark Caster? That didn't sound good.

"Ah, Uncle Macon. You're forgetting that famous Southern hospitality. I didn't break in. I was invited in, on the arm of the handsomest gent in Gat-dung." Ridley turned to me and smiled, pulling her shades from her eyes. They were just wrong, glowing gold, as if they were on fire. They were shaped like a cat's, with black slits in the middle. Light shone from her eyes, and in that light, everything changed.

She looked over at me, with that sinister smile, and her face was twisted into darkness and shadows. The features that had been so feminine and enticing were now sharp and hard, morphing before my eyes. Her skin seemed to be tightening around her bones, accentuating every vein until you could almost see the blood pumping through them. She looked like a monster.

I had brought a monster into the house, into Lena's house.

Almost immediately, the house began to shake violently. The crystal chandeliers were swinging, the lights flickering. The plantation shutters banged open and shut again and again as the rain battered the roof. The sound was so loud, it was almost impossible to hear anything else, like the night I almost hit Lena when she was standing in the road.

Ridley tightened her ice-cold grip on my arm. I tried to shake her loose, but I could barely move. The coldness was spreading; my whole arm was starting to feel numb.

Lena looked up from the table, in horror. "Ethan!"

Aunt Del stamped her foot across the room. The floorboards seemed to roll beneath her feet.

The coldness had spread throughout my body. My throat was frozen. My legs were paralyzed; I couldn't move. I couldn't pull away from Ridley's arm, and I couldn't tell anyone what was happening. In another few minutes, I wouldn't be able to breathe.

A woman's voice floated across the table. Aunt Del. "Ridley. I told you to stay away, child. There's nothing we can do for you now. I'm so sorry."

Macon's voice was harsh. "Ridley, a year can make all the difference in the world. You're Claimed now. You've found your place in the Order of Things. You don't belong here anymore. You have to go."

A second later, he was standing right in front of her. Either that, or I was losing track of what was happening. The voices and faces were starting to spin around me. I could barely catch my breath. I was so cold, my frozen jaw wouldn't even move enough to chatter. "Go!" he shouted.

"No!"

"Ridley! Behave! You must leave this place. Ravenwood is not a place of Dark magic. This is a Bound place, a place of Light. You can't survive here, not for long." Aunt Del's voice was firm.

Ridley answered with a snarl. "I'm not leaving, Mother, and you can't make me."

Macon's voice interrupted her tantrum. "You know that's not true."

"I'm stronger now, Uncle Macon. You can't control me."

"True, your strength is growing, but you are not ready to take me on, and I will do whatever is necessary to protect Lena. Even if that means hurting you, or worse."

The weight of his threat was too much for Ridley. "You would do that to me? Ravenwood's a Dark place of power. It always has been, since Abraham. He was one of us. Ravenwood should be ours. Why are you Binding it to the Light?"

"Ravenwood is Lena's home now."

"You belong with me, Uncle M. *With Her.*"

Ridley stood up, dragging me to my feet. The three of them were standing now—Lena, Macon, and Ridley, the three points of a really frightening triangle. "I'm not scared of your kind."

"That may be, but you have no power here. Not against all of us, and a Natural."

Ridley cackled. "Lena, a Natural? That's the funniest thing you've said all night. I've seen what a Natural can do. Lena could never be one."

"A Cataclyst and a Natural aren't the same."

"Aren't they, though? A Cataclyst is a Natural gone Dark, two sides of the same coin."

What was she talking about? I was in over my head.

And then I felt my body seize up, and I knew I was blacking out—that I was probably going to die. It was like all the life had been sucked out of me, with the warmth of my blood. I could hear the sound of thunder. One—then lightning and the crash of a tree branch just outside the window. The storm was here. It was right on us.

"You're wrong, Uncle M. Lena isn't worth protecting, and she's certainly not a Natural. You won't know her fate until her birthday. You think that just because she's sweet and innocent now, she'll be Claimed by the Light? That means nothing. Wasn't I the same a year ago? And from what Short Straw here has been telling me, she's closer to going Dark than Light. Lightning storms? Terrorizing the high school?"

The wind grew stronger, and Lena was getting angrier. I could see the rage in her eyes. A window shattered, just like in English class. I knew where this was going.

"Shut up! You don't know what you're talking about!" Rain came pouring into the dining room. Wind followed, sending glasses and plates crashing to the floor, black liquid staining the floor in long streaks. No one moved.

Ridley turned back to Macon. "You've always given her too much credit. She's nothing."

I wanted to break free from Ridley's hold, to grab her and drag her out of the house myself, but I couldn't move.

A second window shattered, then another, and another. Glass was breaking everywhere. China, wineglasses, the glass on every picture frame. Furniture was banging against the walls. And the wind, it was like a tornado had been sucked into the room with us. The sound was so loud, I couldn't hear anything else. The tablecloth blew right off the table, with every candle, platter, and plate still on it, throwing everything against the wall. The room was spinning, I think. Everything was being sucked out into the foyer, toward the front door. Boo Radley screamed, that horrible human scream. Ridley's grip seemed to loosen around my arm. I blinked hard, trying not to pass out.

And there, standing in the middle of it all, was Lena. She was perfectly still, her hair whipping in the wind around her. What was happening?

I felt my legs buckle. Just as I lost consciousness, I felt the wind, a surge of power that literally ripped my arm out of Ridley's hand, as she was sucked out of the room, toward the front door. I collapsed to the floor, as I heard Lena's voice, or thought I did.

"Get the hell away from my boyfriend, witch."

Boyfriend.

Was that what I was?

I tried to smile. Instead, I blacked out.

A Crack in the Plaster

When I woke up, I had no idea where I was. I tried to focus on the first few things that came into view. Words. Phrases handwritten in what looked like carefully scripted Sharpie, right on the ceiling over the bed.

moments bleed together, no span to time

There were hundreds of others, too, written everywhere, parts of sentences, parts of verses, random collections of words. On one closet door was scrawled *fate decides.* On the other, it said *until challenged by the fated.* Up and down the door I could see the words *desperate / relentless / condemned / empowered.* The mirror said *open your eyes;* the window-panes said *and see.*

Even the pale white lampshade was scribbled with the words *illuminatethedarknessilluminatethedarkness* over and over again, in an endlessly repeating pattern.

Lena's poetry. I was finally getting to read some of it. Even if you ignored the distinctive ink, this room didn't look like the rest of the house. It was small and cozy, tucked up under the eaves. A ceiling fan swirled slowly above my head, cutting through the phrases. There were stacks of spiral notebooks on every surface, and a stack of books on the nightstand. Poetry books. Plath, Eliot, Bukowski, Frost, Cummings—at least I recognized the names.

I was lying in a small white iron bed, my legs spilling over the edge. This was Lena's room, and I was lying in her bed. Lena was curled in a chair at the foot of the bed, her head resting on the arm.

I sat up, groggy. "Hey. What happened?"

I was pretty sure I had passed out, but I was fuzzy on the details. The last thing I remembered was the freezing cold moving up my body, my throat closing up, and Lena's voice. I thought she had said something about me being her boyfriend, but since I was about to pass out at the time and nothing had really happened between us, that was doubtful. Wishful thinking, I guessed.

"Ethan!" She jumped out of the chair and onto the bed next to me, although she seemed careful not to touch me. "Are you okay? Ridley wouldn't let go of you, and I didn't know what to do. You looked like you were in so much pain, and I just reacted."

"You mean that tornado in the middle of your dining room?"

She looked away, miserable. "That's what happens. I feel things, I get angry or scared and then . . . things just happen."

I reached over and put my hand over hers, feeling the warmth move up my arm. "Things like windows breaking?"

She looked back at me, and I curled my hand around hers until I was holding it in mine. A random crack in the old plaster in the corner behind her seemed to grow, until it curled its

180

way across the ceiling, circled the frosted chandelier, and swirled its way back down. It looked like a heart. A giant, looping, girly heart had just appeared in the cracking plaster of her bedroom ceiling.

"Lena."

"Yeah?"

"Is your ceiling about to fall in on our heads?"

She turned and looked at the crack. When she saw it, she bit her lip, and her cheeks turned pink. "I don't think so. It's just a crack in the plaster."

"Were you trying to do that?"

"No." A creeping pink spread across her nose and cheeks. She looked away.

I wanted to ask her what it was she'd been thinking, but I didn't want to embarrass her. I just hoped it had something to do with me, with her hand nestled in mine. With the word I thought I heard her say, the moment before I blacked out.

I looked dubiously at the crack. A lot was riding on that crack in the plaster.

"Can you undo them? These things that just . . . happen?"

Lena sighed, relieved to talk about something else. "Sometimes. It depends. Sometimes I get so overwhelmed that I can't control it and I can't fix it, not even after. I don't think I could have put the glass back into that window at school. I don't think I could have stopped the storm from coming, the day we met."

"I don't think that one was your fault. You can't blame yourself for every storm that rolls through Gatlin County. Hurricane season isn't even over yet."

She flipped over onto her stomach and looked me right in the eye. She didn't let go, and neither did I. My whole body was buzzing with the warmth of her touch. "Didn't you see what happened tonight?"

"Maybe sometimes a hurricane is just a hurricane, Lena."

"As long as I'm around, I am hurricane season in Gatlin County." She tried to pull her hand away, but that only made me hold on more tightly.

"That's funny. You seem more like a girl to me."

"Yeah, well, I'm not. I'm a whole storm system, out of control. Most Casters can control their gifts by the time they're my age, but half the time it feels more like mine control me." She pointed to her own reflection in the mirror on the wall. The Sharpie writing scribbled itself across the reflection as we watched. *Who is this girl?* "I'm still trying to figure it all out, but sometimes it seems like I never will."

"Do all Casters have the same powers, gifts, whatever?"

"No. We can all do simple things like move objects, but each Caster also has more specific abilities related to their gifts."

Right about now, I wished there was some kind of class I could take so I'd be able to follow these conversations, Caster 101, I don't know, because I was always sort of lost. The only person I knew who had any special abilities was Amma. Reading futures and warding off evil spirits had to count for something, right? And for all I knew, maybe Amma could move objects with her mind; she could sure get my butt moving with just a look. "What about Aunt Del? What can she do?"

"She's a Palimpsest. She reads time."

"Reads time?"

"Like, you and I walk into a room and see the present. Aunt Del sees different points in the past and the present, all at once. She can walk into a room and see it as it is today and as it was ten years ago, twenty years ago, fifty years ago, at the same time. Kind of like when we touch the locket. That's why she's always so confused. She never knows exactly when or even where she is."

I thought about how I felt after one of the visions, and what it would be like to feel that way all of the time. "No kidding. How about Ridley?"

"Ridley's a Siren. Her gift is the Power of Persuasion. She can put any idea into anyone's head, get them to tell her anything, do anything. If she used her power on you, and she told you to jump off a cliff—you'd jump." I remembered how it felt in the car with her, like I would've told her almost anything.

"I wouldn't jump."

"You would. You'd have to. A Mortal man is no match for a Siren."

"I wouldn't." I looked at her. Her hair was blowing in the breeze around her face, except there wasn't an open window in the room. I searched her eyes for some kind of sign that maybe she was feeling the same way I was. "You can't jump off a cliff when you've already fallen off a bigger one."

I heard the words coming out of my mouth, and I wanted to take them back as soon as I said them. They had sounded a lot better in my head. She looked back at me, trying to see if I was serious. I was, but I couldn't say that. Instead, I changed the subject. "So what's Reece's superpower?"

"She's a Sybil, she reads faces. She can see what you've seen, who you've seen, what you've done, just by looking into your eyes. She can open up your face and literally read it, like a book." Lena was still studying my face.

"Yeah, who was that? That other woman Ridley turned into for a second, when Reece was staring at her? Did you see that?"

183

Lena nodded. "Macon wouldn't tell me, but it had to be someone Dark. Someone powerful."

I kept asking. I had to know. It was like finding out I'd just had dinner with a bunch of aliens. "What can Larkin do? Charm snakes?"

"Larkin's an Illusionist. It's like a Shifter. But Uncle Barclay's the only Shifter in the family."

"What's the difference?"

"Larkin can Spellcast, or make anything look like anything he wants, for a spell—people, things, places. He creates illusions, but they're not real. Uncle Barclay can Shiftcast, which means he can actually change any object into another object, for as long as he wants."

"So your cousin changes how things seem, and your uncle changes how they are?"

"Yeah. Mostly, Gramma says their powers are too close. It happens sometimes with parents and their children. They're too much alike, so they're always fighting." I knew what she was thinking, that she would never know that for herself. Her face clouded over, and I made a stupid attempt to lighten the mood.

"Ryan? What's her power? Dog fashion designer?"

"Too soon to tell. She's only ten."

"And Macon?"

"He's just . . . Uncle Macon. There's nothing Uncle Macon can't do, or wouldn't do for me. I spent a lot of time with him growing up." She looked away, avoiding the question. She was holding something back, but with Lena, it was impossible to know what. "He's like my father, or how I imagine my father." She didn't have to say anything else. I knew what it was like to lose someone. I wondered if it was worse to never have them at all.

"What about you? What's your gift?"

As if she had just one. As if I hadn't seen them in action since the first day of school. As if I hadn't been trying to get up the nerve to ask her this question since the night she sat on my porch in her purple pajamas.

She paused for a minute, collecting her thoughts, or deciding if she was going to tell me; it was impossible to know which. Then she looked at me, with her endless green eyes. "I'm a Natural. At least Uncle Macon and Aunt Del think I am."

A Natural. I was relieved. It didn't sound as bad as a Siren. I didn't think I could have handled that. "What exactly does that mean?"

"I don't even know. It's not really one thing. I mean, supposedly a Natural can do a lot more than other Casters." She said it quickly, almost like she was hoping I wouldn't hear, but I did.

More than other Casters.

More. I wasn't sure how I felt about more. Less, I could have handled less. Less would've been good.

"But as you saw tonight, I don't even know what I can do." She picked at the quilt between us, nervous. I pulled on her hand until she was lying on the bed next to me, propped up on one elbow.

"I don't care about any of that. I like you just the way you are."

"Ethan, you barely know anything about me."

The drowsy warmth was washing through my body, and to be honest, I couldn't have cared less what she was saying. It felt so good just to be near her, holding her hand, with only the white quilt between us. "That's not true. I know you write poetry and I know about the raven on your necklace and I know you love orange soda and your grandma and Milk Duds mixed into your popcorn."

For a second, I thought she might smile. "That's hardly anything."

"It's a start."

She looked me right in the eye, her green eyes searching my blue ones. "You don't even know my name."

"Your name is Lena Duchannes."

"Okay, well, for starters, it's not."

I pushed myself all the way up, and let go of her hand. "What are you talking about?"

"It's not my name. Ridley wasn't lying about that." Some of the conversation from earlier started to come back to me. I remembered Ridley saying something about Lena not knowing her real name, but I didn't think she had meant literally.

"Well, what is it then?"

"I don't know."

"Is that some kind of Caster thing?"

"Not really. Most Casters know their real names, but my family's different. In my family, we don't learn our birth names until we turn sixteen. Until then, we have other names. Ridley's was Julia. Reece's was Annabel. Mine is Lena."

"So who's Lena Duchannes?"

"I'm a Duchannes, that much I know. But Lena, that's just a name my gramma started calling me, because she thought I was skinny as a string bean. Lena Beana."

I didn't say anything for a second. I was trying to take it all in. "Okay, so you don't know your first name. You'll know in a couple of months."

"It's not that simple. I don't know anything about myself. That's why I'm so crazy all the time. I don't know my name and I don't know what happened to my parents."

"They died in an accident, right?"

"That's what they told me, but nobody really talks about it. I can't find any record of the accident, and I've never seen their graves or anything. How do I even know it's true?"

"Who's going to lie about something as creepy as that?"

"Have you met my family?"

"Right."

"And that monster downstairs, that—witch, who almost killed you? Believe it or not, she used to be my best friend. Ridley and I grew up together living with my gramma. We moved around so much we shared the same suitcase."

"That's why you guys don't have much of an accent. Most people would never believe you had lived in the South."

"What's your excuse?"

"Professor parents, and a jar full of quarters every time I dropped a G." I rolled my eyes. "So Ridley didn't live with Aunt Del?"

"No. Aunt Del just visits on the holidays. In my family, you don't live with your parents. It's too dangerous." I stopped myself from asking my next fifty questions while Lena raced on, as if she'd been waiting to tell this story for about a hundred years. "Ridley and I were like sisters. We slept in the same room and we were home-schooled together. When we moved to Virginia, we convinced my gramma to let us to go to a regular school. We wanted to make friends, be normal. The only time we ever spoke to Mortals was when Gramma took us on one of her outings to museums, the opera, or lunch at Olde Pink House."

"So what happened when you went to school?"

"It was a disaster. Our clothes were wrong, we didn't have a TV, we turned in all our homework. We were total losers."

"But you got to hang out with Mortals."

She wouldn't look at me. "I've never had a Mortal friend until I met you."

"Really?"

"I only had Ridley. Things were just as bad for her, but she didn't care. She was too busy making sure no one bothered me."

I had a hard time imagining Ridley protecting anyone.

People change, Ethan.

Not that much. Not even Casters.

Especially Casters. That's what I'm trying to tell you.

She pulled her hand away from me. "Ridley started acting strange, and then the same guys who had ignored her started following her everywhere, waiting for her after school, fighting over who would walk her home."

"Yeah, well. Some girls are just like that."

"Ridley isn't some girl. I told you, she's a Siren. She could make people do things, things they wouldn't normally want to do. And those boys were jumping off the cliff, one by one." She twisted her necklace around her fingers and kept talking. "The night before Ridley's sixteenth birthday, I followed her to the train station. She was scared out of her mind. She said she could tell she was going Dark, and she had to get away before she hurt someone she loved. Before she hurt me. I'm the only person Ridley ever really loved. She disappeared that night, and I never saw her again until today. I think after what you saw tonight, it's pretty obvious she went Dark."

"Wait a second, what are you talking about? What do you mean going Dark?"

Lena took a deep breath and hesitated, like she wasn't sure if she wanted to tell me the answer.

"You have to tell me, Lena."

"In my family, when you turn sixteen, you're Claimed. Your fate is chosen for you, and you become Light, like Aunt Del and Reece, or you become Dark, like Ridley. Dark or Light, Black or White. There's no gray in my family. We can't choose, and we can't undo it once we're Claimed."

"What do you mean, you can't choose?"

"We can't decide if we want to be Light or Dark, good or evil, like Mortals and other Casters can. In my family, there's no free will. It's decided for us, on our sixteenth birthday."

I tried to understand what she was saying, but it was too crazy. I'd lived with Amma long enough to know there was White and Black magic, but it was hard to believe that Lena had no choice about which one she was.

Who she was.

She was still talking. "That's why we can't live with our parents."

"What does that have to do with it?"

"It didn't used to be that way. But when my gramma's sister, Althea, went Dark, their mother couldn't send Althea away. Back then, if a Caster went Dark, they were supposed to leave their home and their family, for obvious reasons. Althea's mother thought she could help her fight it, but she couldn't, and terrible things started happening in the town where they lived."

"What kind of things?"

"Althea was an Evo. They're incredibly powerful. They can influence people like Ridley can, but they can also Evolve, morph into other people, into anyone. Once she Turned, unexplained accidents started happening in town. People were injured and eventually a girl drowned. That's when Althea's mother finally sent her away."

I thought we had problems in Gatlin. I couldn't imagine a more powerful version of Ridley hanging around, full-time. "So now none of you can live with your parents?"

"Everyone decided it would be too hard for parents to turn their backs on their children if they went Dark. So ever since then, children live with other family members until they're Claimed."

"Then why does Ryan live with her parents?"

"Ryan is . . . Ryan. She's a special case." She shrugged. "At least, that's what Uncle Macon says every time I ask."

It all sounded so surreal, the idea that everyone in her family possessed supernatural powers. They looked like me, like everyone else in Gatlin, well, maybe not everyone, but they were completely different. Weren't they? Even Ridley, hanging out in front of the Stop & Steal—none of the guys had suspected she was anything other than an incredibly hot girl, who was obviously pretty confused if she was looking for me. How did it work? How did you get to be a Caster instead of just some ordinary kid?

"Were your parents gifted?" I hated to bring up her parents. I knew what it was like to talk about your dead parent, but at this point I had to know.

"Yes. Everyone in my family is."

"What were their gifts? Were they anything like yours?"

"I don't know. Gramma's never said anything. I told you, it's like they never existed. Which just makes me think, you know."

"What?"

"Maybe they were Dark, and I'm going to go Dark, too."

"You're not."

"How do you know?"

"How can I have the same dreams you have? How do I know when I walk into a room whether or not you've been there?"

Ethan.

It's true.

I touched her cheek, and said quietly, "I don't know how I know. I just do."

"I know you believe that, but you can't know. I don't even know what's going to happen to me."

"That's the biggest load of crap I've ever heard." It was like everything else tonight; I hadn't meant to say it, at least not out loud, but I was glad I did.

"What?"

"All that destiny garbage. Nobody can decide what happens to you. Nobody but you."

"Not if you're a Duchannes, Ethan. Other Casters, they can choose, but not us, not my family. When we're Claimed at sixteen, we become Light or Dark. There is no free will."

I lifted her chin with my hand. "So you're a Natural. What's wrong with that?"

I looked into her eyes, and I knew I was going to kiss her, and I knew there was nothing to worry about, as long as we stayed together. And I believed, for that one second, we always would.

I stopped thinking about the Jackson basketball playbook and finally let her see how I felt, what was in my mind. What I was about to do, and how long it had taken me to get up the nerve to do it.

Oh.

Her eyes widened, bigger and greener, if that was even possible.

Ethan—I don't know—

I leaned down and kissed her mouth. It tasted salty, like her tears. This time, not warmth, but electricity, shot from my mouth to my toes. I could feel tingling in my fingertips. It was like shoving a pen into an electrical outlet, which Link had dared me to do when I was eight years old. She closed her eyes and pulled me in to her, and for a minute, everything was perfect. She kissed me, her lips smiling beneath mine, and I knew she had been waiting for me, maybe just as long as I had been waiting for her. But then, as quickly as she had opened herself up to me, she shut me out. Or more accurately, pushed me back.

Ethan, we can't do this.

Why? I thought we felt the same way about each other.

Or maybe we didn't. Maybe she didn't.

I was staring at her, from the end of her outstretched hands that were still resting on my chest. She could probably feel how fast my heart was beating.

It's not that. . . .

She started to turn away, and I was sure she was about to run away like she had the day we found the locket at Greenbrier, like the night she left me standing on my porch. I put my hand on her wrist, and instantly felt the heat. "Then what is it?"

She stared back at me, and I tried to hear her thoughts, but I

192

had nothing. "I know you think I have a choice about what's going to happen to me, but I don't. And what Ridley did tonight, that was nothing. She could've killed you, and maybe she would have if I hadn't stopped her." She took a deep breath, her eyes glistening. "That's what I could turn into—a monster—whether you believe it or not."

I slid my arms back around her neck, ignoring her. But she went on. "I don't want you to see me like that."

"I don't care." I kissed her cheek.

She climbed off the bed, sliding her arm out of my hand.

"You don't get it." She held up her hand. 122. One hundred and twenty-two more days, smeared in blue ink, as if that was all we had.

"I get it. You're scared. But we'll figure something out. We're supposed to be together."

"We're not. You're a Mortal. You can't understand. I don't want to see you get hurt, and that's what will happen if you get too close to me."

"Too late."

I'd heard every word she had said, but I only knew one thing.

I was all in.

ᵈ 10.09 ᵇ

The Greats

It had made sense when a beautiful girl was saying it. Now that I was back home, alone, and in my own bed, I was finally losing it. Even Link wouldn't believe any of this. I tried to think about how the conversation would go—the girl I like, whose real name I don't know, is a witch—excuse me, a Caster, from a whole family of Casters, and in five months she's going to find out essentially if she's good or evil. And she can cause hurricanes indoors and break the glass out of windows. And I can see into the past when I touch the crazy locket Amma and Macon Ravenwood, who isn't actually a shut-in at all, want me to bury. A locket that materialized on the neck of a woman in a painting at Ravenwood, which by the way, is not a haunted mansion, but a perfectly restored house that changes completely every time I go there, to see a girl who burns me and shocks me and shatters me with a single touch.

And I kissed her. And she kissed me back.
It was too unbelievable, even for me. I rolled over.

Tearing.

The wind was tearing at my body.

I held onto the tree as it pounded me, the sound of its scream piercing my ears. All around me, the winds swirled, fighting each other, their speed and force multiplying by the second. The hail rained down like Heaven itself had opened up. I had to get out of here.

But there was nowhere to go.

"Let me go, Ethan. Save yourself!"

I couldn't see her. The wind was too strong, but I could feel her. I was holding her wrist so tightly, I was sure it would break. But I didn't care, I wouldn't let go. The wind changed direction, lifting me off the ground. I held the tree tighter, held her wrist tighter. But I could feel the strength of the wind ripping us apart.

Pulling me away from the tree, away from her. I felt her wrist sliding through my fingers.

I couldn't hold on any longer.

I woke up coughing. I could still feel the windburn on my skin. As if my near-death experience at Ravenwood wasn't enough, now the dreams were back. It was too much for one night, even for me. My bedroom door was wide open, which was weird, considering I had been locking my door at night lately. The last thing I needed was Amma planting some crazy voodoo charm on me in my sleep. I was sure I'd closed it.

I stared up at my ceiling. Sleep was not in my future. I sighed and felt around under the bed. I flipped on the old storm lamp next to my bed and pulled the bookmark out from where I'd left off in *Snow Crash* when I heard something. Footsteps? It was coming from the kitchen, faint, but I still heard it. Maybe my dad was taking a break from writing. Maybe this would give us a chance to talk. Maybe.

But when I reached the bottom of the stairs, I knew it wasn't him. The door to his study was shut and light was coming from the crack under the door. It had to be Amma. Just as I ducked under the kitchen doorway, I saw her scampering down the hall toward her room, to the extent that Amma could scamper. I heard the screen door in the back of the house squeak shut. Someone was coming or going. After everything that had happened tonight, it was an important distinction.

I walked around to the front of the house. There was an old, beat-up pickup truck, a fifties Studebaker, idling by the curb. Amma was leaning in the window talking to the driver. She handed the driver her bag and climbed into the truck. Where was she going in the middle of the night?

I had to follow her. And following the woman who may as well have been my mother when she got into a car at night, with a strange man driving a junker, was a hard thing to do if you didn't have a car. I had no choice. I had to take the Volvo. It was the car my mom had been driving when she had the accident; that was the first thing I thought every time I saw it.

I slid behind the wheel. It smelled of old paper and Windex, just like it always had.

♦ ♦ ♦

Driving without the headlights on was trickier than I'd thought it would be, but I could tell the pickup was heading toward Wader's Creek. Amma must have been going home. The truck turned off Route 9, toward the back country. When it finally slowed down and pulled off to the side of the road, I cut the engine and guided the Volvo onto the shoulder.

Amma opened the door and the interior light went on. I squinted in the darkness. I recognized the driver; it was Carlton Eaton, the postmaster. Why would Amma ask Carlton Eaton for a ride in the middle of the night? I'd never even seen them speak to each other before.

Amma said something to Carlton and shut the door. The truck pulled back onto the road without her. I got out of the car and followed her. Amma was a creature of habit. If something had gotten her so worked up that she was creeping out to the swamp in the middle of the night, I could guess it involved more than one of her usual clients.

She disappeared into the brush, along a gravel path someone had gone to a great deal of trouble to make. She walked along the path in the dark, the gravel crunching under her feet. I walked in the grass beside the path to avoid that same crunching sound, which would've given me away for sure. I told myself it was because I wanted to see why Amma was sneaking home in the middle of the night, but mostly I was scared she would catch me following her.

It was easy to see how Wader's Creek got its name; you actually had to wade through black water ponds to get there, at least the way Amma was taking us. If there hadn't been a full moon, I'd have broken my neck trying to follow her through the maze of moss-covered oaks and scrub brush. We were close to the water. I could feel the swamp in the air, hot and sticky like a second skin.

The edge of the swamp was lined with flat wooden platforms made from cypress logs tied together with rope, poor man's ferries. They were lined up along the bank like taxis waiting to carry people across the water. I could see Amma in the moonlight, balanced expertly atop one of the platforms, pushing out from the bank with a long stick she used like an oar to skate it across to the other side.

I hadn't been to Amma's house in years, but I would've remembered this. We must have come another way back then, but it was impossible to tell in the dark. The one thing I could see was how rotted the logs on the platforms were; each one looked as unstable as the next. So I just picked one.

Maneuvering the platform was a lot harder than Amma made it look. Every few minutes, there was a splash, when a gator's tail hit the water as it slid into the swamp. I was glad I hadn't considered wading across.

I pushed into the floor of the swamp with my own long stick one last time, and the edge of the platform hit the bank. When I stepped onto the sand, I could see Amma's house, small and modest, with a single light in the window. The window frames were painted the same shade of haint blue as the ones at Wate's Landing. The house was made of cypress, like it was part of the swamp itself.

There was something else, something in the air. Strong and overpowering, like the lemons and rosemary. And just as unlikely, for two reasons. Confederate jasmine doesn't flower in the fall, only in the spring, and it doesn't grow in the swamp.

Yet, there it was. The smell was unmistakable. There was something impossible about it, like everything else about this night.

I watched the house. Nothing. Maybe she had just decided to go home. Maybe my dad knew she was leaving, and I was wandering around in the middle of the night, risking being eaten by gators for nothing.

I was about to head back through the swamp, wishing I'd dropped breadcrumbs on my way out here, when the door opened again. Amma stood in the light of the doorway, putting things I couldn't see into her good white patent leather pocketbook. She was wearing her best lavender church dress, white gloves, and a fancy matching hat with flowers all around it.

She was on the move again, heading back toward the swamp. Was she going into the swamp wearing that? As much as I didn't enjoy the trek to Amma's house, slogging through the swamp in my jeans was worse. The mud was so thick it felt like I was pulling my feet out of cement every time I took a step. I didn't know how Amma was able to get through it, in her dress, at her age.

Amma seemed to know exactly where she was going, stopping in a clearing of tall grass and mud weeds. The branches of the cypress trees tangled with weeping willows, creating a canopy overhead. A chill ran up my back, though it was still seventy degrees out here. Even after everything I'd seen tonight, there was something creepy about this place. There was a mist coming off the water, seeping up from the sides, like steam pushing out of the lid of a boiling pot. I edged my way closer. She was pulling something out of her bag, the white patent leather shining in the moonlight.

Bones. They looked like chicken bones.

She whispered something over the bones, and put them into a small pouch, not much different from the pouch she had given me to subdue the power of the locket. Fishing around in the bag again, she pulled out a fancy hand towel, the kind you'd find in a powder room, and used it to wipe the mud from her skirt. There were faint white lights in the distance, like fireflies blinking in the dark, and music, slow, sultry music and laughter. Somewhere, not that far away, people were drinking and dancing out in the swamp.

She looked up. Something had caught her attention, but I didn't hear anything.

"May as well show yourself. I know you're out there."

I froze, panicked. She had seen me.

But it wasn't me she was talking to. Out from the sweltering mist stepped Macon Ravenwood, smoking a cigar. He looked relaxed, like he'd just stepped out of a chauffeured car, instead of wading through filthy black water. He was impeccably dressed, as usual, in one of his crisp white shirts.

And he was spotless. Amma and I were covered in mud and swamp grass up to our knees, and Macon Ravenwood was standing there without so much as a speck of dirt on him.

"About time. You know I don't have all night, Melchizedek. I got to get back. And I don't take kindly to bein' summoned out here all the way from town. It's just rude. Not to mention, inconvenient." She sniffed. "Incommodious, you might say."

I. N. C. O. M. M. O. D. I. O. U. S. Twelve down. I spelled it out in my head.

"I've had quite an eventful evening myself, Amarie, but this matter requires our immediate attention." Macon took a few steps forward.

Amma recoiled and pointed a bony finger in his direction. "You stay where you are. I don't like bein' out here with *your kind* on this sorta night. Don't like it one bit. You keep to yourself, and I'll keep to mine."

He stepped back casually, blowing smoke rings into the air. "As I was saying, certain *developments* require our immediate attention." He exhaled, a smoky sigh. "'The moon, when she is fullest, is farthest from the sun.' To quote our good friends, the Clergy."

"Don't talk your high and mighty with me, Melchizedek. What's so important you need to call me outta bed in the middle a the night?"

"Among other things, Genevieve's locket."

Amma nearly howled, holding her scarf over her nose. She clearly couldn't stand to even hear the word *locket*. "What about that *thing*? I told you I Bound it, and I told him to take it back to Greenbrier and bury it. It can't cause any harm if it's back in the ground."

"Wrong on the first count. Wrong on the second. He still has it. He showed it to me in the sanctity of my own home. Aside from which, I'm not sure anything can Bind such a dark talisman."

"At your house . . . when was he at your house? I told him to stay clear a Ravenwood." Now she was noticeably agitated. Great, Amma would find some way to make me pay for this later.

"Well, perhaps you might consider shortening his leash. Clearly, he isn't very obedient. I warned you that this *friendship* would be dangerous, that it could develop into something more. A future between the two of them is an impossibility."

Amma was mumbling under her breath the way she always

did when I didn't listen to her. "He's always minded me till he met your niece. And don't you blame me. We wouldn't be in this fix if you hadn't brought her down here in the first place. I'll take care a this. I'll tell him he can't see her anymore."

"Don't be absurd. They're teenagers. The more we try to keep them apart, the more they will try to be together. This won't be an issue once she is Claimed, if we make it that far. Until then, control the boy, Amarie. It's only a few more months. Things are dangerous enough, without him making an even greater mess of the situation."

"Don't talk to me about messes, Melchizedek Ravenwood. My family's been cleanin' up your family's messes for over a hundred years. I've kept your secrets, just like you've kept mine."

"I'm not the Seer who failed to foresee them finding the locket. How do you explain that? How did your spirit friends manage to miss that?" He gestured around them, with a sarcastic flick of his cigar.

She spun around, eyes wild. "Don't you insult the Greats. Not here, not in this place. They have their reasons. There must've been a reason they didn't reveal it."

She turned away from Macon. "Now don't you listen to him. I brought you some shrimp 'n' grits and lemon meringue pie." She clearly wasn't talking to Macon anymore. "Your favorite," she said, taking the food out of little Tupperware containers and arranging it on a plate. She laid the plate on the ground. There was a small headstone next to the plate, and several others scattered nearby.

"This is our Great House, the great house a my family, you hear? My great-aunt Sissy. My great-great-uncle Abner. My great-great-great-great-grandmamma Sulla. Don't you disrespect the Greats in their House. You want answers, you show some respect."

"I apologize."

She waited.

"Truly."

She sniffed. "And watch your ash. There's no ashtray in this house. Nasty habit."

He flicked his cigar into the moss. "Now, let's get on with it. We don't have much time. We need to know the whereabouts of Saraf—"

"Shh," she hissed. "Don't say Her name—not tonight. We shouldn't be out here. Half-moon's for workin' White magic and full moon's for workin' Black. We're out here on the wrong night."

"We have no choice. There was quite an unpleasant episode this evening, I'm afraid. My niece, who Turned on her Claiming Day, showed up for the Gathering tonight."

"Del's child? That Dark drink a danger?"

"Ridley. Uninvited, obviously. She crossed my threshold with the boy. I need to know if it was a coincidence."

"No good. No good. This is no good." Amma rocked back and forth on her heels, furiously.

"Well?"

"There are no coincidences. You know that."

"At least we can agree on that."

I couldn't get my mind around any of this. Macon Raven-wood never set foot outside of his house, but there he was, in the middle of the swamp, arguing with Amma—who I had no idea he even knew—about me and Lena and the locket.

Amma rummaged around in her pocketbook again. "Did you bring the whiskey? Uncle Abner loves his Wild Turkey."

Macon held out the bottle.

"Just put it right there," she said, pointing at the ground, "and step back yonder."

"I see you're still afraid to touch me after all these years."

"I'm not afraid of anything. You just keep to yourself. I don't ask you about your business, and I don't want to know anything about it."

He set the bottle on the ground a few feet from Amma. She picked it up, poured the whiskey into a shot glass, and drank it. I had never seen Amma drink anything stronger than sweet tea in my whole life. Then she poured some of the liquor in the grass, covering the grave. "Uncle Abner, we are in need a your intercession. I call your spirit to this place."

Macon coughed.

"You're testin' my patience, Melchizedek." Amma closed her eyes and opened her arms to the sky, her head thrown back as if she was talking to the moon itself. She bent down and shook the small pouch she had taken from her pocketbook. The contents spilled out onto the grave. Tiny chicken bones. I hoped they weren't the bones from the basket of fried chicken I'd put away this afternoon, but I had a feeling they might have been.

"What do they say?" Macon asked.

She ran her fingers over the bones, fanning them out over the grass. "I'm not gettin' an answer."

His perfect composure began to crack. "We don't have time for this! What good is a Seer if you can't see anything? We have less than five months before she turns sixteen. If she Turns, she will damn us all, Mortals and Casters alike. We have a responsibility, a responsibility we both took on willingly, a long time ago. You to your Mortals, and me to my Casters."

"I don't need you remindin' me about my responsibilities. And you keep your voice down, you hear me? I don't need any a my clients comin' out here and seein' us together. How would that look? A fine upstanding member a the community like myself? Don't mess with my business, Melchizedek."

"If we don't find out where Saraf—where *She* is—and what she's planning, we'll have bigger problems on our hands than your failing business ventures, Amarie."

"She's a Dark one. Never know which way the wind will blow with that one. It's like tryin' to see where a twister'll hit."

"Even so. I need to know if she's going to try to make contact with Lena."

"Not if. When." Amma closed her eyes again, touching the charm on the necklace she never took off. It was a disc, engraved with what looked like a heart with some kind of cross coming out from the top. The image was worn from the thousands of times Amma must have rubbed it, as she was doing now. She was whispering some sort of chant in a language I didn't understand, but I'd heard somewhere before.

Macon paced impatiently. I shifted in the weeds, trying not to make a sound.

"I can't get a read tonight. It's murky. I think Uncle Abner is in a mood. I'm sure it was somethin' *you* said."

This must have been his breaking point, because Macon's face changed, his pale skin glowing in the shadows. When he stepped forward, the sharp angles of his face became frightening in the moonlight. "Enough of these games. A Dark Caster entered my house tonight; that in itself is impossible. She arrived with your boy, Ethan, which can mean only one thing. He has power, and you have been hiding it from me."

"Nonsense. That boy doesn't have power any more than I have a tail."

"You're wrong, Amarie. Ask the Greats. Consult the bones. There is no other explanation. It had to be Ethan. Ravenwood is protected. A Dark Caster could never circumvent that sort of protection, not without some powerful form of help."

"You've lost your mind. He doesn't have any kind a power. I raised that child. Don't you think I'd know it?"

"You're wrong this time. You're too close to him; it's clouding your vision. And there is too much at stake now for errors. We both have our *talents*. I'm warning you, there is more to the boy than either of us realized."

"I'll ask the Greats. If there's somethin' to know they'll be sure I know it. Don't you forget, Melchizedek, we have to contend with both the dead and the livin' and that's no easy task." She rummaged around in her pocketbook, and pulled out a dirty-looking string with a row of tiny beads on it.

"Graveyard Bone. Take it. The Greats want you to have it. Protects spirit from spirit, and dead from dead. It's no use for us Mortal folk. Give it to your niece, Macon. It won't hurt her, but it might keep a Dark Caster away."

Macon took the string, holding it gingerly between two fingers, then dropping it into his handkerchief, as if he was pocketing a particularly nasty worm. "I'm obliged."

Amma coughed.

"Please. Tell them, I'm obliged. Much." He looked up at the moon as if he were checking his watch. And then he turned and disappeared. Dissolved into the swamp mist as if he had blown away in the breeze.

⚔ 10.10 ⚔

Red Sweater

I had barely made it into my bed before the sun rose, and I was tired—bone tired, as Amma would say. Now I was waiting for Link on the corner. Even though it was a sunny day, I was caught under my own personal shadow. And I was starving. I hadn't been able to face Amma in the kitchen this morning. One look at my face would have given away everything I'd seen last night, and everything I felt, and I couldn't risk that.

I didn't know what to think. Amma, who I trusted more than anyone, as much as my parents, maybe more—she was holding out on me. She knew Macon, and the two of them wanted to keep Lena and me apart. It all had something to do with the locket, and Lena's birthday. And danger.

I couldn't piece it together, not on my own. I had to talk to Lena. It was all I could think about. So when the hearse rolled around the corner instead of the Beater, I shouldn't have been surprised.

"I guess you heard." I slid into the seat, dumping my backpack on the floor in front of me.

"Heard what?" She smiled, almost shyly, pushing a bag across the seat. "Heard you liked doughnuts? I could hear your stomach growling all the way from Ravenwood."

We looked at each other awkwardly. Lena looked down, embarrassed, picking a piece of lint off a soft, red, embroidered sweater that looked like something the Sisters would have in the attic somewhere. Knowing Lena, it wasn't from the mall in Summerville.

Red? Since when did she wear red?

She wasn't under a bad cloud; she had just come out from under one. She hadn't heard me thinking. She didn't know about Amma and Macon. She just wanted to see me. I guess some of what I had said last night had sunk in. Maybe she wanted to give us a chance. I smiled, opening the white paper bag.

"Hope you're hungry. I had to fight the fat cop for them." She pulled the hearse away from the curb.

"So you just felt like picking me up for school?" That was something new.

"Nope." She rolled down the window, the morning breeze blowing her hair into curls. Today, it was just the wind.

"You got something better in mind?"

Her whole face lit up. "Now how could there be anything better than spending a day like this at Stonewall Jackson High?" She was happy. As she turned the wheel, I noticed her hand. No ink. No number. No birthday. She wasn't worried about anything, not today.

120. I knew it, as if it was written in invisible ink on my own hand. One hundred and twenty days until it, whatever Macon and Amma were so afraid of, happened.

I looked out the window as we turned onto Route 9, wishing she could stay like this for just a little bit longer. I closed my eyes, running through the playbook in my mind. Pick 'n' Roll. Picket Fences. Down the Lane. Full Court Press.

By the time we made it to Summerville, I knew where we were headed. There was only one place kids like us went in Summerville, if it wasn't the last three rows of the Cineplex.

The hearse rolled through the dust behind the water tower at the edge of the field. "Parking? We're parking? At the water tower? Now?" Link would never believe this.

The engine died. Our windows were down, everything was quiet, and the breeze blew into her window and out mine.

Isn't this what people do around here?

Yeah, no. Not people like us. Not in the middle of a school day.

For once, can't we be them? Do we always have to be us?

I like being us.

She unclicked her seatbelt and I unclicked mine, pulling her onto my lap. I could feel her, warm and happy, spreading through me.

So this is what parking is like?

She giggled, reaching over to push my hair out of my eyes.

"What's that?" I grabbed her right arm. It was dangling from her wrist, the bracelet Amma had given Macon, last night in the swamp. My stomach clenched, and I knew Lena's mood was about to change. I had to tell her.

"My uncle gave it to me."

"Take it off." I turned the string around her wrist, looking for the knot.

"What?" Her smile faded. "What are you talking about?"

"Take it off."

"Why?" She pulled her arm away from me.

"Something happened last night."

"What happened?"

"After I got home, I followed Amma out to Wader's Creek, where she lives. She snuck out of our house in the middle of the night to meet someone in the swamp."

"Who?"

"Your uncle."

"What were they doing out there?" Her face had turned a chalky white, and I could tell the parking part of the day was over.

"They were talking about you, about us. And the locket."

Now she was paying attention. "What about the locket?"

"It's some kind of Dark talisman, whatever that means, and your uncle told Amma that I never buried it. They were really freaked out about it."

"How would they know it's a talisman?"

I was starting to get annoyed. She didn't seem to be focusing on the right thing. "How about, how do they even know each other? Did you have any idea your uncle knew Amma?"

"No, but I don't know everyone he knows."

"Lena, they were talking about us. About keeping the locket away from us, and keeping us away from each other. I got the feeling they think I'm some kind of threat. Like I'm getting in the way of something. Your uncle thinks—"

"What?"

"He thinks I have some kind of power."

She laughed out loud, which annoyed me even more. "Why would he think that?"

"Because I brought Ridley into Ravenwood. He said I'd have to have power to do that."

She frowned. "He's right." That wasn't the answer I was expecting.

"You're kidding, right? If I had powers, don't you think I'd know it?"

"I don't know."

Maybe she didn't know, but I did. My dad was a writer and my mom had spent her days reading the journals of dead Civil War generals. I was about as far from being a Caster as you could get, unless aggravating Amma counted as a power. There was obviously some kind of loophole that had allowed Ridley to get inside. One of the wires in the Caster security system had blown a fuse.

Lena must have been thinking the same thing. "Relax. I'm sure there's an explanation. So Macon and Amma know each other. Now we know."

"You don't seem very upset about this."

"What do you mean?"

"They've been lying to us. Both of them. Meeting secretly, trying to keep us apart. Trying to get us to get rid of the locket."

"We never asked them if they knew each other." Why was she acting like this? Why wasn't she upset, or angry, something?

"Why would we? Don't you think it's weird that your uncle is out in the swamp in the middle of the night with Amma, talking to spirits and reading chicken bones?"

"It's weird, but I'm sure they're just trying to protect us."

"From what? The truth? They were talking about something else, too. They were trying to find someone, Sara something. And about how you can damn us all if you Turn."

"What are you talking about?"

"I don't know. Why don't you ask your uncle? See if he'll tell you the truth for once."

I had gone too far. "My uncle is risking his life to protect me. He's always been there for me. He took me in when he knew I might turn into a monster in a few months."

"What is he really protecting you from? Do you even know?"

"Myself!" she snapped. That was it. She pushed the door open and climbed off my lap, out into the field. The shade of the massive white water tower shielded us from Summerville, but the day didn't seem so sunny anymore. Where there had been a cloudless blue sky just a few minutes ago, there were streaks of gray.

The storm was moving in. She didn't want to talk about it, but I didn't care. "That doesn't make any sense. Why is he meeting Amma in the middle of the night to tell her we still have the locket? Why don't they want us to have it? And more important, why don't they want us to be together?"

It was just the two of us, shouting in a field. The breeze was churning into a strong wind. Lena's hair started to whip around her face. She shot back, "I don't know. Parents are always trying to keep teenagers apart, it's what they do. If you want to know why, maybe you should ask Amma. She's the one who hates me. I can't even pick you up at your house because you're afraid she'll see us together."

The knot that was building in the pit of my stomach tightened. I was angry at Amma, angrier than I'd ever been at her in

212

my whole life, but I still loved her. She was the one who had left letters from the Tooth Fairy under my pillow, bandaged every scraped knee, thrown me thousands of pitches when I wanted to try out for Little League. And since my mom died and my dad checked out, Amma was the only one who looked out for me, who cared or even noticed if I skipped school or lost a game. I wanted to believe she had an explanation for all of this.

"You just don't understand her. She thinks she's . . . "

"What? Protecting you? Like my uncle is trying to protect me? Did you ever consider that maybe they're both trying to protect us from the same thing . . . me?"

"Why do you always go there?"

She walked away from me, like she would take off if she could. "Where else is there to go? That's what this is about. They're afraid I'll hurt you or someone else."

"You're wrong. This is about the locket. There's something they don't want us to know." I dug around in my pocket, searching for the familiar shape underneath the handkerchief. After last night, there was no way I was letting it out of my sight. I was sure Amma was going to look for it today, and if she found it we'd never see it again. I laid it on the hood of the car. "We need to find out what happens next."

"Now?"

"Why not?"

"You don't even know if it'll work."

I started to unwrap it. "There's only one way to find out."

I grabbed her hand, even as she tried to yank it away. I touched the smooth metal—

The morning light turned brighter and brighter until it was all I could see. I felt the familiar rush that had taken me back a hundred and fifty years. Then a jolt. I opened my eyes. But instead of the muddy field and flames in the distance, all I saw was the shadow of the water tower and the hearse. The locket hadn't shown us anything.

"Did you feel that? It started, and then it cut off."

She nodded, pushing me away. "I think I'm carsick, or whatever kind of sick you'd call it."

"Are you blocking it?"

"What are you talking about? I'm not doing anything."

"Swear? You aren't using your Caster powers, or something?"

"No, I'm too busy trying to deflect your Power of Stupidity. But I don't think I'm strong enough."

It didn't make sense, just pulling us in and then kicking us out of the vision like that. What was different? Lena reached over, folding the handkerchief over the locket. The dirty leather bracelet Amma had given Macon caught my eye.

"Take that thing off." I looped my finger under the string, lifting the bracelet and her arm to eye level.

"Ethan, it's for protection. You said Amma makes these kinds of things all the time."

"I don't think so."

"What are you saying?"

"I'm saying, maybe that thing is the reason the locket doesn't work."

"It doesn't work all the time, you know that."

"But it was starting to, and something stopped it."

She shook her head, wild curls brushing her shoulder. "Do you honestly believe that?"

"Prove me wrong. Take it off."

She looked at me like I was crazy, but she was thinking about it. I could tell.

"If I'm wrong, you can put it back on."

She hesitated for a second, then gave me her arm so I could untie it. I loosened the knot and put the charm in my pocket. I reached for the locket, and she put her hand on mine.

I closed my hand around it, and we spun out into nothing—

The rain began almost immediately. Hard rain, a downpour. Like the sky just opened up. Ivy had always said the rain was God's tears. Today Genevieve believed it. It was only a few feet, but Genevieve couldn't get there fast enough. She knelt down next to Ethan and cradled his head in her hands. His breathing was ragged. He was alive.

"No, no, not that boy, too. You take too much away. Too much. Not this boy, too." Ivy's voice reached a fever pitch and she started to pray.

"Ivy, get help. I need water and whiskey and somethin' to remove the bullet."

Genevieve pressed the wadded material from her skirt into the hole Ethan's chest had filled just a few moments before.

"I love you. And I would've married you, no matter what your family thought," he whispered.

"Don't say that, Ethan Carter Wate. Don't you say that like you're going to die. You're gonna be just fine. Just fine," she repeated, trying to convince herself as much as him.

215

Genevieve closed her eyes and concentrated. Flowers blooming. Newborn babies crying. The sun rising. Birth, not death.

She pictured the images in her mind, willing it to be so. The images ran in a loop over and over in her mind. Birth, not death.

Ethan choked. She opened her eyes, and their eyes met. For an instant, time seemed to stop. Then, Ethan's eyes closed, and his head rolled to one side.

Genevieve closed her eyes again, visualizing the images. It had to be a mistake. He couldn't be dead. She had summoned her power. She had done it a million times before, moving objects in her mother's kitchen to play tricks on Ivy, healing baby birds that had fallen from their nests.

Why not now? When it mattered?

"Ethan, wake up. Please wake up."

I opened my eyes. We were standing in the middle of the field, in exactly the same place we'd been before. I looked over at Lena. Her eyes were shining, about to spill over. "Oh, God."

I bent down and touched the weeds where we had been standing. A reddish stain marked the plants and the ground around us. "It's blood."

"His blood?"

"I think so."

"You were right. The bracelet was keeping us from seeing the vision. But why would Uncle Macon tell me it was for protection?"

"Maybe it is. That's just not the only thing it's for."

"You don't have to try to make me feel better."

"There's obviously something they don't want us to find out, and it involves the locket and, I'm willing to bet, Genevieve. We've got to find out as much as we can about them both, and we have to do it before your birthday."

"Why my birthday?"

"Last night, Amma and your uncle were talking. Whatever they don't want us to know, it has something to do with your birthday."

Lena took a deep breath, like she was trying to hold it together. "They know I'm going to go Dark. That's what this is about."

"What does that have to do with the locket?"

"I don't know, but it doesn't matter. None of it matters. In four months, I'm not going to be me anymore. You saw Ridley. That's what I'm going to turn into, or worse. If my uncle is right and I am a Natural, then I'll make Ridley look like a volunteer for the Red Cross."

I pulled her toward me, wrapping my arms around her like I could protect her from something we both knew I couldn't. "You can't think like that. There has to be a way to stop it, if that's really the truth."

"You don't get it. There's no way to stop it. It just happens." Her voice was rising. The wind was starting to pick up.

"Okay, maybe you're right. Maybe it just happens. But we're going to find a way to make it *not* happen to you."

Her eyes were clouding over like the sky. "Can't we just enjoy the time we have left?" I felt the words for the first time.

The time we have left.

I couldn't lose her. I wouldn't. Just the thought of never being able to touch her again made me crazy. Crazier than losing all my friends. Crazier than being the least popular guy in school. Crazier than having Amma perpetually angry at me. Losing her was the worst thing I could imagine. Like I was falling, but this time I would definitely hit the ground.

I thought about Ethan Carter Wate hitting the ground, the red blood in the field. The wind began to howl. It was time to go. "Don't talk like that. We're going to find a way."

But even as I was saying it, I didn't know if I believed it.

⊰ 10.13 ⊱

Marian the Librarian

It had been three days, and I still couldn't stop thinking about it. Ethan Carter Wate had been shot, and he was probably dead. I had seen it with my own eyes. Well, technically, everyone from back then was dead by now. But, from one Ethan Wate to another, I was having trouble getting over the death of this particular Confederate soldier. More like, Confederate deserter. My great-great-great-great-uncle.

I thought about it during Algebra II, while Savannah choked on her equation in front of the class, but Mr. Bates was too busy reading the latest issue of *Guns and Ammo* to notice. I thought about it during the Future Farmers of America assembly, when I couldn't find Lena and ended up sitting with the band. Link was sitting with the guys a few rows behind me, but I didn't notice until Shawn and Emory started making animal noises.

After a while, I couldn't hear them anymore. My mind kept going back to Ethan Carter Wate.

It wasn't that he was a Confederate. Everyone in Gatlin County was related to the wrong side in the War Between the States. We were used to that by now. It was like being born in Germany after World War II, being from Japan after Pearl Harbor, or America after Hiroshima. History was a bitch sometimes. You couldn't change where you were from. But still, you didn't have to stay there. You didn't have to stay stuck in the past, like the ladies in the DAR, or the Gatlin Historical Society, or the Sisters. And you didn't have to accept that things had to be the way they were, like Lena. Ethan Carter Wate hadn't, and I couldn't, either.

All I knew was, now that we knew about the other Ethan Wate, we had to find out more about Genevieve. Maybe there was a reason we had stumbled across that locket in the first place. Maybe there was a reason we had stumbled across each other in a dream, even if it was more of a nightmare.

Normally, I would've asked my mom what to do, back when things were normal and she was still alive. But she was gone, my dad was too out of it to be any help, and Amma wasn't about to help us with anything that had to do with the locket. Lena was still being moody about Macon; the rain outside was a dead giveaway. I was supposed to be doing my homework, which meant I needed about a half gallon of chocolate milk and as many cookies as I could carry in my other hand.

I walked down the hallway from the kitchen and paused in front of the study. My dad was upstairs taking a shower, which was about the only time he left the study anymore, so the door was probably locked. It always was, ever since the manuscript incident.

I stared at the door handle, looking down the hall in either direction. Balancing my cookies precariously on top of my milk carton, I reached toward it. Before I could so much as touch the handle, I heard the click of the lock moving. The door unlocked, all by itself, as if someone inside was opening the door for me. The cookies hit the floor.

A month ago, I wouldn't have believed it, but now I knew better. This was Gatlin. Not the Gatlin I thought I knew, but some other Gatlin that had apparently been hiding in plain sight all along. A town where the girl I liked was from a long line of Casters, my housekeeper was a Seer who read chicken bones in the swamp and summoned the spirits of her dead ancestors, and even my dad acted like a vampire.

There seemed to be nothing too unbelievable for this Gatlin. It's funny how you can live somewhere your whole life, but not really see it.

I pushed on the door, slowly, tentatively. I could see just a glimpse of the study, a corner of the built-in shelves, stuffed with my mom's books, and the Civil War debris she seemed to collect wherever she went. I took a deep breath and inhaled the air from the study. No wonder my dad never left the room.

I could almost see her, curled up in her old reading chair by the window. She would've been typing, just on the other side of the door. If I opened the door a little more, for all I knew, she might be there now. Only I couldn't hear any typing, and I knew she wasn't there, and she never would be again.

The books I needed were on those shelves. If anyone knew more about the history of Gatlin County than the Sisters, it was my mom. I took a step forward, pushing the door open just a few inches farther.

"Sweet Host a Heaven and Earth, Ethan Wate, if you're fixin' to set one foot in that room, your daddy will knock you clean into next week."

I nearly dropped the milk. Amma. "I'm not doing anything. The door just opened."

"Shame on you. No ghost in Gatlin would dare set foot in your mamma and daddy's study, except your mamma herself." She looked up at me defiantly. There was something in her eyes that made me wonder if she was trying to tell me something, maybe even the truth. Maybe it was my mom, opening the door.

Because one thing was clear. Someone, something, wanted me to get into that study, as much as somebody else wanted to keep me out.

Amma slammed the door and drew a key out of her pocket, locking it. I heard the click and knew my window of opportunity had slammed shut, as quickly as it had opened. She crossed her arms. "It's a school night. Don't you have some studyin' to do?"

I looked at her, annoyed.

"Goin' back to the library? You and Link finished with that report?"

And then it came to me. "Yeah, the library. As a matter a fact, that's where I'm headed right now." I kissed her cheek and ran past her.

"Say hi to Marian for me, and don't you be late for dinner."

Good old Amma. She always had all the answers, whether she knew it or not, and whether or not she would willingly give them up.

Lena was waiting for me at the parking lot of the Gatlin County Library. The cracked concrete was still wet and shiny from the rain. Even though the library was still open for two more hours, the hearse was the only car in the lot, except for a familiar old turquoise truck. Let's just say this wasn't a big library town. There wasn't much we wanted to know about any town but our own, and if your granddaddy or your great-granddaddy couldn't tell you, chances were you didn't need to know.

Lena was huddled against the side of the building, writing in her notebook. She was wearing tattered jeans, enormous rain boots, and a soft black T-shirt. Tiny braids hung down around her face, lost in all the curls. She looked almost like a regular girl. I wasn't sure I wanted her to be a regular girl. I was sure I wanted to kiss her again, but it would have to wait. If Marian had the answers we needed, I'd have a lot more chances to kiss her.

I ran through my playbook again. Pick 'n' Roll.

"You really think there's something here that can help us?" Lena looked over her notebook at me.

I pulled her up with my hand. "Not something. Someone."

The library itself was beautiful. I had spent so many hours in it as a kid, I'd inherited my mother's belief that a library was sort of a temple. This particular library was one of the few buildings that had survived Sherman's March and the Great Burning. The library and the Historical Society were the two oldest buildings in town, aside from Ravenwood. It was a two-story venerable Victorian, old and weathered with peeling white paint and decades worth of vines sleeping along the doors and windows. It smelled like aging wood and creosote, plastic book covers, and old paper. Old paper, which my mom used to say was the smell of time itself.

"I don't get it. Why the library?"

"It's not just the library. It's Marian Ashcroft."

"The librarian? Uncle Macon's friend?"

"Marian was my mom's best friend, and her research partner. She's the only other person who knows as much about Gatlin County as my mom, and she's the smartest person in Gatlin now."

Lena looked at me, skeptically. "Smarter than Uncle Macon?"

"Okay. She's the smartest Mortal in Gatlin."

I could never quite figure out what someone like Marian was doing in a town like Gatlin. "Just because you live in the middle of *nowhere*," Marian would tell me, over a tuna sandwich with my mom, "doesn't mean you can't *know where* you live." I had no idea what she meant. I had no idea what she was talking about, half the time. That's probably why Marian had gotten along so well with my mom; I didn't know what my mom was talking about, either, the other half the time. Like I said, the biggest brain in town, or maybe just the biggest character.

When we walked into the empty library, Marian was wandering around the stacks in her stockings, wailing to herself like a crazy person from a Greek tragedy, which she was prone to reciting. Since the library was pretty much a ghost town, except for the occasional visit from one of the ladies from the DAR checking on questionable genealogy, Marian had free run of the place.

"'Knowest thou aught?'"

I followed her voice deep into the stacks.

"'Hast thou heard?'"

I rounded the corner into Fiction. There she was, swaying, holding a pile of books in her arms, looking right through me.

"'Or is it hidden from thee . . .'"

Lena stepped up behind me.

"'. . . that our friends are threatened . . .'"

Marian looked from me to Lena, over her square, red reading glasses.

"'. . . with the doom of our foes?'"

Marian was there, but not there. I knew that look well and I knew, though she had a quote for everything, she didn't choose them lightly. What doom of my foes threatened me, or my friends? If that friend was Lena, I wasn't sure I wanted to know.

I read a lot, but not Greek tragedy. "*Oedipus?*"

I hugged Marian, over her pile of books. She hugged me so tightly I couldn't breathe, an unwieldy biography of General Sherman cutting into my ribs.

"*Antigone.*" Lena spoke up from behind me.

Show-off.

"Very good." Marian smiled over my shoulder.

I made a face at Lena, who shrugged. "Home school."

"It's always impressive to meet a young person who knows *Antigone.*"

"All I remember is, she just wanted to bury the dead."

Marian smiled at both of us. She shoved half her pile of books into my arms, and half into Lena's. When she smiled, she looked like she could have been on the cover of a magazine. She had white teeth and beautiful brown skin, and she looked more like a model than a librarian. She was that pretty and exotic-looking, a mix of so many bloodlines it was like looking at the history of the South itself, people from the West Indies, the Sugar Islands, England, Scotland, even America, all intermingling until it would take a whole forest of family trees to chart the course.

Even though we were south of Somewhere and north of Nowhere, as Amma would say, Marian Ashcroft was dressed like she could have been teaching one of her classes at Duke. All of her clothes, all of her jewelry, all of her signature, brightly patterned scarves seemed to come from somewhere else and complement her unintentionally cool cropped haircut.

Marian was no more Gatlin County than Lena, and yet she'd been here as long as my mom had. Now longer. "I've missed you so much, Ethan. And you—you must be Macon's niece, Lena. The infamous new girl in town. The girl with the window. Oh yes, I've heard about you. The ladies, they are talking."

We followed Marian back to the front counter and dumped the books on the re-stacking cart.

"Don't believe everything you hear, Dr. Ashcroft."

"Please. Marian." I nearly dropped a book. Aside from my family, Marian was Dr. Ashcroft to nearly everyone around here. Lena was being offered instant access to the inner circle, and I had no idea why.

"Marian." Lena grinned. Aside from Link and me, this was Lena's first taste of our famed Southern hospitality, and from another outsider.

"The only thing I want to know is, when you broke that window with your broomstick, did you take out the future generation of the DAR?" Marian began to lower the blinds, motioning for us to help.

"Of course not. If I did that, where would I get all this free publicity?"

Marian threw back her head and laughed, putting her arm around Lena. "A good sense of humor, Lena. That's what you need to get around in this town."

Lena sighed. "I've heard a lot of jokes. Mostly about me."

"Ah, but—'The monuments of wit survive the monuments of power.'"

"Is that Shakespeare?" I was feeling a little left behind.

"Close, Sir Francis Bacon. Though, if you're one of the people who think he wrote Shakespeare's plays, I suppose you were right the first time."

"I give up."

Marian ruffled my hair. "You've grown about a foot and a half since I've last seen you, EW. What is Amma feeding you these days? Pie for breakfast, lunch, and dinner? I feel like I haven't seen you in a hundred years."

I looked at her. "I know, I'm sorry. I just didn't feel much like . . . reading."

She knew I was lying, but she knew what I meant. Marian went to the door, and flipped the "Open" sign to "Closed." She turned the bolt with a sharp click. It reminded me of the study.

"I thought the library was open till nine?" If it wasn't I would lose a valuable excuse for sneaking out to Lena's.

"Not today. The head librarian has just declared today a Gatlin County Library Holiday. She's rather spontaneous that way." She winked. "For a librarian."

"Thanks, Aunt Marian."

"I know you wouldn't be here if you didn't have a reason, and I suspect Macon Ravenwood's niece is, if nothing else, a reason. So why don't we all go into the back room, make a pot of tea, and try to be reasonable?" Marian loved a good pun.

"It's more like a question, really." I felt in my pocket, where the locket was still wrapped in Sulla the Prophet's handkerchief.

"Question everything. Learn something. Answer nothing."

"Homer?"

"Euripides. You better start coming up with a few of these answers, EW, or I'm going to actually have to go to one of those school board meetings."

"But you just said to answer nothing."

She unlocked a door marked PRIVATE ARCHIVE. "Did I say that?"

Like Amma, Marian always seemed to have the answer. Like any good librarian.

Like my mom.

I'd never been in Marian's private archive, the back room. Come to think of it, I didn't know anyone who had ever been back there, except for my mom. It was the space they shared, the place they wrote and researched and who knows what else. Not even my dad was allowed in. I can remember Marian stopping him in the doorway, when my mother was examining a historical document inside. "Private means private."

"It's a library, Marian. Libraries were created to democratize knowledge and make it public."

"Around here, libraries were created so that Alcoholics Anonymous would have somewhere to meet when the Baptists kicked them out."

"Marian, don't be ridiculous. It's just an archive."

"Don't think of me as a librarian. Think of me as a mad scientist; this is my secret laboratory."

"You're crazy. You two are just looking at some crumbling old papers."

"'If you reveal your secrets to the wind, you should not blame the wind for revealing them to the trees.'"

"Khalil Gibran." He fired back.

"'Three can keep a secret if two of them are dead.'"

"Benjamin Franklin."

Eventually even my father had given up trying to get into their archive. We'd gone home and eaten rocky road ice cream, and after that, I had always thought of my mother and Marian as an unstoppable force of nature. Two mad scientists, as Marian had said, chained to each other in the lab. They had churned out book after book, even once making the short-list for the Voice of the South Award, the Southern equivalent of a Pulitzer Prize. My dad was fiercely proud of my mom, of both of them, even if we were just along for the ride. "Lively of the mind." That's how he used to describe my mom, especially when she was in the middle of a project. That was when she was the most absent, and yet somehow, when he seemed to love her best.

And now here I was, in the private archive, without my dad or my mom, or even a bowl of rocky road ice cream, in sight. Things were changing pretty quickly around here, for a town that never changed at all.

The room was paneled and dark, the most secluded, airless, windowless room of the third-oldest building in Gatlin. Four long oak tables stood in parallel lines down the center of the room. Every inch of every wall was crammed with books. *Civil War Artillery and Munitions. King Cotton: White Gold of the*

South. Flat metal shelving drawers held manuscripts, and overflowing file cabinets lined a smaller room attached to the back of the archive.

Marian busied herself with her teapot and hotplate. Lena walked up to a wall of framed maps of Gatlin County, crumbling behind glass, old as the Sisters themselves.

"Look—Ravenwood." Lena moved her finger across the glass. "And there's Greenbrier. You can see the property line a lot better on this map."

I walked to the far corner of the room, where a lone table stood, covered with a fine layer of dust and the occasional cobweb. An old Historical Society charter lay open, with circled names, a pencil still stuck in the spine. A map made out of tracing paper, tacked to a map of modern-day Gatlin, seemed like someone was trying to mentally excavate the old town from beneath the new. And lying on top of all of it was a photo of the painting in Macon Ravenwood's entry.

The woman with the locket.

Genevieve. It has to be Genevieve. We have to tell her, L. We have to ask.

We can't. We can't trust anyone. We don't even know why we're seeing the visions.

Lena. Trust me.

"What's all this stuff over here, Aunt Marian?"

She looked at me, her face briefly clouding over. "That's our last project. Your mom's and mine."

Why did my mom have a picture of the painting at Ravenwood?

I don't know.

Lena walked over to the table, and picked up the photo of the painting. "Marian, what were you guys doing with this painting?"

Marian handed each of us a proper cup of tea, with a saucer. That was another thing about Gatlin. You used a saucer, at all times, no matter what.

"You should recognize that painting, Lena. It belongs to your Uncle Macon. In fact, he sent me that photo himself."

"But who's the woman?"

"Genevieve Duchannes, but I expect you know that."

"I didn't, actually."

"Hasn't your uncle taught you anything about your genealogy?"

"We don't talk much about my dead relatives. No one wants to bring up my parents."

Marian walked over to one of the flat archival drawers, searching for something. "Genevieve Duchannes was your great-great-great-great-grandmother. She was an interesting character, really. Lila and I were tracing the entire Duchannes family tree, for a project your Uncle Macon had been helping us with, right up until—" she looked down. "Last year."

My mom had known Macon Ravenwood? I thought he had said he only knew her through her work.

"You really should know your genealogy." Marian turned a few yellowed pages of parchment. Lena's family tree stared back at us, right next to Macon's.

I pointed to Lena's family tree. "That's weird. All the girls in your family have the last name Duchannes, even the ones who were married."

DUCHANNES FAMILY TREE

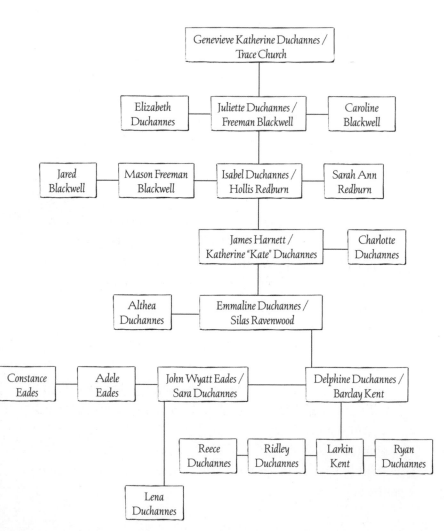

Genevieve Katherine Duchannes / Trace Church

Elizabeth Duchannes — Juliette Duchannes / Freeman Blackwell — Caroline Blackwell

Jared Blackwell — Mason Freeman Blackwell — Isabel Duchannes / Hollis Redburn — Sarah Ann Redburn

James Harnett / Katherine "Kate" Duchannes — Charlotte Duchannes

Althea Duchannes — Emmaline Duchannes / Silas Ravenwood

Constance Eades — Adele Eades — John Wyatt Eades / Sara Duchannes — Delphine Duchannes / Barclay Kent

Reece Duchannes — Ridley Duchannes — Larkin Kent — Ryan Duchannes

Lena Duchannes

RAVENWOOD FAMILY TREE

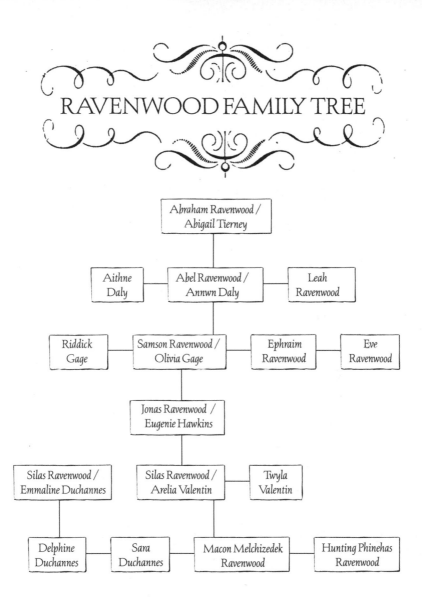

Abraham Ravenwood / Abigail Tierney

Aithne Daly — Abel Ravenwood / Annwn Daly — Leah Ravenwood

Riddick Gage — Samson Ravenwood / Olivia Gage — Ephraim Ravenwood — Eve Ravenwood

Jonas Ravenwood / Eugenie Hawkins

Silas Ravenwood / Emmaline Duchannes — Silas Ravenwood / Arelia Valentin — Twyla Valentin

Delphine Duchannes — Sara Duchannes — Macon Melchizedek Ravenwood — Hunting Phinehas Ravenwood

"It's just a thing in my family. The women keep the family name even after they're married. It's always been that way."

Marian turned the page, and looked at Lena. "It's often the case in bloodlines where the women are considered particularly powerful."

I wanted to change the subject. I didn't want to dig too deep into the powerful women in Lena's family with Marian, especially considering Lena was definitely one of them. "Why were you and Mom tracing the Duchannes tree? What was the project?"

Marian stirred her tea. "Sugar?"

She looked away as I spooned it into my cup. "We were actually mostly interested in this locket." She pointed to another photograph of Genevieve. In this one, she was wearing the locket.

"One story in particular. It was a simple story, really, a love story." She smiled sadly. "Your mother was a great romantic, Ethan."

I locked eyes with Lena. We both knew what Marian was about to say.

"Interestingly enough for you two, this love story involves both a Wate and a Duchannes. A Confederate soldier, and a beautiful mistress of Greenbrier."

The locket visions. The burning of Greenbrier. My mom's last book was about everything we had seen happen between Genevieve and Ethan, Lena's great-great-great-great-grandmother and my great-great-great-great-uncle.

My mom was working on that book when she died. My head was reeling. Gatlin was like that. Nothing here ever happened only once.

Lena looked pale. She leaned over and touched my hand,

where it rested on the dusty table. Instantly, I felt the familiar prick of electricity.

"Here. This is the letter that got us started on the whole project." Marian lay out two parchment sheets on the next oak table. Secretly, I was glad she didn't disturb my mom's worktable. I thought of it as a fitting memorial, more like her than the carnations everyone had laid on her casket. Even the DAR, they were there for the funeral, laying those carnations down like crazy, though my mom would have hated it. The whole town, the Baptists, the Methodists, even the Pentecostals, turned out for a death, a birth, or a wedding.

"You can read it, just don't touch it. It's one of the oldest things in Gatlin."

Lena bent over the letter, holding her hair back to keep it from brushing the old parchment. "They're desperately in love, but they're too different." She scanned the letter. "'A Species Apart,' he calls them. Her family is trying to keep them apart, and he's gone to enlist, even though he doesn't believe in the war, in the hope that fighting for the South will win him the approval of her family."

Marian closed her eyes, reciting:

"I might as well be a monkey as a man, for all the good it does me at Greenbrier. Though merely Mortal, my heart breaks with such pain at the thought of spending the rest of my life without you, Genevieve."

It was like poetry, like something I imagined Lena would write.

Marian opened her eyes again. "As if he were Atlas carrying the weight of the world on his shoulders."

"It's all so sad," said Lena, looking at me.

"They were in love. There was a war. I hate to tell you, but it ends badly, or so it seems." Marian finished her tea.

"What about this locket?" I pointed at the photo, almost afraid to ask.

"Supposedly, Ethan gave it to Genevieve, as a troth of secret engagement. We'll never know what happened to it. Nobody ever saw it again, after the night Ethan died. Genevieve's father forced her to marry someone else, but legend has it, she kept the locket and it was buried with her. It was said to be a powerful talisman, the broken bond of a broken heart."

I shivered. The powerful talisman wasn't buried with Genevieve; it was in my pocket, and a Dark talisman according to Macon and Amma. I could feel it throbbing, as if it had been baking in hot coals.

Ethan, don't.

We have to. She can help us. My mom would have helped us.

I shoved one hand in my pocket, pushing past the handkerchief to touch the battered cameo, and took Marian's hand, hoping this was one of those times the locket would work. Her cup of tea crashed to the floor. The room started to swirl.

"Ethan!" Marian shouted.

Lena took Marian's hand. The light in the room was dissolving into night. "Don't worry. We'll be with you the whole time." Lena's voice sounded far away, and I heard the sound of distant gunfire.

In moments, the library filled with rain—

The rain battered down upon them. The winds kicked up, beginning to quell the flames, even though it was too late.

Genevieve stared at what was left of the great house. She had lost everything today. Mamma. Evangeline. She couldn't lose Ethan, too.

Ivy ran through the mud toward her, using her skirt to carry the things Genevieve had asked for.

"I'm too late, Lord in Heaven, I'm too late," Ivy cried. She looked around nervously. "Come, Miss Genevieve, there's nothin' more we can do here."

But Ivy was wrong. There was one thing.

"It's not too late. It's not too late." Genevieve kept repeating the words.

"You're talkin' crazy, child."

She looked at Ivy, desperate. "I need the book."

Ivy backed away, shaking her head. "No. You can't mess with that book. You don't know what you doin'."

Genevieve grabbed the old woman by the shoulders. "Ivy, it's the only way. You have to give it to me."

"You don't know what you askin'. You don't know nothin' about that book—"

"Give it to me or I'll find it myself."

Black smoke was billowing up behind them, the fire still spitting as it swallowed up what was left of the house.

Ivy relented, picking up her tattered skirts and leading Genevieve out past what used to be her mother's lemon grove. Genevieve had never been past that point. There was nothing out there but cotton fields, or at least that's what she had always been told. And she had never had a reason to be in those fields, except on the rare occasions when she and Evangeline played a game of hide-and-seek.

But Ivy's path was purposeful. She knew exactly where she was going. In the distance, Genevieve could still hear the sound of gunshots and the piercing cries of her neighbors, as they watched their own homes burn.

Ivy stopped near a bramble of wild vines, rosemary, and jasmine, snaking their way up the side of an old stone wall. There was a small archway, hidden beneath the overgrowth. Ivy ducked down and walked under the arch. Genevieve followed. The arch must have been attached to a wall because the area was enclosed. A perfect circle—its walls obscured by years of wild vines.

"What is this place?"

"A place your mamma didn't want you to know nothin' about, or you'd know what it was."

In the distance, Genevieve could see tiny stones jutting from the tall grass. Of course. The family cemetery. Genevieve remembered being out there, once, when she was very young, when her great-grandmother had died. She remembered the funeral was at night, and her mother had stood in the tall grass, in the moonlight, whispering words in a language Genevieve and her sister hadn't recognized. "What are we doin' out here?"

"You said you wanted that book. Didn't ya?"

"It's out here?"

Ivy stopped and looked at Genevieve, confused. "Where else would it be?"

Farther back, there was another structure being

238

strangled by wild vines. A crypt. Ivy stopped at the door. "You sure ya want to—"

"We don't have time for this!" Genevieve reached for the handle, but there wasn't one. "How does it open?"

The old woman stood on her toes, reaching high above the door. There, illuminated by the distant light of the fires, Genevieve could see a small piece of smooth stone above the door, with a crescent moon carved into it. Ivy put her hand over the small moon and pushed. The stone door began to move, opening with the sound of stone scraping stone. Ivy reached for something on the other side of the doorway. A candle.

The candlelight illuminated the small room. It couldn't have been bigger than a few feet wide all around. But there were old wooden shelves on every side, piled high with tiny vials and bottles, filled with plant blossoms, powders, and murky liquids. In the center of the room, there was a weathered stone table, with an old wooden box lying on it. The box was modest by any standard, the only adornment a tiny crescent moon carved on its lid. The same carving from the stone above the door.

"I'm not touchin' it," Ivy said quietly, as if she thought the box itself could hear her.

"Ivy, it's just a book."

"No such thing as just a book, 'specially in your family."

Genevieve lifted the lid gently. The book's jacket was cracked black leather, now more gray than black. There was no title, just the same crescent moon embossed on the front. Genevieve lifted the book tentatively from the box. She knew Ivy was superstitious. Although she had mocked the old woman, she also knew that Ivy was wise. She read cards and tea leaves, and Genevieve's mother consulted Ivy and her tea leaves for almost everything, the best day to plant her vegetables to avoid a freeze, the right herbs to cure a cold.

The book was warm. As if it were alive, breathing.

"Why doesn't it have a name?" Genevieve asked.

"Just 'cause a book don't have a title, don't mean it don't have a name. That right there is The Book a Moons."

There was no more time to lose. She followed the flames through the darkness. Back to what was left of Greenbrier, and Ethan.

She flipped through the pages. There were hundreds of Casts. How would she find the right one? Then she saw it. It was in Latin, a language she knew well; her mother had brought a special tutor in from up North to make sure she and Evangeline learned it. The most important language as far as her family was concerned.

The Binding Spell. To Bind Death To Life.

Genevieve rested the Book on the ground next to Ethan, her finger under the first verse of the incantation.

Ivy grabbed her wrist and held it tight. "This isn't any night for this. Half moon's for workin' White magic, full moon's for workin' Black. No moon is somethin' else altogether."

Genevieve jerked her arm from the old woman's grip. "I don't have a choice. This is the only night we have."

"Miss Genevieve, you need to understand. Those words are more than a Cast. They're a bargain. You can't use The Book a Moons, *without givin' somethin' in return."*

"I don't care about the price. We're talkin' about Ethan's life. I've lost everyone else."

"That boy don't have no more life. It's been shot right out of 'im. What you tryin' to do is unnatural. And there can't be no right in that."

Genevieve knew Ivy was right. Her mother had warned her and Evangeline often enough about respecting the Natural Laws. She was crossing a line none of the Casters in her family would ever have dared.

But they were all gone now. She was the only one left.

And she had to try.

"No!" Lena let go of our hands, breaking the circle. "She went Dark, don't you get it? Genevieve, she was using Dark magic."

I grabbed her hands. She tried to pull away from me. Usually all I could feel from Lena was a sunny sort of warmth, but this time she felt more like a tornado. "Lena, she's not you. He's not me. This all happened more than a hundred years ago."

She was hysterical. "She *is* me, that's why the locket wants me to see this. It's warning me to stay away from you. So I don't hurt you after I go Dark."

Marian opened her eyes, which were bigger than I'd ever seen them. Her short hair, normally neat and perfectly in place, was wild and windblown. She looked exhausted, but exhilarated. I knew that look. It was like my mom was haunting her, especially around the eyes. "You are not Claimed, Lena. You're neither good nor bad. This is just what it feels like to be fifteen and a half, in the Duchannes family. I've known a lot of Casters in my day and a whole lot of Duchannes, both Dark and Light."

Lena looked at Marian, stunned.

Marian tried to catch her breath. "You are not going Dark. You're as melodramatic as Macon. Now calm down."

How did she know about Lena's birthday? How did she know about Casters?

"You two have Genevieve's locket. Why didn't you tell me?"

"We don't know what to do. Everyone tells us something different."

"Let me see it."

I reached into my pocket. Lena put her hand on my arm, and I hesitated. Marian was my mom's closest friend, and she was like family. I knew I shouldn't question her motives, but then I had just followed Amma into the swamp to meet Macon Ravenwood, and I would never have seen that coming. "How do we know we can trust you?" I asked, feeling sick even asking the question.

"'The best way to find out if you can trust somebody is to trust them.'"

"Elton John?"

"Close. Ernest Hemingway. In his own way, sort of the rock star of his time."

I smiled, but Lena was not so willing to have her doubts charmed away. "Why should we trust you when everyone else has been hiding things from us?"

Marian grew serious. "Precisely because I'm not Amma, and I'm not Uncle Macon. I'm not your Gramma or your Aunt Delphine. I'm Mortal. I'm neutral. Between Black magic and White magic, Light and Dark, there has to be something in between— something to resist the pull—and that something is me."

Lena backed away from her. It was inconceivable, to both of us. How did Marian know so much about Lena's family?

"What are you?" In Lena's family, that was a loaded question.

"I'm the Gatlin County Head Librarian, same as I've been since I moved here, same as I always will be. I'm not a Caster. I just keep the records. I just keep the books." Marian smoothed her hair. "I'm the Keeper, just one in a long line of Mortals entrusted with the history and the secrets of a world we can never entirely be a part of. There must always be one, and now that one is me."

"Aunt Marian? What are you talking about?" I was lost.

"Let's just say, there are libraries, and then there are *libraries*. I serve all the good citizens of Gatlin, whether they are Casters or Mortals. Which works out just fine since the other branch is more of a night job, really."

"You mean—?"

"The Gatlin County Caster Library. I am, of course, the Caster Librarian. The *Head* Caster Librarian."

I stared at Marian as if I was seeing her for the first time. She looked back at me with the same brown eyes, the same knowing smile. She looked the same, but somehow she was completely different. I had always wondered why Marian stayed in Gatlin all these years. I thought it was because of my mom. Now I realized there was another reason.

I didn't know what I was feeling, but whatever it was, Lena was feeling the opposite. "Then you can help us. We have to find out what happened to Ethan and Genevieve, and what it has to do with Ethan and me, and we have to find out before my birthday." Lena looked at her expectantly. "The Caster Library must have records. Maybe *The Book of Moons* is there. Do you think it could have the answers?"

Marian looked away. "Maybe, maybe not. I'm afraid I can't help you. I'm so sorry."

"What are you talking about?" She wasn't making sense. I'd never seen Marian refuse help to anyone, especially me.

"I can't get involved, even if I want to. It's part of the job description. I don't write the books, or the rules, I just keep them. I can't interfere."

"Is this job more important than helping us?" I stepped in front of her, so she had to look me in the eye when she answered. "More important than me?"

"It's not that simple, Ethan. There's a balance between the Mortal world and the Caster world, between Light and Dark. The Keeper is part of that balance, part of the Order of Things. If I defy the laws by which I'm Bound, that balance is jeopardized." She looked back at me, her voice shaky. "I can't interfere, even if it kills me. Even if it hurts the people I love."

I didn't understand what she was talking about, but I knew Marian loved me, like she had loved my mom. If she couldn't help us, there had to be a reason. "Fine. You can't help us. Just take me to this Caster Library, and I'll figure it out myself."

"You're not a Caster, Ethan. This isn't your decision to make."

Lena stepped next to me, and took my hand. "It's mine. And I want to go."

Marian nodded. "All right, I'll take you, the next time it's open. The Caster Library doesn't operate on the same schedule as the Gatlin County Library. It's a bit more *irregular*."

Of course it was.

Hallow E'en

The only days of the year that the Gatlin County Library was closed were bank holidays—like Thanksgiving Day, Christmas Day, New Year's Day, Easter. As a result, these were the only days the Gatlin County Caster Library was open, which apparently wasn't something Marian could control.

"Take it up with the county. Like I said, I don't make the rules." I wondered what county she was talking about—the one I had lived in my whole life, or the one that had been hidden from me for just as long.

Still, Lena seemed almost hopeful. For the first time, it was as if she actually believed there might be a way to prevent what she had considered the inevitable. Marian couldn't give us any answers, but she anchored us in the absence of the two people we relied on most, who hadn't gone anywhere, but seemed far away just the same. I didn't say anything to Lena, but without

Amma I was lost. And without Macon, I knew Lena couldn't even find her way to lost.

Marian did give us something, Ethan and Genevieve's letters, so old and delicate they were almost transparent, and everything she and my mother had collected about the two of them. A whole stack of papers in a dusty brown box, with cardboard printed to look like wood paneling on the sides. Although Lena loved poring over the prose—*"the days without you bleed together until time is nothing more than another obstacle we must overcome,"*—all it seemed to amount to was a love story with a really bad, and really Black ending. But it was all we had.

Now all we had to do was figure out what we were looking for. The needle in the haystack, or in this case, the cardboard box. So we did the only thing we could do. We started looking.

———

After two weeks, I'd spent more time with Lena on the locket papers than I would have thought possible. The more we read through the papers, the more it seemed like we were reading about ourselves. At night, we stayed up late trying to solve the mystery of Ethan and Genevieve, a Mortal and a Caster, desperate to find a way to be together, against impossible odds. At school, we faced some steep odds ourselves, just getting through another eight hours at Jackson, and it was only getting harder. Every day, there was another scheme to drive Lena away, or us apart. Especially if that day was Halloween.

Halloween was generally a pretty loaded holiday at Jackson. For a guy, anything involving costumes was an accident waiting to happen. And then, there was always the stress of whether or not you made the guest list to Savannah Snow's annual blowout. But Halloween took on a whole new level of stress when the girl you were crazy about was a Caster.

I had no idea what to expect when Lena picked me up for school, a couple of blocks from my house, safely around the corner from the eyes in the back of Amma's head.

"You're not dressed up," I said, surprised.

"What are you talking about?"

"I thought you'd be wearing a costume or something." I knew I sounded like an idiot the second the words came out of my mouth.

"Oh, you think Casters dress up on Halloween and fly around on brooms?" She laughed.

"I didn't mean—"

"Sorry to disappoint you. We just dress for dinner like we do on any other holiday."

"So it's a holiday for you guys, too."

"It's the most sacred night of the year, and the most dangerous—the most important of the four High Holidays. It's our version of New Year's Eve, the end of the old year and the beginning of the new."

"What do you mean by dangerous?"

"My gramma says it's the night when the veil between this world and the Otherworld, the world of spirits, is the thinnest. It's a night of power and a night of remembrance."

"The Otherworld? Is that like the afterlife?"

"Sort of. It's the realm of spirits."

"So Halloween really is all about spirits and ghosts." She rolled her eyes.

"We remember the Casters who were persecuted for their

differences. Men and women who were burned for using their gifts."

"Are you talking about the Salem Witch Trials?'

"I guess that's what you call them. There were Witch Trials all along the eastern seaboard, not just in Salem. All over the world, even. The Salem Witch Trials are just the ones *your* textbooks mention." She said "your" like it was a dirty word, and today of all days, maybe it was.

We drove past the Stop & Steal. Boo was sitting by the stop sign at the corner. Waiting. He saw the hearse and loped slowly after the car. "We should just give that dog a ride already. He must be tired, following you around day and night."

Lena glanced in her rearview mirror. "He'd never get in."

I knew she was right. But as I turned back to look at him, I could have sworn he nodded.

I spotted Link in the parking lot. He was wearing a blond wig and a blue sweater with a Wildcats patch sewn on it. He was even carrying pom-poms. He looked scary and sort of like his mom, actually. The basketball team had decided to dress up like Jackson cheerleaders this year. With everything else that had been going on, it had slipped my mind—at least that's what I told myself. I was going to get a lot of crap for this, and Earl was just waiting for a reason to jump all over me. Since I had started hanging out with Lena, I had developed a hot hand on the court. Now I was starting center instead of Earl, who was not too happy about it.

Lena swore there was nothing magic about it, at least not Caster magic. She came to one game and I made every shot. The drawback was, she was in my head throughout the game, asking me a thousand questions about foul shots and assists and the three-second rule. Turns out, she had never been to a game. It was worse than taking the Sisters to the County Fair. After that, she skipped the games. I could tell she was listening, though, when I played. I could feel her there.

On the other hand, maybe she was the reason the cheer squad was having a tougher year than usual. Emily was having a hard time staying on top of the Wildcats pyramid, but I didn't ask Lena about that.

Today it was hard to pick out my teammates, until you got close enough to see the hairy legs and facial hair. Link caught up to us. He looked worse up close. He had tried to put on makeup, smeared pink lipstick and all. He hitched up his skirt, tugging on the straining pantyhose underneath.

"You suck," he said, pointing at me across a row of cars. "Where's your costume?"

"I'm sorry, man. I forgot."

"Bull. You just didn't want to put all this crap on. I know you, Wate. You wussed out."

"I swear, I just forgot."

Lena smiled at Link. "I think you look great."

"I don't know how you girls wear all this junk all over your face. It itches like hell."

Lena made a face. She almost never wore makeup; she didn't have to. "You know, it's not like we all sign a contract with Maybelline when we turn thirteen."

Link patted his wig and stuffed another sock down his sweater. "Tell that to Savannah."

We walked up the front steps, and Boo was sitting on the lawn, next to the flagpole. I almost asked how that dog could

250

have possibly beaten us to school, but by now I knew not to bother.

The halls were packed. It looked like half the school had skipped first period. The rest of the basketball team was hanging out in front of Link's locker, also in drag, which was a big hit. Just not with me.

"Where're your pom-poms, Wate?" Emory shook one in my face. "What's the matter? Those chicken legs a yours didn't look good in the skirt?"

Shawn pulled on his sweater. "I bet none a the girls on the squad would lend him a skirt." A few of the guys laughed.

Emory put his arm around me, leaning in toward me. "Was that it, Wate? Or is it Halloween every day, when you're hookin' up with a girl who lives in the Haunted Mansion?"

I grabbed him by the back of his sweater. One of the socks in his bra fell down to the floor. "You want to do this now, Em?"

He shrugged. "Your call. Bound to happen sooner or later."

Link stepped in between us. "Ladies, ladies. We're here to cheer. And you don't want to mess up that pretty face, Em."

Earl shook his head, pushing Emory down the hall in front of him. As usual, he didn't say a word, but I knew the look.

Once you go down that road, Wate, there's no goin' back.

It seemed like the basketball team was the talk of the school, until I saw the real cheer squad. Turns out, my teammates weren't the only ones who had come up with a group costume. Lena and I were on our way to English when we saw them.

"Holy crap." Link hit my arm with the back of his hand.

"What?"

They were marching down the hall single file. Emily, Savannah, Eden, and Charlotte, followed by every member of the Jackson Wildcats' cheerleading squad. They were dressed exactly alike in ridiculously short black dresses, of course, pointy black boots, and tall, bent witches' hats. But that wasn't the worst part. Their long black wigs were curled into wild ringlets. And in black makeup, just below their right eyes were painstakingly drawn exaggerated crescent moons. Lena's unmistakable birthmark. To complete the effect, they were carrying brooms, pretending to frantically sweep around people's feet as they walked down the hall, in procession.

Witches? On Halloween? How creative.

I squeezed her hand. Her expression didn't change, but I could feel her hand shaking.

I'm sorry, Lena.

If they only knew.

I waited for the building to start shaking, the windows to blow out, something. But nothing happened. Lena just stood there, seething.

The future generation of the DAR headed toward us. I decided to meet them halfway. "Where's your costume, Emily? Did you forget it was Halloween?"

Emily looked confused. Then she smiled at me, the sticky sweet smile of someone a little too proud of herself. "What are you talkin' about, Ethan? Isn't this what you're into now?"

"We were just tryin' to make your *girlfriend* feel at home," Savannah said, smacking her gum.

Lena shot me a look.

Ethan, stop. You'll just make it worse for yourself.

I don't care.

I can handle this.

What happens to you happens to me.

Link walked up beside me, yanking up his stockings. "Hey girls, I thought we were comin' as bitches. Oh wait, that's every day."

Lena smiled at Link in spite of herself.

"You shut your mouth, Wesley Lincoln. I'm gonna tell your mamma that you're hangin' out with that freak, and she won't let you outta your house till Christmas."

"You know what that thing on her face is, don't you?" Emily smirked, pointing from Lena's birthmark to the crescent she'd drawn on her cheek. "It's called a witch's mark."

"Did you look that up online last night? You're an even bigger idiot than I thought." I laughed.

"You're the idiot. You're goin' out with her." I was turning red, which was the last thing I wanted to do. This wasn't a conversation I wanted to have in front of the whole school, not to mention the fact that I had no idea if Lena and I were even going out. We had kissed once. And we were always together, in one way or another. But she wasn't my girlfriend, at least I didn't think she was, even though I thought I'd heard her say that at the Gathering. And what could I do, ask? Maybe it was one of those things that if you had to ask, the answer was probably no. There was some part of her that still seemed to be holding back from me, a part of her I just couldn't reach.

Emily jabbed me with the end of her broom. I could tell the whole "stake in the heart" concept would be attractive to her, just about now.

"Emily, why don't you all go jump out a window. See if you can fly. Or not."

Her eyes narrowed. "I hope you enjoy yourselves sittin' around the house together tonight, while the rest a the school is at Savannah's party. This will be the last holiday *she* spends at Jackson." Emily spun around and marched back down the hall toward her locker, Savannah and their minions trailing behind her.

Link was joking around with Lena, trying to cheer her up, which wasn't hard, considering how ridiculous he looked. Like I said, I could always count on Link.

"They really hate me. It's never going to get old, is it?" Lena sighed.

Link broke into a cheer, jumping around and waving his pom-poms. "They really hate you, yes they do. They hate everyone, how 'bout you?"

"I'd be more worried if they liked you." I leaned over and put my arm around her awkwardly, or tried to. She turned away, my hand barely brushing her shoulder. Great.

Not here.

Why not?

You're just making it worse for yourself.

I'm a glutton for punishment.

"Enough of the PDA." Link elbowed me in the ribs. "You're gonna make me start feelin' bad for myself, now that I've doomed myself to another year without a date. We're gonna be late for English, and I gotta take these pantyhose off on the way. I'm gettin' a serious wedgie."

"I just have to stop at my locker and get my book," Lena

said. Her hair began to curl around her shoulders. I was suspicious, but I didn't say anything.

Emily, Savannah, Charlotte, and Eden were standing in front of their lockers, primping in front of the mirrors hanging inside the doors. Lena's locker was only a little farther down the hall.

"Just ignore them," I said.

Emily was rubbing her cheek with a Kleenex. The black moon-shaped mark was only smearing bigger and blacker, not coming off at all. "Charlotte, do you have any makeup remover?"

"Sure."

Emily wiped her cheek a few more times. "This isn't comin' off. Savannah, I thought you said this stuff came off with soap and water."

"It does."

"Then why isn't it comin' off?" Emily slammed her locker door, annoyed.

The drama got Link's attention. "What are those four doin' over there?"

"Look's like they're having some kind of *problem*," Lena said, leaning against her locker.

Savannah tried to wipe the black moon off her own cheek. "Mine isn't comin' off, either." The moon was now smeared across half her face. Savannah started digging around in her purse. "I have the pencil right here."

Emily pulled her purse out of her locker, searching through it. "Forget it. I have mine in my bag."

"What the—" Savannah pulled something out of her bag.

"You used Sharpie?" Emily laughed.

Savannah held the marker up in front of her. "Of course not. I have no idea how this got in here."

"You're so lame. That will never come off before the party tonight."

"I can't have this *thing* on my face all night. I'm goin' dressed as a Greek Goddess, Aphrodite. This will completely ruin my costume."

"You should've been more careful." Emily dug around in her little silver purse some more. She dumped her purse on the ground under her locker, lip gloss and nail polish bottles rolling around on the floor. "It has to be here."

"What are you talkin' about?" Charlotte asked.

"The makeup I used this mornin', it's not here." By now, Emily was attracting an audience; people were stopping to see what was going on. A Sharpie rolled out of Emily's purse into the middle of the hall.

"You used Sharpie, too?"

"Of course I didn't!" Emily shrieked, rubbing her face frantically. But the black moon only grew bigger and blacker like the others. "What the hell is goin' on?"

"I know I have mine," Charlotte said, turning the lock on her locker door. She opened the door and stood there for a few seconds, staring inside.

"What is it?" Savannah demanded. Charlotte pulled her hand back out of her locker. She was holding a Sharpie.

Link shook his pom-pom. "Cheerleaders rock!"

I looked at Lena.

Sharpie?

A mischievous smile spread across her face.

I thought you said you couldn't control your powers.
Beginner's luck.

By the end of the day, everyone at Jackson was talking about the cheer squad. Apparently, every one of the cheerleaders who dressed up as Lena had somehow used a Sharpie to draw the innocuous crescent moon on her face, instead of eyeliner. Cheerleaders. The jokes were endless.

All of them would be walking around school and the rest of town, singing in the church youth choirs, and cheering at the games, with Sharpie on their cheeks for the next few days, until it faded away. Mrs. Lincoln and Mrs. Snow were going to have a fit.

I just wished I could be there to see it.

———

After school, I walked Lena back to her car, which was really just an excuse to try to hold her hand a little longer. The intense physical feelings I had when I touched her weren't the deterrent you might have expected. No matter what it felt like, whether I was burning or blowing out light bulbs or getting struck by lightning, I had to be close to her. It was like eating, or breathing. I didn't have a choice. And that was scarier than a month of Halloweens, and it was killing me.

"What are you doing tonight?" As she spoke, she pulled her hand absentmindedly through her hair. She was sitting on the hood of the hearse and I was standing in front of her.

"I thought maybe you'd come over, and we'd stay home and answer the door for trick-or-treaters. You can help me watch the lawn to make sure no one burns a cross on it." I tried not to think too clearly about the rest of my plan, which involved Lena and our couch and old movies and Amma being gone for the night.

"I can't. It's a High Holiday. I have relatives coming in from all over. Uncle M won't let me out of the house for five minutes, not to mention the danger. I'd never open my door to strangers on a night of such Dark power."

"I never thought of it that way." Until now.

By the time I got home, Amma was getting ready to leave. She was boiling a chicken on the stove and mixing biscuit batter with her hands, "the only way any self-respectin' woman makes her biscuits." I looked at the pot suspiciously, wondering if this meal was going to make it to our dinner table or the Greats'.

I pinched some dough, and she caught my hand.

"P. U. R. L. O. I. N. E. R." I smiled.

"As in, keep your thievin' hands off a my biscuits, Ethan Wate. I've got hungry people to feed." Guess I wouldn't be eating chicken and biscuits tonight.

Amma always went home on Halloween. She said it was a special night at church, but my mom used to say it was just a good night for business. What better night to have your cards read than Halloween? You weren't going to get quite the same crowd on Easter or Valentine's Day.

But in light of recent events, I wondered if there wasn't another reason. Maybe it was a good night for reading chicken bones in the graveyard, too. I couldn't ask, and I wasn't sure I wanted to know. I missed Amma, missed talking to her, missed trusting her. If she felt the difference, she didn't let on. Maybe she just thought I was growing up, or maybe I was.

"You goin' to that party over at the Snows'?"

"No, I'm just gonna stay home this year."

She raised an eyebrow, but she wasn't going to ask. She already knew why I wasn't going. "You make your bed, you better be ready to lie in it."

I didn't say anything. I knew better. She wasn't expecting a response.

"I'm fixin' to go in a few minutes. You answer the door for those young'uns when they come around. Your daddy's busy workin'." Like my dad was going to come out of his self-imposed exile to answer the door for trick-or-treaters.

"Sure."

The bags of candy were in the hall. I ripped them open and turned them over into a big glass bowl. I couldn't get Lena's words out of my head. *A night of such Dark power.* I remembered Ridley standing in front of her car, outside the Stop & Steal, all sticky sweet smiles and legs. Obviously, identifying Dark forces wasn't one of my talents, or deciding who you should and shouldn't open your front door for. Like I said, when the girl you couldn't stop thinking about was a Caster, Halloween took on a whole new meaning. I looked at the bowl of candy in my hands. Then I opened the front door, put the bowl out on the porch, and went back inside.

As I settled in to watch *The Shining*, I found myself missing Lena. I let my mind wander, because it usually found a way of wandering over to wherever she was, but she wasn't there. I fell asleep on the couch waiting for her to dream me, or something.

A knock at the door startled me. I looked at my watch. It was nearly ten, too late for trick-or-treaters.

"Amma?"

No answer. I heard knocking again.

"Is that you?"

The den was dark, and only the light of the TV was flickering. It was the moment in *The Shining* when the dad chops down the hotel room door with his bloody axe to bludgeon his family. Not a great moment for answering any door, especially on Halloween. Another knock.

"Link?" I clicked off the TV and looked around for something to pick up, but there was nothing. I picked up an old game console, lying on the floor in a pile of video games. It wasn't a baseball bat, but some decently solid old-school Japanese technology. It had to weigh at least five pounds. I raised it over my head and took a step closer to the wall separating the den from the front hall. Another step, and I moved the lace curtain covering the glass-paned door, just a millimeter.

In the darkness of the unlit porch, I couldn't see her face. But I would recognize that old beige van, still running in the street in front of my house, anywhere. "Desert Sand," she used to say. It was Link's mom, holding a plate of brownies. I was still carrying the console. If Link saw me, he'd never let me live this down.

"Just a minute, Mrs. Lincoln." I flipped on the porch light, and unbolted the front door. But when I tried to pull it open, the door jammed. I checked the lock again, and it was still bolted, even though I had just unbolted it.

"Ethan?"

I unbolted the lock again. It bolted shut with a snap, before I could take my hand away from it. "Mrs. Lincoln, I'm sorry, my door seems to be stuck." I rattled the door with all my weight, juggling the console. Something fell to the floor in front of me. I stopped to pick it up. Garlic, wrapped in one of Amma's handkerchiefs. If I had to guess, there was one over every door and every windowsill. Amma's little Halloween tradition.

Still, something was keeping the door from opening, just like something had tried to open the study door for me just days ago. How many bolts in this house were going to just keep locking and unlocking themselves? What was going on?

I unbolted the lock one more time and gave the door a final pull. It flung open, banging against the wall in the front hall. Mrs. Lincoln was lit from behind, a dark figure in a pool of pale lamplight. The silhouette was unsettling.

She stared at the game console in my hand. "Video games will rot your brain, Ethan."

"Yes, ma'am."

"I brought you some brownies. A peace offerin'." She held them out expectantly. I should've asked her to come in. There was a formula for everything. I guess you could call it manners, Southern hospitality. But I had tried that with Ridley, and it hadn't gone so well. I hesitated. "What are you doing out tonight, ma'am? Link's not here."

"Of course he's not. He's at the Snows', which is where every upstandin' member a the Jackson High student body should be lucky enough to be. It took quite a number a phone calls on my part to get him an invitation, in light a his recent behavior."

I still didn't get it. I'd known Mrs. Lincoln my whole life. She had always been an odd duck. Busy getting books taken off the library shelves, teachers fired from the schools, reputations ruined in a single afternoon. Lately, she was different. The crusade against Lena was different. Mrs. Lincoln had always had conviction, but this was personal.

"Ma'am?"

She looked agitated. "I made you brownies. I thought I could come in, and we could talk. My fight's not with you, Ethan. It's not your fault that girl is usin' her deviltry on you. You should be at the party, with your friends. With the kids who belong here." She held out the brownies, the gooey double chocolate chip fudge brownies that were always the first thing to go at the Baptist Church Bake Sale. I had grown up on those brownies. "Ethan?"

"Ma'am."

"Can I come in?"

I didn't move a muscle. My grip tightened around the console. I stared at the brownies, and suddenly I didn't feel hungry at all. Not even the plate, not a crumb of that woman was welcome in my house. My house, like Ravenwood, was starting to have a mind of its own, and there was no part of me or my house that was going to let her in.

"No, ma'am."

"What was that, Ethan?"

"No. Ma'am."

Her eyes narrowed. She pushed the plate toward me, as if she was going to come in anyway, but it jerked like it had hit an invisible wall between her and me. I saw the plate tumble, falling slowly to the ground until it shattered into a million bits of ceramic and chocolate, all over our Happy Halloween doormat. Amma would pitch a fit in the morning.

Mrs. Lincoln backed down the porch steps warily, and disappeared into the darkness of the old Desert Sand.

Ethan!

Her voice ripped me right out of my sleep. I must have drifted off. The horror marathon was over and the television had broken down into a loud, gray fuzz.

Uncle Macon! Ethan! Help!

Lena was screaming. Somewhere. I could hear the terror in her voice, and my head was pounding with such pain for a second I forgot where I was.

Someone please help me!

My front door was wide open, swinging and banging in the wind. The sound ricocheted off the walls, like gunfire.

I thought you said I was safe here!

Ravenwood.

I grabbed the car keys to the old Volvo, and ran.

I can't remember how I got to Ravenwood, but I know I nearly drove off the road a few times. My eyes could barely focus. Lena was in such intense pain, our connection so close, that I nearly blacked out just from feeling it through her.

And the screaming.

There was always the screaming, from the moment I'd woken up, until the moment I pressed the crescent and let myself into Ravenwood Manor.

As the front door swung open, I could see Ravenwood had transformed itself once again. Tonight, it was almost like some kind of ancient castle. Candelabras cast strange shadows down on the throngs of black-robed, black-gowned, black-jacketed guests, far outnumbering the guests at the Gathering.

Ethan! Hurry! I can't hold on . . .

"Lena!" I yelled. "Macon! Where is she?"

No one so much as looked my way. I didn't see anyone I recognized, though the front hall was crowded with guests, flowing from room to room like ghosts at a haunted dinner party. They were not from around here, at least not for hundreds of years. I saw men in dark kilts and rough Gaelic robes, women in corseted gowns. Everything was black, wrapped in shadow.

I pushed through the crowd and into what looked like a grand ballroom. I couldn't see any of them—no Aunt Del, no Reece, not even little Ryan. Candles sputtered into flame in the corners of the room, and what seemed to be a translucent orchestra of strange musical instruments shifted in and out of focus, playing themselves, while shadowy couples went spinning and gliding across the now stone floor. The dancers didn't even seem to be aware of me.

The music was clearly Caster music, conjuring a spell of its own. It was the strings, mostly. I could hear the violin, the viola, the cello. I could almost see the web that spun from dancer to dancer, the way they pulled each other in and out, as if there was a deliberate pattern, and they were all a part of the design. And I wasn't.

Ethan—

I had to find her.

A sudden surge of pain. Her voice was growing quieter now. I stumbled, grabbing onto the shoulder of the robed guest next to me. All I did was touch him and the pain, Lena's pain, flowed through me and into him. He staggered, bumping into the couple dancing next to him.

"Macon!" I screamed at the top of my lungs.

I saw Boo Radley at the head of the stairs, like he was waiting for me. His round, human eyes looked terrified.

"Boo! Where is she?" Boo looked at me, and I saw the clouded, steely gray eyes of Macon Ravenwood; at least, I could've have sworn I did. Then Boo turned and ran. I chased him, or I thought I was chasing him, running up the spiraling stone stairs of what was now Ravenwood Castle. At the landing, he waited for me to catch up, then ran toward a dark room at the end of the hall. From Boo, that was practically an invitation.

He barked, and two massive oaken doors groaned open by themselves. They were so far away from the party, I couldn't hear the music or the chatter of the guests. It was as if we had entered a different place and time. Even the castle was changing under my feet, the rock crumbling, the walls growing mossy and cold. The lights had become torches, hung on the walls.

I knew about old. Gatlin was old. I had grown up with old. This was something altogether different. Like Lena had said, a New Year. A night out of time.

When I entered the main chamber, I was struck by the sky. The room opened wide to the heavens, like a conservatory. The sky above it was black, the blackest sky I'd ever seen. Like we were in the middle of a terrible storm, yet the room was silent.

Lena lay on a heavy stone table, curled in a fetal position. She was soaking wet, drenched in her own sweat and writhing in pain. They were all standing around her—Macon, Aunt Del, Barclay, Reece, Larkin, even Ryan, and a woman I didn't recognize, holding hands, forming a circle.

Their eyes were open, but they weren't seeing. They didn't even notice I was in the room. I could see their mouths moving, mumbling something. As I stepped closer to Macon, I realized that they weren't speaking in English. I couldn't be sure, but I'd spent enough time with Marian to think it was Latin.

"Sanguis sanguinis mei, tutela tua est.
Sanguis sanguinis mei, tutela tua est.
Sanguis sanguinis mei, tutela tua est.
Sanguis sanguinis mei, tutela tua est."

All I could hear was the quiet mumbling, the chanting. I couldn't hear Lena anymore. My head was empty. She was gone.

Lena! Answer me!

Nothing. She just lay there, moaning softly, twisting slowly like she was trying to shed her own skin. Still sweating, sweat mixed with tears.

Del broke the silence, hysterical. "Macon, do something! It's not working."

"I'm trying, Delphine." There was something in his voice I'd never heard before. Fear.

"I don't understand. We Bound this place together. This house is the one place she was supposed to be safe." Aunt Del looked at Macon for answers.

"We were wrong. There's no safe haven for her here." A beautiful woman about my grandmother's age with spirals of black hair spoke. She wore strands of beads around her neck, piled one on top of the other, and ornate silver rings on her thumbs. She had the same exotic quality Marian possessed, as if she was from somewhere far from here.

"You don't know that, Aunt Arelia," Del snapped, turning to Reece. "Reece, what's happening? Can you see anything?"

Reece's eyes were closed, tears streaming down her face. "I can't see anything, Mamma."

Lena's body seized and she screamed—at least she opened her mouth and looked as if she was screaming, but she didn't make a sound. I couldn't take it.

"Do something! Help her!" I shouted.

"What are you doin' here? Get out of here. It's not safe," Larkin warned. The family had noticed me for the first time.

"Concentrate!" Macon sounded desperate. His voice rose over the others', louder and louder, until he was shouting—

"Sanguis sanguinis mei, tutela tua est!
Sanguis sanguinis mei, tutela tua est!
Sanguis sanguinis mei, tutela tua est!
Blood of my blood, protection is thine!"

The members of the circle tensed their arms as if to give the circle more strength, but it didn't work. Lena was still screaming, silent screams of terror. This was worse than the dreams. This was real. And if they weren't going to stop it, I would. I ran toward her, ducking under Reece and Larkin's arms.

"Ethan, NO!"

As I entered the circle, I could hear it. A howl. Sinister, haunting, like the voice of the wind itself. Or was it a voice? I couldn't be sure. Even though it was only a few feet to the table where she was lying, it felt like it was a million miles away. Something was trying to push me back, something more powerful than anything I'd ever felt before. Even more powerful than when

267

Ridley was freezing the life out of me. I pushed against it with everything I had in me.

I'm coming, Lena! Hold on!

I threw my body forward, reaching, like I reached in the dreams. The black abyss in the sky began to spin.

I closed my eyes and lunged forward. Our fingers touched, barely.

I heard her voice.

Ethan. I . . .

The air inside the circle whipped around us violently, like a vortex. Swirling up toward the sky, if you could still call it a sky. Into the blackness. There was a surge, like an explosion, slamming Uncle Macon, Aunt Del, everyone onto their backs, into the walls behind them. In the same moment, the spinning air within the broken circle was sucked up into the blackness above.

Then it was over. The castle dissolved into a regular attic, with a regular window, swinging open under the eaves. Lena lay on the floor, in a tangle of hair and limbs and unconsciousness, but she was breathing.

Macon pulled himself up from the floor, staring at me, stunned. Then he walked over to the window and slammed it shut.

Aunt Del looked at me, tears still streaming down her face. "If I hadn't seen it myself . . ."

I knelt at Lena's side. She couldn't move, couldn't speak. But she was alive. I could feel her, a tiny throb pulsing in her hand. I lay my head down next to her. It was all I could do not to collapse.

Lena's family slowly contracted around us, a dark circle talking over my head.

"I told you. The boy has power."

"It's not possible. He's a Mortal. He's not one of us."

"How could a Mortal break a *Sanguinis* Circle? How could a Mortal ward off a *Mentem Interficere* so powerful that Ravenwood itself came all but Unbound?"

"I don't know, but there has to be an explanation." Del raised her hand above her head. *"Evinco, contineo, colligo, includo."* She opened her eyes. "The house is still Bound, Macon. I can feel it. But she got to Lena anyway."

"Of course she did. We can't stop her from coming for the child."

"Sarafine's powers are growing by the day. Reece can see her now, when she looks in Lena's eyes." Del's voice was shaky.

"Striking us here, on this night. She was just making a point."

"And what point would that be, Macon?"

"That she can."

I could feel a hand at my temple. It caressed me, moving across my forehead. I tried to listen, but the hand made me sleepy. I wanted to crawl home to my bed.

"Or that she can't." I looked up. Arelia was rubbing my temples, as if I were a little broken sparrow. Only I could tell she was feeling for me, for what was inside me. She was searching for something, rummaging around in my mind as if she was looking for a lost button or an old sock. "She was foolish. She made a critical error. We've learned the only thing we really needed to know," Arelia said.

"So you agree with Macon? The boy has power?" Del sounded even more frantic now.

"You were right before, Delphine. There must be some other explanation. He's a Mortal, and we all know Mortals can't possess power on their own," Macon snapped, as if he was try-ing to convince himself as much as anyone.

But I had begun to wonder if it wasn't true. He had said the same thing to Amma in the swamp, that I had some kind of power. It just didn't make sense, even to me. I wasn't one of them, that much I knew. I wasn't a Caster.

Arelia looked up at Macon. "You can Bind the house all you want, Macon. But I'm your mother and I'm tellin' you that you can bring in every Duchannes, every Ravenwood, make the Circle as wide as this godforsaken county if you want. Cast all the *Vincula* you can. It's not the house that protects her. It's the boy. I've never seen anything like it. No Caster can come be-tween them."

"So it would seem." Macon sounded angry, but he didn't challenge his mother. I was too tired to care. I didn't even lift my head.

I could hear Arelia whispering something in my ear. It seemed like she was speaking Latin again, but the words sounded different.

"Cruor pectoris mei, tutela tua est!
Blood of my heart, protection is thine!"

‑‑ 11.01 ‑‑

The Writing on the Wall

In the morning, I had no idea where I was. Then I saw the words covering the walls and the old iron bed and the windows and the mirrors, all scrawled with Sharpie in Lena's handwriting, and I remembered.

I lifted my head up, and wiped the drool off my cheek. Lena was still sacked out; I could just see the edge of her foot hanging over the side of the bed. I pushed myself up, my back stiff from sleeping on the floor. I wondered who had brought us down from the attic, or how.

My cell phone went off; my default alarm clock, so Amma would only have to yell up the stairs three times to get me up. Only today, it wasn't blaring "Bohemian Rhapsody." It was the song. Lena sat up, startled, groggy.

"What happ—"

"Shh. Listen."

The song had changed.

> *Sixteen moons, sixteen years,*
> *Sixteen times you dreamed my fears,*
> *Sixteen will try to Bind the spheres,*
> *Sixteen screams but just one hears . . .*

"Stop it!" She grabbed my cell and turned it off, but the verse kept playing.

"It's about you, I think. But what's Binding the spheres?"

"I almost died last night. I'm sick of everything being about me. I'm sick of all these weird things happening to me. Maybe the stupid song is about you, for a change. You're actually the only sixteen-year-old here." Frustrated, Lena flung her hand up in the air and opened it. She closed it into a fist, and banged it against the floor like she was killing a spider.

The music stopped. There was no messing with Lena today. I couldn't blame her, to be honest. She looked green and wobbly, maybe even worse than Link did the morning after Savannah had dared him to drink the old bottle of peppermint schnapps out of her mom's pantry, on the last day of school before winter break. Three years later and he still wouldn't eat a candy cane.

Lena's hair was sticking out in about fifteen directions, and her eyes were all small and puffy from crying. So this was what girls looked like in the morning. I had never seen one, not up close. I tried not to think about Amma and the hell I was going to pay when I got home.

I crawled up onto the bed and pulled Lena into my lap, running my hand through her crazy hair. "Are you okay?"

She shut her eyes and buried her face in my sweatshirt. I knew I must reek like a wild possum by now. "I think so."

"I could hear you screaming, all the way from my house."

"Who knew Kelting would save my life."

I had missed something, as usual. "What's Kelting?"

"That's what it's called, the way we're able to communicate with each other no matter where we are. Some Casters can Kelt, some can't. Ridley and I used to be able to talk to each other in school that way, but—"

"I thought you said it had never happened to you before?"

"It's never happened to me before with a Mortal. Uncle Macon says it's really rare."

I like the sound of that.

Lena nudged me. "It's from the Celtic side of our family. It's how Casters used to get messages to each other, during the Trials. In the States, they used to call it 'The Whispering.'"

"But I'm not a Caster."

"I know, it's really weird. It's not supposed to work with Mortals." Of course it wasn't.

"Don't you think it's a little more than weird? We can do this Kelting thing, Ridley got into Ravenwood because of me, even your uncle said I can protect you somehow. How is that possible? I mean, I'm not a Caster. My parents are different, but they're not *that* different."

She leaned into my shoulder. "Maybe you don't have to be a Caster to have power."

I pushed her hair behind her ear. "Maybe you just have to fall for one."

I said it, just like that. No stupid jokes, no changing the subject. For once, I wasn't embarrassed, because it was the truth. I had fallen. I think I had always been falling. And she might as well know, if she didn't already, because there was no going back now. Not for me.

She looked up at me, and the whole world disappeared. Like there was just us, like there would always be just us, and we didn't need magic for that. It was sort of happy and sad, all at the same time. I couldn't be around her without feeling things, without feeling everything.

What are you thinking?

She smiled.

I think you can figure it out. You can read the writing on the wall.

And as she said it, there was writing on the wall. It appeared slowly, one word at a time.

You're
not
the
only
one
falling.

It wrote itself out, in the same curling black script as the rest of the room. Lena's cheeks flushed a little, and she covered her face with her hands. "It's going to be really embarrassing if everything I think starts showing up on the walls."

"You didn't mean to do that?"

"No."

You don't need to be embarrassed, L.

I pulled her hands away.

Because I feel the same way about you.

Her eyes were closed, and I leaned in to kiss her. It was a tiny kiss, a nothing of a kiss. But it made my heart race just the same.

She opened her eyes and smiled. "I want to hear the rest. I want to hear how you saved my life."

"I don't even remember how I got here, and then I couldn't find you, and your house was full of all these creepy people who looked like they were at a costume party."

"They weren't."

"I figured."

"Then you found me?" She laid her head in my lap, looking up at me with a smile. "You rode into the room on your white stallion and saved me from certain death at the hands of a Dark Caster?"

"Don't joke. It was really scary. And there was no stallion, it was more like a dog."

"The last thing I remember was Uncle Macon talking about the Binding." Lena twirled her hair, thinking.

"What was the Circle thing?"

"The *Sanguinis* Circle. The Circle of Blood."

I tried not to look freaked out. I could barely stomach the idea of Amma and the chicken bones. I didn't think I could handle real chicken blood; at least, I hoped it was just chicken blood. "I didn't see the blood."

"Not actual blood, you idiot. Blood as in kin, family. My whole family is here for the holiday, remember?"

"Right. Sorry."

"I told you. Halloween is a powerful night for Casting."

"So that's what you were all doing up here? In that Circle?"

"Macon wanted to Bind Ravenwood. It's always Bound, but he Binds it again every Halloween for the New Year."

"But something went wrong."

"I guess so, because we were in the circle, and then I could hear Uncle Macon talking to Aunt Del, and then everyone was shouting, and they were all talking about a woman. Sara something."

"Sarafine. I heard it, too."

"Sarafine. Was that the name? I've never heard it before."

"She must be a Dark Caster. They all seemed, I don't know, scared. I've never heard your uncle talk like that before. Do you know what was happening? Was she really trying to kill you?" I wasn't sure I wanted to know the answer.

"I don't know. I don't remember much, except this voice, like someone was talking to me from really far away. But I can't remember what they were saying." She squirmed into my lap, awkwardly leaning against my chest. It almost seemed like I could feel her heart beating on top of mine, like a little fluttering bird in a cage. We were as close as two people could be, without looking at each other. Which was, this morning, the way I think we both needed it to be. "Ethan. We're running out of time. It's no use. Whatever it was, whatever she was, don't you think she was coming for me, because in four months I'm going to go Dark?"

"No."

"No? That's all you have to say about the worst night of my whole life, when I almost died?" Lena pulled back.

"Think about it. Would this Sarafine, whoever she is, be hunting you down if you were one of the bad guys? No, the good guys would be coming after you. Look at Ridley. Nobody in your family was exactly pulling out the welcome mat for her."

"Except you. Jerk." She jabbed me playfully in the ribs.

"Exactly. Because I'm not a Caster, I'm a puny Mortal. And you said yourself, if she told me to jump off a cliff, I'd do it."

Lena tossed her hair. "Didn't your mamma ever ask you, Ethan Wate, if your friends were about to jump right off a cliff, would you jump, too?"

I drew my arms around her, feeling happier than I should've, given last night. Or maybe it was Lena who was feeling better, and I was just picking up on it. These days, such a strong current flowed between us that it was hard to sort out what was me, and what was her.

All I knew was, I wanted to kiss her.

You're going Light.

And so I did.

Definitely, Light.

I kissed her again, pulling her up into my arms. Kissing her was like breathing. I had to do it. I couldn't help myself. I pressed my body against hers. I could hear her breathing, feel her heart beating against my chest. My whole nervous system started firing at once. My hair was standing on end. Her black hair spilled into my hands, and she relaxed into my body. Every touch of her hair was like a prick of electricity. I had been waiting to do this since I had first met her, since I had first dreamed about her.

It was like lightning striking. We were one thing.

Ethan.

Even in my head, I could hear the urgency in her voice. I felt it too, like I couldn't get close enough to her. Her skin was soft and hot. I could feel the pinpricks intensifying. Our lips were raw; we couldn't kiss each other any harder. The bed started to shake, and then lift. I could feel it swaying underneath us. I felt like my lungs were collapsing. My skin went cold. The lights in the room flashed on and off, and the room was spinning, or maybe growing dark, only I couldn't tell and I didn't know if it was me, or if it was the light in the room.

Ethan!

The bed crashed to the floor. I heard the sound of splintering glass, in the distance, as if a window had shattered. I heard Lena crying.

Then the voice of a child. "What's wrong, Lena Beana? Why are you so sad?"

I felt a small, warm hand on my chest. The warmth radiated out from the hand, through my body, and the room stopped spinning, and I could breathe again, and I opened my eyes.

Ryan.

I sat up, my head pounding. Lena was next to me, her head pressed against my chest, just like she had been an hour before. Only this time, her windows were broken, her bed had collapsed, and a little blond ten-year-old was standing in front of me with her hand on my chest. Lena, still sniffling, tried to push part of a broken mirror away from me, and what was left of her bed.

"I think we figured out what Ryan is."

Lena smiled, wiping her eyes. She pulled Ryan close. "A Thaumaturge. We've never had one in our family."

"I'm guessing that's a fancy Caster name for a healer," I said, rubbing my head.

Lena nodded and kissed Ryan's cheek.

"Something like that."

Just Your Average
American Holiday

After Halloween, it felt like the calm after the storm. We settled into a routine, even though we knew the clock was ticking.
I walked to the corner to hide from Amma, Lena picked me up
in the hearse, Boo Radley caught up with us in front of the Stop
& Steal and followed us to school. With the occasional exception of Winnie Reid, the only member of the Jackson Debate team,
which made debating difficult, or Robert Lester Tate, who had
won the State Spelling Bee two years in a row, the only person
who would even sit with us in the cafeteria was Link. When we
weren't at school eating on the bleachers, or being spied on by
Principal Harper, we were holed up in the library rereading the
locket papers and hoping Marian might slip up and tell us something. No sign of flirty Siren cousins bearing lollipops and death
grips, no unexplained Category 3 storms or ominous black clouds

in the sky, not even a weird meal with Macon. Nothing out of the ordinary.

Except for one thing. The most important thing. I was crazy about a girl who actually felt the same way about me. When did that ever happen? The fact that she was a Caster was almost easier to believe than the fact that she existed at all.

I had Lena. She was powerful and she was beautiful. Every day was terrifying, and every day was perfect.

Until out of nowhere, the unthinkable happened. Amma invited Lena to Thanksgiving dinner.

"I don't know why you want to come over for Thanksgiving anyway. It's pretty boring." I was nervous. Amma was obviously up to something.

Lena smiled, and I relaxed. There was nothing better than when she smiled. It blew me away every time. "I don't think it sounds boring."

"You've never been to Thanksgiving at my house."

"I've never been to Thanksgiving at anyone's house. Casters don't celebrate Thanksgiving. It's a Mortal holiday."

"Are you kidding? No turkey? No pumpkin pie?"

"Nope."

"You didn't eat much today, did you?"

"Not really."

"Then you'll be okay."

I had prepped Lena ahead of time so she wouldn't be surprised when the Sisters wrapped extra biscuits in their dinner napkins and slipped them into their purses. Or when my Aunt

Caroline and Marian spent half the night debating the location of the first public library in the U.S. (Charleston) or the proper proportions for "Charleston green" paint (two parts "Yankee" black and one part "Rebel" yellow). Aunt Caroline was a museum curator in Savannah and she knew as much about period architecture and antiques as my mom had known about Civil War ammunition and battle strategy. Because that's what Lena had to be ready for—Amma, my crazy relatives, Marian, and Harlon James thrown in for good measure.

I left out the one detail she actually needed to know. Given how things had been lately, Thanksgiving probably also meant dinner with my dad in his pajamas. But that was something I just couldn't explain.

Amma took Thanksgiving really seriously, which meant two things. My dad would finally come out of his study, although technically it was after dark so that wasn't a big exception, and he would eat at the table with us. No Shredded Wheat. That was the absolute minimum Amma would allow. So in honor of my dad's pilgrimage into the world the rest of us inhabited every day, Amma cooked up a storm. Turkey, mashed potatoes with gravy, butter beans and creamed corn, sweet potatoes with marshmallows, honey ham and biscuits, pumpkin and lemon meringue pie, which, after my evening in the swamp, I was pretty sure she was making more for Uncle Abner than the rest of us.

I stopped for a second on the porch, remembering how I felt standing on the veranda at Ravenwood the first night I showed up there. Now it was Lena's turn. She had pulled her dark hair away from her face, and I touched the place where it managed to escape, curling around her chin.

You ready?

She pulled her black dress loose from her tights. She was nervous.

I'm not.

You should be.

I grinned and pushed open the door. "Ready or not." The house smelled like my childhood. Like mashed potatoes and hard work.

"Ethan Wate, is that you?" Amma called from the kitchen.

"Yes, ma'am."

"You have that girl with you? Bring her in here so we can get a look at her."

The kitchen was sizzling. Amma was standing in front of the stove, in her apron, a wooden spoon in each hand. Aunt Prue was puttering around, sticking her fingers in the mixing bowls on the counter. Aunt Mercy and Aunt Grace were playing Scrabble at the kitchen table; neither one of them seemed to notice they weren't actually making any words.

"Well, don't just stand there. Bring her on in here."

Every muscle in my body tensed. There was no way to predict what Amma, or the Sisters, were going to say. I still had no idea why Amma had insisted I invite Lena in the first place.

Lena stepped forward. "It's nice to finally meet you."

Amma looked Lena up and down, wiping her hands on her apron. "So you're the one keepin' my boy so busy. Postman was right. Pretty as a picture." I wondered if Carlton Eaton had mentioned that on their ride to Wader's Creek.

Lena blushed. "Thank you."

"Heard you've shaken things up at that school." Aunt Grace smiled. "A good thing, too. I don't know what they're teachin' you kids over there."

Aunt Mercy put down her tiles, one at a time. I-T-C-H-I-N.

Aunt Grace leaned closer to the board, squinting. "Mercy Lynne, you're cheatin' again! What kinda word is that? Use it in a sentence."

"I'm itchin' ta have some a that white cake."

"That's not how you spell it." At least one of them could spell. Aunt Grace pulled one of the tiles off the board. "There's no T in itchin'." Or not.

You weren't exaggerating.

I told you.

"Is that Ethan I hear?" Aunt Caroline walked into the kitchen just in time, her arms open wide. "Come on over here and give your aunt a hug." It always caught me off guard for a second, just how much she looked like my mother. The same long brown hair, always pulled back, the same dark brown eyes. But my mom had always preferred bare feet and jeans, while Aunt Caroline was more of a Southern Belle in sundresses and little sweaters. I think my aunt liked to see the expression on people's faces when they found out she was curator of the Savannah History Museum and not some aging debutante.

"How're things up North?" Aunt Caroline always referred to Gatlin as "up North" since it was north of Savannah.

"All right. Did you bring me some pralines?"

"Don't I always?"

I took Lena's hand, pulling her toward us. "Lena, this is my Aunt Caroline and my great-aunts, Prudence, Mercy, and Grace."

"It's a pleasure to meet you all." Lena reached out her hand, but my Aunt Caroline pulled her in for a hug instead.

The front door slammed.

"Happy Thanksgiving." Marian came in carrying a casserole dish and a pie plate stacked on top of one another. "What did I miss?"

"Squirrels." Aunt Prue shuffled over and looped her arm through Marian's. "What do you know about 'em?"

"All right, every one a you, clear on outta my kitchen. I need some space to work my magic, and Mercy Statham, I see you eatin' my Red Hots." Aunt Mercy stopped crunching for a second. Lena looked over at me, trying not to smile.

I could call Kitchen.

Trust me, Amma doesn't need any help when it comes to cooking. She's got some magic of her own.

Everyone crowded into the living room. Aunt Caroline and Aunt Prue were discussing how to grow persimmons on a sun porch and Aunt Grace and Aunt Mercy were still fighting over how to spell "itchin'," while Marian refereed. It was enough to make anyone crazy, but when I saw Lena wedged between the Sisters, she looked happy, even content.

This is nice.

Are you kidding?

Was this her idea of a family holiday? Casseroles and Scrabble and old ladies bickering? I wasn't sure, but I knew this was about as far from the Gathering as you could get.

At least no one is trying to kill anyone.

Give them about fifteen minutes, L.

I caught Amma's eye through the kitchen doorway, but it wasn't me she was looking at. It was Lena.

She was definitely up to something.

Thanksgiving dinner unfolded as it had every year. Except nothing was the same. My father was in pajamas, my mom's chair was empty, and I was holding hands with a Caster girl under the table. For a second, it was overwhelming—feeling happy and sad at the same time—as if they were tied together somehow. But I only had a second to think about it; we had barely said "amen" before the Sisters started swiping biscuits, Amma was spooning heaping mounds of mashed potatoes and gravy on our plates, and Aunt Caroline started with the small talk.

I knew what was going on. If there was enough work, enough talk, enough pie, maybe nobody would notice the empty chair. There wasn't enough pie in the world for that, not even in Amma's kitchen.

Either way, Aunt Caroline was determined to keep me talking. "Ethan, do you need to borrow anything for the reenactment? I've got some remarkably authentic-looking shell jackets in the attic."

"Don't remind me." I'd almost forgotten I had to dress up as a Confederate soldier for the Reenactment of the Battle of Honey Hill if I wanted to pass history this year. Every February, there was a Civil War reenactment in Gatlin; it was the only reason tourists ever showed up here.

Lena reached for a biscuit. "I don't really understand why the reenactment is such a big deal. It seems like a lot of work to re-create a battle that happened over a hundred years ago, considering we can just read about it in our history books."

Uh-oh.

Aunt Prue gasped; that was blasphemy as far as she was concerned. "They should burn that school a yours ta the ground! They're not teachin' any kind a his'try over there. You can't learn 'bout the War for Southern Independence in any textbook. You have ta see it for yourself, and every one a you kids should, because the same country that fought together in the American Revolution for independence, turned clear against itself in the War."

Ethan, say something. Change the subject.

Too late. She's going to break into the "Star Spangled Banner" any second now.

Marian split a biscuit and filled it with ham. "Miss Statham is right. The Civil War turned this country against itself, oftentimes brother against brother. It was a tragic chapter in American history. Over half a million men died, although more of them died from sickness than battle."

"A tragic chapter, that's what it was." Aunt Prue nodded.

"Now don't get all worked up, Prudence Jane." Aunt Grace patted her sister's arm.

Aunt Prue swatted her hand away. "Don't tell me when I'm worked up. I'm just tryin' ta make sure they know the pig's head from its tail. I'm the only one doin' any teachin'. That school should be payin' me."

I should have warned you not to get them started.

Now you tell me.

Lena shifted uncomfortably in her seat. "I'm sorry. I didn't mean any disrespect. I've just never known anyone who was so knowledgeable about the War."

Nice one. If by knowledgeable you mean obsessed.

"Now don't you feel bad, sweetheart. Prudence Jane just gets her britches in a twist every now and again." Aunt Grace elbowed Aunt Prue.

That's why we put whiskey in her tea.

"It's all that peanut brittle Carlton brought by." Aunt Prue looked at Lena apologetically. "I have a hard time with too much sugar."

A hard time staying away from it.

My dad coughed and absentmindedly pushed his mashed potatoes around his plate. Lena saw an opportunity to change the subject. "So Ethan says you're a writer, Mr. Wate. What kind of books do you write?"

My dad looked up at her, but didn't say anything. He probably didn't even realize Lena was talking to him.

"Mitchell's workin' on a new book. It's a big one. Maybe the most important one he's ever written. And Mitchell's written a mess a books. How many is it now, Mitchell?" Amma asked, like she was talking to a child. She knew how many books my dad had published.

"Thirteen," he mumbled.

Lena wasn't discouraged by my dad's frightening social skills, even though I was. I looked at him, hair uncombed, black circles under his eyes. When had it gotten this bad?

Lena pressed on. "What's your book about?"

My dad came back to life, animated for the first time this evening. "It's a love story. It's really been a journey, this book. The great American novel. Some might say *The Sound and the Fury* of my career, but I can't really talk about the plot. Not really. Not at this point. Not when I'm so close . . . to . . ." He was rambling. Then he just stopped talking, like someone had flipped a switch in his back. He stared at my mom's empty chair as he drifted away.

Amma looked anxious. Aunt Caroline tried to distract

everyone from what was quickly becoming the most embarrassing night of my life. "Lena, where did you say you moved here from?"

But I couldn't hear her answer. I couldn't hear anything. Instead, all I could see was everything moving in slow motion. Blurring, expanding and contracting, like the way heat waves look as they move through the air.

Then—

The room was frozen, except it wasn't. I was frozen. My father was frozen. His eyes were narrow, his lips rounded to form sounds that hadn't had a chance to escape his lips. Still staring at the plateful of mashed potatoes, untouched. The Sisters, Aunt Caroline, and Marian were like statues. Even the air was perfectly still. The pendulum of the grandfather clock had stopped in mid-swing.

Ethan? Are you all right?

I tried to answer her, but I couldn't. When Ridley had me in her death grip, I had been sure I was going to freeze to death. Now I was frozen, except I wasn't cold and I wasn't dead.

"Did I do this?" Lena asked aloud.

Only Amma could answer. "Cast a Time Bind? You? About as likely as this turkey hatchin' a gator." She snorted. "No, you didn't do this, child. This is bigger than you. The Greats figured it was time we had ourselves a talk, woman to woman. Nobody can hear us now."

Except me. I can hear you.

But the words didn't come out. I could hear them talking, but I couldn't make a sound.

Amma looked up at the ceiling, "Thank you, Aunt Delilah. 'Preciate the help." She walked over to the buffet and cut a piece of pumpkin pie. She put it on a fancy china plate and laid the plate in the center of the table. "Now I'm gonna leave this piece for you and the Greats, and you be sure to remember I did."

"What's going on? What did you do to them?"

"Didn't do anything to *them*. Just bought us some time, I reckon."

"Are you a Caster?"

"No, I'm just a Seer. I see what needs to be seen, what no one else can see, or wants to."

"Did you stop time?" Casters could do that, stop time. Lena had told me. But only incredibly powerful ones.

"I didn't do a thing. I only asked the Greats for some *assistance* and Aunt Delilah obliged."

Lena looked confused, or frightened. "Who are the Greats?"

"The Greats are my family from the Otherworld. They give me some help every now and again, and they're not alone. They've got others with them." Amma leaned across the table, looking Lena in the eye. "Why aren't you wearin' the bracelet?"

"What?"

"Didn't Melchizedek give it to you? I told him you needed to wear it."

"He gave it to me, but I took it off."

"Now why would you go and do a thing like that?"

"We figured out it was blocking the visions."

"It was blockin' somethin' all right. Until you stopped wearin' it."

"What was it blocking?"

Amma reached out and took Lena's hand in her own, turning it over to reveal her palm. "I didn't want to be the one to tell you this, child. But Melchizedek, your family, they aren't gonna tell you, not one a them. And you need to be told. You need to be prepared."

"Prepared for what?"

Amma looked at the ceiling, mumbling under her breath. "She's comin', child. She's comin' for you, and she's a force to be reckoned with. As Dark as night."

"Who? Who's coming for me?"

"I wish they'd told you themselves. I didn't want to be the one. But the Greats, they say somebody has to tell you before it's too late."

"Tell me what? Who's coming, Amma?"

Amma pulled a small pouch that was dangling from a leather cord around her neck out of her shirt and clutched it, lowering her voice like she was afraid someone might hear her. "Sarafine. The Dark One."

"Who's Sarafine?"

Amma hesitated, clutching the pouch even tighter.

"Your mamma."

"I don't understand. My parents died when I was a child, and my mother's name was Sara. I've seen it on my family tree."

"Your daddy died, that's the truth, but your mamma's alive as sure as I'm standin' here. And you know the thing about family trees down South, they're never quite as right as they claim to be."

The color drained from Lena's face. I strained to reach out and take her hand, but only my finger trembled. I was powerless. I couldn't do anything but watch as she tumbled into a dark place, alone. Just like in the dreams. "And she's Dark?"

"She's the Darkest Caster livin' today."

"Why didn't my uncle tell me? Or my gramma? They said she was dead. Why would they lie to me?"

"There's the truth and then there's the *truth*. They aren't likely the same thing. I reckon they were tryin' to protect you. They still think they can. But the Greats, they're not so sure. I didn't want to be the one to tell you, but Melchizedek's a stubborn one."

"Why are you trying to help me? I thought—I thought you didn't like me."

"Doesn't have anything to do with likin' or not likin'. She's comin' for you, and you don't need any distractions." Amma raised an eyebrow. "And I don't want anything to happen to my boy. This is bigger than you, bigger than the both a you."

"What's bigger than both of us?"

"All of it. You and Ethan just aren't meant to be."

Lena looked confused. Amma was talking in riddles again. "What do you mean?"

Amma jerked around as if someone behind her had tapped her on the shoulder. "What'd you say, Aunt Delilah?" Amma turned to Lena. "We don't have much time left."

The pendulum on the clock began to move almost imperceptibly. The room began to come back to life. My dad's eyes started to blink slowly, so that it took seconds for his lashes to brush his cheeks.

"You put that bracelet back on. You need all the help you can get."

Time snapped back into place—

I blinked a few times, glancing around the room. My father was still staring at his potatoes. Aunt Mercy was still wrapping a biscuit in her napkin. I lifted my hands in front of my face, wiggling my fingers. "What the hell was that?"

"Ethan Wate!" Aunt Grace gasped.

Amma was splitting her biscuits and filling them with ham. She looked up at me, caught off guard. It was obvious she hadn't intended for me to hear their little girl talk. She gave me the Look. Meaning, you keep your mouth shut, Ethan Wate.

"Don't you use that kinda language at my table. You're not too old for me to wash your mouth out with a bar a soap. What do you think it is? Ham and biscuits. Turkey and stuffing. Now I been cookin' all day, I expect you to eat."

I looked over at Lena. The smile was gone. She was staring at her plate.

Lena Beana. Come back to me. I won't let anything happen to you. You'll be okay.

But she was too far away.

Lena didn't say a word the whole way home. When we got to Ravenwood, she yanked open the car door, slammed it behind her, and took off toward the house without a word.

I almost didn't follow her in. My head was reeling. I couldn't imagine what Lena was feeling. It was bad enough to lose your mother, but even I couldn't guess what it would feel like to find out your mother wanted you dead.

My mother was lost to me, but I wasn't lost. She had anchored me, to Amma, my father, Link, Gatlin, before she left. I felt her in the streets, my house, the library, even the pantry. Lena had never had that. She was cut loose and coming unmoored, Amma would say, like the poor man's ferries on the swamp.

I wanted to be her anchor. But right now, I didn't think anyone could.

Lena stalked past Boo, who was sitting on the front veranda not even panting, even though he had dutifully run behind our car the whole way home. He had also sat in my front yard all through dinner. He seemed to like the sweet potatoes and little marshmallows, which I had chucked out the front door when Amma went into the kitchen for more gravy.

I could hear her shouting from inside the house. I sighed, got out of the car, and sat down on the porch steps next to the dog. My head was already pounding, a sugar low. "Uncle Macon! Uncle Macon! Wake up! The sun's down, I know you're not asleep in there!"

I could hear Lena yelling from inside my head, too.

The sun's down, I know you're not asleep!

I was waiting for the day Lena was going to spring it on me and tell me the truth about Macon, like she'd told me the truth about herself. Whatever he was, he didn't seem like an ordinary Caster, if there even was such a thing. The way he slept all day and just appeared and disappeared wherever he felt like it, you didn't need to be a genius to see where that was going. Still, I wasn't sure I wanted to go there today.

Boo stared at me. I reached out my hand to pet him, and he twisted his head away, as if to say, we're good. Please don't touch me, boy. When we heard things start to break inside, Boo and I got up and followed the noise. Lena was banging on one of the doors upstairs.

The house had reverted to what I suspected was Macon's preferred state, dilapidated antebellum finery. I was secretly relieved not to be standing in a castle. I wished I could stop time and go back three hours. To be honest, I would have been perfectly happy if Lena's house had transformed into a doublewide trailer, and we were all sitting in front of a bowl of leftover stuffing, like the rest of Gatlin.

"My mother? My own mother?"

The door flung open. Macon stood there in the doorway, a disheveled mess. He was in rumpled linen pajamas, only what it really was, I hate to say, was more of a nightdress. His eyes were redder than usual and his skin whiter, his hair tousled. He looked like he had been run over by a Mack truck.

In his own way, he wasn't all that different from my dad, a fine mess. Maybe a finer mess. Except the nightdress; my dad wouldn't be caught dead in a dress.

"My mother is Sarafine? That *thing* that tried to kill me on Halloween? How could you keep this from me?"

Macon shook his head and rubbed his hand over his hair, annoyed. "Amarie." I would've paid anything to see Macon and Amma square off in a fight. My money would be on Amma, all the way.

Macon stepped across his doorway, pulling the door shut behind him. I caught a glimpse of his bedroom. It looked like something out of *Phantom of the Opera*, with wrought iron candelabras standing taller than I was and a black four-poster bed draped with gray and black velvet. The windows were draped with the same material, hanging sullenly over the black plantation shutters. Even the walls were upholstered in fraying black and gray fabric that was probably a hundred years old. The room was pitch dark, dark as night. The effect was chilling.

Darkness, real darkness, was something more than just a lack of light.

As Macon stepped through the doorway, he emerged into the hall perfectly dressed, not a hair out of place on his head, not a wrinkle in his slacks or crisp white shirt. Even the smooth buckskin shoes were without a scuff. He looked nothing like he had a moment before, and all he'd done was step through his own bedroom door.

I looked at Lena. She hadn't even noticed, and I felt cold, remembering for a moment how different her life must have always been than mine. "My mother's alive?"

"I'm afraid it's a bit more complicated than that."

"You mean, the part about how my own mother wants to kill me? When were you going to tell me, Uncle Macon? When I was already Claimed?"

"Please don't start this again. You're not going Dark." Macon sighed.

"I can't imagine how you can think otherwise. Since I am the daughter of, and I quote, 'the Darkest Caster living today'."

"I understand you're upset. This is a lot to take in, and I should have told you myself. But you have to believe I was trying to protect you."

Lena was more than just angry now. "Protect me! You let me believe that Halloween was just some random attack, but it was my mother! My mother is alive, and she was trying to kill me, and you didn't think I should know about it?"

"We don't know that she's trying to kill you."

Picture frames started to bang against the walls. The bulbs in the fixtures lining the hallway shorted out one by one, down the length of the hallway. The sound of rain pelted the shutters.

"Haven't we had enough bad weather in the last few weeks?"

"What else have you been lying about? What am I going to find out next? That my father is alive, too?"

"I'm afraid not." He said it like it was a tragedy, something too sad to talk about. It was the same tone people used when they talked about my mother's death.

"You have to help me." Her voice was cracking.

"I will do everything in my power to help you, Lena. I always have."

"That's not true," she spat back at him. "You haven't told me about my powers. You haven't taught me how to protect myself."

"I don't know the scope of your powers. You're a Natural. When you need to do something, you'll do it. In your own way, in your own time."

"My own mother wants to kill me. I don't have any time."

"As I said before, we don't know that she's trying to kill you."

"Then how do you explain Halloween?"

"There are other possibilities. Del and I are trying to work that out." Macon turned away from her, as if he was going to go back into his room. "You need to calm down. We can talk about this later."

Lena turned toward a vase, sitting on the credenza at the end of the hall. As if pulled by a string, the vase followed her eyes to the wall next to Macon's bedroom door, flying across the room and smashing against the plaster. It was far enough from Macon to be sure it wouldn't have hit him, but close enough to make a point. It wasn't an accident.

It wasn't one of those times Lena had lost control and

things just *happened*. She had done this on purpose. She was in control.

Macon spun around so fast I didn't even see him move, but he was standing in front of Lena. He was as shocked as I was, and he had come to the same realization; it was no accident. And the look on her face told me she was just as surprised. He looked hurt, as hurt as Macon Ravenwood was capable of looking. "As I said, when you need to do something, you'll do it."

Macon turned to me. "It will be even more dangerous, I'm afraid, in the coming weeks. Things have changed. Don't leave her alone. When she is here, I can protect her, but my mother was right. It seems you can also protect her, perhaps better than I can."

"Hello? I can hear you!" Lena had recovered from her display of power and the look on Macon's face. I knew she'd torture herself over it later, but right now she was too angry to see that. "Don't talk about me like I'm not in the room."

A lightbulb exploded behind him, and he didn't even flinch.

"Are you listening to yourself? I need to know! I'm the one being hunted. I'm the one she wants, and I don't even know why."

They stared at each other, a Ravenwood and a Duchannes, two branches of the same twisted Caster tree. I wondered if this would be a good time for me to go.

Macon looked at me. His face said yes.

Lena looked at me. Hers said no.

She grabbed me by the hand, and I could feel the heat, burning. She was on fire, as angry as I'd ever seen her. I couldn't believe every window in the house hadn't blown out.

"You know why she's hunting me, don't you?"

"It's—"

"Let me guess, complicated?" The two of them stared at each other. Lena's hair was curling. Macon was twisting his silver ring.

Boo was backing away on his belly. Smart dog. I wished I could crawl out of the room, too. The last of the bulbs blew, and we were standing in the dark.

"You have to tell me everything you know about my powers." Those were her terms.

Macon sighed, and the darkness began to dissipate. "Lena. It's not as if I don't want to tell you. After your little *demonstration*, it's clear that I don't even know what you're capable of. No one does. I suspect, not even you." She wasn't completely convinced, but she was listening. "That's what it means to be a Natural. It's part of the gift."

She began to relax. The battle was over, and she had won it, for now. "Then what am I going to do?"

Macon looked distressingly like my father when he came into my room when I was in fifth grade to explain the birds and the bees. "Coming into your powers can be a very confusing time. Perhaps there is a book on the subject. If you like, we can go see Marian."

Yeah, right. *Choices and Changes. A Modern Girl's Guide to Casting. My Mom Wants to Kill Me: A Self-Help Book for Teens.*

It was going to be a long few weeks.

Domus Lunae Libri

Today? But it's not a holiday." When I opened the front door, Marian was the last person I had expected to see, standing on my doorstep in her coat. Now I was sitting with Lena on the cold bench seat of Marian's old turquoise truck, on our way to the Caster Library.

"A promise is a promise. It's the day after Thanksgiving. Black Friday. It may not seem like a holiday, but it is a bank holiday, and that's all we need." Marian was right. Amma had probably been in the line at the mall with a handful of coupons since before dawn; it was dark out now, and she still wasn't back. "The Gatlin County Library is closed, so the Caster Library is open."

"Same hours?" I asked Marian, as she turned onto Main.

She nodded. "Nine to six." Then, winking, "Nine p.m. to six a.m. Not all my clientele can venture out in the daylight."

"That hardly seems fair," complained Lena. "The Mortals get so much more time, and they don't even read around here."

Marian shrugged. "Like I said, I do get paid by Gatlin County. Take it up with them. But think how much longer you'll have until your *Lunae Libri* are due back."

I looked blank.

"*Lunae Libri.* Roughly translated, Books of the Moon. You might call them Caster Scrolls."

I didn't care what you called them. I couldn't wait to see what the books in the Caster Library would tell us, or one book in particular. Because we were short on two things: answers and time.

When we piled out of the truck, I couldn't believe where we were. Marian's truck was parked at the curb, not ten feet from the Gatlin Historical Society, or, as my mom and Marian liked to say, the Gatlin Hysterical Society. The Historical Society was also the DAR headquarters. Marian had pulled her truck forward enough to avoid the puddle of light spilling down to the pavement from the lamppost.

Boo Radley was sitting on the sidewalk, as if he had known.

"Here? The *Lunae* whatever is at the DAR headquarters?"

"*Domus Lunae Libri.* The House of *The Book of Moons. Lunae Libri,* for short. And no, just the Gatlin entrance." I burst out laughing. "You have your mother's appreciation for irony." We walked up to the deserted building. We couldn't have picked a better night.

"But it's not a joke. The Historical Society is the oldest building in the County, next to Ravenwood itself. Nothing else survived the Great Burning," Marian added.

"But the DAR and the Casters? How could they have anything in common?" Lena was dumbfounded.

"I expect you'll find they have quite a bit more in common than you think." Marian hurried toward the old stone building, drawing out her familiar key ring. "I, for example, am a member of both societies." I looked at Marian in disbelief. "I'm neutral. I thought I made myself perfectly clear. I'm not like you. You're like Lila, you get too involved. . . ." I could finish that sentence for myself. And look what happened to her.

Marian froze, but the words hung in the air. There was nothing she could say or do to take them back. I felt numb, but I didn't say anything. Lena reached for my hand, and I could feel her pulling me out of myself.

Ethan. Are you okay?

Marian looked at her watch again. "It's five to nine. Technically, I shouldn't let you in yet. But I need to be downstairs by nine, in case we have any other visitors this evening. Follow me."

We made our way into the dark yard behind the building. She fumbled through her keys until she drew out what I had always thought was a keychain, because it didn't look like a key at all. It was an iron ring, with one hinged side. With an expert hand, Marian twisted the hinge until it snapped back upon itself, turning the circle into a crescent. A Caster moon.

She pushed the key into what appeared to be an iron grating, in the foundation at the back of the building. She twisted the key, and the grating slid open. Behind the grating was a dark stone staircase leading down into even more darkness, the basement beneath the basement of the DAR. As she snapped the key one more rotation to the left, a row of torches lit themselves along the sides of the wall. Now the stairwell was fully illuminated with flickering light, and I could even see a glimpse of the words DOMUS LUNAE LIBRI etched into the stone archway of the entrance below. Marian snapped the key once more, and the stairs disappeared, replaced by the iron grating once again.

"That's it? We aren't going to go in?" Lena sounded annoyed.

Marian stuck her hand through the grating. It was an illusion. "I can't Cast, as you know, but something had to be done. Strays kept wandering in at night. Macon had Larkin rig it for me, and he stops by to keep it intact, every now and then."

Marian looked at us, suddenly somber. "All right, then. If you're sure this is what you want to do, I can't stop you. Nor can I guide you in any way, once you're downstairs. I can't prevent you from taking a book, or take one back from you before the *Lunae Libri* opens itself again."

She put her hand on my shoulder. "Do you understand, Ethan? This isn't a game. There are powerful books down there—Binding books, Caster scrolls, Dark and Light talismans, objects of power. Things no Mortal has ever seen, except me, and my predecessors. Many of the books are charmed, others are jinxed. You have to be careful. Touch nothing. Let Lena handle the books for you."

Lena's hair was waving. She was already feeling the magic of this place. I nodded, wary. What I was feeling was less magical, my stomach churning like I was the one who drank too much peppermint schnapps. I wondered how often Mrs. Lincoln and her cronies had paced back and forth on the floor above us, oblivious to what was below them.

"No matter what you find, remember we have to be out before sunrise. Nine to six. Those are the library hours, and the entrance can only be made to open during that time. The sun will rise precisely at six; it always does, on a Library Day. If you aren't up the stairs by sunrise, you will be trapped until the next Library Day, and I have no way of knowing how well a Mortal could survive that experience. Have I made myself perfectly clear?"

Lena nodded, taking my hand. "Can we go in now? I can't wait."

"I can't believe I'm doing this. Your Uncle Macon and Amma would kill me if they knew." Marian checked her watch. "After you."

"Marian? Have you—did my mother ever see this?" I couldn't let it go. I couldn't think about anything else.

Marian looked at me, her eyes strangely sparkling. "Your mother was the person who gave me the job."

And with that, she disappeared in front of us through the illusionary grating, and down into the *Lunae Libri* below. Boo Radley barked, but it was too late to turn back now.

———◌

The steps were cold and mossy, the air dank. Wet things, scurrying things, burrowing things—it wasn't hard to imagine them making themselves comfortable down here.

I tried not to think about Marian's last words. I couldn't imagine my mother coming down these stairs. I couldn't imagine her knowing anything about this world I'd just stumbled onto, more like, this world that had stumbled onto me. But she had, and I couldn't stop wondering how. Had she stumbled onto it too, or had someone invited her in? Somehow, it made it all seem more real, that my mother and I shared this secret, even if she wasn't here to share it with me.

But I was the one here now, walking down the stone steps, carved and flat like the floor of an old church. Along either side of the stairs I could see rough stone boulders, the foundations of an ancient room that had existed on the site of the DAR building, long before the structure itself had been built. I looked down the stairs, but all I could see were rough outlines, shapes in the dark. It didn't look like a library. It looked like what it probably was, what it had always been. A crypt.

At the bottom of the stairs, in the shadows of the crypt, countless tiny domes curved overhead where the columns jutted up into the vaulted ceiling, forty or fifty in all. As my eyes adjusted to the dark, I could see that each column was different, and some of them were tilted, like crooked old oaks. Their shadows made the circular chamber seem like some kind of quiet, dark forest. It was a terrifying room to be in. There was no way of knowing how far back it went, since every direction dissolved into darkness.

Marian inserted her key into the first column, marked with a moon. The torches along the walls lit themselves, illuminating the room with flickering light.

"They're beautiful," Lena breathed. I could see her hair still twisting, and wondered how this place must feel to her, in ways I could never know.

Alive. Powerful. Like the truth, every truth, is here, somewhere.

"Collected from all over the world, long before my time. Istanbul." Marian pointed to the tops of the columns, the decorated parts, the capitals. "Taken from Babylon." She pointed to another one, with four hawk heads poking out from each side. "Egypt, the Eye of God." She patted another, dramatically carved with a lion's head. "Assyria."

I felt along the wall with my hand. Even the stones of the walls were carved. Some were cut with faces, of men, creatures, birds, staring from between the forest of columns, like predators. Other stones were carved with symbols I didn't recognize, hieroglyphs of Casters and cultures I'd never know.

We moved farther into the chamber, out of the crypt, which seemed to serve as some sort of lobby, and again torches burst into flame, one after another, as if they were following us. I could see that the columns curved around a stone table in the middle of the room. The stacks, or what I guessed were the stacks, radiated out from the central circle like the spokes of a wheel, and seemed to rise up almost to the ceiling, creating a frightening maze I imagined a Mortal could get lost in. In the room itself, there was nothing but the columns, and the circular stone table.

Marian calmly picked up a torch from an iron crescent on the wall and handed it to me. She handed another to Lena, and took one for herself. "Have a look around. I have to check the mail. I may have a transfer request from another branch."

"For the *Lunae Libri*?" I hadn't considered that there might be other Caster libraries.

"Of course." Marian turned back toward the stairs.

"Wait. How do you get mail here?"

"The same way you do. Carlton Eaton delivers it, rain or shine." Carlton Eaton was in the know. Of course he was. That probably explained why he'd picked Amma up in the middle of the night. I wondered if he opened the Casters' mail, too. I wondered what else I didn't know about Gatlin, and the people in it. I didn't have to ask.

"There aren't too many of us, but more than you'd think. You have to remember, Ravenwood has been here longer than this old building. This was a Caster county before it was ever a Mortal one."

"Maybe that's why you're all so weird around here." Lena poked me. I was still stuck back on Carlton Eaton.

Who else knew what was really going on in Gatlin, in the other Gatlin, the one with magical underground libraries and girls who could control the weather or make you jump off a cliff? Who else was in the Caster loop, like Marian and Carlton Eaton? Like my mom?

Fatty? Mrs. English? Mr. Lee?

Definitely not Mr. Lee.

"Don't worry. When you need them, they'll find you. That's how it works, how it always has."

"Wait." I grabbed Marian's arm. "Does my dad know?"

"No." At least there was one person in my house who wasn't living a double life, even if he was crazy.

Marian issued a final piece of advice. "Now, you'd better get started. The *Lunae Libri* is thousands of times bigger than any library you've ever seen. If you get lost, immediately trace your steps backward. That's why the stacks radiate out from this one chamber. If you only go forward or back, you have less chance of getting lost."

"How can you get lost, if you can only go in a straight line?"

"Try it for yourself. You'll see."

Lena interrupted, "What's at the end of the stacks? I mean, at the end of the aisles?"

Marian looked at her oddly. "Nobody knows. No one has ever made it far enough to find out. Some of the aisles turn into tunnels. Parts of the *Lunae Libri* are still uncharted. There are many things down here even I've never seen. One day, perhaps."

"What are you talking about? Everything ends somewhere. There can't be rows and rows of books tunneling under the whole town. What, do you come up for tea at Mrs. Lincoln's house? Make a left turn and drop a book off to Aunt Del in the next town? Tunnel to the right for a chat with Amma?" I was skeptical.

Marian smiled at me, amused. "How do you think Macon gets his books? How do you think the DAR never sees any visitors going in or out? Gatlin is Gatlin. Folks like it fine the way it is, the way they *think* it is. Mortals only see what they want to see. There's been a thriving Caster community in and around this county since before the Civil War. That's hundreds of years, Ethan, and that's not going to change suddenly. Not just because you know about it."

"I can't believe Uncle Macon never told me about this place. Think of all the Casters that have come through here." Lena held up her torch, pulling a bound volume from the shelf. The book was ornately bound, heavy in her hands, and sent a cloud of gray dust exploding out in every direction. I started to cough.

"*Casting, A Briefe Historie.*" She drew out another. "We're in the C's, I guess." This one was a leather box that opened on top to reveal the standing scroll inside. Lena pulled out the scroll. Even the dust looked older, and grayer. "*Castyng to Creyate & Confounde.* That's an old one."

"Careful. More than a few hundred years. Gutenberg didn't invent the printing press until 1455." Marian took the scroll out of her hand gingerly, as if she was handling a newborn baby.

Lena pulled out another book, bound in gray leather. "*Casting the Confederacy.* Were there Casters in the War?"

Marian nodded. "Both sides, the Blue and the Gray. It was one of the great divisions in the Caster Community, I'm afraid. Just as it was for us Mortals."

Lena looked up at Marian, shoving the dusty book back on the shelf. "The Casters in our family, we're still in a war, aren't we?"

Marian looked at her sadly. "A House Divided, that's what President Lincoln called it. And yes, Lena, I'm afraid you are." She touched Lena's cheek. "Which is why you're here, if you recall. To find what you need, to make sense of something senseless. Now, you'd better get started."

"There are so many books, Marian. Can't you just point us in the right direction?"

"Don't look at me. Like I said, I don't have the answers, just the books. Get going. We're on the lunar clock down here, and you may lose track of time. Things aren't exactly as they seem when you're down below."

I looked from Lena to Marian. I was afraid to let either one of them out of my sight. The *Lunae Libri* was more intimidating than I had imagined. Less like a library, and more like, well, catacombs. And *The Book of Moons* could be anywhere.

Lena and I faced the endless stacks, but neither one of us took even a single step.

"How are we going to find it? There must be a million books in here."

"I have no idea. Maybe . . ." I knew what she was thinking.

"Should we try the locket?"

"Do you have it?" I nodded, and pulled the warm lump out of my jeans pocket. I handed Lena the torch.

"We need to see what happens. There has to be something else." I unwrapped the locket and placed it on the round stone table in the center of the room. I saw a familiar look in Marian's eyes, the look she and my mother shared when they dug up a particularly good find. "Do you want to see this?"

"More than you know." Marian slowly took my hand, and I took Lena's. I reached over, with my fingers intertwined with Lena's, and touched the locket.

A blinding flash forced my eyes shut.

And then I could see the smoke and smell the fire, and we were gone—

Genevieve lifted the Book so she could read the words through the rain. She knew speaking the words would defy the Natural Laws. She could almost hear her mother's voice willing her to stop—to think about the choice she was making.

But Genevieve couldn't stop. She couldn't lose Ethan.

She began to chant.

"CRUOR PECTORIS MEI, TUTELA TUA EST.
VITA VITAE MEAE, CORRIPIENS TUAM, CORRIPIENS
    MEAM.
CORPUS CORPORIS MEI, MEDULLA MENSQUE,
ANIMA ANIMAE MEAE, ANIMAM NOSTRAM
    CONECTE.

CRUOR PECTORIS MEI, LUNA MEA, AESTUS MEUS.

CRUOR PECTORIS MEI. FATUM MEUM, MEA SALUS."

"Stop, child, 'fore it's too late!" Ivy's voice was frantic.

The rain poured down and lightning sliced through the smoke. Genevieve held her breath and waited. Nothing. She must have done it wrong. She squinted to read the words more clearly in the dark. She screamed them into the darkness, in the language she knew best.

"BLOOD OF MY HEART, PROTECTION IS THINE.

LIFE OF MY LIFE, TAKING YOURS, TAKING MINE.

BODY OF MY BODY, MARROW AND MIND,

SOUL OF MY SOUL, TO OUR SPIRIT BIND.

BLOOD OF MY HEART, MY TIDES, MY MOON.

BLOOD OF MY HEART. MY SALVATION, MY DOOM."

She thought her eyes were playing tricks on her, when she saw Ethan's eyelids struggling to open.

"Ethan!" For a split second, their eyes met.

Ethan fought for breath, clearly trying to speak. Genevieve pressed her ear closer to his lips and she could feel his warm breath on her cheek.

"I never believed your daddy when he said it was impossible for a Caster and a Mortal to be together. We would have found a way. I love you, Genevieve." He pressed something into her hand. A locket.

And as suddenly as his eyes opened, they closed again, his chest failing to rise and fall.

Before Genevieve could react, a jolt of electricity surged through her body. She could feel the blood pulsing through her veins. She must have been struck by lightning. The waves of pain crashed down on her.

Genevieve tried to hold on.

Then everything went black.

"Sweet God in Heaven, don't take her, too."

Genevieve recognized Ivy's voice. Where was she? The smell brought her back. Burnt lemons. She tried to speak, but her throat felt like she had swallowed sand. Her eyes fluttered.

"Oh Lord, thank you!" Ivy was staring down at her, kneeling beside her in the dirt.

Genevieve coughed and reached for Ivy, trying to pull her closer.

"Ethan, is he . . ." she whispered.

"I'm sorry, child. He's gone."

Genevieve struggled to open her eyes. Ivy jumped back, as if she'd seen the Devil himself.

"Lord have mercy!"

"What? What's wrong, Ivy?"

The old woman struggled to make sense of what she saw. "Your eyes, child. They're . . . they've changed."

"What are you talkin' about?"

"They ain't green no more. They're yellow, as yellow as the sun."

Genevieve didn't care what color her eyes were. She didn't care about anything now that she'd lost Ethan. She started to sob.

The rain picked up, turning the ground under them to mud.

"You've got to get up, Miss Genevieve. We have to commune with the Ones in the Otherworld." Ivy tried to pull her to her feet.

"Ivy, you're not makin' sense."

"Your eyes—I warned you. I told you about that moon, no moon. We have to find out what it means. We have to consult the Spirits."

"If there's something wrong with my eyes, I'm sure it was because I was struck by lightnin'."

"What did you see?" Ivy looked panicked.

"Ivy, what's goin' on? Why are you actin' so strange?"

"You weren't struck by lightnin'. It was somethin' else."

Ivy ran back toward the burning cotton fields. Genevieve called after her, trying to get up, but she was still reeling. She leaned her head back in the thick mud, rain falling steadily on her face. Rain mixed with the tears of defeat. She drifted in and out of the moment, in and out of consciousness. She heard Ivy's voice, faint, in the distance, calling her name. When her eyes focused again, the old woman was next to her, her skirt gathered in her hands.

Ivy was carrying something in the folds of her skirt, and she dumped it out on the wet ground next to Genevieve. Tiny vials of powder and bottles of what looked like sand and dirt knocked against each other.

"What are you doin'?"

"Makin' an offerin'. To the Spirits. They're the only ones who can tell us what this means."

"Ivy, calm down. You're talkin' gibberish."

The old woman pulled something from the pocket of her housedress. It was a shard of mirror. She thrust it in front of Genevieve.

It was dark, but there was no mistaking it. Genevieve's eyes were blazing. They had turned from deep green to a fiery gold, and they didn't look like her eyes in another unmistakable way. In the center, where a round black pupil should have been, there were almond-shaped slits, like the pupils of a cat. Genevieve threw the mirror to the ground and turned to Ivy.

But the old woman wasn't paying attention. She had already mixed the powders and the earth and she was sifting them from hand to hand, whispering in the old Gullah language of her ancestors.

"Ivy, what are you—"

"Shh," the old woman hissed, "I'm listenin' to the Spirits. They know what you've done. They're gonna tell us what this means."

"From the earth a her bones and the blood a my blood." Ivy pricked her finger with the edge of the broken mirror and smeared the tiny drops of blood into the earth she was sifting. "Lemme hear what ya hear. See what ya see. Know what ya know."

Ivy stood up, arms open to the heavens. The rain poured down upon her, the dirt running down her dress in streaks. She began to speak again in the strange language and then—

313

"It can't be. She didn't know no better," she wailed at the dark sky above.

"Ivy, what is it?"

Ivy was shaking, hugging herself, and moaning, "It can't be. It can't be."

Genevieve grabbed Ivy by her shoulders. "What? What is it? What's wrong with me?"

"I told you not to mess with that book. I told you it was the wrong kinda night for Castin', but it's too late now, child. There's no way to take it back."

"What are you talkin' about?"

"You're cursed now, Miss Genevieve. You been Claimed. You've Turned, and there's nothin' we can do to stop it. A bargain. You can't get nothin' from The Book a Moons *without givin' somethin' in return."*

"What? What did I give?"

"Your fate, child. Your fate and the fate a every other Duchannes child that's born after you."

Genevieve didn't understand. But she understood enough to know that what she had done couldn't be undone. "What do you mean?"

"On the Sixteenth Moon, the Sixteenth Year, the Book will take what it's been promised. What you bargained. The blood of a Duchannes child, and that child will go Dark."

"Every Duchannes child?"

Ivy bowed her head. Genevieve wasn't the only one who was defeated on this night. "Not every one."

Genevieve looked hopeful. "Which ones? How will we know which ones?"

"The Book will choose. On the Sixteenth Moon, the child's sixteenth birthday."

"It didn't work." Lena's voice sounded strangled, far away. All I could see was smoke, and all I could hear was her voice. We weren't in the library, and we weren't in the vision. We were somewhere in between, and it was awful.

"Lena!"

And then, for a moment, I saw her face in the smoke. Her eyes were huge and dark—only now, the green looked almost black. Her voice was now more like a whisper. "Two seconds. He was alive for two seconds, and then she lost him."

She closed her eyes and disappeared.

"L! Where are you?"

"Ethan. The locket." I could hear Marian, as if from a great distance.

I could feel the hardness of the locket in my hands. I understood.

I dropped it.

I opened my eyes, coughing from the smoke still in my lungs. The room was swirling, blurry.

"What the hell are you children doing here?"

I fixed my eyes on the locket and the room came back into focus. It lay on the stone floor, looking small and harmless. Marian dropped my hand.

Macon Ravenwood stood in the middle of the crypt, his overcoat twisting around him. Amma was standing next to him, her good coat buttoned on the wrong buttons, clutching her pocketbook. I don't know who was angrier.

315

"I'm sorry, Macon. You know the rules. They asked for help, and I am Bound to give it." Marian looked stricken.

Amma was all over Marian, like she had doused our house in gasoline. "The way I see it, you're Bound to take care a Lila's boy, and Macon's niece. And I don't see how what you're doin' does either."

I waited for Macon to lay into Marian, too, but he didn't say a word. Then I realized why. He was shaking Lena. She had collapsed across the stone table in the center of the room. Her arms were spread wide, her face down against the rough stone. She didn't look conscious.

"Lena!" I pulled her into my arms, ignoring Macon, who was already next to her. Her eyes were still black, staring up at me.

"She's not dead. She's drifting. I believe I can reach her." Macon was working quietly. I could see him twisting his ring. His eyes were strangely alight.

"Lena! Come back!" I pulled her limp body into my arms, leaning her against my chest.

Macon was mumbling. I couldn't make out the words, but I could see Lena's hair begin to stir in the now familiar, supernatural wind I'd come to think of as a Casting breeze.

"Not here, Macon. Your Casting won't work here." Marian was tearing through the pages of a dusty book, her voice unsteady.

"He's not Castin', Marian. He's Travelin'. Even a Caster can't do that. Where she's gone, only Macon's kind can go. Under." Amma was trying to be reassuring, but she wasn't very convincing.

I felt the cold settling over Lena's empty body and knew

Amma was right. Wherever Lena was, it wasn't in my arms. She was far away. I could feel it myself, and I was just a Mortal.

"I told you, Macon. This is a neutral place. There is no Binding you can work in a room of earth." Marian was pacing, clutching the book as if it made her feel like she was helping in some way. But there were no answers inside. She had said it herself. Casting couldn't help us here.

I remembered the dreams, remembered pulling Lena through the mud. I wondered if this was the place where I lost her.

Macon spoke. His eyes were open, but he wasn't seeing. It was like they were turned inward, to wherever Lena was. "Lena. Listen to me. She can't hold you."

She. I stared into Lena's empty eyes.

Sarafine.

"You're strong, Lena; break through. She knows I can't help you here. She was waiting for you in the shadows. You have to do this yourself."

Marian appeared with a glass of water. Macon poured it onto Lena's face, into her mouth, but she didn't move.

I couldn't stand it anymore.

I grabbed her mouth and kissed her, hard. The water dribbled out of our mouths, like I was giving mouth-to-mouth to a drowning victim.

Wake up, L. You can't leave me now. Not like this. I need you more than she does.

Lena's eyelids fluttered.

Ethan. I'm tired.

She sputtered back to life, choking, spitting water across her jacket. I smiled in spite of everything, and she smiled back at me. If this was what the dreams were about, we had changed the way they ended. This time, I had held on. But in the back of my mind, I think I knew. This wasn't the moment when she slipped out of my arms. It was only the beginning.

Even if that was true, I had saved her this time.

I reached down to pull her into my arms. I wanted to feel the familiar current between us. Before I could wrap my arms around her, she jerked up and out of my arms. "Uncle Macon!"

Macon stood across the room, propped against the crypt wall, barely able to support his own weight. He leaned his head back against the stone. He was sweating, breathing heavily, and his face was chalk white.

Lena ran and clung to him, a child worried for her father. "You shouldn't have done that. She could have killed you." Whatever he was doing when he was Traveling, whatever that meant, the effort had cost him.

So this was Sarafine. This thing, whoever She was, was Lena's mother.

If this was a trip to the library, I didn't know if I was ready for what might happen in the next few months.

Or as of tomorrow morning, 74 days.

———

Lena sat, still dripping wet, wrapped in a blanket. She looked about five years old. I glanced at the old oaken door behind her, wondering if I could ever find my way out alone. Unlikely. We'd gone about thirty paces down one of the aisles, and then disappeared down a stairwell, through a series of small doors, into a cozy study that was apparently some sort of reading room. The passageway had seemed endless, with a door every few feet like some sort of underground hotel.

The moment Macon sat down, a silver tea service appeared in the center of the table, with exactly five cups and a platter of sweet breads. Maybe Kitchen was here, too.

I looked around. I had no idea where I was, but I knew one thing. I was somewhere in Gatlin, yet somewhere further away from Gatlin than I'd ever been.

Either way, I was out of my league.

I tried to find a comfortable spot in an upholstered chair that looked like it could have belonged to Henry VIII. Actually, there was no way of knowing that it hadn't. The tapestry on the wall also looked as if had come from an old castle, or Ravenwood. It was woven into the shape of a constellation, midnight blue and silver thread. Every time I looked at it, the moon appeared in a different stage.

Macon, Marian, and Amma sat across the table. Saying Lena and I were in trouble was putting the best possible spin on it. Macon was furious, his teacup rattling in front of him. Amma was beyond that. "What makes you think you can take it upon yourself to decide when my boy is ready for the Underground? Lila would skin you herself, if she was here. You've got some nerve, Marian Ashcroft."

Marian's hands were shaking as she lifted her teacup.

"Your boy? What about my niece? Since I believe she was the one who was attacked." Macon and Amma, having ripped us to shreds, were starting in on each other. I didn't dare look at Lena.

"You've been trouble since the day you were born, Macon." Amma turned to Lena. "But I can't believe you would drag my boy into this, Lena Duchannes."

Lena lost it. "Of course I dragged him into this. I do bad things. When are you going to understand that? And it's only going to get worse!"

The tea set flew off the table and into the air, where it froze. Macon looked at it, without so much as blinking. A challenge. The entire set righted itself and landed gently back on the table. Lena looked at Macon as if there were no one else in the room. "I'm going to go Dark, and there's nothing you can do to stop it."

"That's not true."

"Isn't it? I'm going to end up just like my—" She couldn't say it.

The blanket fell from her shoulders, and she took my hand. "You have to get away from me, Ethan. Before it's too late."

Macon looked at her, irritated. "You're not going to go Dark. Don't be so gullible. She only wants you to think that." The way he said *She* reminded me of the way he said *Gatlin.*

Marian put her teacup down on the table. "Teenagers— everything is so apocalyptic."

Amma shook her head. "Some things are meant to be and some take some doin'. This one isn't done just yet."

I could feel Lena's hand shaking in mine. "They're right, L. Everything's going to be okay."

She yanked her hand away. "Everything's going to be okay? My mother, a Cataclyst, is trying to kill me. A vision from a hundred years ago just clarified that my whole family has been cursed since the Civil War. My sixteenth birthday is in two months, and that's the best you can do?"

I took her hand again, gently, because she let me. "I saw the same vision you did. The Book chooses who it takes. Maybe it won't choose you." I was clutching at straws, but they were all I had.

Amma looked at Marian, slamming her saucer on the table. The cup rattled against it.

"The Book?" Macon's eyes drilled down on me.

I tried to look him in the eye, but I couldn't do it. "The Book in the vision."

Don't say another word, Ethan.

We should tell them. We can't do this alone.

"It's nothing, Uncle M. We don't even know what the visions mean." Lena wasn't going to give in, but after tonight I felt like I had to. We had to. Everything was spiraling out of control. I felt like I was drowning and I couldn't even save myself, let alone Lena.

"Maybe the visions mean not everyone in your family goes Dark when they're Claimed. What about Aunt Del? Reece? Think cute little Ryan is going to the dark side when she can heal people?" I said, moving closer to her.

Lena shrank back into her chair. "You don't know anything about my family."

"But he's not wrong, Lena." Macon looked at her, exasperated.

"You're not Ridley. And you're not your mother," I said, as convincingly as I could.

"How do you know? You've never even met my mother. And by the way, neither have I, except in psychic attacks that no one can seem to prevent."

Macon tried to sound reassuring. "We were unprepared for these sorts of attacks. I didn't know she could Travel. I didn't know she shared some of my powers. It is not a gift afforded to Casters."

"Nobody seems to know anything about my mother, or me."

"That's why we need the Book." This time, I looked right at Macon as I said it.

"What is this book you keep talking about?" Macon was losing his patience.

Don't tell him, Ethan.

We have to.

"The Book that cursed Genevieve." Macon and Amma looked at each other. They already knew what I was going to say. "*The Book of Moons.* If that's how the curse was Cast, something in it should tell us how to break it. Right?" The room fell silent.

Marian looked at Macon. "Macon—"

"Marian. Stay out of this. You've interfered more than enough already, and the sun will rise just minutes from now." Marian knew. She knew where to find *The Book of Moons*, and Macon wanted to make sure she kept her mouth shut.

"Aunt Marian, where's the Book?" I looked her in the eye. "You have to help us. My mom would've helped us, and you're not supposed to take sides, right?" I wasn't playing fair, but it was true.

Amma raised her hands, then dropped them into her lap. A rare sign of surrender. "What's done is done. They've already started pullin' the thread, Melchizedek. That old sweater's bound to unravel, anyhow."

"Macon, there are *protocols*. If they ask, I'm Bound to tell them," Marian said. Then she looked up at me. "*The Book of Moons* isn't in the *Lunae Libri*."

"How do you know?"

Macon stood to leave, turning to both of us. His jaw was clenched, his eyes dark and angry. When he finally spoke, his voice echoed over the chamber, over all of us. "Because that's the book for which this archive was named. It is the most powerful book from here to the Otherworld. It is also the book that cursed our family, for eternity. And it's been missing for over a hundred years."

⊰ 12.01 ⊱

It Rhymes with Witch

O n Monday morning, Link and I drove down Route 9, stopping at the fork in the road to pick up Lena. Link liked Lena, but there was no way he was driving up to Ravenwood Manor. It was still the Haunted Mansion to him.

If he only knew. Thanksgiving break had only been a long weekend, but it felt a lot longer, considering that Twilight Zone of a Thanksgiving dinner, the vases flying between Macon and Lena, and our journey to the center of the earth, all without leaving the Gatlin city limits. Unlike Link, who had spent the weekend watching football, beating up his cousins, and trying to determine whether or not the cheese ball had onions in it this year.

But according to Link, there was trouble of another kind brewing, and this morning it sounded equally dangerous. Link's mom had been burning up the lines for the last twenty-four hours, whispering on the phone with the long cord and the kitchen door closed. Mrs. Snow and Mrs. Asher had shown up after dinner, and the three of them had disappeared into the kitchen—the War Room. When Link went in, pretending to grab a Mountain Dew, he didn't catch much. But it was enough to figure out his mom's end game. "We'll get her outta our school, one way or another." And her little dog, too.

It wasn't much, but if I knew Mrs. Lincoln, I knew enough to be worried. You could never underestimate the lengths women like Mrs. Lincoln would go to protect their children and their town from the one thing they hated most—anyone different from them. I should know. My mom had told me the stories about the first few years she'd lived here. The way she told it, she was such a criminal even the most God-fearing church ladies got bored of reporting on her; she did the marketing on Sunday, dropped by any church she liked or none at all, was a feminist (which Mrs. Asher sometimes confused with communist), a Democrat (which Mrs. Lincoln pointed out practically had "demon" in the word itself), and worst of all, a vegetarian (which ruled out any dinner invitations from Mrs. Snow). Beyond that, beyond not being a member of the right church or the DAR or the National Rifle Association, was the fact that my mom was an outsider.

But my dad had grown up here and was considered one of Gatlin's sons. So when my mom died, all the same women who had been so judgmental of her when she was alive dropped off cream-of-something casseroles and crock pot roasts and chili-ghetti with a vengeance. Like they were finally getting the last word. My mom would have hated it, and they knew it. That was the first time my dad went into his study and locked the door for days. Amma and I had let the casseroles pile up on the porch until they took them away and went back to judging us, like they always had.

They always got the last word. Link and I both knew it, even if Lena didn't.

Lena was sandwiched between Link and me in the front seat of the Beater, writing on her hand. I could just make out the words *shattered like everything else.* She wrote all the time, the way some people chewed gum or twirled their hair; I don't even think she realized it. I wondered if she would ever let me read one of her poems, if any of them were about me.

Link glanced down. "When are you gonna write me a song?"

"Right after I finish the one I'm writing for Bob Dylan."

"Holy crap." Link slammed on the brakes at the front entrance of the parking lot. I couldn't blame him. The sight of his mother in the parking lot before eight in the morning was terrifying. And there she was.

The parking lot was crowded with people, way more than usual. And parents; other than after the window incident, there hadn't been a parent in the parking lot since Jocelyn Walker's mom came to yank her out of school during the film about the reproductive cycle in Human Development.

Something was definitely going on.

Link's mom handed a box to Emily, who had the whole cheerleading squad—Varsity and JV—papering every car in the parking lot with some kind of neon flyer. Some were flapping in the wind, but I could make out a few from the relative safety of the Beater. It was like they were running some kind of campaign, only without a candidate.

SAY NO TO VIOLENCE AT JACKSON!

ZERO TOLERANCE!

Link turned bright red. "Sorry. You guys gotta get out." He crouched down in the driver's seat, so low it looked like nobody was driving the car. "I don't want my mom to beat the crap outta me in front a the whole cheerleadin' squad."

I slunk down, reaching across the seat to open the door for Lena. "We'll see you inside, man."

I grabbed Lena's hand and squeezed it.

Ready?

As ready as I'm going to be.

We ducked down between the cars around the side of the lot. We couldn't see Emily, but we could hear her voice from behind Emory's pickup.

"Know the signs!" Emily was approaching Carrie Jensen's window. "We're formin' a new club at school, the Jackson High Guardian Angels. We're goin' to help keep our school safe by reportin' acts a violence or any *unusual* behavior we see around school. Personally, I think it's the responsibility a every student at Jackson to keep our school safe. If you want to join, we're havin' a meetin' in the cafeteria after eighth period." As Emily's voice faded in the distance, Lena's hand tightened around mine.

What does that even mean?

I have no idea. But they've totally lost it. Come on.

I tried to pull her up, but she pulled me back down. She shrunk back next to the tire. "I just need a minute."

"Are you okay?"

"Look at them. They think I'm a monster. They formed a club."

"They just can't stand outsiders, and you're the new girl. A window broke. They need someone to blame. This is just a—"

"Witch hunt."

I wasn't going to say that.

But you were thinking it.

I squeezed her hand and my hair stood on end.

You don't have to do this.

Yes I do. I let people like them run me out of my last school. I'm not going to let it happen again.

As we stepped out from the last row of cars, there they were. Mrs. Asher and Emily were packing the extra boxes of flyers into the back of their minivan. Eden and Savannah were handing out flyers to the cheerleaders and any guy who wanted to see a little of Savannah's legs or her cleavage. Mrs. Lincoln was a few feet away talking to the other mothers, most likely promising to add their houses to the Southern Heritage Tour if they made a couple of phone calls to Principal Harper. She handed Earl Petty's mom a clipboard with a pen attached to it. It took me a minute to realize what it was—there was no way.

It looked like a petition.

Mrs. Lincoln noticed us standing there and zeroed in on us. The other mothers followed her gaze. For a second, they didn't say anything. I thought maybe they felt bad for me and they were going to put down their flyers, pack up their minivans and station wagons, and go home. Mrs. Lincoln, whose house I'd slept at almost as many times as my own. Mrs. Snow, who was technically my third cousin to some degree removed. Mrs. Asher, who bandaged my hand after I sliced it open on a fishing hook when I was ten. Miss Ellery, who gave me my first real haircut. These women knew me. They'd known me since I was a kid. There was no way they were going to do this, not to me. They were going to back down.

If I said it enough times maybe it would be true.

It's going to be okay.

By the time I realized I was wrong, it was too late. They recovered from the momentary shock of seeing Lena and me.

When Mrs. Lincoln saw us, her eyes narrowed. "Principal Harper—" She looked from Lena to me, and shook her head. Let's just say I wouldn't be invited to Link's for dinner again anytime soon. She raised her voice. "Principal Harper has promised his full support. We won't tolerate the violence at Jackson that has plagued the city schools in this country. You young people are doin' the right thing, protectin' your school, and as concerned parents" —she looked at us— "we'll do *anything* we can to support you."

Still holding hands, Lena and I walked past them. Emily stepped in front of us, shoving a flyer at me and ignoring Lena. "Ethan, come to the meetin' today. The Guardian Angels could really use you."

It was the first time she had spoken to me in weeks. I got the message. You're one of us, last chance.

I pushed her hand away. "That's just what Jackson needs, a little more of your *angelic* behavior. Why don't you go torture some children. Rip the wings off a butterfly. Knock a baby bird out of its nest." I pulled Lena past her.

"What would your poor mamma say, Ethan Wate? What would she think about the company you're keepin'?" I turned around. Mrs. Lincoln was standing right behind me. She was dressed the way she always was, like some kind of punishing librarian out of a movie, with cheap drugstore glasses and angry-looking hair that couldn't decide if it was brown or gray. You had to wonder, where did Link come from? "I'll tell you what your mamma would say. She would cry. She would be turnin' over in her grave."

She had crossed the line.

Mrs. Lincoln didn't know anything about my mother. She didn't know my mom was the one who had sent the School Superintendent a copy of every ruling against book banning in the U.S. She didn't know my mom cringed every time Mrs. Lincoln invited her to a Women's Auxiliary or DAR meeting. Not because my mom hated the Women's Auxiliary or the DAR, but because she hated what Mrs. Lincoln stood for. That small-minded brand of superiority women in Gatlin, like Mrs. Lincoln and Mrs. Asher, were so famous for.

My mom had always said, "The right thing and the easy thing are never the same." And now, at this very second, I knew the right thing to do, even if it wasn't going to be easy. Or at least, the fallout wasn't going to be.

I turned to Mrs. Lincoln and looked her in the eye. "'Good for you, Ethan.' That's what my poor mamma would've said. Ma'am."

I turned back toward the door of the administration building and kept walking, pulling Lena along beside me. We were only a few feet away. Lena was shaking, even though she didn't look scared. I kept squeezing her hand, trying to reassure her. Her long black hair was curling and uncurling, as if she was about to explode, or maybe I was. I never thought I'd be so happy to set foot in the halls of Jackson, until I saw Principal Harper standing in the doorway. He was glaring at us like he wished he wasn't the principal so he could pass out a flyer of his own.

Lena's hair blew around her shoulders as we walked past him. Only he didn't even look at us. He was too busy looking past us. "What the—"

I turned and looked over my shoulder just in time to see hundreds of neon green flyers, curling away from windshields and out of stacks and boxes and vans and hands. Flying away in a sudden gust of wind, as if they were a flock of birds soaring into the clouds. Escaping and beautiful and free. Kind of like that Hitchcock movie *The Birds*, only in reverse.

We could hear the shrieking until the heavy metal doors closed behind us.

Lena smoothed her hair. "Crazy weather you have down here."

⊰ 12.06 ⊱

Lost and Found

I was almost relieved it was Saturday. There was something comforting about spending the day with women whose only magical powers were forgetting their own names. When I arrived at the Sisters', Aunt Mercy's Siamese cat, Lucille Ball—the Sisters loved *I Love Lucy*—was "exercising" in the front yard. The Sisters had a clothesline that ran the length of the yard, and every morning Aunt Mercy put Lucille Ball on a leash and hooked it onto the clothesline so the cat could exercise. I had tried to explain that you could let cats outside and they would come back whenever they felt like it, but Aunt Mercy had looked at me like I'd suggested she shack up with a married man. "I can't just let Lucille Ball wander the streets alone. I'm sure someone would snatch her." There hadn't been a lot of catnappings in town, but it was an argument I'd never win.

I opened the door, expecting the usual commotion, but today the house was noticeably quiet. A bad sign. "Aunt Prue?"

I heard her familiar drawl coming from the back of the house. "We're on the sun porch, Ethan."

I ducked under the doorway of the screened-in porch to see the Sisters scuttling around the room, carrying what looked like little hairless rats.

"What the heck are those?" I said without even thinking.

"Ethan Wate, you watch your mouth, or I'll have ta wash it out with soap. You know better than ta use pro-fanity," Aunt Grace said. Which, as far as she was concerned, included words like *panties, naked,* and *bladder.*

"I'm sorry, ma'am. But what is that you've got in your hand?"

Aunt Mercy rushed forward and thrust her hand out, with two little rodents sleeping in it. "They're baby squirrels. Ruby Wilcox found them in her attic last Tuesday."

"Wild squirrels?"

"There are six of 'em. Aren't they just the cutest things you ever saw?"

All I could see was an accident waiting to happen. The idea of my ancient aunts handling wild animals, babies or otherwise, was a frightening thought. "Where did you get them?"

"Well, Ruby couldn't take care of 'em—" Aunt Mercy started.

"On account a that awful husban' a hers. He won't even let her go ta the Stop & Shop without tellin' him."

"So Ruby gave them ta us, on account a the fact that we already had a cage."

The Sisters had rescued an injured raccoon after a hurricane and nursed it back to health. Afterward, the raccoon ate Aunt

Prudence's lovebirds, Sonny and Cher, and Thelma put the raccoon out of the house, never to be spoken of again. But they still had the cage.

"You know squirrels can carry rabies. You can't handle these things. What if one of them bites you?"

Aunt Prue frowned. "Ethan, these are our babies and they are just the sweetest things. They wouldn't bite us. We're their mammas."

"They are just as tame as they can be, aren't y'all?" Aunt Grace said, nuzzling one of them.

All I could imagine was one of those little vermin latching onto one of the Sisters' necks and me having to drive them to the emergency room to get the twenty shots in the stomach you have to get if you're bitten by a rabid animal. Shots that I'm sure at their age might kill any one of them.

I tried to reason with them, a complete waste of time. "You never know. They're wild animals."

"Ethan Wate, clearly you are *not* an animal lover. These babies would never hurt us." Aunt Grace scowled at me disapprovingly. "And what would you have us do with 'em? Their mamma is gone. They'll die if we don't take care of 'em."

"I can take them over to the ASPCA."

Aunt Mercy clutched them against her chest protectively. "The ASPCA! Those murderers. They'll kill 'em for sure!"

"That's enough talk about the ASPCA. Ethan, hand me that eye dropper over there."

"What for?"

"We have ta feed them every four hours with this little dropper," Aunt Grace explained. Aunt Prue was holding one of the squirrels in her hand, while it sucked ferociously on the end of the dropper. "And once a day, we have ta clean their little private parts with a Q-tip, so they'll learn ta clean themselves." That was a visual I didn't need.

"How could you possibly know that?"

"We looked it up on the E-nternet." Aunt Mercy smiled proudly.

I couldn't imagine how my aunts knew anything about the Internet. The Sisters didn't even own a toaster oven. "How did you get on the Internet?"

"Thelma took us ta the library and Miss Marian helped us. They have computers over there. Did you know that?"

"And you can look up just about anything, even dirty pictures. Every now and again, the dirtiest pictures you ever saw would pop up on the screen. Imagine!" By "dirty," Aunt Grace probably meant naked, which I would've thought would keep them off the Internet forever.

"I just want to go on record as saying I think this is a bad idea. You can't keep them forever. They're going to get bigger and more aggressive."

"Well, of course we aren't plannin' on lookin' after 'em forever." Aunt Prue was shaking her head, as if it was a ridiculous thought. "We're going ta let 'em go in the backyard just as soon as they can look after themselves."

"But they won't know how to find food. That's why it's a bad idea to take in wild animals. Once you let them go, they'll starve." This seemed like an argument that would appeal to the Sisters and keep me out of the emergency room.

"That's where you're wrong. It tells all about that on the E-nternet," Aunt Grace said. Where was this Web site about raising wild squirrels and cleaning their private parts with Q-tips?

"You have ta teach 'em ta gather nuts. You bury nuts in the yard and you let the squirrels practice findin' 'em."

I could see where this was going. Which led to the part of the day that had me in the backyard burying mixed cocktail nuts for baby squirrels. I wondered how many of these little holes I'd have to dig before the Sisters would be satisfied.

A half hour into my digging, I started finding things. A thimble, a silver spoon, and an amethyst ring that didn't look particularly valuable, but gave me a good excuse to stop hiding peanuts in the backyard. When I came back into the house, Aunt Prue was wearing her extra thick reading glasses, laboring over a pile of yellowed papers. "What are you reading?"

"I'm just lookin' up some things for your friend Link's mamma. The DAR needs some notes on Gatlin's hist'ry for the Southern Heritage Tour." She shuffled through one of the piles. "But it's hard ta find much about the hist'ry a Gatlin that doesn't include the Ravenwoods." Which was the last name the DAR wanted to hear.

"What do you mean?"

"Well, without them, I reckon Gatlin wouldn't be here at all. So it's hard ta write a town hist'ry and leave 'em outta it."

"Were they really the first ones here?" I had heard Marian say it, but it was hard to believe.

Aunt Mercy lifted one of the papers out of the pile and held it so close to her face she must have been seeing double. Aunt Prue snatched it back. "Give me that. I've got myself a system goin'."

"Well, if you don't want any help." Aunt Mercy turned back to me. "The Ravenwoods were the first in these parts, all right. Got themselves a land grant from the King a Scotland, sometime around 1800."

"1781. I've got the paper right here." Aunt Prue waved a yellow sheet in the air. "They were farmers, and it turned out Gatlin County had the most fertile soil in all a South Carolina. Cotton, tobacco, rice, indigo—it all grew here, which was peculiar on account a those crops don't usually grow in the same place. Once folks figured out you could grow just 'bout anything here, the Ravenwoods had themselves a town."

"Whether they liked it or not," Aunt Grace added, looking up from her cross-stitch.

It was ironic; without the Ravenwoods Gatlin might not even exist. The folks that shunned Macon Ravenwood and his family had them to thank for the fact they even had a town at all. I wondered how Mrs. Lincoln would feel about that. I bet she already knew, and it had something to do with why they all hated Macon Ravenwood so much.

I stared down at my hand, covered in that inexplicably fertile soil. I was still holding the junk I'd unearthed in the backyard.

"Aunt Prue, does this belong to one of you?" I rinsed the ring off in the sink and held it up.

"Why, that's the ring my second husband Wallace Pritchard gave me for our first, and only, weddin' anniversary." She dropped her voice to a whisper. "He was a cheap, cheap man. Where in the world did you find it?"

"Buried in the backyard. I also found a spoon and a thimble."

"Mercy, look what Ethan found, your Tennessee Collector's spoon. I told you I didn't take it!" Aunt Prue hollered.

"Let me see that." Mercy put her glasses on to inspect the spoon. "Well, I'll be. I finally have all eleven states."

"There are more than eleven states, Aunt Mercy."

"I only collect the states a the Confed'racy." Aunt Grace and Aunt Prue nodded in agreement.

"Speakin' a buryin' things, can you believe that Eunice Honeycutt made 'em bury her with her recipe book? She didn't want anyone in church ta get her hands on her cobbler recipe." Aunt Mercy shook her head.

"She was a spiteful thing, just like her sister." Aunt Grace was prying open a Whitman's Sampler with the Tennessee Collector's spoon.

"And that recipe wasn't any good, anyhow," said Aunt Mercy.

Aunt Grace turned the lid over on the Whitman's Sampler so she could read the names of the candies inside. "Mercy, which one is the butter cream?"

"When I die, I want ta be buried with my fur stole and my Bible," Aunt Prue said.

"You aren't goin' ta get extra points with the Good Lord for that, Prudence Jane."

"I'm not tryin' ta get points, I just want ta have somethin' ta read durin' the wait. But if there were points bein' handed out, Grace Ann, I'd have more than you."

Buried with her recipe book . . .

What if *The Book of Moons* was buried somewhere? What if someone didn't want anyone to find it, so they hid it? Maybe the person who understood its power better than anyone else. Genevieve.

Lena, I think I know where the Book is.

For a second, there was only silence, and then Lena's thoughts found her way to mine.

What are you talking about?

338

The Book of Moons. *I think it's with Genevieve.*

Genevieve is dead.

I know.

What are you saying, Ethan?

I think you know what I'm saying.

Harlon James limped up to the table, looking pitiful. His leg was still wrapped in bandages. Aunt Mercy started feeding him the dark chocolates out of the box.

"Mercy, don't feed that dog chocolate! You'll kill him. I saw it on the Oprah show. Chocolate, or was it onion dip?"

"Ethan, you want me ta save you the toffees?" Aunt Mercy asked. "Ethan?"

I wasn't listening anymore. I was thinking about how to dig up a grave.

Grave Digging

It was Lena's idea. Today was Aunt Del's birthday, and at the last minute, Lena decided to throw a family party at Ravenwood. It was also Lena who invited Amma, knowing full well nothing short of divine intervention could get Amma to set foot through the door of Ravenwood Manor. Whatever it was about Macon, Amma reacted only slightly better to his presence than she did to the locket. And she preferred to keep Macon just as far away.

Boo Radley had shown up in the afternoon with a scroll in his mouth, lettered in careful calligraphy. Amma wouldn't touch the thing, even if it was an invitation, and almost didn't let me go. Good thing she didn't see me get into the hearse with my mom's old garden shovel. That would have raised a flag or two.

I was glad to get out of my house, for any reason, even if the reason involved grave robbing. After Thanksgiving, my father had shut himself in the study, and since Macon and Amma caught us at the *Lunae Libri*, all I was getting from Amma was stinkeye.

Lena and I weren't allowed to go back to the *Lunae Libri*, either, at least, not for the next sixty-eight days. Macon and Amma didn't seem to want us digging up any more information they hadn't planned on telling us in the first place.

"After the eleventh a February, you can do what you like," Amma had harrumphed. "Until then, you can do what everyone else your age does. Listen to music. Watch the television. Just keep your nose away from those books."

My mom would have laughed, the idea that I wasn't allowed to read a book. Things had obviously gotten pretty bad around here.

It's worse here, Ethan. Boo even sleeps at the foot of my bed now.

That doesn't sound so bad to me.

He waits for me outside the bathroom door.

That's just Macon being Macon.

It's like house arrest.

It was, and we both knew it.

We had to find *The Book of Moons*, and it had to be with Genevieve. It was more than possible Genevieve had been buried at Greenbrier. There were some weathered headstones in the clearing just outside the garden. You could see them from the stone where we usually sat, which had turned out to be a hearthstone. Our spot, that's how I thought of it, even if I had never said it out loud. Genevieve had to be buried out there, unless she'd moved away after the War, but nobody ever left Gatlin.

I always thought I'd be the first.

But now that I had gotten out of the house, how was I going to find a lost Casting book that may or may not save Lena's life, that may or may not be buried in the grave of a cursed ancestral Caster, that may or may not be next door to Macon Ravenwood's house? Without her uncle seeing me, stopping me, or killing me first?

The rest was up to Lena.

—⟨⟩

"What sort of history project requires visiting a graveyard at night?" Aunt Del asked, tripping over a bramble of vines. "Oh my!"

"Mamma, be careful." Reece looped her arm through her mother's, helping her negotiate the overgrowth. Aunt Del had a hard enough time walking around without bumping into anything in the daylight, but in the dark it was asking too much.

"We have to make a rubbing from one of our ancestors' tombstones. We're studying genealogy." Well, that was sort of true.

"Why Genevieve?" Reece asked, looking suspicious.

Reece looked at Lena, but Lena immediately turned away. Lena had warned me not to let Reece see my face. Apparently, one look was all it took for a Sybil to know if you were lying. Lying to a Sybil was even trickier than lying to Amma.

"She's the one in the painting, in the hall. I just thought it would be cool to use her. It's not like we have a big family cemetery to choose from, like most people around here."

The hypnotic Caster music from the party was starting to fade in the distance, replaced by the sound of dry leaves crackling under our feet. We had crossed over into Greenbrier. We

342

were getting close. It was dark, but the full moon was so bright we didn't even need our flashlights. I remembered what Amma had said to Macon at the graveyard. *Half moon's for workin' White magic, full moon's for workin' Black.* We weren't going to be working any magic, I hoped, but it didn't make it seem any less spooky.

"I'm not sure Macon would want us wandering out here in the dark. Did you tell him where we were going?" Aunt Del was apprehensive. She pulled on the collar of her high-necked lace blouse.

"I told him we were going for a walk. He just told me to stay with you."

"I don't know that I'm in good enough shape for this. I have to admit, I'm a bit winded." Aunt Del was out of breath, and the hair around her face had escaped from her always slightly off-center bun.

Then I smelled that familiar scent. "We're here."

"Thank goodness."

We walked toward the crumbling stone wall of the garden, where I'd found Lena crying the day the window shattered. I ducked under the archway of vines, into the garden. It looked different at night, less like a spot for cloud gazing and more like the place a cursed Caster would be buried.

This is it, Ethan. She's here. I can feel it.

Me, too.

Where do you think her grave is?

As we crossed over the hearthstone where I'd found the locket, I could see another stone in the clearing a few yards just beyond it. A headstone, with a hazy looking figure sitting on it.

I heard Lena gasp, just barely loud enough for me to hear.

Ethan, can you see her?

Yeah.

Genevieve. She was only partially materialized, a mix of cloudy haze and light, fading in and out as the air moved through her ghostly form, but there was no mistaking it. It was Genevieve, the woman in the painting. She had the same golden eyes and long, wavy red hair. Her hair blew gently in the wind, as if she was just a woman sitting on a bench at the bus stop, instead of an apparition sitting on a headstone in a graveyard. She was beautiful, even in her present state, and terrifying at the same time. The hair on the back of my neck stood on end.

Maybe this was a mistake.

Aunt Del stopped dead in her tracks. She saw Genevieve, too, but it was clear she didn't think anyone else could see her. She probably thought the apparition was just the result of seeing too many times at once, the muddled images of this place in twenty different decades.

"I think we should go back to the house. I'm not feeling very well." Aunt Del clearly didn't want to mess with a hundred-and-fifty-year-old ghost in a Caster graveyard.

Lena tripped over a loose vine and stumbled. I grabbed her arm to catch her, but I wasn't fast enough. "Are you okay?"

She caught herself and looked up at me for a split second, but a split second was all Reece needed. She zeroed in on Lena's eyes, looking into her face, her expression, her thoughts.

"Mamma, they're lyin'! They aren't doin' a history project at all. They're lookin' for somethin'." Reece put her hand to her temple as if she was adjusting a piece of equipment. "A book!"

Aunt Del looked confused, even more confused than she usually looked. "What sort of book would you be looking for in a graveyard?"

Lena broke away from Reece's gaze and her hold. "It's a book that belonged to Genevieve."

I unzipped the duffel bag I'd been carrying and pulled out a shovel. I walked toward the grave slowly, trying to ignore the fact that Genevieve's ghost was watching me the whole time. Maybe I was going to get struck by lightning or something; it wouldn't have surprised me. But we'd come this far. I pushed the shovel into the ground, scooping out a pile of earth.

"Oh, Great Mother! Ethan, what are you doing?" Apparently, grave digging brought Aunt Del back to the present.

"I'm looking for the book."

"In there?" Aunt Del looked faint. "What sort of book would be in there?"

"It's a Casting book, a really old one. We don't even know if it's in there. It's just a hunch," Lena said, glancing at Genevieve, who was still perched on the tombstone only a foot away.

I tried not to look at Genevieve. It was disturbing the way her body faded in and out, and she stared at us with those creepy golden cat eyes, vacant and lifeless like they were made of glass.

The ground wasn't that hard, especially considering it was December. Within a few minutes, I had already dug a foot deep. Aunt Del was pacing back and forth, looking worried. Every once in a while, she'd look around to be sure none of us were watching, then she'd glance over at Genevieve. At least I wasn't the only one freaked out about her.

345

"We should go back. This is disgustin'," Reece said, trying to make eye contact with me.

"Don't be such a Girl Scout," Lena said, kneeling over the hole.

Does Reece see her?

I don't think so. Just don't make eye contact with her.

What if Reece reads Aunt Del's face?

She can't. No one can. Aunt Del sees too much at once. No one but a Palimpsest can process all that information and make any sense of it.

"Mamma, are you really going to let them dig up a grave?"

"For star's sake, this is ridiculous. Let's stop this foolishness right now and go back to the party."

"We can't. We have to know if the book is down there." Lena turned to Aunt Del. "You could show us."

What are you talking about?

She can show us what's down there. She can project what she sees.

"I don't know. Macon wouldn't like it." Aunt Del was biting her lip uneasily.

"Do you think he'd prefer we dig up a grave?" Lena countered.

"All right, all right. Get out of that hole, Ethan."

I stepped out of the hole, wiping the dirt on my pants. I looked over at Genevieve. She had a peculiar look on her face, almost as if she was interested to see what was about to happen, or maybe she was just about to vaporize us.

"Everyone, have a seat. This might make you dizzy. If you feel queasy, put your head between your knees," Aunt Del instructed, like some kind of supernatural flight attendant. "The first time is always the hardest." Aunt Del reached out so we could take her hands.

"I can't believe you are participatin' in this, Mamma."

Aunt Del took the clip out of her bun, letting her hair spill down around her shoulders. "Don't be such a Girl Scout, Reece."

Reece rolled her eyes and took my hand. I glanced up at Genevieve. She looked right at me, right into me, and held a finger to her lips as if to say, "Shh."

The air began to dissolve around us. Then we were spinning like one of those rides where they strap you against the wall and the whole thing spins so fast you think you're going to puke.

Then flashes—

One after the next, opening and closing like doors. One after another, second after second.

Two girls in white petticoats running in the grass, holding hands, laughing. Yellow ribbons tied in their hair.

Another door opened.

A young woman with caramel-colored skin, hanging clothes on a wash line, humming quietly, the breeze lifting the sheets into the wind. The woman turns toward a grand white Federal-style house and calls out, *"Genevieve! Evangeline!"*

And another.

A young girl moving across the clearing at dusk. She looks back to see if anyone is following her, red hair swinging behind her. Genevieve. She runs into the arms of a tall, lanky boy—a boy who could've been me. He leans down and kisses her. *"I love you, Genevieve. And one day I'm goin' to marry you. I don't care what your family says. It can't be impossible."* She touches his lips, gently.

"Shh. We don't have much time."

347

The door closes and another opens.

Rain, smoke, and the crackling sound of fire, eating, breathing. Genevieve stands in the darkness; black smoke and tears streak her face. There's a black leather-bound book in her hand. It has no title, just a crescent moon embossed on the cover. She looks at the woman, the same woman who was hanging laundry on the clothesline. Ivy. *"Why doesn't it have a name?"* The old woman's eyes are filled with fear. *"Just 'cause a book don't have a title, don't mean it don't have a name. That right there is* The Book a Moons."

The door slams shut.

Ivy, older and sadder, standing over a freshly dug grave, a pine box resting deep in the hole. *"Though I walk through the valley a the shadow a death, I fear no evil."* There is something in her hand. The Book, black leather with the crescent moon on the cover. *"Take this with ya, Miss Genevieve. So it can't cause nobody else any harm."* She tosses the Book into the hole with the casket.

Another door.

The four of us sitting around the half-dug hole, and below the dirt, farther down where we can't see without Del's help, the pine box. The Book rests against it. Then farther down, into the casket, Genevieve's body, lying there in the darkness. Her eyes closed, her skin pale porcelain, as if she was still breathing, perfectly preserved in a way no corpse could ever be. Her long, fiery hair cascading onto her shoulders.

The view spirals back up, out of the ground. Back up to the four of us, sitting around the half-dug hole, holding hands. Up to the headstone and Genevieve's faded figure, staring down at us.

Reece screamed. The last door slammed shut.

♦ ♦ ♦

I tried to open my eyes, but I was dizzy. Del had been right, I felt like I was going to be sick. I tried to get my bearings, but my eyes wouldn't focus. I felt Reece drop my hand, backing away from me, trying to get far away from Genevieve and her terrifying golden gaze.

Are you okay?

I think so.

Lena's head was between her knees.

"Is everyone all right?" Aunt Del asked, her voice even and unshaken. Aunt Del didn't seem so confused or clumsy anymore. If I had to see all that every time I looked at something, I'd pass out, or go crazy.

"I can't believe that's what you see," I said, looking at Del, my eyes finally beginning to refocus.

"The gift of Palimpsestry is a great honor, and a greater burden."

"The Book, it's down there," I said.

"That it is, but it appears it belongs to this woman," Del said, gesturing toward Genevieve's apparition, "who the two of you don't seem particularly surprised to see."

"We saw her before," Lena admitted.

"Well, then, she chose to reveal herself to you. Seeing the dead is not one of the gifts of a Caster, even a Natural, and certainly not within the realm of Mortal talents. One can only see the dead if the dead so will it."

I was scared. Not standing on the steps of Ravenwood scared, or having Ridley freeze the life out of me scared. This was something else. It was closer to the fear I felt when I awoke from the dreams, and the thought of losing Lena. It was a paralyzing fear. The kind you feel when you realize the powerful ghost of a cursed Dark Caster is staring down at you, in the middle of the night, watching you dig up her grave to steal a book from on top of her coffin. What was I thinking? What were we doing coming out here, digging up a grave under a full moon?

You were trying to right a wrong. There was a voice in my head, but it wasn't Lena's.

I turned to Lena. She was pale. Reece and Aunt Del were both staring at what was left of Genevieve. They could hear her, too. I looked up at the glowing golden eyes as she continued to fade in and out. She seemed to sense what we were here for.

Take it.

I looked at Genevieve, unsure. She closed her eyes and nodded ever so slightly.

"She wants us to take the Book," Lena said. I guessed I wasn't losing my mind.

"How do we know we can trust her?" She was a Dark Caster after all. With the same golden eyes as Ridley.

Lena looked back at me, with a glint of excitement. "We don't."

There was only one thing to do.

Dig.

The Book looked exactly as it had in the vision, cracked black leather, embossed with a tiny crescent moon. It smelled like desperation and it felt heavy, not just physically, but psychically. This was a Dark book; I knew it just from the seconds I managed to hold it, before it singed the skin off my fingertips. It felt like the Book was stealing a little bit of my breath each time I inhaled.

I reached my arm out of the hole, holding it above my head. Lena took it from my hand and I climbed back out. I wanted to get out of there, as quickly as possible. It wasn't lost on me that I was standing on Genevieve's casket.

Aunt Del gasped. "Great Mother, I never thought I would see it. *The Book of Moons*. Be careful. That book is as old as time, maybe older. Macon will never believe we—"

"He's never going to know." Lena brushed the dirt from the cover gently.

"Okay now, you've seriously lost it. If you think for one minute we're not goin' to tell Uncle Macon—" Reece crossed her arms like an irritated babysitter.

Lena held the Book up higher, right in front of Reece's face. "About what?" Lena was staring at Reece the same way Reece had stared into Ridley's eyes at the Gathering, intently, with purpose. Reece's expression changed—she looked confused, almost disoriented. She stared at the Book, but it was like she couldn't see it.

"What is there to tell, Reece?"

Reece squeezed her eyes shut, as if she was trying to shake off a bad dream. She opened her mouth to say something, then shut it abruptly. A hint of a smile twitched across Lena's face, as she turned slowly toward her aunt. "Aunt Del?"

Aunt Del looked as confused as Reece, which was how she looked most of the time, anyway, but something was different. And she didn't answer Lena, either.

Lena turned slightly and dropped the Book on top of my bag. As she did, I saw green sparks in her eyes, and the curling motion of her hair as it caught the moonlight, the Casting breeze. It was almost as if I could see the magic churning around her in the darkness. I didn't understand what was happening, but the three of them seemed to be locked in a dark, wordless conversation I couldn't hear or understand.

Then it was over, and the moonlight became moonlight again, and the night faded back into night. I looked behind Reece, at Genevieve's headstone. Genevieve was gone, as if she had never been there at all.

Reece shifted her weight, and her usual sanctimonious expression returned. "If you think for a minute I'm not goin' to tell Uncle Macon you dragged us out to a graveyard for no good reason, because of some stupid school project you didn't even end up doin'—" What the hell was she talking about? But Reece was dead serious. She didn't remember what had just happened, any more than I understood it.

What did you just do?

Uncle Macon and I have been practicing.

Lena zipped up my duffel bag, with the Book inside. "I know. I'm sorry. It's just this place is really creepy at night. Let's get out of here."

Reece turned back toward Ravenwood, dragging Aunt Del behind her. "You're such a baby."

Lena winked at me.

Practicing what? Mind control?

Little things. Teletossing Pebbles. Interior Illusions. Time Binds, but those are hard.

That was easy?

I Shifted the Book out of their minds. I guess you could say I erased it. They won't remember it, because in their reality, it never happened.

I knew we needed the Book. I knew why Lena did it. But

somehow it felt like a line had been crossed, and now I didn't know where we stood, or if she could ever cross back over to where I was. Where she used to be.

Reece and Aunt Del were already back in the garden. I didn't need to be a Sybil to tell Reece wanted to get the hell out of there. Lena started to follow them, but something stopped me.

L, wait.

I walked back over to the hole and reached into my pocket. I opened the handkerchief with the familiar initials, and lifted the locket up by its chain. Nothing. No visions, and something told me there weren't going to be any more. The locket had led us here, showed us what we needed to see.

I held the locket over the grave. It seemed only right, a fair trade. I was about to drop it when I heard Genevieve's voice again, softer this time.

No. It doesn't belong with me.

I looked back at the headstone. Genevieve was there again, what was left of her breaking into nothingness each time the wind blew through her. She didn't look as terrifying.

She looked broken. The way you would look if you lost the only person you ever loved.

I understood.

⊰ 12.08 ⊱

Waist Deep

There was only so much trouble you could get into before the threat of more trouble wasn't even a threat anymore. At some point, you'd waded so far in you had no choice but to paddle through the middle, if you had any chance of making it to the other side. It was classic Link logic, but I was starting to see the genius in it. Maybe you can't really understand it yourself until you're waist deep in it.

By the next day, that's where we were, Lena and me. Waist deep. It started with forging a note with one of Amma's #2 pencils, then cutting school to read a stolen book we weren't supposed to have in the first place, and ended with a pack of lies about an extra-credit "project" we were working on together. I was pretty sure Amma was going to catch on about two seconds after I said the words extra credit, but she had been on the phone with my Aunt Caroline discussing my dad's "condition."

I felt guilty about all the lying, not to mention the stealing, forging, and mind erasing, but we didn't have time for school; we had too much actual studying to do.

Because we had *The Book of Moons*. It was real. I could hold it in my hands—

"Ouch!" It burned my hand, like I had touched a hot stove. The Book dropped to the floor of Lena's bedroom. Boo Radley barked from somewhere in the house. I could hear his paws click their way up the stairs, toward us.

"Door." Lena spoke without looking up from an old Latin dictionary. Her bedroom door slammed shut, just as Boo reached the landing. He protested with a resentful bark. "Stay out of my room, Boo. We're not doing anything. I'm about to start practicing."

I stared at the door, surprised. Another lesson from Macon, I guessed. Lena didn't even react, as if she'd done it a thousand times. It was like the stunt she had pulled on Reece and Aunt Del last night. I was starting to think the closer we got to her birthday, the more the Caster was coming out in the girl.

I was trying not to notice. But the more I tried, the more I noticed.

She looked over at me, rubbing my hands on my jeans. They still hurt. "What part about 'you can't touch it if you're not a Caster' are you not getting?"

"Right. That part."

She opened a battered black case and pulled out her viola. "It's almost five. I've got to start practicing or Uncle Macon will know when he gets up. He always knows."

"What? Now?" She smiled and sat on a chair in the corner of her room. Adjusting the instrument with her chin, she picked up a long bow and set it to the strings. For a moment she didn't move, and closed her eyes like we were at a philharmonic, instead of sitting in her bedroom. And then she began to play. The music crawled up from her hands and out into the room, moving through the air like another one of her undiscovered powers. The sheer white curtains hanging at her window began to stir, and I heard the song—

> *Sixteen moons, sixteen years,*
> *The Claiming Moon, the hour nears,*
> *In these pages Darkness clears,*
> *Powers Bind what fire sears . . .*

As I watched, Lena slid herself out of the chair and carefully placed her viola back where she had been sitting. She wasn't playing it anymore, but the music was still pouring out of it. She leaned the bow against the chair, and sat down next to me on the floor.

Shh.

That's practicing?

"Uncle M doesn't seem to know the difference. And look—" She pointed over to the door, where I could see a shadow, and hear a rhythmic thump. Boo's tail. "He likes it, and I like to have him in front of my door. Think of it as a sort of an anti-adult alarm system." She had a point.

Lena knelt by the Book and picked it up easily in her hands. When she opened the pages again, we saw the same thing we had been staring at all day. Hundreds of Casts, careful lists written in English, Latin, Gaelic, and other languages I didn't recognize, one composed of strange curling letters I had never seen before. The thin brown pages were fragile, almost translucent. The parchment was covered with dark brown ink, in an ancient and delicate script. At least I hoped it was ink.

She tapped her finger on the strange writing and handed me the Latin dictionary. "It's not Latin. See for yourself."

"I think its Gaelic. Have you ever seen anything like that before?" I pointed to the curling script.

"No. Maybe it's some kind of old Caster language."

"Too bad we don't have a Caster dictionary."

"We do, I mean, my uncle should. He has hundreds of Caster books, down in his library. It's no *Lunae Libri*, but it probably has what we're looking for."

"How long do we have before he's up?"

"Not long enough."

I pulled the sleeve of my sweatshirt down over my palm and used the material to handle the Book, as if I was using one of Amma's oven mitts. I flipped through the thin pages; they bent noisily under my touch as if they were made of dry leaves, instead of paper. "Does any of this mean anything to you?"

Lena shook her head. "In my family, before your Claiming you aren't really allowed to know anything." She pretended to pore over the pages. "In case you go Dark, I guess." I knew enough to let it drop.

Page after page, there was nothing we could even begin to comprehend. There were pictures, some frightening, some beautiful. Creatures, symbols, animals—even the human-looking faces somehow managed to look anything but human in *The Book of Moons*. As far as I was concerned, it was like an encyclopedia from another planet.

Lena pulled the Book into her lap. "There's so much I don't know, and it's all so—"

"Trippy?"

I leaned against her bed, looking at the ceiling. There were words everywhere, new words, and numbers. I could see the countdown, the numbers scribbled against the walls of her room as if it was a jail cell.

100, 78, 50 . . .

How much longer would we be able to sit around like this? Lena's birthday was getting closer, and her powers were already growing. What if she was right, and she grew into something unrecognizable, something so Dark she wouldn't even know or care about me? I stared at the viola in the corner until I just didn't want to see it anymore. I closed my eyes and listened to the Caster melody. And then I heard Lena's voice—

". . . UNTIL THE DARKENING BRINGES THE TYME OF CLAYMING, AT THE SIXTEENTHE MOONE, WHEN THE PERSON OF POWERE HAS THE FREEDOME OF WILLE & AGENCIE TO CASTE THE ETERNAL CHOICE, IN THE END OF DAYE, OR THE LASTE MOMENT OF THE LAST OURE, UNDER THE CLAYMING MOONE . . ."

We looked at each other.

"How did you just—" I looked over her shoulder.

She turned the page. "It's English. These pages are written in English. Someone started to translate it, here in the back. See how the ink is a different color?" She was right.

Even the pages in English must have been hundreds of years old. The page was written in another elegant script, but it wasn't the same writing, and it wasn't written in the same brownish ink, or whatever it was.

"Flip to the back."

She held up the Book, reading,

"THE CLAYMING, ONCE BOUND, CANNOT BE UNBOUND. THE CHOICE, ONCE CAST, CANNOT BE RECAST. A PERSON OF POWERE FALLES INTO THE GREAT DARKENING OR THE GREAT LIGHT, FOR ALL TYME. IF TYME PASSES & THE LASTE OURE OF THE SIXTEENTHE MOONE FLEES UNBOUND, THE ORDER OF THINGS IS UNDONE. THIS MUST NOT BE. THE BOOKE WILLE BINDE THAT WHICHE IS UNBOUND, FOR ALL TYME."

"So there's really no getting around this Claiming thing?"

"That's what I've been trying to tell you."

I stared at the words that didn't bring me any closer to understanding. "But what happens, exactly, during the Claiming? Does this Claiming Moon send down some kind of Caster beam, or something?"

She scanned the page. "It doesn't exactly say. All I know is it takes place under the moon, at midnight— 'IN THE MIDST OF THE GREAT DARKNESSE & UNDERE THE GREAT LIGHT, FROM WHICHE WE CAME.' But it can happen anywhere. It's nothing you can really see, it just happens. No Caster beam involved."

"But what happens exactly?" I wanted to know everything, and it still felt like she was holding something back. She kept her eyes on the page.

"For most Casters, it's a conscious thing, just like it says here. The Person of Power, the Caster, Casts the Eternal Choice. They choose if they want to Claim themselves Light or Dark. That's what the free will and agency is all about, like Mortals choose to be good or bad, except Casters make the Choice for all time. They choose the life they want to lead, the way they will interact with the magical universe, and one another. It's a covenant they make with the natural world, the Order of Things. I know that sounds crazy."

"When you're sixteen? How are you supposed to know who you are and who you want to be for the rest of your life by then?"

"Yeah, well, those are the lucky ones. I don't even get a choice."

I almost couldn't bring myself to ask the next question. "So what will happen to you?"

"Reece says you just change. It happens in a second, like a heartbeat. You feel this energy, this power moving through your body, almost like you're coming to life for the first time." She looked wistful. "At least, that's what Reece said."

"That's doesn't sound so bad."

"Reece described it as an overwhelming warmth. She said it felt like the sun was shining on her, and no one else. And at that moment, she said you just know which path has been chosen for you." It sounded too easy, too painless, like she was leaving something out. Like the part about what it felt like when a Caster went Dark. But I didn't want to put it out there, even if I knew we were both thinking about it.

Just like that?

Just like that. It doesn't hurt or anything, if that's what you're worried about.

That was one of the things I was worried about, but it wasn't the only thing.

I'm not worried.

Me neither.

And this time, we made a point of staying away from what we were thinking, even to ourselves.

The sun crept across the braided rug on Lena's floor, the orange light turning all the colors of the braid into a hundred different kinds of gold. For a moment, Lena's face, her eyes, her hair, everything the light touched turned to gold. She was beautiful, a hundred years and a hundred miles away, and just like the faces in the Book, somehow not quite human.

"Sundown. Uncle Macon will be up, any minute. We have to put the Book away." She closed it, zipping it back into my bag. "You take it. If my uncle finds it, he'll just try to keep it from me, like everything else."

"I just can't figure out what he and Amma are hiding. If all this stuff is going to happen and there's nothing anyone can do to stop it, why not tell us everything?"

She wouldn't look at me. I pulled her into my arms, and she lay her head against my chest. She didn't say a word, but between two layers of sweatshirts and sweaters, I could still feel her heart beating against mine.

She looked over at the viola until the music died out, dimming like the sun in the window.

⎯⎯ ☙

The next day at school, it was clear we were the only people thinking about anything that had to do with any kind of book. No hands were raised in any classes, unless someone needed the hall pass for the bathroom. Not a single pen touched a scrap of paper, unless it was to write a note about who had been asked, who didn't have a prayer of being asked, and who had already been shot down.

December only meant one thing at Jackson High: the winter formal. We were in the cafeteria when Lena brought the subject up for the first time.

"Did you ask anyone to go to the dance?" Lena wasn't familiar with Link's not-so-secret strategy of going to all the dances stag so he could flirt with Coach Cross, the girls' track coach. Link had been in love with Maggie Cross, who had graduated five years ago and came back after college to become Coach Cross, since we were in fifth grade.

"No, I like to fly solo." Link grinned, his mouth full of fries.

"Coach Cross chaperones, so Link always goes by himself so he can loiter around her all night," I explained.

"Don't wanna disappoint the ladies. They'll be fightin' over me once somebody spikes the punch."

"I've never been to a school dance before." Lena looked down at her tray and picked at her sandwich. She looked almost disappointed.

I hadn't asked her to the dance. It hadn't occurred to me that she'd want to go. So much was going on between us, and every part of it was so much bigger than a school dance.

Link shot me a look. He had warned me this would happen. "Every girl wants to be asked to the dance, man. I have no idea why, but even I know that much." Who knew Link might actually be right, considering his Coach Cross Master Plan had never panned out?

Link drained the rest of his Coke. "A pretty girl like you? You could be the Snow Queen."

Lena tried to smile, but it wasn't even close. "So what's with the whole Snow Queen thing? Don't you just have a Homecoming Queen like everywhere else?"

"No. This is the winter formal, so it's an Ice Queen, but Savannah's cousin, Suzanne, won every year until she graduated and Savannah won last year, so everyone just calls it the Snow Queen." Link reached over and grabbed a slice of pizza from my plate.

It was pretty obvious Lena wanted to be asked. Another mysterious thing about girls—they want to be asked to stuff even if they don't want to go. But I had a feeling that wasn't the case with Lena. It was almost like she had a list of all the things she imagined a regular girl was supposed to do in high school, and she was determined to do them. It was crazy. The formal was the last place I wanted to go right now. We weren't the most popular people at Jackson lately. I didn't mind that everyone stared when we walked down the hall, even if we weren't holding hands. I didn't mind that people were probably saying things right now, cruel things, while the three of us sat alone at the only empty table in the crowded lunchroom, or that a whole club full of Jackson Angels was patrolling the halls just waiting for us to screw up.

But the thing is, before Lena, I would've cared. I was just starting to wonder, I mean, if maybe I was under some kind of spell myself.

I don't do that.

I didn't say you did.

You just did.

I didn't say you had Cast a spell. I just said, maybe I was under one.

You think I'm Ridley?

I think . . . forget it.

Lena searched my face even more intently, like she was trying to read it. Maybe she could do that, too, now, for all I knew.

What?

The thing you said the morning after Halloween, in your room. Did you mean it, L?

What thing?

The writing on the wall.

What wall?

The wall in your bedroom. Don't act like you don't know what I'm talking about. You said you were feeling the same way I was.

She started fidgeting with her necklace.

I don't know what you're talking about.

Falling.

Falling?

Falling . . . you know.

What?

Never mind.

Say it, Ethan.

I just did.

Look at me.

I'm looking right at you.

I looked down into my chocolate milk.

"Get it? Savannah Snow? Ice Queen?" Link dumped vanilla ice cream on top of his French fries.

Lena caught my eye, blushing. She reached her hand under the table. I took it in mine, then almost yanked my hand away, the shock of her touch was so strong. It really was like sticking my hand in a wall socket. The way she looked at me, even if I couldn't hear what she was thinking, I would've known.

If you have something to say, Ethan, just say it.

Yeah. That.

Say it.

But we didn't need to say it. We were all by ourselves, in the middle of the crowded lunchroom, in the middle of a conversation with Link. Between the two of us, we had no idea what Link was even talking about, anymore. "Get it? It's only funny because it's true. You know, Ice Queen, Savannah is one."

Lena let go of my hand and threw a carrot at Link. She couldn't stop smiling. He thought she was smiling at him. "Okay. I get it, Ice Queen. It's still stupid." Link stuck a fork into the gloppy mess on his tray.

"It makes no sense. It doesn't even snow here."

Link smiled at me over his ice cream fries. "She's jealous. You better watch out. Lena just wants to be elected Ice Queen so she can dance with me when they make me Ice King."

Lena laughed in spite of herself. "You? I thought you were saving yourself for the track coach."

"I am, and this is gonna be the year she falls for me."

"Link spends the whole night trying to come up with witty things to say when she walks by."

"She thinks I'm funny."

"Funny looking."

"This is my year. I can feel it. I'm gonna get Snow King this year, and Coach Cross is finally gonna see me up there on the stage with Savannah Snow."

"I can't really see how it plays out from there." Lena began to peel a blood orange.

"Oh, you know, she'll be struck by my good looks and charm and musical talent, especially if you write me a song. Then she'll give in and dance with me and follow me up to New York after graduation, to be my groupie."

"What is that, like an after-school special?" The orange peel came off in one long spiral.

"Your girlfriend thinks I'm special, dude." Fries were falling out of his mouth.

Lena looked at me. Girlfriend. We both heard him say it.

Is that what I am?

Is that what you want to be?

Are you asking me something?

It wasn't the first time I'd thought about it. Lena had felt like my girlfriend for a while now. When you considered everything we'd been through together, it was sort of a given. So I don't know why I had never said it, and I don't know why it was hard to say it now. But there was something about saying the words that made it more real.

I guess I am.

You don't sound so sure.

I grabbed her other hand under the table and found her green eyes.

I'm sure, L.

Then I guess I'm your girlfriend.

Link was still talking. "You'll think I'm special when Coach Cross is hangin' all over me at the dance." Link got up and tossed his tray.

"Just don't be thinking my girlfriend's saving you a dance." I tossed mine.

Lena's eyes lit up. I was right; she not only wanted to be asked, she wanted to go. In that moment, I knew I didn't care what was on her regular-high-school-girl to-do list. I was going to make sure she got to do everything on it.

"Are you guys goin'?"

I looked at her expectantly and she squeezed my hand. "Yeah, I guess."

This time she smiled for real. "And Link, how about I save you two dances? My boyfriend won't mind. He would never tell me who I can and can't dance with." I rolled my eyes.

Link put his fist up and I tapped my knuckles against his. "Yeah, I bet."

The bell rang and lunch was over. Just like that, I not only had a date to the winter formal, I had a girlfriend. And not just a girlfriend, for the first time in my whole life, I had almost used the L word. In the middle of the cafeteria, in front of Link.

Talk about hot lunch.

Melting

I don't see why she can't meet you here. I was hopin' to see Melchizedek's niece all dolled up in her fancy dress." I was standing in front of Amma so she could tie my bow tie. Amma was so short, she had to stand three stairs up from me to reach my collar. When I was a kid, she used to comb my hair and tie my necktie before we went to church on Sundays. She had always looked like she was so proud, and that's how she was looking at me now.

"Sorry. No time for a photo session. I'm picking her up from her house. The guy is supposed to pick up the girl, remember?" That was a stretch, considering I was picking her up in the Beater. Link was catching a ride with Shawn. The guys on the team were still saving him a seat at their new lunch table, even though he usually sat with Lena and me.

Amma yanked on my tie and snorted a laugh. I don't know what she thought was so funny, but it made me edgy.

"It's too tight. I feel like it's strangling me." I tried to wedge a finger in between my neck and the collar of my rented jacket from Buck's Tux, but I couldn't.

"Isn't the tie, it's your nerves. You'll do fine." She surveyed me approvingly, like I imagined my mom would have if she'd been here. "Now, let me see those flowers." I reached behind me for a small box, a red rose surrounded by white baby's breath inside. They looked pretty ugly to me, but you couldn't get much better from Gardens of Eden, the only place in Gatlin.

"About the sorriest flowers I've ever seen." Amma took one look and tossed them into the wastebasket at the bottom of the stairs. She turned on her heel and disappeared into the kitchen.

"What did you do that for?"

She opened the refrigerator and pulled out a wrist corsage, small and delicate. White Confederate jasmine and wild rosemary, tied with a pale silver ribbon. Silver and white, the colors of the winter formal. It was perfect.

As much as I knew that Amma wasn't crazy about my relationship with Lena, she had done this anyway. She'd done it for me. It was something my mom would have done. It was only since my mom had died that I realized how much I relied on Amma, how much I had always relied on her. She was the only thing that had kept me afloat. Without her, I probably would have drowned, like my dad.

"Everything means somethin'. Don't try to change somethin' wild into somethin' tame."

I held the corsage up to the kitchen lamp. I felt the length of

369

the ribbon, carefully probing it with my fingers. Under the ribbon, there was a tiny bone.

"Amma!"

She shrugged. "What, are you gonna take issue with a teeny little graveyard bone like that? After all this time growin' up in this house, after seein' the things you've seen, where's your sense? A little protection never hurt anybody—not even you, Ethan Wate."

I sighed and put the corsage back in the box. "I love you, too, Amma."

She gave me a bone-crushing hug, and I ran down the steps and into the night. "You be careful, you hear? Don't get carried away."

I had no idea what she meant, but I smiled at her anyway. "Yes, ma'am."

My father's light was on in the study as I drove away. I wondered if he even knew tonight was the winter formal.

When Lena pulled the door open, my heart almost stopped, which was saying something considering she wasn't even touching me. I knew she looked nothing like any of the other girls at the dance would look tonight. There were only two kinds of prom dresses in Gatlin County, and they all came from one of two places: Little Miss, the local pageant gown supplier, or Southern Belle, the bridal shop two towns over.

The girls who went to Little Miss wore the slutty mermaid dresses, all slits and plunging necklines and sequins; those were the girls that Amma would never have allowed me to be seen with at a church picnic, let alone the winter formal. They were sometimes the local pageant girls or the daughters of local pageant girls, like Eden, whose mom had been First Runner Up Miss South Carolina, or more often just the daughters of the women who wished they had been pageant girls. These were the same girls you might eventually see holding their babies at the Jackson High School graduation in a couple of years.

Southern Belle dresses were the Scarlett O'Hara dresses, shaped like giant cowbells. The Southern Belle girls were the daughters of the DAR and the Ladies Auxiliary members—the Emily Ashers and the Savannah Snows—and you could take them anywhere, if you could stomach it, stomach them, and stomach the way it looked like you were dancing with a bride at her own wedding.

Either way, everything was shiny, everything was colorful, and everything involved a lot of metallic trim and a particular shade of orange folks called Gatlin Peach, that was probably reserved for tacky bridesmaids' dresses everywhere else but Gatlin County.

For guys, there was less obvious pressure, but it wasn't really any easier. We had to match, usually our date, which could involve the dreaded Gatlin Peach. This year, the basketball team was going in silver bow ties and silver cummerbunds, sparing them the humiliation of pink or purple or peach bow ties.

Lena had definitely never worn Gatlin Peach in her life. As I looked at her, my knees started to buckle, which was starting to become a familiar feeling. She was so pretty it hurt.

Wow.

Like it?

She spun around. Her hair curled around her shoulders, long and loose, held back with glinting clips, in one of those magical ways girls have of making their hair look like it is supposed to be up, but also sort of falling down. I wanted to run my fingers through it, but I didn't dare touch her, not a single hair. Lena's dress fell from her body, clinging to all the right places without looking Little Miss, in silvery gray strands, as delicate as a silver cobweb, spun by silver spiders.

Was it? Spun by silver spiders?

Who knows? It could've been. It was a gift from Uncle Macon.

She laughed and pulled me into the house. Even Ravenwood seemed to reflect the wintry theme of the formal. Tonight, the entry hall looked like old Hollywood; tiles of black and white checkered the floor, and silver snowflakes sparkled, floating in the air above us. A black lacquered antique table stood in front of iridescent silver curtains, and beyond them, I could see something that glinted like the ocean, though I knew it couldn't be. Flickering candles hovered over the furniture, tossing little pools of moonlight everywhere I looked.

"Really? Spiders?"

I could see the candlelight reflecting off her shining lips. I tried not to think about it. I tried not to want to kiss the little moon-shaped crescent on her cheekbone. The most subtle dusting of silver shone on her shoulders, her face, her hair. Even her birthmark seemed to be silver tonight.

"Just kidding. It was probably just something he found in some little shop in Paris or Rome or New York City. Uncle Macon likes beautiful things." She touched the silver crescent moon at her neckline, dangling just above her chain of memories. Another gift from Macon, I guessed.

The familiar drawl came out of the dark hallway, accompanied by a single silver candlestick. "Budapest, not Paris. Other than that, guilty as charged." Macon emerged in a smoking jacket over neat black pants and a white dress shirt. The silver studs in his shirt caught the glint of the candlelight.

"Ethan, I would appreciate it greatly if you could take every precaution with my niece tonight. As you know, I prefer her home in the evenings." He handed me a corsage for Lena, a small wreath of Confederate jasmine. "Every possible precaution."

"Uncle M!" Lena sounded annoyed.

I looked at the corsage more closely. A silver ring dangled from the pin that held the flowers. It had an inscription in a language I didn't understand, but recognized from *The Book of Moons*. I didn't have to look too closely to see it was the ring he had worn night and day, until now. I pulled out Amma's nearly identical corsage. Between the hundred Casters probably Bound to the ring, and all of Amma's extended Greats, there wasn't a spirit in town that would mess with us. I hoped.

"I think, between you and Amma, sir, Lena will survive the Jackson High winter formal all right." I smiled.

Macon didn't. "It's not the formal I worry about, but I'm grateful to Amarie just the same."

Lena frowned, looking from her uncle to me. Maybe we didn't look like the two happiest guys in town. "Your turn." She picked up a boutonniere from the hall table, a plain white rose with a tiny sprig of jasmine, and pinned it on my jacket. "I wish you would all stop worrying for one minute. This is getting embarrassing. I can take care of myself."

Macon looked unconvinced. "In any event, I wouldn't want anyone to get hurt."

I didn't know if he was referring to the witches of Jackson High, or the powerful Dark Caster, Sarafine. Either way, I'd seen enough in the last few months to take a warning like that seriously.

"And have her back by midnight."

"Is that some powerful Caster hour?"

"No. It's her curfew."

I stifled a smile.

Lena seemed anxious on the way to school. She sat stiffly in the front seat, fiddling with the radio, her dress, her seatbelt.

"Relax."

"Is it crazy that we're going tonight?" Lena looked at me expectantly.

"What do you mean?"

"I mean everyone hates me." She looked down at her hands.

"You mean everyone hates us."

"Okay, everyone hates us."

"We don't have to go."

"No, I want to go. That's the thing . . ." She twisted the corsage around her wrist a few times "Last year, Ridley and I had planned to go together. But then . . ."

I couldn't hear her answer, not even in my head.

"Things had already gone wrong by then. Ridley turned sixteen. Then she was gone, and I had to leave school."

"Well, this isn't last year. It's just a dance. Nothing's gone wrong."

She frowned and shut the mirror.

Not yet.

When we walked into the gym, even I was impressed by how hard Student Council must have worked all weekend. Jackson

374

had gone all the way with the whole Midwinter Night's Dream concept. Hundreds of tiny paper snowflakes—some white, some shimmering with tinfoil, glitter, sequins, and anything else that could be made to sparkle—hung on fishing wire from the ceiling of the gym. Powdery soap flake "snow" drifted into the corners of the gym, and twinkling white lights fell in strands from the risers.

"Hi, Ethan. Lena, you look lovely." Coach Cross handed us both cups of Gatlin Peach Punch. She was in a black dress that showed just a little too much leg, I thought, for Link's sake.

I looked at Lena, thinking of the silver snowflakes floating through the air at Ravenwood, without fishing wire or silver tinfoil. Still, her eyes were shining and she clung to my hand tightly, like she was a kid at her first birthday party. I had never believed Link when he claimed school dances had some sort of inexplicable effect on girls. But it was clear it was true of all girls, even Caster girls.

"It's beautiful." Honestly, it wasn't. What it was, was a plain old Jackson High dance, but I guess to Lena, that was something beautiful. Maybe magic wasn't the magic thing, when you grew up with it.

Then I heard a familiar voice. It couldn't be.

"Let's get this party started!"

Ethan, look—

I turned around and almost choked on my punch. Link grinned at me, wearing what looked like a silver sharkskin tuxedo. He had one of those black T-shirts with a picture of the front of a tuxedo shirt screened on it underneath, and his black high-tops. He looked like a Charleston street performer.

"Hey, Short Straw! Hey, Cuz!" I heard that unmistakable

voice again, over the crowd, over the DJ, over the thumping of pounding bass, and the couples on the dance floor. Honey, sugar, molasses, and cherry lollipops, all rolled into one. It was the only time in my life I'd ever thought something was too sweet.

Lena's hand tightened on mine. On Link's arm, unbelievably, in the smallest splash of silver sequins ever worn to a Jackson High formal, maybe any formal, was Ridley. I didn't even know where to look; she was all legs and curves and blond hair spilling everywhere. I could feel the temperature in the room rising just by looking at her. From the number of guys who had stopped dancing with their wedding cake–topper dates, who were fuming, it was obvious I wasn't the only one. In a world where all the prom dresses came from one of two stores, Ridley had out–Little Missed even the Little Misses. She made Coach Cross look like the Reverend Mother. In other words, Link was doomed.

Lena looked from me to her cousin, ill. "Ridley, what are you doing here?"

"Cuz. We finally got to that dance after all. Aren't you *ecstatic*? Isn't it *fantastic*?"

I could see Lena's hair starting to curl in the nonexistent wind. She blinked and half the string of twinkling white lights went dark. I had to act fast. I pulled Link over to the punch bowl. "What are you doing with her?"

"Dude, can you believe it? She's the hottest chick in Gatlin, no offense. Third Degree Burns. And she was just hangin' out at the Stop & Steal when I went in to buy Slim Jims on the way here. She even had a dress on."

"Don't you think that's a little weird?"

"Do you think I care?"

"What if she's some kind of psycho?"

"You think she'll tie me up or somethin'?" He grinned, already picturing it.

"I'm not joking."

"You're always jokin'. What's up? Oh, I get it, you're jealous. 'Cause I seem to remember you gettin' in her car pretty fast yourself. Don't tell me you tried to get with her or somethin'—"

"No way. She's Lena's cousin."

"Whatever. All I know is, I'm here at the formal with the hottest hotness in three counties. It's like, what are the odds of a meteor hittin' this town? This'll never happen again. Be cool, okay? Don't ruin it for me." He was under her spell already, not that she had needed much of one with Link. It didn't matter what I said.

I gave it another half-hearted try. "She's bad news, man. She's messing with your head. She'll suck you in and spit you out when she's done."

He grabbed my shoulders with both hands. "Suck away."

Link put his arm around Ridley's waist and went out onto the dance floor. He didn't so much as look at Coach Cross as they walked by.

I pulled Lena away in the other direction, toward the corner where the photographer was taking pictures of the couples in front of a fake snowdrift with a fake snowman, while members of Student Council took turns shaking fake snow down onto the scene. I bumped right into Emily.

She looked at Lena. "Lena. You look . . . shiny."

Lena just looked at her. "Emily. You look . . . puffy."

It was true. Ethan-Hating Southern Belle Emily looked like a silver and peach-filled cream puff, plucked and primped and puckered into taffeta. Her hair, in scary little piggy ringlets, looked like it was made out of yellow curling ribbon. Her face looked like it had been stretched a little too tightly while she was getting her hair done at the Snip 'n' Curl, stabbed in the head one too many times with a bobby pin.

What had I ever seen in any of them?

"I didn't know your kind danced."

"We do." Lena stared at her.

"Around a bonfire?" Emily's face twisted into a nasty smile.

Lena's hair began to curl again. "Why? Looking for a bonfire so you can burn that dress?" The other half of the twinkle lights shorted out. I could see Student Council scrambling to check the cord connections.

Don't let her win. She's the only witch here.

She's not the only one, Ethan.

Savannah appeared next to Emily, dragging Earl behind her. She looked exactly like Emily, only she was silver and pink, rather than silver and peach. Her skirt was just as fluffy. If you squinted, you could visualize both of their weddings now. It was horrifying.

Earl looked at the ground, trying to avoid making eye contact with me.

"Come on, Em, they're announcin' the Royal Court." Savannah looked at Emily meaningfully.

"Don't let me hold ya up." Savannah gestured to the line for pictures. "I mean, will you even show up on film, Lena?" She flounced off, massive cream puff dress and all.

"Next!"

Lena's hair was still curling.

They're idiots. It doesn't matter. None of it matters.

I heard the photographer's voice again. "Next!"

I grabbed Lena's hand and pulled her into the fake snowdrift. She looked up at me, her eyes clouded. And then, the clouds passed, and she was back. I could feel the storm settle.

"Cue the snow," I heard in the background.

You're right. It doesn't matter.

I leaned in to kiss her.

You're what matters.

We kissed, and the flash from the camera went off. For one second, one perfect second, it seemed like there was nobody else in the world, and nothing else mattered.

The blinding light of a flashbulb and then, sticky white goop was pouring everywhere, all over the two of us.

What the—?

Lena gasped. I tried to clear the glop out of my eyes, but it was everywhere. When I saw Lena, it was even worse, her hair, her face, her beautiful dress. Her first dance. Ruined.

It was foaming up, the consistency of pancake mix, dripping down from a bucket over our heads, the one that was supposed to release the flakes of fake snow so it could drift down gently for the photo. I looked up, only to get another face full of the stuff. The bucket rattled to the floor.

"Who put water in the snow?" The photographer was furious. No one said a word, and I was willing to bet the Jackson Angels hadn't seen a thing.

"She's melting!" someone shouted. We stood in a puddle of white soap or glue or whatever, wishing we could shrink until we disappeared; at least, that's how it must have looked to the crowd standing around us laughing. Savannah and Emily were standing off to the side, enjoying every minute of what was maybe the most humiliating moment of Lena's life.

A guy called out over the din. "You shoulda stayed home."

I would've known that stupid voice anywhere. I'd heard it enough times on the court, about the only place he ever used it. Earl was whispering in Savannah's ear, his arm slung around her shoulder.

I snapped. I was across the room so fast Earl didn't even see me coming at him. I slammed my soap-covered fist into his jaw and he hit the ground, knocking Savannah on her hoop-skirted butt in the process.

"What the hell? Have you lost your mind, Wate?" Earl started to get up, but I pushed him back down with my foot.

"You better stay down."

Earl sat up and pulled on the collar of his jacket to straighten it, as if he could still look cool sitting on the gym floor. "You better hope you know what you're doin'." But he didn't get back up. He could say what he wanted, but we both knew if he got up, he was the one who would end up back on the ground.

"I do." I pulled Lena out of the growing slush puddle of what used to be the fake snowdrift.

"Let's go, Earl, they're announcin' the court," Savannah said, annoyed. Earl got up and brushed himself off.

I wiped my eyes, shaking out my wet hair. Lena stood there shivering, dripping fake snow like whitewash. Even in the crowd, there was a little puddle of space around her. No one dared get too close, except me. I tried to wipe her face with my sleeve, but she backed away.

This is the way it always is.

"Lena."

I should've known better.

380

Ridley appeared at her side, with Link right behind her. She was furious, I could see that much. "I don't get it, Cuz. I don't see why you want to hang out with *their kind*." She spat the words out, sounding just like Emily. "No one treats us like this, Light or Dark—not one of *them*. Where's your self-respect, Lena Beana?"

"It's not worth it. Not tonight. I just want to go home." Lena was too embarrassed to be as angry as Ridley. It was fight or flight, and right now, Lena was choosing flight. "Take me home, Ethan."

Link took off his silver jacket and put it around her shoulders. "That was messed up."

Ridley couldn't calm down, or wouldn't. "They're bad news, Cuz, except Short Straw. And my new boyfriend, Shrinky Dink."

"Link. I told you, it's Link."

"Shut up, Ridley. She's had enough." The Siren effect wasn't working on me anymore.

Ridley looked over my shoulder, and smiled, a dark smile. "Come to think of it, I've had enough, too."

I followed her gaze. The Ice Queen and her Court had made their way up to the stage, and were grinning from the catbird seat. Once again, Savannah was the Snow Queen. Nothing ever changed. She was beaming at Emily, once again her Ice Princess, just like last year.

Ridley took off her movie star sunglasses, just a little. Her eyes began to glow—you could almost feel the heat coming off her. A lollipop appeared in her hand, and I smelled the thick, sickly sweetness in the air.

Don't, Ridley.

This isn't about you, Cuz. It's bigger than that. Things are about to change in this back-assward town.

I could hear Ridley's voice in my head as clearly as Lena's. I shook my head.

Leave it alone, Ridley. You're only going to make things worse.

Open your eyes; they can't get any worse. Or maybe they can.

She patted Lena on the shoulder.

Watch and learn.

She was staring at the Royal Court, sucking on her cherry lollipop. I hoped it was too dark for them to see her creepy cat eyes.

No! They'll just blame me, Ridley. Don't.

Gat-dung needs to learn a lesson. And I'm just the one to teach it to them.

Ridley strode toward the stage, her glitter heels clicking against the floor.

"Hey, babe, where ya goin'?" Link was right behind her.

Charlotte was walking up the stairs, in yards of shiny lavender taffeta two sizes too small, toward her sparkly, plastic silver crown and her usual place in fourth position of the Royal Court, behind Eden—Ice Handmaiden, I guess. Just as she was taking the last step, her gigantic lavender sweatshop creation caught the edge of the riser, and when she stepped up onto the last stair, the back of her dress tore right off, right at the feebly sewn seam. It took Charlotte a couple of seconds to realize it and by then, half the school was staring at her hot pink panties, the size of the state of Texas. Charlotte screamed a bloodcurdling, now-everyone-knows-how-fat-I-really-am scream.

Ridley grinned.

Oopsies!

Ridley, stop!

I'm just getting started.

Charlotte was screaming, while Emily, Eden, and Savannah tried to shield her from view with their teen wedding dresses. The sound of a record scratching ripped across the speakers, as the record that was playing abruptly changed to the Stones.

"Sympathy for the Devil." It could've been Ridley's theme song. She was introducing herself, in a big way.

The people on the dance floor just assumed it was another one of Dickey Wix's screw-ups, on his way to becoming the most famous thirty-five-year-old DJ on the prom circuit. But the joke was on them. Forget light strands shorting out; within seconds all the bulbs above the stage and the track lighting along the dance floor began to blow, one by one, like dominoes.

Ridley led Link onto the dance floor, and he twirled her around as Jackson students screamed, pushing their way off the floor, under the spray of sparks. I'm sure they all thought they were in the middle of some kind of electrical wiring disaster that Red Sweet, Gatlin's only electrician, would get blamed for. Ridley threw her head back, laughing and undulating around Link in that loincloth of a dress.

Ethan—we have to do something!

What?

It was too late to do anything. Lena turned and ran, and I was right behind her. Before either of us reached the doors to the gym, the sprinklers went off, all along the ceiling. Water poured into the gym. The audio equipment started to short out, sparking like an electrocution just waiting to happen. Wet snowflakes dropped to the floor like soaked pancakes, and soap-flake snow turned into a bubbling mess.

Everyone started to scream, and girls dripping mascara and hair product ran toward the door in their soggy taffeta skirts. In the mess, you couldn't tell a Little Miss from a Southern Belle. They all looked like pastel-colored drowned rats.

As I reached the door, I heard a loud crash. I turned to the stage just as the giant glitter snowflake backdrop toppled. Emily flopped out of position, off her step on the slippery stage. Still waving to the crowd, she tried to catch herself, but her feet slipped out from under her and she fell to the gym floor. She collapsed into a pile of peach and silver taffeta. Coach Cross went running.

I didn't feel sorry for her, even though I did feel sorry for the people who would be blamed for this nightmare: the Student Council for their dangerously unstable backdrop, Dickey Wix for capitalizing on the misfortune of a fat teenage cheerleader in her underwear, and Red Sweet for his unprofessional and potentially life-threatening wiring of the lighting in the Jackson High gym.

See you later, Cuz. This was even better than a prom.

I pushed Lena out the door in front of me. "Go!"

She was so cold I could barely stand to touch her. By the time we got to the car, Boo Radley was already catching up to us.

Macon shouldn't have worried about her curfew.

It wasn't even half past nine.

Macon was infuriated, or maybe he was just worried. I couldn't tell which, because every time he looked at me, I looked away. Even Boo didn't dare look at him, lying at Lena's feet, thumping his tail on the floor.

The house no longer resembled the dance. I bet Macon would never allow a silver snowflake through the doors of Ravenwood again. Everything was black now. Everything: the floors, the furniture, the curtains, the ceiling. Only the fire in the study fireplace burned steadily, casting light out into the room from the hearth. Maybe the house reflected his changing moods, and this was a dark one.

"Kitchen!" A black mug of cocoa appeared in Macon's hand. He handed it to Lena, who sat wrapped in a scratchy woolen blanket in front of the fire. She clutched the mug with both hands, her wet hair tucked behind her ears, clinging to the warmth. He paced in front of her. "You should have left the moment you saw her, Lena."

"I was kind of busy getting doused with soap and laughed at by everyone in school."

"Well, you won't be busy anymore. You're grounded until your birthday, for your own good."

"My own good is so clearly not the point here." She was still shaking, but I didn't think it was from the cold, not anymore.

He stared at me, his eyes cold and dark. He was furious, I was sure now. "You should have made her leave."

"I didn't know what to do, sir. I didn't know Ridley was going to destroy the gym. And Lena had never been to a dance." It sounded stupid even as I was saying it.

Macon just stared back at me, swirling the scotch in his glass. "Interesting to note, you didn't even dance. Not a single dance."

"How do you know that?" Lena put down her mug.

Macon paced. "That's not important."

"Actually, it's important to me."

Macon shrugged. "It's Boo. He is, for lack of a better word, my eyes."

"What?"

"He sees what I see. I see what he sees. He's a Caster dog, you know."

"Uncle Macon! You've been spying on me!"

"Not on you, in particular. How do you think I manage as the town shut-in? I wouldn't get far without man's best friend. Boo here sees everything, so I see everything." I looked at Boo. I could see the eyes, human eyes. I should have known, maybe I had always known. He had Macon's eyes.

And something else, something he was chewing. He had a ball of something in his mouth. I bent down to take it from him. It was a crumpled, soggy Polaroid. He had carried it all the way from the gym.

Our picture from the formal. I was standing there, with Lena, in the middle of the fake snow. Emily was wrong. Lena's kind did show up on film, only she was shimmering, transparent, as if from the waist down she had already begun to dissolve into some kind of ghostly apparition. Like she really was melting, before the snow had even hit her.

I patted Boo's head and pocketed the photo. This wasn't something Lena needed to see, not right now. Two months until her birthday. I didn't need the picture to know we were running out of time.

⊰ 12.16 ⊱

When the Saints Go Marching In

Lena was sitting on the porch when I pulled up. I insisted on driving because Link wanted to ride with us, and he couldn't risk being seen in the hearse. And I didn't want Lena to have to walk in alone. I didn't even want her to go, but there was no talking her out of it. She looked like she was ready for battle. She was wearing a black turtleneck sweater, black jeans, and a black vest with a fur-trimmed hood. She was about to face the firing squad, and she knew it.

It had only been three days since the dance, and the DAR hadn't wasted any time. The Jackson Disciplinary Committee meeting this afternoon wasn't going to be much different than a witch trial, and you didn't have to be a Caster to know that. Emily was limping around in a cast, the winter formal disaster had become the talk of the town, and Mrs. Lincoln finally had all the support she needed. Witnesses had come forward.

And if you twisted everything everyone claimed they saw, heard, or remembered far enough, you could squint, slant your head just right, and try to see the logic: that Lena Duchannes was responsible.

Everything was fine until she came to town.

Link jumped out and opened the door for Lena. He was so riddled with guilt, he looked like he was going to puke. "Hey, Lena. How ya doin'?"

"I'm okay."

Liar.

I don't want him to feel bad. It's not his fault.

Link cleared his throat. "I'm real sorry about this. I've been fightin' with my mom all weekend. She's always been crazy, but this time it's different."

"It's not your fault, but I appreciate you trying to talk to her."

"It might have made a difference if all those hags from the DAR weren't talkin' her other ear off. Mrs. Snow and Mrs. Asher must've called my house a hundred times in the last two days."

We drove past the Stop & Steal. Even Fatty wasn't there. The roads were deserted, like we were driving through a ghost town. The Disciplinary Committee meeting was scheduled for five o'clock sharp, and we were going to be right on time. The meeting was in the gym because it was the only place at Jackson big enough to accommodate the number of people that were likely to show up. That was another thing about Gatlin, everything that went on involved everyone. There were no closed proceedings around here. From the look of the streets, the whole town had all but shut down, which meant just about everyone was going to be at the meeting.

"I just don't get how your mom pulled this off so quickly. This is fast even for her."

"From what I overheard, Doc Asher got involved. He hunts with Principal Harper and some bigwig on the School Board." Doc Asher was Emily's dad and the only real doctor in town.

"Great."

"You guys know I'm probably going to get kicked out, right? I'll bet it's already been decided. This meeting is just for show."

Link looked confused. "They can't kick you out without hearin' your side a the story. You didn't even do anything."

"None of that matters. These things are decided behind closed doors. Nothing I say is going to matter."

She was right, and we both knew it. So I didn't say anything. Instead, I pulled her hand up to my mouth and kissed it, wishing for the hundredth time that it was me going up against the whole School Board, instead of Lena.

But the thing was, it would never have been me. No matter what I did, no matter what I said, I would always be one of them. Lena never would. And I think that was the thing that made me the angriest, and the most embarrassed. I hated them even more because deep down, they still claimed me as one of their own, even when I dated Old Man Ravenwood's niece and took on Mrs. Lincoln and wasn't invited to Savannah Snow's parties. I was one of them. I belonged to them, and there was nothing I could do to change that. And if the opposite were true, and in some way they belonged to me, then what Lena was up against wasn't just them. It was me.

The truth was killing me. Maybe Lena was going to be Claimed on her sixteenth birthday, but I had been claimed since birth. I had no more control over my fate than she did. Maybe none of us did.

I pulled the car into the parking lot. It was full. There was a crowd of people lined up at the main entrance, waiting to get in. I hadn't seen this many people in one place since the opening of *Gods and Generals*, the longest and most boring Civil War movie ever made and one that half my relatives starred in as extras, because they owned their own uniforms.

Link ducked down in the backseat. "I'm gonna slide out here. I'll see y'all in there." He pushed open the door and crawled out between the cars. "Good luck."

Lena's hands were in her lap, shaking. It killed me to see her this nervous. "You don't have to go in there. We can turn around and I can drive you right back to your house."

"No. I'm going in."

"Why do you want to subject yourself to this? You said it yourself, this is probably just for show."

"I'm not going to let them think I'm scared to face them. I left my last school, but I'm not going to run away this time." She took a deep breath.

"It's not running away."

"It is to me."

"Is your uncle coming at least?"

"He can't."

"Why the hell not?" She was all alone in this, even though I was standing right next to her.

"It's too early. I didn't even tell him."

"Too early? What is that about, anyway? Is he locked up in his crypt or something?"

"More like, *or something*."

It wasn't worth trying to talk about now. She was going to have enough to deal with in a few minutes.

We walked toward the building. It started to rain. I looked at her.

Believe me, I'm trying. If I let go, it would be a tornado.

People were staring, even pointing, not that I was surprised. So much for common decency. I looked around, half expecting to see Boo Radley sitting by the door, but tonight, he was nowhere in sight.

We entered the gym from the side, coincidentally—the Visitor's entrance, Link's idea, which turned out to be a good one. Because once we got inside, I realized people weren't standing out front waiting to get in, they were just hoping to hear the meeting. Inside, it was standing room only.

It looked like a pathetic version of a grand jury hearing from an episode of one of those courtroom dramas on TV. There was a big plastic folding table in the front of the room, and a few teachers—Mr. Lee of course, sporting a red bow tie and his own backwoods brand of prejudice; Principal Harper; and a couple of people who must have been members of the School Board—sitting in a row at the tables. They all looked old and annoyed, like they wished they could be at home watching QVC or religious programming.

The bleachers were filled with Gatlin's finest. Mrs. Lincoln and her DAR lynch mob were taking up the first three rows, with the members of the Sisters of the Confederacy, the First Methodist Choir, and the Historical Society taking up the next few. Right behind them were the Jackson Angels—also known as, the girls who wanted to be Emily and Savannah, and the guys who wanted to get into Emily's and Savannah's pants—sporting their freshly screened Guardian tees. The front of the shirts had a picture of an angel that looked suspiciously like Emily Asher, with her huge white angel wings spread wide open, wearing what else—a Jackson High Wildcats T-shirt. On the back, there was simply a pair of white wings designed to look like they were sprouting right out of the person's back, and the Angels' battle cry, "We'll Be Watching You."

Emily was sitting next to Mrs. Asher, her leg and its huge cast propped up on one of the orange cafeteria chairs. Mrs. Lincoln narrowed her eyes when she saw us, and Mrs. Asher put her arm around Emily protectively, as if one of us might run over there and beat her with a club like a defenseless baby seal pup. I saw Emily slip her phone out of her tiny silver bag, text-ready. Soon, her fingers would be flying. Our school gym was probably the epicenter of local gossip for four counties tonight.

Amma was sitting a few rows back, fiddling with the charm around her neck. Hopefully, it would make Mrs. Lincoln grow the horns she'd been so artfully hiding all these years. Of course, my dad wasn't there, but the Sisters were sitting next to Thelma, across the aisle from Amma. Things must have been worse than I thought. The Sisters hadn't been out of the house this late since 1980, when Aunt Grace ate too much spicy Hoppin' John and thought she was having a heart attack. Aunt Mercy caught my eye and waved her handkerchief.

I walked Lena to the seat in the front of the room obviously reserved for her. It was right in front of the firing squad, dead center.

It's going to be okay.

Promise?

I could hear the rain pounding on the roof outside.

I promise this doesn't matter. I promise these people are idiots. I promise nothing they say will ever change the way I feel about you.

I'll take that as a no.

The rain beat down harder on the roof, not a good sign. I took her hand and pressed something into it. The little silver button from Lena's vest, that I'd found in the Beater's cracked upholstery, the night we met in the rain. It looked like a piece of junk, but I had carried it in my jeans pocket ever since.

Here. It's sort of a good luck charm. At least it brought something good to me.

I could see how hard she was trying not to crack. Without a word, Lena took off her chain and added it to her own collection of valuable junk.

Thanks. If she could have smiled, she would have.

I made my way back toward the row where the Sisters and Amma were sitting. Aunt Grace stood up, resting on her cane. "Ethan, over here. We saved you a seat, darlin'."

"Why don't you sit down, Grace Statham," an old blue-haired woman sitting behind the Sisters hissed.

Aunt Prue turned around. "Why don't you mind your own business, Sadie Honeycutt, or I will mind it for you."

Aunt Grace turned to Mrs. Honeycutt and smiled. "Now you come right on over here, Ethan."

I squeezed in between Aunt Mercy and Aunt Grace. "How you holdin' up, Sweet Meat?" Thelma smiled and pinched my arm.

Thunder crashed outside, and the lights flickered. A few old women gasped.

393

An uptight-looking guy sitting in the middle of the big folding table cleared his throat. "Just a little hiccup in the power is all. Why doesn't everyone kindly take their seats so we can get started. My name is Bertrand Hollingsworth, and I'm Head a the School Board. This meeting's been called to respond to the petition requestin' the expulsion of a Jackson student, a Miss Lena Duchannes, is that right?"

Principal Harper addressed Mr. Hollingsworth from his seat at the table, the Prosecution, or more accurately, Mrs. Lincoln's hangman. "Yes, sir. The petition was brought to my attention by several *concerned* parents, and it was signed by over two hundred a Gatlin's most respected parents and citizens, and a number of Jackson students." Of course it was.

"What are the grounds for expulsion?"

Mr. Harper flipped some pages on his yellow legal pad like he was reading a rap sheet. "Assault. Destruction a school property. And Miss Duchannes was already on probation."

Assault? I didn't assault anyone.

It's just an accusation. They can't prove anything.

I was on my feet before he even finished. "None of that's true!"

Another jumpy-looking guy at the other end of the table raised his voice to be heard over the rain, and the twenty or thirty old women whispering about my bad manners. "Young man, have a seat. This is not a free-for-all."

Mr. Hollingsworth pressed on over the din. "Do we have any witnesses to substantiate these accusations?" Now there were more than a few people whispering to each other to see if anyone knew what "substantiate" meant.

Principal Harper cleared his throat awkwardly. "Yes. And recently, I received information that indicates Miss Duchannes had similar problems at the school she previously attended."

What is he talking about? How do they know anything about my old school?

I don't know. What happened at your old school?

Nothing.

A woman from the School Board flipped through some papers in front of her. "I think we'd like to hear from Jackson's Parent Partnership President, Mrs. Lincoln, first."

Link's mom stood up dramatically and walked down the aisle toward the Gatlin Grand Jury. She had seen a few courtroom dramas on TV, herself. "Good evenin', ladies and gentlemen."

"Mrs. Lincoln, can you tell us what you know about this situation, since you are one of the original petitioners?"

"Of course. Miss Ravenwood, I mean, Miss Duchannes, moved here several months ago, and since then there have been all sorts a *problems* at Jackson. First, she broke a window in the English class—"

"That came close to cuttin' my baby to shreds," Mrs. Snow called out.

"It came close to seriously injurin' several children, and many a them suffered cuts from the broken glass."

"No one except Lena was injured and that was an accident!" Link yelled from where he was standing in the back of the room.

"Wesley Jefferson Lincoln, you better go home right now if you know what's good for you!" Mrs. Lincoln hissed.

She regained her composure, smoothing her skirt, and turned to face the Disciplinary Committee. "Miss Duchannes' charms seem to work quite well on the weaker sex," Mrs. Lincoln said with a smile. "As I was sayin', she broke a window in the English classroom, which frightened the students so much that a number of civically minded young ladies took it upon *themselves* to form the Jackson Guardian Angels—a group whose sole purpose is to protect the students at Jackson. Like a Neighborhood Watch."

The Fallen Angels nodded in unison from their seats on the bleachers like someone was pulling invisible strings attached to their heads, which, in a way, someone was.

Mr. Hollingsworth was scribbling on a yellow legal pad. "Was this the only incident involvin' Miss Duchannes?"

Mrs. Lincoln tried to look shocked. "Heavens, no! At the winter formal, she pulled the fire alarm, ruinin' the dance and destroyin' four thousand dollars worth a audio equipment. As if that weren't enough, she pushed Miss Asher off a the stage, causin' her to break her leg, which I've been told, on good authority, will take months to heal."

Lena stared straight ahead, refusing to look at anyone.

"Thank you, Mrs. Lincoln." Link's mom turned and smiled at Lena. Not a genuine smile or even a sarcastic smile, but an I'm-going-to-ruin-your-life-and-enjoy-doing-it smile.

Mrs. Lincoln walked back to her seat. Then she stopped and looked right at Lena. "I almost forgot. There is one last thing." She pulled some loose papers from her purse. "I have records from Miss Duchannes' previous school in Virginia. Although it might be more accurate to call it an *institution*."

I wasn't in an institution. It was a private school.

"As Principal Harper mentioned, this is not the first time Miss Duchannes has had violent episodes."

Lena's voice in my head was bordering on hysterical. I tried to reassure her.

Don't worry.

But I was worried. Mrs. Lincoln wouldn't be saying this here if she couldn't prove it somehow.

"Miss Duchannes is a very *disturbed* girl. She suffers from a mental illness. Let me see . . ." Mrs. Lincoln ran her finger down the page as if she was looking for something. I waited to hear the diagnosis for the mental illness Mrs. Lincoln thought Lena suffered from—the state of being different. "Ah, yes, here it is. It appears Miss Duchannes suffers from bipolar disorder, which Doctor Asher can tell you is a very serious mental condition. These *people* who suffer from this affliction are prone to violence and unpredictable behavior. These things run in families; her mother was afflicted as well."

This can't be happening.

The rain hammered down on the roof. The wind picked up, lashing the door of the gym.

"In fact, her mother murdered her father fourteen years ago." The entire room gasped.

Game. Set. Match.

Everyone started talking at once.

"Ladies and gentlemen, please." Principal Harper tried to calm everyone down, but it was like taking a match to dry brush. Once the fire got started, there was no stopping it.

—☌

It took ten minutes for the gym to settle back down again, but Lena never did. I could feel her heart racing like it was my own, and the knot in her throat from choking back her tears. Although judging by the downpour outside, she was having a tough time with that. I was surprised she hadn't run out of the gym already, but she was either too brave or too stunned to move.

I knew Mrs. Lincoln was lying. I didn't believe Lena had been in an institution any more than I believed the Angels wanted to protect the students at Jackson. What I didn't know was if Mrs. Lincoln was lying about the rest, the part about Lena's mother murdering her father.

But I knew I wanted to kill Mrs. Lincoln. I'd known Link's mom my whole life, but lately I hadn't even been able to think of her like that anymore. She didn't seem like the woman who ripped the cable box out of the wall or lectured us for hours on the virtues of abstinence. This didn't seem like one of her annoying, yet ultimately innocent causes. This seemed more vindictive and more personal. I just couldn't figure out why she hated Lena so much.

Mr. Hollingsworth tried to regain control. "All right, everyone, let's settle down. Mrs. Lincoln, thank you for takin' the time to be here tonight. I'd like to review those documents, if you don't mind."

I stood up again. "This whole thing is ridiculous. Why don't you just set her on fire and see if she burns?"

Mr. Hollingsworth tried to gain control of the meeting, which was bordering on becoming an episode of *Jerry Springer*. "Mr. Wate, have a seat or you will be asked to leave. There will be no more outbursts during this meetin'. I have reviewed the witnesses' written accounts a what happened, and it seems this matter is quite straightforward and there is only one sensible thing to do."

There was a crash, and the huge metal doors in the back of the room flew open. A gust of wind blew in, along with sheets of rain.

And something else.

Macon Ravenwood strode casually into the gym, dressed in a black cashmere overcoat and sharp-looking gray pinstripe suit, with Marian Ashcroft on his arm. Marian was carrying a small, checkered umbrella just large enough to shield her from the downpour. Macon didn't have an umbrella, but he was still bone-dry. Boo lumbered in behind them, his black hair wet and standing on end, making it obvious he was more wolf than dog.

Lena turned around in her orange plastic chair, and for a second she looked as vulnerable as she felt. I could see the relief in her eyes, and I could see how hard she was trying to stay in her seat, to keep from throwing herself, sobbing, into his arms.

Macon's eyes flickered in her direction, and she settled back in her chair. He walked down the aisle toward the members of the School Board. "I'm so sorry we are late. The weather is just treacherous out there tonight. Don't let me interrupt. You were just about to do something *sensible* if I heard correctly."

Mr. Hollingsworth looked confused. Actually, most of the people in the gym looked confused. None of them had ever seen Macon Ravenwood in the flesh. "Excuse me, sir. I don't know who you think you are, but we are in the middle of proceedin's. And you can't bring that . . . that dog in here. Only service animals are permitted on school grounds."

"I understand completely. It just so happens that Boo Radley is my Seeing-Eye dog." I couldn't help but smile. I guess technically, that was true. Boo shook his huge body, water from his soaking wet fur showering everyone sitting close to the aisle.

"Well, Mister . . . ?"

"Ravenwood. Macon Ravenwood."

There was another audible gasp from the bleachers, followed by the buzz of whispering moving down the rows. The whole town had been waiting for this day since before I was born. You could feel the energy in the room pick up, from the sheer spectacle of it all. There was nothing, *nothing*, Gatlin loved better than a spectacle.

"Ladies and gentlemen of Gatlin. How nice to finally meet you all. I trust you know my dear friend, the beautiful Dr. Ashcroft. She has been kind enough to escort me this evening, as I don't quite know my way around our fair town."

Marian waved.

"Let me apologize once again for being late; please do continue. I'm sure you were just about to explain that the accusations against my niece are completely unfounded and encourage these children to go home and get a good night's sleep for school tomorrow."

For a minute, Mr. Hollingsworth looked like he might be convinced to do just that, and I wondered if maybe Uncle Macon had the same Power of Persuasion Ridley possessed. A woman with a beehive whispered something to Mr. Hollingsworth and he seemed to remember his original train of thought. "No, sir, that's not what I was about to do, not at all. In fact, the accusations against your niece are quite serious. It seems there are several witnesses to the events that transpired. Based on the written accounts and the information presented at this meetin', I'm afraid we are faced with no choice but to expel her."

Macon waved his hand toward Emily, Savannah, Charlotte, and Eden. "Are these your *witnesses*? An *imaginative* band of little girls suffering from a bad case of sour grapes."

Mrs. Snow leapt to her feet. "Are you insinuatin' that my daughter is lyin'?"

Macon smiled his movie star smile. "Not at all, my dear. I'm *saying* that your daughter is lying. I'm sure you can appreciate the difference."

"How dare you!" Link's mother pounced like a wildcat. "You have no right to be here, railroadin' these proceedin's."

Marian smiled and stepped forward. "As the great man said, 'Injustice anywhere is a threat to Justice everywhere.' And I see no justice in this room, Mrs. Lincoln."

"Don't you talk your Harvard talk around here."

Marian snapped her umbrella shut. "I don't believe Martin Luther King Jr. went to Harvard."

Mr. Hollingsworth spoke up authoritatively. "The fact remains that accordin' to witnesses, Miss Duchannes pulled the fire alarm, resultin' in thousands a dollars in damages to Jackson High School property, and pushed Miss Asher off the stage, resultin' in injuries to Miss Asher. Based on these events alone, we have grounds to expel her."

Marian sighed loudly, snapping her umbrella shut. "'It is difficult to free fools from the chains they revere.'" She looked pointedly at Mrs. Lincoln. "Voltaire, another man who did not go to Harvard."

Macon remained calm, which seemed to aggravate everyone even more. "Mister?"

"Hollingsworth."

"Mr. Hollingsworth, it would be a shame for you to continue on this course of action. You see, it's illegal to prevent a minor from attending school in the Great State of South Carolina. Education is compulsory, that means required. You cannot dismiss an innocent girl from school without grounds. Those days are over, even in the South."

"As I have explained, Mr. Ravenwood, we do have grounds, and we are well within our power to expel your niece."

Mrs. Lincoln jumped to her feet. "You can't just show up here out a the blue, interferin' with town business. You haven't left your house in years! What gives you the right to have a say in what happens in this town, or with our children?"

"Are you referring to your little collection of marionettes, dressed like, what is it—unicorns? You'll have to forgive my poor eyesight." Macon gestured toward the Angels.

"They are angels, Mr. Ravenwood, not unicorns. Not that I expect *you* to recognize Our Lord's messengers, since I don't ever recall seein' you in church."

"'Let he who is without sin cast the first stone,' Mrs. Lincoln." Macon paused for a second, as if he thought Mrs. Lincoln might need a moment or two to get her mind around that.

"As for your original point, you're absolutely right, Mrs. Lincoln. I spend a great deal of time in my house, which I don't mind. It's an enchanting place, really. But perhaps I should spend more time in town, spend some more time with all of you. Shake things up a bit, for lack of a better expression."

Mrs. Lincoln looked horrified, and the DAR members were turning around in their seats, looking at one another nervously at the thought of it.

"In fact, if Lena will not be returning to Jackson, she will have to be home schooled. Perhaps I should invite a few of her cousins to stay with me, as well. I wouldn't want her to miss out on the social aspect of her education. Some of her cousins are quite captivating. In fact, I believe you met one of them at your little Midwinter's Eve Masquerade Ball."

"It wasn't a masquerade ball—"

"My apologies. I only assumed those dresses were costumes, based on the garish nature of the plumage."

Mrs. Lincoln reddened. She was no longer just a woman trying to ban books. This was not a woman to be messed with. I was worried for Macon. I was worried for all of us.

"Let's be honest, Mr. Ravenwood. You have no place in this town. You are not part of it and clearly, neither is your niece. I don't think you are in any position to make demands."

Macon's expression changed slightly. He turned his ring around on his finger. "Mrs. Lincoln, I appreciate your candor, and I will try to be as frank with you as you have been with me. It would be a grave error for you, for anyone in this town, really, to pursue this matter. You see, I have a great deal of means. I'm a bit of a spendthrift, if you will. If you try to prevent my niece from returning to Stonewall Jackson High School, I will be forced to spend some of that money. Who knows, perhaps I'll bring in a Wal-Mart." There was another gasp from the bleachers.

"Is that a threat?"

"Not at all. Quite coincidentally, I also own the land upon which the Southern Comfort Hotel resides. Its closure would be most inconvenient for you, Mrs. Snow, as your husband would have to drive a great deal farther to meet his lady friends, which

I'm sure would make him late for supper on a regular basis. Now we couldn't have that, could we?"

Mr. Snow turned beet red and scrunched down behind a couple of guys on the football team, but Macon was just getting started. "And Mr. Hollingsworth, you look very familiar, sir. As does that striking Confederate flower to your left." Macon gestured to the lady from the School Board sitting next to him. "Haven't I seen you two somewhere before? I could swear—"

Mr. Hollingsworth swayed a little. "Absolutely not, Mr. Ravenwood. I am a married man!"

Macon turned his attention to the balding man sitting on the other side of Mr. Hollingsworth. "And Mr. Ebitt, if I decide to stop leasing the land to the Wayward Dog, where will you spend the evenings drinking, when your wife thinks you're studying at the Good Book Bible Group?"

"Wilson, how could you! To use Our Lord Almighty as an alibi. You will burn in the fires of Hell, sure as I'm standin' here!" Mrs. Ebitt collected her purse and started to push her way toward the aisle.

"It's not true, Rosalie!"

"Isn't it, though?" Macon smiled. "I can't even imagine what Boo here would tell me if he could talk. You know, he's been in and out of every yard and parking lot in your fair town, and I'll bet he's seen a thing or two." I stifled a laugh.

Boo's ears perked up at the sound of his name, and more than a few people started to squirm in their seats, as if Boo might open his mouth and start talking. After Halloween night, it wouldn't have surprised me, and considering Macon Ravenwood's reputation, nobody in Gatlin would have been too shocked, either.

"As you can see, there are more than a few people in this town who are less than honest. So you can imagine my concern when I learned that four teenage girls are the only witnesses to these scathing accusations made against my own family. Wouldn't it be in all of our interests to drop this matter? Wouldn't it be the *gentlemanly* thing to do, sir?"

Mr. Hollingsworth looked like he was going to be sick, and the woman next to him looked like she was hoping she'd get sucked down into the ground. Mr. Ebitt, whose name I realized was never mentioned before Macon said it, had already left, chasing after his wife. The remaining members of the tribunal looked scared to death, as if any minute now, Macon Ravenwood, or his dog, might start telling the whole town their dirty little secrets.

"I think you may be right, Mr. Ravenwood. Perhaps we need to *investigate* these accusations further before pursuin' this matter. There may, in fact, be *inconsistencies*."

"A wise choice, Mr. Hollingsworth. A very wise choice." Macon walked toward the tiny table where Lena was sitting and offered his arm. "Come now, Lena. It's late. You have school tomorrow." Lena stood up, standing even straighter than usual. The rain faded to a gentle patter. Marian tied a scarf around her hair and the three of them walked back up the aisle, Boo trailing behind them. They didn't look at anyone else in the room.

Mrs. Lincoln was on her feet. "Her mother is a murderer!" she screamed, pointing at Lena.

Macon spun around and their eyes met. There was something about his expression—it was the same expression he'd had when I showed him Genevieve's locket. Boo growled menacingly.

"Be careful, Martha. You never know when we'll run into each other again."

"Oh, but I do, Macon." She smiled, but it was nothing like a smile. I don't know what passed between them, but it didn't look like Macon was just battling Mrs. Lincoln anymore.

Marian opened her umbrella again, even though they weren't outside yet. She smiled diplomatically at the crowd. "Now, I hope to see all of you at the library. Don't forget, we're open till six o'clock on the weekdays."

She nodded to the room. "'Without libraries what have we? We have no past and no future.' Just ask Ray Bradbury. Or go to Charlotte, and read it for yourself on the wall of the public library." Macon took Marian's arm, but she wasn't finished. "And he didn't go to Harvard, either, Mrs. Lincoln. He didn't even go to college."

With that, they were gone.

White Christmas

After the Disciplinary Committee meeting, I don't think anyone believed Lena would show up at school the next day. But she did, just like I knew she would. No one else knew she had given up the right to go to school once. She wasn't going to let anyone take it away from her again. To everyone else, school was prison. To Lena, it was freedom. Only it didn't matter, because that was the day Lena became a ghost at Jackson—nobody looked at her, spoke to her, sat near her at any table, bleacher, or desk. By Thursday, half the kids at school were wearing the Jackson Angels T-shirt, with those white wings on their backs. The way they looked at her, it seemed half the teachers wished they could wear them, too. On Friday, I turned in my basketball jersey. It just didn't feel like we were all on the same team anymore.

Coach was furious. After all the hollering died down, he just shook his head. "You're crazy, Wate. Look at the season you're havin', and you're throwin' it away on some girl." I could hear it in his voice. *Some girl.* Old Man Ravenwood's niece.

Still, nobody said an unkind word to either one of us, at least not to our faces. If Mrs. Lincoln had put the fear of God into them, Macon Ravenwood had given people in Gatlin a reason to fear something even worse. The truth.

As I watched the numbers on Lena's wall and hand get smaller and smaller, the possibility became more real. What if we couldn't stop it? What if Lena had been right all along, and after her birthday the girl I knew disappeared? Like she had never been here at all.

All we had was *The Book of Moons.* And more and more, there was one thought I was trying to keep out of Lena's head and mine.

I wasn't sure the Book was enough.

"AMONGST PERSONNES OF POWERE, THERE BEING TWINNE FORCES FROM WHYCHE SPRING ALL MAGICK, THE DARKNESSE & THE LIGHT."

"I think we've got the whole Darkness and Light thing worked out. You think we could get to the good part? The part called, Loopholes for Your Claiming Day? How to Vanquish a Rogue Cataclyst? How to Reverse the Passage of Time?" I was frustrated, and Lena wasn't talking.

From where we sat on the cold bleachers, the school looked deserted. We were supposed to be at the science fair, watching Alice Milkhouse soak an egg in vinegar, listening to Jackson Freeman argue there was no such thing as global warming, and

Annie Honeycutt counter with how to make Jackson a green school. Maybe the Angels were going to have to start recycling their flyers.

I stared at the Algebra II book hanging out of my backpack. It didn't seem like there was anything worth learning at this place anymore. I'd learned enough in the last few months. Lena was a million miles away, still buried in the Book. I had started carrying it around in my backpack, out of fear Amma would find it if I left it in my room.

"Here's more about Cataclysts.

"THE GREATEST OF THE DARKNESSE BEING THE POWERE CLOSEST TO THE WOLD & THE UNDYRWOLD, THE CATACLYSTE. THE GREATEST OF THE LIGHT BEING THE POWERE CLOSEST TO THE WOLD & THE UNDYRWOLD, THE NATURAL. WHERE THERE IS NOT ONNE THERE CANNOT BE THE OTHERE, AS WITHOUTE DARKNESSE THERE CAN BE NO LIGHT."

"See? You're not going Dark. You're Light because you're the Natural."

Lena shook her head and pointed at the next paragraph. "Not necessarily. That's what my uncle thinks. But listen to this—

"AT THE TYME OF CLAIMING, THE TRUTHE WILL BE MADE MANIFESTE. WHAT APPEARS DARKNESSE MAYE BE THE GREATEST LIGHT, WHAT APPEARS LIGHT MAYE BE THE GREATEST DARKNESSE."

She was right, there was no way to be sure.

"Then it gets really complicated. I'm not even sure I understand the words.

"FOR THE DARKE MATTERE MAYDE THE DARKE FYRE, & THE DARKE FYRE MAYDE THE POWERES OF ALL LILUM IN THE DAEMON WOLD & CASTERS OF DARKNESSE & LIGHT. WITHOUT ALL

POWERE THERE CAN BE NO POWERE. THE DARKE FYRE MAYDE THE GREAT DARKNESSE & THE GREAT LIGHT. ALL POWERE IS DARKE POWERE, AS DARKE POWERE IS EVEN THE LIGHT."

"Dark Matter? Dark Fire? What is this, the Big Bang for Casters?"

"What about Lilum? I've never heard of any of this, but then again, nobody tells me anything. I didn't even know my own mother was alive." She tried to sound sarcastic, but I could hear the pain in her voice.

"Maybe Lilum is an old word for Casters, or something."

"The more I find out, the less I understand."

And the less time we have.

Don't say that.

The bell rang and I stood up. "You coming?"

She shook her head. "I'm going to stay out here a while longer." Alone, in the cold. More and more, it was like that; she hadn't even looked me in the eye since the Disciplinary Committee meeting, almost as if I were one of them. I couldn't really blame her, considering the whole school and half the town had basically decided she was the institutionalized, bipolar child of a murderer.

"You better show up in class sooner or later. Don't give Principal Harper any more ammunition."

She looked back toward the building. "I don't see how it matters now."

For the rest of the afternoon, she was nowhere to be found. At least, if she was, she wasn't listening. In chemistry, she wasn't there for our quiz on the periodic table.

You're not Dark, L. I would know.

In history, she wasn't there while we reenacted the Lincoln-Douglas Debate, and Mr. Lee tried to make me argue the Pro-Slavery side, most likely as punishment for some future "liberally minded" paper I was bound to write.

Don't let them get to you like this. They don't matter.

In ASL, she wasn't there while I had to stand up in front of the class and sign "Twinkle, Twinkle, Little Star" while the rest of the basketball team just sat there, smirking.

I'm not going anywhere, L. You can't shut me out.

That's when I realized she could.

By lunch, I couldn't take it anymore. I waited for her to come out of Trig and I pulled her over to the side of the hall, dropping my backpack to the floor. I took her face in my hands, and drew her in to me.

Ethan, what are you doing?

This.

I pulled her face into mine with both hands. When our lips touched, I could feel the warmth from my body seep into the coldness of hers. I could feel her body melting into mine, the inexplicable pull that had bound us together from the beginning, bringing us together again. Lena dropped her books and wrapped her arms around my neck, responding to my touch. I was becoming light-headed.

The bell rang. She pushed away from me, gasping. I bent down to pick up her copy of Bukowski's *Pleasures of the Damned* and her battered spiral notebook. The notebook was practically falling apart, but then again, she'd had a lot to write about lately.

You shouldn't have done that.

Why not? You're my girlfriend, and I miss you.

Fifty-four days, Ethan. That's all I have. It's time to stop pretending we can change things. It'll be easier if we both accept it.

There was something about the way she said it, like she was talking about more than just her birthday. She was talking about other things we couldn't change.

She turned away, but I caught her arm before she could turn her back on me. If she was saying what I thought she was saying, I wanted her to look at me when she said it.

"What do you mean, L?" I almost couldn't ask.

She looked away. "Ethan, I know you think this can have a happy ending, and for a while maybe I did, too. But we don't live in the same world, and in mine, wanting something badly enough won't make it happen." She wouldn't look at me. "We're just too different."

"Now we're too different? After everything we've been through?" My voice was getting louder. A couple of people turned and stared at me. They didn't even look at Lena.

We are different. You're a Mortal and I'm a Caster, and those worlds might intersect, but they'll never be the same. We aren't meant to live in both.

What she was saying was *she* wasn't meant to live in both. Emily and Savannah, the basketball team, Mrs. Lincoln, Mr. Harper, the Jackson Angels, they were all finally getting what they wanted.

This is about the disciplinary meeting, isn't it? Don't let them—

It isn't just about the meeting. It's everything. I don't belong here, Ethan. And you do.

So now I'm one of them. Is that what you're saying?

She closed her eyes and I could almost see her thoughts, tangled up in her mind.

I'm not saying you're like them, but you are one of them. This is where you've lived your whole life. And after this is all over, after I'm Claimed, you're still going to be here. You're going to have to walk down these halls and those streets again, and I probably won't be there. But you will, for who knows how long, and you said it yourself—people in Gatlin never forget anything.

Two years.

What?

That's how long I'll be here.

Two years is a long time to be invisible. Trust me, I know.

For a minute, neither of us said anything. She just stood there, pulling shreds of paper from the wire spine of her notebook. "I'm tired of fighting it. I'm tired of trying to pretend I'm normal."

"You can't give up. Not now, not after everything. You can't let them win."

"They already have. They won the day I broke the window in English."

There was something about her voice that told me she was giving up on more than just Jackson. "Are you breaking up with me?" I was holding my breath.

"Please don't make this harder. It's not what I want, either."

Then don't do it.

I couldn't breathe. I couldn't think. It was like time had stopped again, the way it had at Thanksgiving dinner. Only this time, it wasn't magic. It was the opposite of magic.

"I just think things will be easier this way. It doesn't change the way I feel about you." She looked up at me, her big green

eyes sparkling with tears. Then she turned and fled down a hallway that was so quiet you could've heard a pencil drop.

Merry Christmas, Lena.

But there was nothing to hear. She was gone, and that wasn't
something I would have been ready for, not in fifty-three days,
not in fifty-three years, not in fifty-three centuries.

Fifty-three minutes later, I sat alone, staring out the window,
which was a statement right there, considering how crowded the
lunchroom was. Gatlin was gray; the clouds had drifted in. I
wouldn't call it a storm, exactly; it hadn't snowed in years. If we
were lucky, we got a flurry or two, maybe once a year. But it
hadn't snowed a single day since I was twelve.

I wished it would snow. I wished I could hit rewind and be
back in the hallway with Lena. I wished I could tell her I didn't
care if everyone in this town hated me, because it didn't matter.
I was lost before I found her in my dreams, and she found me
that day in the rain. I knew it seemed like I was always the one
trying to save Lena, but the truth was she had saved me, and I
wasn't ready for her to stop now.

"Hey, man." Link slid onto the bench across from me at the
empty table. "Where's Lena? I wanted to thank her."

"For what?"

Link pulled a piece of folded notebook paper out of his
pocket. "She wrote me a song. Pretty cool, huh?" I couldn't
even look at it. She was talking to Link, just not to me.

Link grabbed a slice of my untouched pizza. "Listen, I got a
favor to ask you."

"Sure. What do you need?"

"Ridley and I are goin' up to New York over break. If anyone asks, I'm at church camp in Savannah, far as you know."

"There's no church camp in Savannah."

"Yeah, but my mom doesn't know that. I told her I signed up because they have some kind of Baptist rock band."

"And she believed that?"

"She's been actin' a little weird lately, but what do I care. She said I could go."

"It doesn't matter what your mom said, you can't go. There are things you don't know about Ridley. She's . . . dangerous. Stuff could happen to you."

His eyes lit up. I had never seen Link like this. Then again, I hadn't seen him too much lately. I'd been spending all my time with Lena, or thinking about Lena, the Book, her birthday. The stuff my world revolved around now, or did, until an hour ago.

"That's what I'm hopin'. Besides, I got it bad for that girl. She really does somethin' to me, ya know?" He took the last slice of pizza off my tray.

For a second I considered telling Link everything, just like the old days—about Lena and her family, Ridley, Genevieve, and Ethan Carter Wate. Link had known everything in the beginning, but I didn't know if he would believe the rest, or if he could. Some things were just asking too much, even from your best friend. Right now I couldn't risk losing Link, too, but I had to do something. I couldn't let him go to New York, or anywhere else, with Ridley. "Listen man, you've gotta trust me. Don't get mixed up with her. She's just using you. You're gonna get hurt."

He crushed a Coke can in his hand. "Oh, I get it. If the hottest girl in town is hangin' out with me, she must be usin' me? I guess you think you're the only one who can pull a hot chick. When did you get so full of yourself?"

"That's not what I'm saying."

Link got up. "I think we both know what you're sayin'. Forget I asked."

It was too late. Ridley had already gotten to him. Nothing I said was going to change his mind. And I couldn't lose my girlfriend and my best friend in the same day. "Listen, I didn't mean it like that. I won't say anything, not like your mom is speaking to me anyway."

"It's cool. It's gotta be hard to have a best friend who's good lookin' and as talented as me." Link took the cookie off my tray and broke it in half. It might as well have been the dirty Twinkie off the floor of the bus. It was over. It would take a lot more than a girl, even a Siren, to come between us.

Emily was eyeing him. "You'd better go before Emily rats you out to your mom. Then you won't be going to any church camp, real or imaginary."

"I'm not worried about her." But he was. He didn't want to be stuck in the house with his mom the whole winter break. And he didn't want to be frozen out by the team, by everyone at Jackson, even if he was too stupid or too loyal to realize it.

On Monday, I helped Amma bring the boxes of holiday decorations down from the attic. The dust made my eyes water; at least, that's what I told myself. I found a whole little town, lit by little white lights, that my Mom used to lay out every year under the Christmas tree, on a piece of cotton we pretended was snow.

The houses were her grandmother's, and she had loved them so much that I had loved them, even though they were made of flimsy cardboard, glue, and glitter, and half the time they fell over when I tried to stand them up. "Old things are better than new things, because they've got stories in them, Ethan." She would hold up an old tin car and say, "Imagine my great-grand-mother playing with this same car, arranging this same town under her tree, just like we are now."

I hadn't seen the town since, when? Since I'd seen my mom, at least. It looked smaller than before, the cardboard more warped and tattered. I couldn't find the people in any of the boxes, or even the animals. The town looked lonely, and it made me sad. Somehow the magic was gone, without her. I found myself reaching for Lena, in spite of everything.

Everything's missing. The boxes are there, but it's all wrong. She's not here. It's not even a town anymore. And she's never going to meet you.

But there was no response. Lena had vanished, or banished me. I didn't know which was worse. I really was alone, and the only thing worse than being alone was having everyone else see how lonely you were. So I went to the only place in town where I knew I wouldn't run into anyone. The Gatlin County Library.

———෴

"Aunt Marian?"

The library was freezing, and completely empty, as usual. After the way the Disciplinary Committee meeting had gone, I was guessing Marian hadn't had any visitors.

"I'm back here." She was sitting on the floor in her overcoat, waist high amidst a pile of open books, as if they had just fallen off the shelves around her. She was holding a book, reading aloud, in one of her familiar book-trances.

"'We see Him come, and know Him ours,
Who, with His Sun-shine, and His showers,
Turns all the patient ground to flowers.
The Darling of the world is come . . .'"

She closed the book. "Robert Herrick. It's a Christmas carol, sung for the king at Whitehall Palace." She sounded as far away as Lena had been lately, and I felt now.

"Sorry, don't know the guy." It was so cold I could see her breath when she spoke.

"Who does it remind you of? Turning the ground to flowers, the darling of the world."

"You mean Lena? I bet Mrs. Lincoln would have something to say about that." I sat down next to Marian, scattering books in the aisle.

"Mrs. Lincoln. What a sad creature." She shook her head, and pulled out another book. "Dickens thinks Christmas is a time for people 'to open their shut-up hearts freely, and to think of people below them as if they really were fellow passengers to the grave, and not another race of creatures.'"

"Is the heater broken? Do you want me to call Gatlin Electric?"

"I never turned it on. I guess I got distracted." She tossed the book back onto the pile surrounding her. "Pity Dickens never came to Gatlin. We've got more than our share of shut-up hearts around here."

I picked up a book. Richard Wilbur. I opened it, burying my face in the smell of the pages. I glanced at the words. "'What is the opposite of two? A lonely me, a lonely you.'" Weird, that was exactly how I was feeling. I snapped the book shut and looked at Marian.

"Thanks for coming to the meeting, Aunt Marian. I hope it didn't make trouble for you. I feel like it was all my fault."

"It wasn't."

"Feels like it was." I tossed the book down.

"What, now you're the author of all ignorance? You taught Mrs. Lincoln to hate, and Mr. Hollingsworth to fear?"

We both just sat there, surrounded by a mountain of books. She reached over and squeezed my hand. "This battle didn't start with you, Ethan. It won't end with you either, I'm afraid, or me, for that matter." Her face grew serious. "When I walked in this morning, these books were in a pile on the floor. I don't know how they got there, or why. I locked the doors when I left last night, and they were still locked this morning. All I know is, I sat down to look through them, and every single book, every one of them, had some kind of message for me about this moment, in this town, right now. About Lena, you, even me."

I shook my head. "It's a coincidence. Books are like that."

She plucked a random book out of the pile and handed it to me. "You try. Open it."

I took the book from her hand. "What is it?"

"Shakespeare. *Julius Caesar.*"

I opened it, and began to read.

"'Men at some time are masters of their fates:
The fault, dear Brutus, is not in our stars,

419

But in ourselves, that we are underlings.'

"What does that have to do with me?"

Marian peered at me, over her glasses. "I'm just the librarian. I can only give you the books. I can't give you the answers." But she smiled, all the same. "The thing about fate is, are you the master of your fate, or are the stars?"

"Are you talking about Lena, or Julius Caesar? Because I hate to break it to you, but I never read the play."

"You tell me."

We spent the rest of the hour going through the pile, taking turns reading to each other. Finally, I knew why I had come. "Aunt Marian, I think I need to go back into the archive."

"Today? Don't you have things you need to be doing? Holiday shopping at least?"

"I don't shop."

"Spoken wisely. As for myself, 'I do like Christmas on the whole. . . . In its clumsy way, it does approach Peace and Goodwill. But it is clumsier every year.'"

"More Dickens?"

"E. M. Forster."

I sighed. "I can't explain it. I think I need to be with my mom."

"I know. I miss her, too." I hadn't really thought about what I would say to Marian about how I was feeling. About the town, and how everything was wrong. Now the words seemed stuck in my throat, like another person was stumbling through them. "I just thought, if I could be around her books, maybe I could feel how it was before. Maybe I could talk to her. I tried to go to the graveyard once, but it didn't make me feel like she was there, in the ground." I stared at a random speck on the carpet.

"I know."

"I still can't think about her being there. It doesn't make sense. Why would you stick someone you love down in a lonely old hole in the dirt? Where it's cold, and dirty, and full of bugs? That can't be how it ends, after everything, after everything she was." I tried not to think about it, her body turning into bone and mud and dust down there. I hated the idea that she had to go through it alone, like I was going through everything alone now.

"How do you want it to end?" Marian laid her hand on my shoulder.

"I don't know. I should, somebody should build her a monument or something."

"Like the General? Your mom would have had a good laugh about that." Marian pulled her arm around me. "I know what you mean. She's not there, she's here."

She held out her hand, and I pulled her up. We held hands all the way back to the archive, as if I was still a kid she was babysitting while my mom was at work in the back. She pulled out a thick ring of keys and opened the door. She didn't follow me inside.

Back in the archive, I sank into the chair in front of my mom's desk. My mom's chair. It was wooden, and bore the insignia of Duke University. I think they had given it to her for graduating with honors, or something like that. It wasn't comfortable, but comforting, and familiar. I smelled the old varnish, the same varnish I'd probably chewed on as a baby, and right away I felt better than I had in months. I could breathe in the smell of the stacks of books wrapped in crackling plastic, the old crumbling parchment, the dust and the cheap file cabinets. I could breathe in the particular air of the particular atmosphere of my mother's very particular planet. To me, it was the same as if I was seven years old, sitting in her lap, burying my face in her shoulder.

I wanted to go home. Without Lena, I had nowhere else to go.

I picked up a small, framed photograph on my mom's desk, almost hidden among the books. It was her, and my father, in the study at our house. Someone had taken it in black and white, a long time ago. Probably for the back of a book jacket, on one of their early projects, when my dad was still a historian, and they had worked together. Back when they had funny hair, and ugly pants, and you could see the happiness on their faces. It was hard to look at, but harder to put down. When I went to return it to my mom's desk, next to the dusty stacks of books, one book caught my eye. I pulled it out from under an encyclopedia of Civil War weapons and a catalog of native plants of South Carolina. I didn't know what the book was. I only knew it was bookmarked with a long sprig of rosemary. I smiled. At least it wasn't a sock, or a dirty pudding spoon.

The Gatlin County Junior League cookbook, *Fried Chicken and Sass*. It opened, by itself, to a single page. "Betty Burton's Buttermilk Pan Fried Tomatoes," my mom's favorite. The scent of rosemary rose up from the pages. I looked at the rosemary more closely. It was fresh, as if it had been plucked from a garden yesterday. My mom couldn't have put it there, but no one else would use rosemary as a bookmark. My mom's favorite recipe was bookmarked with Lena's familiar scent. Maybe the books really were trying to tell me something.

"Aunt Marian? Were you looking to fry up some tomatoes?"

She stuck her head in the doorway. "Do you think I would touch a tomato, let alone cook one?"

I stared at the rosemary in my hand. "That's what I thought."

"I think that was the one thing your mother and I disagreed on."

"Can I borrow this book? Just for a few days?"

"Ethan, you don't have to ask. Those are your mother's things; there isn't anything in this room she wouldn't have wanted you to have."

I wanted to ask Marian about the rosemary in the cookbook, but I couldn't. I couldn't bear to show it to anyone else, or to part with it. Even though I had never and probably would never fry a tomato in my entire life. I stuck the book under my arm as Marian walked me to the door.

"If you need me, I'm here for you. You and Lena. You know that. There's nothing I wouldn't do for you." She pushed the hair out of my eyes and gave me a smile. It wasn't my mother's smile, but it was one of my mother's favorite smiles.

Marian hugged me, and wrinkled her nose. "Do you smell rosemary?"

I shrugged and slipped out the door, into the gray day. Maybe Julius Caesar was right. Maybe it was time to confront my fate, and Lena's fate. Whether it was up to us or the stars, I couldn't just sit around and wait to find out.

───ᗡჂ───

When I walked outside, it was snowing. I couldn't believe it. I looked up into the sky and let snow fall on my freezing face. The thick, white powdery flakes were drifting down with no particular purpose. It wasn't a storm, not at all. It was a gift, maybe even a miracle: a white Christmas, just like the song.

When I walked up to my front porch, there she was, sitting bareheaded on my front steps with her hood down. The moment I saw her, I recognized the snow for what it really was. A peace offering.

Lena smiled at me. In that second, the pieces of my life that had been falling apart fell back in place. Everything that was wrong just righted itself; maybe not everything, but enough.

I sat down next to her on the step. "Thanks, L."

She leaned against me. "I just wanted to make you feel better. I'm so confused, Ethan. I don't want you to get hurt. I don't know what I'd do if anything happened to you."

I ran my hand through her damp hair. "Don't push me away, please. I can't stand to lose anyone else I care about." I unzipped her parka, slipping my arm around her waist, inside her jacket, and pulled her toward me. I kissed her as she pressed into me, until I felt like we would melt the whole front yard if we didn't stop.

"What was that?" she asked, catching her breath. I kissed her again, until I couldn't take it any longer, and pulled back.

"I think that's called fate. I've been waiting to do that since the winter formal, and I'm not going to wait any longer."

"You're not?"

"Nope."

"Well, you'll have to wait a little longer. I'm still grounded. Uncle M thinks I'm at the library."

"I don't care if you're grounded. I'm not. I'll move into your house if I have to, and sleep with Boo in his dog bed."

"He has a bedroom. He sleeps in a four-poster bed."

"Even better."

She smiled and held onto my hand. The snowflakes melted as they landed on our warm skin.

"I've missed you, Ethan Wate." She kissed me back. The snow fell harder, dripping off us. We were practically radioactive. "Maybe you were right. We should spend as much time together as we can before—" she stopped, but I knew what she was thinking.

"We're gonna figure something out, L. I promise."

She nodded half-heartedly, and snuggled inside my arms. I could feel the calm beginning to spread between us. "I don't want to think about that today." She pushed me away, playfully, back among the living.

"Yeah? What do you want to think about, then?"

"Snow angels. I've never made one."

"Really? You guys don't do angels?"

"It's not the angels. We only moved to Virginia for a few months, so I've never lived anywhere it snows."

An hour later, we were soggy and wet and sitting around the kitchen table. Amma had gone to the Stop & Steal, and we were drinking the sorry hot chocolate I had attempted to make myself.

"I'm not sure this is the way you make hot chocolate," Lena teased me as I scraped a microwaved bowl of chocolate chips into hot milk. The result was brown and white and lumpy. It looked great to me.

"Yeah? How would you know? 'Kitchen, hot chocolate, please.'" I mimicked her high voice with my low one and the result was a strange cracking falsetto. She smiled. I had missed that smile, even though it had only been days; I missed it even when it had only been minutes.

"Speaking of Kitchen, I have to go. I told my uncle I was at the library, and it's closed by now."

I pulled her onto my lap, sitting at the kitchen table. I was having trouble not touching her every second, now that I could again. I found myself making excuses to tickle her, anything to touch her hair, her hands, her knees. The pull between us was like a magnet. She leaned against my chest and we just sat there until I heard feet padding across the floor upstairs. She bolted out of my lap like a frightened cat.

"Don't worry, that's my dad. He's just taking a shower. It's the only time he comes out of his study anymore."

"He's getting worse, isn't he?" She took my hand. We both knew it wasn't really a question.

"My dad wasn't like this until my mom died. He just flipped out after that." I didn't have to say the rest; she'd heard me think it enough times. About how my mom died, and we stopped cooking fried tomatoes, and we lost the little pieces of the Christmas town, and she wasn't there to stand up to Mrs. Lincoln, and nothing was ever the same again.

"I'm sorry."

"I know."

"Is that why you went to the library today? To look for your mom?"

I looked at Lena, pushing her hair out of her face. I nodded, pulling the rosemary out of my pocket and placing it carefully on the counter. "Come on. I want to show you something." I pulled her out of the chair and took her hand. We slid across the old wood flooring in our damp socks and stopped at the door to the study. I looked up the stairs to my dad's bedroom. I didn't even hear the shower yet; we still had plenty of time. I tried the door handle.

"It's locked." Lena frowned. "Do you have the key?"

"Wait, watch what happens." We stood there, staring at the door. I felt stupid standing there, and Lena must have too because she started to giggle. Just when I was about to laugh, the door began to unbolt itself. She stopped laughing.

That's not a Cast. I would be able to feel it.

I think I'm supposed to go in, or we are.

I stepped back and the door bolted itself again. Lena held up her hand, as if she was going to use her powers to open the door for me. I touched her back, gently. "L. I think I need to do it."

I touched the handle again. The door unbolted and swung open, and I stepped into the study for the first time in years. It was still a dark, frightening place. The painting, covered with a sheet, was still hanging over the faded sofa. Under the window, my dad's carved mahogany desk was papered with his latest novel, stacked on his computer, stacked on his chair, stacked meticulously across the Persian rug on the floor.

"Don't touch anything. He'll know."

Lena squatted down and stared at the nearest pile. Then, she picked up a piece of paper and turned on the brass desk lamp. "Ethan."

"Don't turn on the light. I don't want him to come down here and freak out on us. He'd kill me if he knew we were in here. All he cares about is his book."

She handed me the paper, without a word. I took it. It was covered with scribbles. Not scribbled words, just scribbles. I grabbed a handful of the papers closest to me. They were

427

covered with squiggly lines and shapes, and more scribbles. I picked up a piece of paper from the floor, nothing but tiny rows of circles. I tore through the stacks of white paper littering his desk and the floor. More scribbles and shapes, pages and pages of them. Not a single word.

Then I understood. There was no book.

My father wasn't a writer. He wasn't even a vampire.

He was a madman.

I bent down, my hands on my knees. I was going to be sick. I should have seen this coming. Lena rubbed my back.

It's okay. He's just going through a hard time. He'll come back to you.

He won't. He's gone. She's gone, and now I'm losing him, too.

What had my father been doing all this time, avoiding me? What was the point of sleeping all day and working all night, if you weren't working on the great American novel? If you were scribbling rows and rows of circles? Escaping from your only child? Did Amma know? Was everyone in on the joke but me?

It's not your fault. Don't do this to yourself.

This time I was the one out of control. The anger welled up inside me, and I pushed his laptop off his desk, sending his papers flying. I knocked over the brass lamp, and without even thinking, yanked the sheet off the painting over the couch. The painting went tumbling to the ground, knocking over a low bookshelf. A pile of books went flying to the floor, sprawling open on the rug.

"Look at the painting." She righted it, amidst the books on the floor.

It was a painting of me.

428

Me, as a Confederate soldier, in 1865. But it was me, none-theless.

Neither one of us needed to read the penciled label on the back of the frame to know who it was. He even had the lanky brown hair hanging down in his face.

"About time we met you, Ethan Carter Wate," I said, just as I heard my father lumbering down the stairs.

"Ethan Wate!"

Lena looked at the door, panicking. "Door!" It slammed shut and bolted. I raised an eyebrow. I didn't think I was ever going to get used to that.

There was pounding on the door. "Ethan, are you okay? What's goin' on in there?" I ignored him. I couldn't figure out what else to do, and I couldn't stand to look at him right now. Then I noticed the books.

"Look." I knelt on the floor in front of the nearest one. It was open to page 3. I flipped the page to 4 and it flipped back to 3. Just like the bolt on the study door. "Did you just do that?"

"What are you talking about? We can't stay in here all night."

"Marian and I spent the day in the library. And as crazy as it sounds, she thought the books were telling us things."

"What things?"

"I don't know. Stuff about fate, and Mrs. Lincoln, and you."

"Me?"

"Ethan! Open this door!" My dad was pounding now, but he had kept me out long enough. It was my turn.

"In the archive, I found a picture of my mom in this study and then a cookbook, opened to her favorite recipe, with a bookmark made of rosemary. Fresh rosemary. Don't you get it? It has to do with you, somehow, and my mom. And now we're here, like something wanted me to come here. Or, I don't know—someone."

"Or maybe you just thought of it because you saw her picture."

"Maybe, but look at this." I flipped the page of the *Constitutional History* book in front of me, turning it from page 3 to page 4. Once again, no sooner had I turned it than the page flipped back by itself.

"That's weird." She turned to the next book. *South Carolina: Cradle to Grave.* It was open to page 12. She flipped it back to 11. It flipped to 12.

I pushed my hair out of my eyes. "But this page doesn't say anything, it's a chart. Marian's books were open to certain pages because they were trying to tell us something, like messages. My mom's books don't seem to be telling us anything."

"Maybe it's some kind of code."

"My mom was terrible at math. She was a *writer*," I said, as if that was explanation enough. But I wasn't, and my mom knew that better than anyone.

Lena considered the next book. "Page 1. This is just the title page. It can't be the content."

"Why would she leave me a code?" I was thinking out loud, but Lena still had the answer.

"Because you always know the end of the movie. Because you grew up with Amma and the mystery novels and the crosswords. Maybe your mom thought you would figure out something that no one else would get."

My father half-heartedly banged away at the door. I looked at the next book. Page 9, and then 13. None of the numbers went higher than 26. And yet, lots of the books had way more pages than that. . . .

"There are 26 letters in the alphabet, right?"

"Yeah."

"That's it. When I was little, and couldn't sit still in church with the Sisters, my mom would make up games for me to play on the back of the church program. Hangman, scrambled words, and this, the alphabet code."

"Wait, let me get a pen." She grabbed a pen from the desk. "If A is 1 and B is 2—let me write it out."

"Careful. Sometimes I used to do it backward, where Z was 1."

Lena and I sat in the middle of the circle of the books, moving from book to book, while my father banged on the door outside. I ignored him, just like he had been ignoring me. I wasn't going to answer to him, or give him an explanation. Let him see how it felt for a change.

"3, 12, 1, 9, 13 . . ."

"Ethan! What are you doin' in there? What was all that racket?"

"25, 15, 21, 18, 19, 5, 12, 6."

I looked at Lena, and held out the paper. I was already a step ahead. "I think—it's meant for you."

It was as clear as if my mom was standing in the study, telling us in her own words, with her own voice.

CLAIM YOURSELF

It was a message for Lena.

My mom was there, in some form, in some sense, in some universe. My mom was still my mom, even if she only lived in books and door locks and the smell of fried tomatoes and old paper.

She lived.

When I finally opened the door, my dad was standing there in his bathrobe. He stared past me, into the study, where the pages of his imaginary novel were scattered all over the floor and the painting of Ethan Carter Wate was resting against the sofa, uncovered.

"Ethan, I—"

"What? Were going to tell me that you've been locked in your study for months doing this?" I held up one of the crumpled pages in my hand.

He looked down at the floor. My dad may have been crazy, but he was still sane enough to know that I had figured out the truth. Lena sat down on the sofa, looking uncomfortable.

"Why? That's all I want to know. Was there ever a book or were you just trying to avoid me?"

My dad raised his head slowly, his eyes tired and bloodshot. He looked old, like life had worn him down one disappointment at a time. "I just wanted to be close to her. When I'm in there, with her books and her things, it feels like she isn't really gone. I can still smell her. Fried tomatoes . . ." His voice trailed off, as if he was lost in his own mind again and the rare moment of clarity was gone.

He walked past me, back into the study, and bent down to pick up one of the pages covered with circles. His hand was shaking. "I was tryin' to write." He looked over at my mom's chair. "I just don't know what to write anymore."

It wasn't about me. It had never been about me. It was about my mom. A few hours ago I had felt the same way in the library, sitting among her things, trying to feel her there with me. But now I knew she wasn't gone, and everything was different. My dad didn't know. She wasn't unlocking doors for him and leaving him messages. He didn't even have that.

—⟋☊

The next week, on Christmas Eve, the weathered and warped cardboard town didn't seem so small. The lopsided steeple stayed on the church, and the farmhouse even stood up by itself, if you set it just right. The white glitter glue sparkled and the same old piece of cotton snow secured the town, constant as time.

I lay on my stomach on the floor, with my head tucked under the lowest branches of the fat white pine, just as I always had. The blue-green needles scratched my neck as I carefully pushed a string of tiny white lights, one by one, into the circular holes in the back of the broken village. I sat back to take a look, the soft white light turning colors through the painted paper windows of the town. We never found the people, and the tin cars and animals were still gone. The town was empty, but for the first time it didn't seem deserted, and I didn't feel alone.

As I sat there, listening to Amma's pencil scratching, and my dad's scratchy old holiday record, something caught my eye. It was small and dark, and snagged in a fold, between layers of the cotton snow. It was a star, about the size of a penny, painted silver and gold, and surrounded by a twisted halo made of what looked like a paper clip. It was from the town's pipe-cleaner

Christmas tree, which we hadn't been able to find in years. My mom had made it in school, as a little girl in Savannah.

I put it in my pocket. I'd give it to Lena next time I saw her, for her charm necklace, for safekeeping. So it didn't get lost again. So I didn't get lost again.

My mom would have liked that. Would like that. Just like she would have liked Lena—or maybe even, did.

Claim yourself.

The answer had been in front of us, all along. It was just locked away with all the books in my father's study, stuck between the pages of my mother's cookbook.

Snagged a little in the dusty snow.

⊰ 1.12 ⊱

Promise

There was something in the air. Usually, when you heard that, there wasn't really something in the air. But the closer it got to Lena's birthday, the more I had to wonder. When we came back from winter break, the halls had been tagged with spray paint, covering the lockers and walls. Only it wasn't the usual graffiti; the words didn't even look like English. You wouldn't have thought they were words at all, unless you had seen *The Book of Moons.*

A week later, every window in our English classroom was busted out. Again, it could have been the wind, except there wasn't even a breeze. How could the wind target a single class-room, anyway?

Now that I wasn't playing basketball, I had to take P.E. for the rest of the year, by far the worst class at Jackson. After an hour of timed sprints and rope burn from climbing a knotted rope to the gym ceiling, I got back to my locker to find the door open and my papers scattered all over the hall. My backpack was gone. Though Link found it a few hours later, dumped in a trash-can outside the gym, I had learned my lesson. Jackson High was no place for *The Book of Moons*.

From then on, we kept the Book in my closet. I waited for Amma to discover it, to say something, to cover my room with salt, but she never did. I had pored over the old leather book, with and without Lena, using my mom's battered Latin diction-ary, for the past six weeks. Amma's oven mitts helped me keep the burns to a minimum. There were hundreds of Casts, and only a few of them were in English. The rest were written in languages I couldn't read, and the Caster language we couldn't hope to decipher. As we grew more familiar with the pages, Lena grew more restless.

"Claim yourself. That doesn't even mean anything."

"Of course it does."

"None of the chapters say anything about it. It's not in any description of the Claiming in the Book."

"We just have to keep looking. It's not like we're going to read it in the Cliff Notes." *The Book of Moons* had to have the answer, if we could just find it. We couldn't think about any-thing else, except the fact that a month from now we could lose it all.

At night, we stayed up late talking, from our respective beds, because even now, every night seemed closer to the night that could be our last.

What are you thinking, L?

Do you really want to know?

436

I always want to know.

Did I? I stared at the creased map on my wall, the thin green line connecting all the places I had read about. There they were, all the cities of my imaginary future, held together with tape and marker and pins. In six months, a lot had changed. There was no thin green line that could lead me to my future anymore. Just a girl.

But now, her voice was small, and I had to strain to hear her.

There's a part of me that wishes we'd never met.

You're kidding, right?

She didn't answer. Not right away.

It just makes everything so much harder. I thought I had a lot to lose before, but now I have you.

I know what you mean.

I knocked the shade off the lamp next to my bed and stared straight into the bulb. If I stared right at it, the brightness would sting my eyes and keep me from crying.

And I could lose you.

That's not gonna happen, L.

She was quiet. My eyes were temporarily blinded by swirls and streaks of light. I couldn't even see the blue of my bedroom ceiling, though I was staring right at it.

Promise?

I promise.

It was a promise she knew I might not be able to keep. But I made it anyway because I was going to find a way to make it true.

I burned my hand as I tried to turn out the light.

The Sandman or Something Like Him

Lena's birthday was in a week.

Seven days.

One hundred and sixty-eight hours.

Ten thousand and eight seconds.

Claim yourself.

Lena and I were exhausted, but we ditched school anyway to spend the day with *The Book of Moons*. I had become an expert at Amma's signature, and Miss Hester wouldn't dare to ask Lena for a note from Macon Ravenwood. It was a cold, clear day, and we curled together in the freezing garden at Greenbrier, huddled under the old sleeping bag from the Beater, trying to figure out for the thousandth time if anything in the Book could help.

I could tell Lena was starting to give up. Her ceiling was completely covered in Sharpie, wallpapered with the words she couldn't say and thoughts she was too scared to express.

darkfire, lightdark / dark matter, what matters? the great darkness swallows the great light, as they swallow my life / caster/girl super/natural before/first sight seven days seven days seven days 777777777777777.

I couldn't blame her. It did seem pretty hopeless, but I wasn't ready to give up. I never would be. Lena slumped against the old stone wall, crumbling like what little chance we had left. "This is impossible. There are too many Casts. We don't even know what we're looking for."

There were Casts for every conceivable purpose: *Blinding the Unfaithful, Bringing Forth Water from the Sea, Binding the Runes.*

But nothing that said *Cast to Uncurse Your Family from a Dark Binding*, or *Cast to Undo the Act of Trying to Bring Great-Great-Great-Great-Grandmother Genevieve's War Hero Back to Life*, or *Cast to Avoid Going Dark at Your Claiming.* Or the one I was really looking for—*Cast to Save Your Girlfriend (Now That You Finally Have One) Before It's Too Late.*

I turned back to the Table of Contents: OBSECRATIONES, IN-CANTAMINA, NECTENTES, MALEDICENTES, MALEFICIA.

"Don't worry, L. We'll figure it out." But even as I said it, I wasn't so sure.

———⟲

The longer the Book stayed on the top shelf of my closet, the more I felt like my room was becoming haunted. It was happening to both of us, every night; the dreams, which felt more like nightmares, were getting worse. I hadn't slept for more than a couple of hours in days. Every time I closed my eyes, every time I fell asleep, they were there. Waiting. But even worse, it was the same nightmare replayed again and again in a constant loop. Every night, I lost Lena over and over again, and it was killing me.

My only strategy was to stay awake. Jacked up on sugar and caffeine from drinking Coke and Red Bull, playing video games. Reading everything from *Heart of Darkness* to my favorite issue of *Silver Surfer*, the one where Galactus swallows the universe, over and over. But as anyone who hasn't slept in days knows, by the third or fourth night you're so tired you could fall asleep standing up.

Even Galactus didn't stand a chance.

Burning.

There was fire everywhere.

And smoke. I choked on the smoke and ash. It was pitch-black, impossible to see. And the heat was like sandpaper scraping against my skin.

I couldn't hear anything except the roar of the fire.

I couldn't even hear Lena screaming, except in my head.

Let go! You have to get out!

I could feel the bones in my wrist snapping, like tiny guitar strings breaking one by one. She let go of my wrist like she was preparing for me to release her, but I'd never let go.

Don't do that, L! Don't you let go!

Let me go! Please . . . save yourself!

I'd never let go.

But I could feel her sliding through my fingers. I tried to hold on tighter, but she was slipping. . . .

I bolted upright in bed, coughing. It was so real, I could taste the smoke. But my room wasn't hot; it was cold. My window was open again. The moonlight allowed my eyes to adjust more quickly than usual to the darkness.

I noticed something out of the corner of my eye. Something was moving, in the shadows.

There was someone in my room.

"Holy crap!"

He tried to get out before I noticed him, but he wasn't fast enough. He knew I'd seen him. So he did the only thing he could do. He turned to face me.

"Although I myself don't consider it particularly holy, who am I to correct you after such an *ungraceful* exit?" Macon smiled his Cary Grant smile and approached the end of my bed. He was wearing a long black coat and dark slacks. He looked like he was dressed for some kind of turn-of-the-century night on the town, instead of a modern-day breaking and entering. "Hello, Ethan."

"What the hell are you doing in my bedroom?"

He seemed at a loss, for Macon, which just meant he didn't have an immediate and charming explanation on the tip of his tongue. "It's complicated."

"Well, uncomplicate it. Because you climbed in my window in the middle of the night, so either you're some kind of vampire or some kind of perv, or both. Which is it?"

"Mortals, everything is so black and white to you. I'm not

a Hunter, nor a Harmer. You would be confusing me with my brother, Hunting. Blood doesn't interest me." He shuddered at the thought. "Neither blood nor flesh." He lit a cigar, rolling it between his fingers. Amma was going to have a fit when she smelled that tomorrow. "In fact, it all makes me a bit squeamish."

I was losing my patience. I hadn't slept in days and I was tired of everyone dodging my questions all the time. I wanted answers, and I wanted them now. "I've had enough of your riddles. Answer the question. What are you doing in my room?"

He walked over to the cheap swivel chair next to my desk and sat down in one sweeping movement. "Let's just say I was eavesdropping."

I picked up the old Jackson High basketball T-shirt balled up on the floor and pulled it over my head. "Eavesdropping on what, exactly? There's no one here. I was sleeping."

"No, actually you were dreaming."

"How do you know that? Is that one of your Caster powers?"

"I'm afraid not. I'm not a Caster, not technically."

My breath caught in my throat. Macon Ravenwood never left his house during the day; he could make himself appear out of nowhere, watch people through the eyes of his wolf that masqueraded as a dog, and nearly squeeze the life out of a Dark Caster without flinching. If he wasn't a Caster, then there was only one explanation.

"So you are a vampire."

"I most certainly am not." He looked annoyed. "That's such a common phrase, such a cliché, and so unflattering. There are no such things as vampires. I suppose you believe in werewolves and aliens, too. I blame television." He inhaled deeply from his cigar. "I hate to disappoint you. I'm an Incubus. I'm sure it was just a matter of time before Amarie told you herself, since she seems so intent on revealing all my secrets."

An Incubus? I didn't even know if I should be scared. I must have looked confused, because Macon felt compelled to elaborate. "By nature, gentlemen like myself do have certain *powers*, but those powers are only relative to our strength, which we must *replenish* regularly." There was something disturbing about the way he said replenish.

"What do you mean by replenish?"

"We feed, for lack of a better word, on Mortals to replenish our strength."

The room started to sway. Or maybe Macon was swaying.

"Ethan, sit down. You look absolutely pallid." Macon strode over and guided me to the edge of the bed. "As I said, I use the word 'feed' for lack of a better term. Only a Blood Incubus feeds on Mortal blood, and I am not a Blood Incubus. Although we are both Lilum—those who dwell in the Absolute Darkness—I am something entirely more *evolved*. I take something you Mortals have in abundance, something you don't even need."

"What?"

"Dreams. Fragmented bits and pieces. Ideas, desires, fears, memories—nothing you miss." The words came rolling out of his mouth as if he was speaking a charm. I found myself struggling to process them, trying to understand what he was saying. My mind felt like it was wrapped in thick wool.

But then, I understood. I could feel the pieces clicking together like a puzzle in my mind. "The dreams—you've been taking part of them? Sucking them out of my head? That's the reason I can't remember the whole dream?"

He smiled and stubbed his cigar out on an empty Coke can on my desk. "Guilty as charged. Except for the 'sucking.' Not the most polite phraseology."

"If you're the one sucking—stealing my dreams, then you know the rest. You know what happens, in the end. You can tell us, so we can stop it."

"I'm afraid not. I selected the bits and pieces I took rather intentionally."

"Why don't you want us to know what happens? If we know the rest of the dream, maybe we can stop it from happening."

"It seems you know too much already, not that I understand it completely myself."

"Stop talking in riddles for once. You keep saying I can protect Lena, that I have power. Why don't you tell me what the hell is really going on, Mr. Ravenwood, because I'm tired, and I'm sick of being jerked around."

"I can't tell you what I don't know, son. You're a bit of a mystery."

"I'm not your son."

"Melchizedek Ravenwood!" Amma's voice rang out like a bell.

Macon started losing his composure.

"How dare you come into this house without my permission!" She was standing in her bathrobe holding a long rope of beads. If I didn't know better I'd have thought it was a necklace. Amma shook the beaded charm angrily in her fist. "We have an agreement. This house is off-limits. You find somewhere else to do your dirty business."

"It's not that simple, Amarie. The boy is seeing things in his dreams, things that are dangerous for *both* of them."

Amma's eyes were wild. "Are you feedin' offa my boy? Is that what you're sayin'? Is that supposed to make me feel better?"

"Calm down. Don't be so literal. I am merely doing what is necessary to protect them both."

"I know what you do and what you are, Melchizedek, and you will deal with the Devil in due time. Don't you bring that evil into my house."

"I made a choice long ago, Amarie. I've fought what I was destined to be. I fight it every night of my life. But I am not Dark, not as long as I have the child to concern me."

"Doesn't change what you are. That's not a choice you get to make."

Macon's eyes narrowed. It was clear that the bargain between the two of them was a delicate one, and he had jeopardized it by coming here. How many times? I didn't even know.

"Why don't you just tell me what happens at the end of the dream? I have a right to know. It's my dream."

"It's a powerful dream, a disturbing dream, and Lena doesn't need to see it. She's not ready to see it, and you two are so inexplicably connected. She sees what you see. So you can understand why I had to take it."

The rage welled up inside me. I was so angry, angrier than when Mrs. Lincoln stood up and lied about Lena at the Disciplinary Committee meeting, angrier then when I found the pages and pages of scribble in my father's study.

"No. I don't understand. If you know something that can help her, why won't you tell us? Or just stop using your Jedi mind tricks on me and my dreams and let me see it for myself?"

"I am only trying to protect her. I love Lena, and I would never—"

"—I know, I've heard it. You'd never do anything to hurt her. What you forgot to say is that you won't do anything to help her, either."

His jaw tightened. Now he was the one who was angry; I knew how to recognize it now. But he didn't break character, not even for a minute. "I am trying to protect her, Ethan, and you as well. I know you care for Lena, and you do offer her some sort of protection, but there are things you don't see right now, things that are beyond any of our control. One day you will understand. You and Lena are just too different."

A *Species Apart*. Just like the other Ethan wrote to Genevieve. I understood all right. Nothing had changed in over a hundred years.

His eyes softened. I thought maybe he pitied me, but it was something else. "Ultimately, it will be your burden to bear. It's always the Mortal who bears it. Trust me, I know."

"I don't trust you and you're wrong. We aren't too different."

"Mortals. I envy you. You think you can change things. Stop the universe. Undo what was done long before you came along. You are such beautiful creatures." He was talking to me, but it didn't feel like he was talking about me anymore. "I apologize for the intrusion. I'll leave you to your sleep."

"Just stay out of my room, Mr. Ravenwood. And out of my head."

He turned toward the door, which surprised me. I expected him to leave the way he had arrived.

"One more thing. Does Lena know what you are?"

He smiled. "Of course. We have no secrets between us."

I didn't smile back. There were more than a few secrets between them, even if this wasn't one of them, and both Macon and I knew it.

He turned away from me with a swirl of his overcoat, and was gone.

Just like that.

The Battle of Honey Hill

The next morning, I woke up with a pounding headache. I did not, as so often happens in stories, think that the whole thing had never happened. I did not believe that Macon Ravenwood appearing and disappearing in my bedroom the night before had been a dream. Every morning for months after my mom's accident, I had woken up believing it had all been a bad dream. I would never make that mistake again.

This time around, I knew if it seemed like everything had changed, it was because it had. If it seemed like things were getting weirder and weirder, it was because they were. If it seemed like Lena and I were running out of time, it was because we were.

Six days and counting. Things didn't look good for us. That was all there was to say. So of course, we didn't say it. At school, we did what we always did. We held hands in the hallway. We kissed by the back lockers until our lips ached and I felt close to being electrocuted. We stayed in our bubble, enjoyed what we tried to pretend were our ordinary lives, or what little we had left of them. And we talked, all day long, through every minute of every class, even the ones we didn't have together.

Lena told me about Barbados, where the water and the sky met in a thin blue line until you couldn't tell which was which, while I was supposed to be making a clay rope bowl in ceramics.

Lena told me about her Gramma, who let her drink 7-Up using red licorice as a straw, while we wrote our in-class *Dr. Jekyll and Mr. Hyde* essays in English, and Savannah Snow smacked her gum.

Lena told me about Macon, who, despite everything, had been there for every birthday, wherever she'd been, since she could remember.

That night, after staying up for hour after hour with *The Book of Moons*, we watched the sun rise—even though she was at Ravenwood, and I was at home.

Ethan?

I'm here.

I'm scared.

I know. You should try to get some sleep, L.

I don't want to waste time sleeping.

Me neither.

But we both knew that wasn't it. Neither one of us felt much like dreaming.

"THE NYGHT OF THE CLAYMYNG BEING THE NYGHT OF
GREATESTE WEAKNESSE, WHENNE THE DARKENESSE WITHINNE
ENJOINS THE DARKENESSE WITHOUTE & THE PERSONNE OF
POWERE OPENNES TO THE GREATE DARKNESSE, SO STRIPPED
OF PROTECTIONS, BINDINGS & CASTS OF SHIELDE & IMMUNI-
TIE. DEATH, AT THE HOURE OF CLAYMING, IS MOST FINALE
& ETERNALLE . . ."

Lena shut the Book. "I can't read any more of this."

"No kidding. No wonder your uncle is so worried all the time."

"It's not enough that I could turn into some kind of evil demon. I could also suffer eternal death. Add that to the list under impending doom."

"Got it. Demon. Death. Doom."

We were in the garden at Greenbrier again. Lena handed me the Book and flopped on her back, staring up at the sky. I hoped she was playing with the clouds instead of thinking about how little we had figured out during these afternoons with the Book. But I didn't ask her to help me as I paged through it, wearing Amma's old garden gloves that were way too small.

There were thousands of pages in *The Book of Moons*, and some pages contained more than one Cast. There was no rhyme or reason to the way it was organized, at least none that I could see. The Table of Contents had turned out to be some kind of hoax that only loosely corresponded to some of what could actually be found inside. I turned the pages, hoping I would stumble across something. But most of the pages just looked like gibberish. I stared at the words I couldn't understand.

I DDARGANFOD YR HYN SYDD AR GOLL

DATODWCH Y CWLWM, TROELLWCH A THROWCH EF

BWRIWCH Y RHWYMYN HWN

FEL Y CAF GANFOD

YR HYN RWY'N DYHEU AMDANO

YR HYN RWY'N EI GEISIO.

Something jumped out at me, a word I recognized from a quote tacked on the wall of my parents' study: "PETE ET INVENIES." Seek and you shall find. "INVENIES." Find.

UT INVENIAS QUOD ABEST

EXPEDI NODUM, TORQUE ET CONVOLVE

ELICE HOC VINCULUM

UT INVENIAM

QUOD DESIDERO

QUOD PETO.

I tore through the pages of my mom's Latin dictionary, scrawling the words in the back as I translated them. The words of the Cast stared back at me.

To Find What is Missing
Unravel the tie, twist and wind
Cast this Bind
So I may find
That which I yearn for
That which I seek.

451

"I found something!"

Lena sat up, peering over my shoulder. "What are you talking about?" She sounded less than convinced.

I held my chicken scratch handwriting up for her to read. "I translated this. It seems like you use it to find something."

Lena leaned closer, checking my translation. Her eyes widened. "It's a Locator Cast."

"That sounds like something we can use to find the answer, so we can figure out how to undo the curse."

Lena pulled the Book into her lap, staring at the page. She pointed to the other Cast above it. "That's the same Cast in Welsh, I think."

"But can it help us?"

"I don't know. We don't even really know what we're looking for." She frowned, suddenly less enthusiastic. "Besides, Spoken Casting isn't as easy as it looks, and I've never done it before. Things can go wrong." Was she kidding?

"Things can go wrong? Things worse than turning into a Dark Caster on your sixteenth birthday?" I grabbed the Book out of her hands, burning the daisies off the tips of the gloves. "Why did we dig up a grave to find this thing and waste weeks trying to figure out what it says, if we aren't even going to try?" I held the Book up until one of the gloves started to smoke.

Lena shook her head. "Give me that." She took a deep breath. "Okay, I'll try, but I have no idea what will happen. This isn't usually how I do it."

"It?"

"You know, the way I use my powers, all the Natural stuff. I mean, that's the whole point, isn't it? It's supposed to be natural. I don't even know what I'm doing, half the time."

"Okay, so this time you do, and I'll help. What do I need to do? Draw a circle? Light some candles?"

Lena rolled her eyes. "How about sit over there." She pointed to a spot a few feet away. "Just in case."

I was expecting a little bit more preparation, but I was just a Mortal. What did I know? I ignored Lena's order to put some distance between myself and her first Spoken Cast, but I did take a few steps back. Lena held the Book in one hand, which was a feat in itself because it was incredibly heavy, and took a deep breath. Her eyes ran slowly down the page as she read.

"'Unravel the tie, twist and wind

Cast this Bind

So I may find

That which I yearn for . . .'"

She looked up and spoke the last line, clear and strong.

"'That which I seek.'"

For a second, nothing happened. The clouds still lingered overhead, the air was still cold. It didn't work. Lena shrugged her shoulders. I knew she was thinking the same thing. Until we both heard it, a sound like a rush of air echoing through a tunnel. The tree behind me caught fire. It actually ignited, from the bottom up. Flames raced up the trunk, roaring, spreading out to every branch. I had never seen anything catch fire that quickly.

The wood started to smoke immediately. I pulled Lena away from the fire, coughing. "Are you okay?" She was coughing, too. I pushed her black curls away from her face. "Well, obviously that didn't work. Unless you were looking to toast some really big marshmallows."

Lena smiled weakly. "I told you things could go wrong."

"That's an understatement."

We stared up at the burning cypress. That was five days and counting.

Four days and counting, the storm clouds rolled in, and Lena stayed home sick. The Santee flooded and the roads were washed out north of town. The local news chalked it up to global warming, but I knew better. As I sat in Algebra II, Lena and I argued about the Book, which wasn't going to help my grade on the pop quiz.

Forget about the Book, Ethan. I'm sick of it. It's not helping.

We can't forget about it. It's your only chance. You heard your uncle. It's the most powerful book in the Caster world.

It's also the Book that cursed my whole family.

Don't give up. The answer has to be somewhere in the Book.

I was losing her, she wouldn't listen to me, and I was about to fail my third quiz of the semester. Great.

By the way, can you simplify 7x – 2(4x – 6)?

I knew she could. She was already in Trig.

What does that have to do with anything?

Nothing. But I'm failing this quiz.

She sighed.

A Caster girlfriend had some perks.

Three days and counting, the mudslides started and the upper field slid into the gym. The squad wouldn't be cheering for a while, and the Disciplinary Committee was going to have to find a new place to hold their witch trials. Lena was still not back in school, but she was in my head the whole day. Her voice grew smaller, until I could barely hear it over the chaos of another day at Jackson High.

I sat alone in the lunchroom. I couldn't eat. For the first time since I met Lena, I looked at everyone around me and felt a pang of, I don't know, something. What was it? Jealousy? Their lives were so simple, so easy. Their problems were Mortal-sized, tiny. The way mine used to be. I caught Emily looking at me. Savannah bounced into Emily's lap, and with Savannah came the familiar snarl. It wasn't jealousy. I wouldn't trade Lena for any of this.

I couldn't imagine going back to such a tiny life.

_____ᘒ

Two days and counting, Lena wouldn't even speak to me. Half the roof blew off the DAR headquarters when the high winds hit. The Member Registries Mrs. Lincoln and Mrs. Asher had spent years compiling, the family trees going back to the Mayflower and the Revolution, were destroyed. The Gatlin County patriots would have to prove their blood was better than the rest of ours, all over again.

I drove to Ravenwood on my way to school and banged on the door as hard as I could. Lena wouldn't come out of the house. When I finally got her to open the door, I could see why.

Ravenwood had changed again. Inside, it looked like a maximum-security prison. The windows had bars and the walls were smooth concrete, except for in the front hallway, where they were orange and padded. Lena was wearing an orange jumpsuit with the numbers 0211, her birthday, stamped on it, her hands covered in writing. She looked kind of cool, actually, her messy black hair falling around her. She could even make a prison jumpsuit look good.

"What's going on, L?"

She followed my gaze over her shoulder. "Oh, this? Nothing. It's a joke."

"I didn't know Macon joked."

She pulled at a loose string on her sleeve. "He doesn't. It's my joke."

"Since when can you control Ravenwood?"

She shrugged. "I just woke up yesterday and this is what it looked like. It must have been on my mind. The house just listened, I guess."

"Let's get out of here. Prison is only making you more depressed."

"I could be Ridley in two days. It's pretty depressing." She shook her head sadly and sat down on the edge of the veranda. I sat down next to her. She didn't look at me, but instead stared down at her prison-issue white sneakers. I wondered how she knew what prison sneakers looked like.

"Shoelaces. You got that part wrong."

"What?"

I pointed. "They take away your shoelaces in real prisons."

"You have to let go, Ethan. It's over. I can't stop my birthday from coming, or the curse. I can't pretend I'm a regular girl anymore. I'm not like Savannah Snow or Emily Asher. I'm a Caster."

I picked up a handful of pebbles from the bottom step of the veranda and chucked one as far as I could.

I won't say good-bye, L. I can't.

She took a pebble from my hand and threw it. Her fingers brushed against mine and I felt the tiny pulse of warmth. I tried to memorize it.

You won't have a chance to. I'll be gone, and I won't even remember I cared about you.

I was stubborn. I couldn't listen to this. This time, the pebble hit a tree. "Nothing will change the way we feel about each other. That's the one thing I know for sure."

"Ethan, I may not even be capable of feeling."

"I don't believe that." I flung the rest of the stones out into the overgrown yard. I don't know where they landed; they didn't make a sound. But I stared out that way, as hard as I could, swallowing the lump in my throat.

Lena reached out toward me, then hesitated. She put her hand down without so much as a touch. "Don't be mad at me. I didn't ask for any of this."

That's when I snapped. "Maybe not, but what if tomorrow is our last day together? And I could be spending it with you, but instead you're here, moping around like you're already Claimed."

She got up. "You don't understand." I heard the door slam behind me as she went back into the house, her cellblock, whatever.

I hadn't had a girlfriend before so I wasn't prepared to deal with all this—I didn't even know what to call it. Especially not with a Caster girl. Not having a better idea of what to do, I stood up, gave up, and drove back to school—late, as usual.

Twenty-four hours and counting. A low-pressure system settled over Gatlin. You couldn't tell if it was going to snow or hail, but the skies didn't look right. Today anything could happen. I looked out the window during history and saw what looked like some kind of funeral procession, only for a funeral that hadn't happened yet. It was Macon Ravenwood's hearse followed by seven black Lincoln town cars. They drove past Jackson High as they made their way through town and out to Ravenwood. Nobody was listening to Mr. Lee drone on about the upcoming Reenactment of the Battle of Honey Hill—not the most well-known of Civil War battles, but it was the one the people of Gatlin County were most proud of.

"In 1864, Sherman ordered Union Major General John Hatch and his troops to cut off the Charleston and Savannah Railroad to keep Confederate soldiers from interferin' with his 'March to the Sea.' But, due to several 'navigational miscalculations,' the Union forces were delayed."

He smiled proudly, writing NAVIGATIONAL MISCALCULA-TIONS out on the chalkboard. Okay, the Union was stupid. We got it. That was the point of the Battle of Honey Hill, the point of the War Between the States, as it had been taught to all of us, since kindergarten. Neglecting, of course, the fact that the Union had actually won the war. In Gatlin, everyone kind of talked about it like a gentlemanly concession on the part of the more gentlemanly South. The South had taken, historically speaking, the high road, at least according to Mr. Lee.

But today, nobody was looking at the board. Everyone was staring out the windows. The black Lincolns followed the hearse in a convoy down the street, behind the athletic field. Now that Macon had come out, so to speak, he seemed to enjoy making a spectacle of himself. For a guy who only came out at night, he managed to command a lot of attention.

I felt a kick in my shin. Link was hunched over the desk, so Mr. Lee couldn't see his face. "Dude. Who do you think is in all those cars?"

"Mr. Lincoln, would you like to tell us what happened next? Especially since your father will be commandin' the Cavalry tomorrow?" Mr. Lee was staring at us with his arms crossed.

Link pretended to cough. Link's dad, a browbeaten shell of a man, had the honor of commanding the Cavalry in the Reenactment since Big Earl Eaton died last year, which was the only way a reenactor ever advanced in rank. Someone had to die. It would have been a big deal in Savannah Snow's family. Link, he wasn't too big on the whole Living History scene.

"Let's see, Mr. Lee. Wait, I got it. We, uh, won the battle and lost the war, or was it the other way around? 'Cause around here, it's hard to tell sometimes."

Mr. Lee ignored Link's comment. He probably hung the Stars and Bars, the Confederate flag, in front of his house all year round, I mean his doublewide. "Mr. Lincoln, by the time Hatch and the Fed'rals reached Honey Hill, Colonel Colcock—" the class snickered, while Mr. Lee glared. "Yes, that was his real name. The Colonel and his brigade of Confederate soldiers and militia formed an impassable battery a seven guns across the road." How many times were we going to have to hear about the seven guns? You would have thought it was the miracle of the fish and the loaves.

459

Link looked back to me, nodding in the direction of Main. "Well?"

"I think it's Lena's family. They were supposed to be coming in for her birthday."

"Yeah. Ridley said somethin' about that."

"You guys still hanging out?" I was almost afraid to ask.

"Yeah, man. Can you keep a secret?"

"Haven't I always?"

Link pulled up the sleeve of his Ramones T-shirt to reveal a tattoo of what looked like an anime version of Ridley, complete with the Catholic schoolgirl mini and knee socks. I was hoping Link's fascination with Ridley had lost some steam, but deep down I knew the truth. Link would only get over Ridley when she was good and done with him, if she didn't make him jump headlong off a cliff first. And even then, he might not get over her.

"I got it over Christmas break. Pretty cool, huh? Ridley drew it for me herself. She's a killer artist." The killer part I believed. What could I say? You tattooed a comic book version of a Dark Caster on your arm, who by the way has you under some kind of love spell and who also happens to be your girlfriend?

"Your mom is gonna freak when she sees that."

"She's not gonna see it. My sleeve covers it, and we have a new privacy rule in my house. She has to knock."

"Before she barges in and does whatever she wants?"

"Yeah, well, at least she knocks first."

"I hope so, for your sake."

"Anyway, Ridley and I have a surprise for Lena. Don't tell Rid I told you, she'll kill me, but we're throwin' Lena a party tomorrow. In that big field at Ravenwood."

"That better be a joke."

"Surprise." He actually looked excited, as if this party was ever going to happen, as if Lena would ever go, or Macon would ever let her.

"What were you thinking? Lena would hate that. She and Ridley don't even speak."

"That's on Lena, man. She should get over it, they're family." I knew he was under the influence, a Ridley-fied zombie, but he was still pissing me off.

"You don't know what you're talking about. Just stay out of it. Trust me."

He opened a Slim Jim and took a bite. "Whatever, man. We were just tryin' to do somethin' nice for Lena. It's not like she has that many people willin' to throw her a party."

"All the more reason not to have one. No one would come."

He grinned and stuffed the rest of the Slim Jim into his mouth. "Everyone will come. Everyone's already comin'. At least, that's what Rid says."

Ridley. Of course. She'd have the whole damn town following her around, like the Pied Piper, at the suck of her first lollipop.

That didn't seem to be Link's understanding of the situation. "My band, the Holy Rollers, are gonna play for the very first time ever."

"The what?"

"My new band. I started it, you know, at church camp." I didn't want to know anything else about what had happened over winter break. I was just happy he had made it back in one piece.

Mr. Lee banged on the blackboard for emphasis, drawing a big number eight in chalk. "In the end, Hatch could not move the Confederates and withdrew his forces with a count of eighty-nine dead and six hundred and twenty-nine wounded. The Confederates won the battle, only losin' eight men. And that"—Mr. Lee pounded proudly on the number eight—"is why you all will be joinin' me at the Livin' History Reenactment of the Battle of Honey Hill tomorrow."

Living History. That's what people like Mr. Lee called Civil War reenactments, and they weren't kidding. Every detail was accurate, from the uniforms to the ammunition to the position of the soldiers on the battlefield.

Link grinned at me, all Slim Jim. "Don't tell Lena. We want her to be surprised. It's, like, her birthday present from the two of us."

I just stared at him. I thought about Lena in her dark mood and her orange prison jumpsuit. Then, Link's no doubt terrible band, a Jackson High party, Emily Asher and Savannah Snow, the Fallen Angels, Ridley, and Ravenwood, not to mention Honey Hill blowing up in the distance. All under the disapproving eye of Macon, Lena's other crazy relatives, and the mother who was trying to kill her. And the dog that allowed Macon to see every move we made.

The bell rang. Surprise wouldn't even begin to describe how she would feel. And I was the one who'd have to tell her.

"Don't forget to sign in when you arrive at the Reenactment. You don't get credit if you don't sign in! And remember to stay inside the ropes of the Safe Zone. Gettin' shot won't get you an A in this class," Mr. Lee called as we filed out the door.

Right about now, getting shot didn't seem like the worst thing in the world.

Civil War reenactments are a seriously strange phenomenon, and the Reenactment of the Battle of Honey Hill was no exception. Who would actually be interested in dressing up in what looked like really sweaty wool Halloween costumes? Who wanted to run around shooting antique firearms so unstable they had been known to blow people's limbs off when fired? Which is, by the way, how Big Earl Eaton had died. Who cared about recreating battles that happened in a war that took place almost a hundred and fifty years ago and that, in fact, the South didn't actually win? Who would do that?

In Gatlin, and most of the South, the answer would be: your doctor, your lawyer, your preacher, the guy who fixes your car and the one who delivers your mail, most likely your dad, all your uncles and cousins, your history teacher (especially if you happen to have Mr. Lee), and most definitely, the guy who owns the gun shop over in town. Come the second week of February, rain or shine, Gatlin thought about, talked about, and fussed about nothing but the Reenactment of the Battle of Honey Hill.

Honey Hill was Our Battle. I don't know how they decided that, but I'm pretty sure it had something to do with the seven guns. People in town spent weeks preparing for Honey Hill. Now that it was down to the last minute, Confederate uniforms were being steamed and pressed all over the county, the smell of warm wool wafting through the air. Whitworth rifles were cleaned and swords polished, and half the men in town had spent last weekend at Buford Radford's place making homemade ammunition, because his wife didn't mind the smell. The widows were busy washing sheets and freezing pies for the hundreds of tourists descending on the town to witness Living History. The members of the DAR had spent weeks preparing for their version of the Reenactment, the Southern Heritage Tours, and their daughters had spent two Saturdays baking pound cakes to serve after the tours.

This was particularly amusing because the DAR members, including Mrs. Lincoln, conducted these tours in period dress; they squeezed into girdles and layers of petticoats that made them look like sausages about to burst from their casings. And they weren't the only ones; their daughters, including Savannah and Emily, the future generation of the DAR, had to putter around the historic plantation houses dressed like characters from *Little House on the Prairie*. The tour had always started at the DAR headquarters, since it was the second-oldest house in Gatlin. I wondered if the roof would be fixed in time. I couldn't help imagining all those women wandering around the Gatlin Historical Society, pointing out starburst quilt patterns above the hundreds of Caster scrolls and documents awaiting the next bank holiday below.

But the DAR weren't the only ones to get into the act. The War Between the States was often referred to as the "first modern war," but if you took a walk around Gatlin the week before the Reenactment, there was nothing modern looking about it. Every Civil War relic in town was on display, from horse-drawn wagons to Howitzers, which any preschooler in town could tell you were artillery cannons resting on a set of old wagon wheels. The Sisters even dragged out their original Confederate flag and tacked it up on their front door, after I refused to hang it on the porch for them. Even though it was all for show, that's where I drew the line.

There was a big parade the day before the Reenactment, which gave the reenactors an opportunity to march through town in full regalia in front of all the tourists, because the next day they'd be so covered in smoke and dirt that no one would notice the shiny brass buttons on their authentic shell jackets.

After the parade, there was a huge festival, with a pig pick, a kissing booth, and an old-fashioned pie sale. Amma spent days baking. Outside of the County Fair, this was her biggest pie show, and her biggest opportunity to claim victory over her enemies. Her pies were always bestsellers, which drove Mrs. Lincoln and Mrs. Snow crazy—Amma's primary motivation for all that baking in the first place. There was nothing she liked better than showing up the women of the DAR and rubbing their noses in their second-rate pies.

So every year when the second week of February rolled around, life as we knew it ceased to exist, and we all found ourselves back at the Battle of Honey Hill, circa 1864. This year was no exception, with one peculiar addition. This year, as pickups pulled into town towing double-barreled cannons and horse trailers—any self-respecting cavalry reenactor owned his own horse—different preparations were also under way, for a different battle.

Only this one didn't begin at the second-oldest house in Gatlin, but the oldest. There were Howitzers, and then there were Howitzers. This battle wasn't concerned with guns and horses, but that didn't make it any less of a battle. To be honest, it was the only real battle in town.

As for the eight casualties of Honey Hill, I couldn't really compare. I was only worried about one. Because if I lost her, I would be lost, too.

So forget the Battle of Honey Hill. To me, this felt more like D-Day.

⊰ 2.11 ⊱

Sweet Sixteen

*L*eave me alone! I told all of you! There's nothing you can do!

Lena's voice woke me from a few hours of fitful sleep. I pulled on my jeans and a gray T-shirt without even stopping to think about it. About anything other than this: Day One. We could stop waiting for the end to come.

The end was here.

not with a bang but a whimper not with a bang but a whimper not with a bang but a whimper

Lena was losing it, and it was barely daylight.

The Book. Damn, I'd forgotten it. I ran back up into my room, two stairs at a time. I reached up to the top shelf of my closet, where I'd hidden it, bracing myself for the scorching that went along with touching a Caster book.

Only it didn't happen. Because it wasn't there.

The Book of Moons, our book, was gone. We needed that

book, today of all days. But Lena's voice was pounding in my head.

this is the way the world ends not with a bang but a whimper

Lena reciting T. S. Eliot was not a good sign. I grabbed the keys to the Volvo and ran.

The sun was rising as I drove down Dove Street. Greenbrier, or the only empty field in Gatlin to everyone else in town—making it the location of the Battle of Honey Hill—was beginning to come to life, too. The funny thing was, I couldn't even hear the artillery outside my car window, because of the artillery going off in my head.

By the time I ran up the steps of Ravenwood's veranda, Boo was waiting for me, barking. Larkin was on the steps, too, leaning against one of the pillars. He was in his leather jacket, playing with the snake that curled and uncurled its way around his arm. First it was his arm, then it was a snake. He Shifted idly between shapes, like a dealer shuffling a deck of cards. The sight of it caught me off guard for a second. That, and the way he made Boo bark. Come to think of it, I couldn't tell if Boo was barking at me or Larkin. Boo belonged to Macon, and Macon and I hadn't exactly left things on speaking terms.

"Hey, Larkin." He nodded, disinterested. It was cold, and a puff of breath crept out of his mouth, as if from an imaginary cigarette. The puff stretched out into a circle that became a tiny white snake, which then bit into its own tail, devouring itself until it disappeared.

"I wouldn't go in there if I was you. Your girlfriend is a little, how should I put it? Venomous?" The snake curved its length around his neck, then became the collar of his leather jacket.

Aunt Del flung the door open. "Finally, we've been waiting for you. Lena's in her room and she won't let any of us in."

I looked at Aunt Del, so muddled, her scarf dangling lopsidedly from one shoulder, her glasses askew, even her off-kilter gray bun coming unraveled from its twist. I leaned in to give her a hug. She smelled like one of the Sisters' antique cabinets, full of lavender sachets and old linens, handed down from Sister to Sister. Reece and Ryan stood behind her like a mournful family in a grim hospital lobby, waiting for bad news.

Again, Ravenwood seemed more attuned to Lena and her mood than to Macon's, or maybe this was a mood they shared. Macon was nowhere to be found, so I couldn't tell. If you could imagine the color of anger, it had been splashed over every wall. Rage, or something equally dense and seething, was hanging from every chandelier, resentment woven into thick carpets padding the room, hatred flickering underneath every lampshade. The floor was bathed in a creeping shadow, a particular darkness that had seeped up into the walls, and right now was rolling across my Converse so I almost couldn't see them. Absolute darkness.

I can't say for sure how the room looked. I was too distracted by how it felt, and it felt pretty rank. I took a tentative step onto the grand flying staircase that led up to Lena's bedroom. I'd gone up those stairs a hundred times before; it's not like I didn't know where they went. And yet somehow, today felt different. Aunt Del looked at Reece and Ryan, following behind me, as if I was leading the way into an unknown war front.

When I stepped onto the second stair, the whole house shook. The thousand candles of the ancient chandelier swinging over my head shuddered and dripped wax down onto my face. I winced

469

and jerked back. Without warning, the stairway curled up beneath my feet and snapped underneath me, tossing me back onto my butt, sending me skidding halfway across the polished floors of the entry hall. Reece and Aunt Del made it out of the way, but I took poor Ryan with me like a bowling ball hitting the pins at County Line Lanes.

I stood up and shouted up the stairs. "Lena Duchannes. If you sic those stairs on me again, I'm gonna report you to the Disciplinary Committee myself."

I took a step onto the first stair, and then the second. Nothing happened. "I will call Mr. Hollingsworth and personally testify that you're a dangerous lunatic." I double-jumped the stairs, all the way up to the first landing. "Because if you do that to me again, you will be, you hear me?" Then I heard it, her voice, uncurling in my mind.

You don't understand.

I know you're scared, L, but shutting everyone out isn't going to make things any better.

Go away.

No.

I mean it, Ethan. Go away. I don't want anything to happen to you.

I can't.

Now I was standing at her bedroom door, leaning my cheek against the cold white wood of the paneling. I wanted to be with her, as close to her as I could get without having another heart attack. And if this was as near as she would let me get, it was enough for me, for now.

Are you there, Ethan?

I'm right here.
I'm afraid.
I know, L.
I don't want you to get hurt.
I won't.
Ethan, I don't want to leave you.
You won't.
What if I do?
I'll wait for you.
Even if I'm Dark?
Even if you're very, very Dark.

She pulled the door open and pulled me inside. Music was blasting. I knew the song. This was an angry, almost metal version of it, but I recognized it all the same.

> *Sixteen moons, sixteen years*
> *Sixteen of your deepest fears*
> *Sixteen times you dreamed my tears*
> *Falling, falling through the years . . .*

It looked like she had been crying all night. She probably had. When I touched her face, I saw it was still striped with tears. I held her in my arms, and we swayed while the song played on.

> *Sixteen moons, sixteen years*
> *Sound of thunder in your ears*
> *Sixteen miles before she nears*
> *Sixteen seeks what sixteen fears . . .*

Over her shoulder, I could see her room was in shambles. The plaster on her walls was cracked and falling and her dresser was overturned, the way a thief tosses a room during a break-in. Her windows were shattered. Without the glass the small metal panes looked like prison bars from some ancient castle. The prisoner clung to me as the melody wrapped around us.

Still, the music didn't stop.

> *Sixteen moons, sixteen years,*
> *Sixteen times you dreamed my fears,*
> *Sixteen will try to Bind the spheres,*
> *Sixteen screams but just one hears . . .*

The last time I was here, the ceiling had been almost completely covered in words detailing Lena's innermost thoughts. But now, every surface of the room was covered in her distinctive black handwriting. The edges of the ceiling now read: *Loneliness is holding the one you love / When you know you might never hold him again.* The walls: *Even lost in the darkness / My heart will find you.* The doorjambs: *The soul dies at the hand of the one who carries it.* The mirrors: *If I could find a place to run away / Hidden safely, I would be there today.* Even the dresser was marred with phrases: *The darkest daylight finds me here, those who wait are always watching,* and the one that seemed to say it all, *How do you escape from yourself?* I could see her story in the words, hear it in the music.

> *Sixteen moons, sixteen years,*
> *The Claiming Moon, the hour nears,*

472

In these pages Darkness clears,
Powers Bind what fire sears . . .

Then the electric guitar slowed, and I heard a new verse, the end of the song. Finally, something had an ending. I tried to put the earth and fire and water and wind dreams out of my head as I listened.

Sixteenth Moon, Sixteenth Year,
Now has come the day you fear,
Claim or be Claimed,
Shed blood, shed tear,
Moon or Sun—destroy, revere.

The guitar died out, and now we were standing in silence.

"What do you think—"

She put her hand on my lips. She couldn't bear to talk about it. She was as raw as I had ever seen her. A cold breeze was blowing past her, surrounding her, and exhaling out through the open door behind me. I didn't know if her cheeks were red from the cold or from her tears, and I didn't ask. We fell onto her bed and curled into one ball, until it would have been hard to sort out whose limbs were whose. We weren't kissing, but it was like we were. We were closer than I'd ever realized two people could be.

I guess this was what it felt like to love someone, and feel like you had lost them. Even when you were still holding them in your arms.

Lena was shivering. I could feel every rib, every bone in her body, and her movements seemed involuntary. I untangled my arm from around her neck and twisted so I could grab the pieced quilt from the foot of her bed and pull it up over us. She burrowed into my chest and I pulled the quilt higher. Now it was over our heads, and we were in a dark little cave together, the two of us.

The cave became warm with our breath. I kissed her cold mouth and she kissed me back. The current between us intensified and she nuzzled her way into the hollow of my neck.

Do you think we can stay like this forever, Ethan?

We can do whatever you want. It's your birthday.

I felt her stiffen in my arms.

Don't remind me.

But I brought you a present.

She held up the cover, to let just a crack of light in. "You did? I told you not to."

"Since when did I ever listen to anything you say? Besides, Link says if a girl says not to get her a birthday present that means get me a birthday present and make sure it's jewelry."

"That's not true of all girls."

"Okay. Forget it."

She let the quilt drop, then snuggled back into my arms.

Is it?

What?

Jewelry.

I thought you didn't want a present?

Just curious.

I smiled to myself and pulled down the quilt. The cold air hit us both at the same time, and I quickly pulled a small box out of my jeans and dove back under the covers. I lifted the quilt up so she could see the box.

"Put it down, it's too cold."

I let it fall, and we were surrounded by darkness again. The box began to glow with green light, and I could make out Lena's slender fingertips as she pulled off the silver ribbon. The glow spread, warm and bright, until her face was softly lit across from mine.

"That's a new one." I smiled at her in the green light.

"I know. It's been happening ever since I woke up this morning. Whatever I think, just sort of happens."

"Not bad."

She stared at the box wistfully, as if she was waiting as long as she could to open it. It occurred to me that this was possibly the only present Lena would get today. Aside from the surprise party I was holding off telling her about until the last minute.

Surprise party?

Whoops.

You'd better be joking.

Tell that to Ridley and Link.

Yeah? The surprise is, there isn't going to be a party.

Just open the box.

She glared at me and opened the box, and more light came pouring out, even though the gift had nothing to do with that. Her face softened and I knew I was off the hook about the party. It was that thing, about girls and jewelry. Who knew? Link was right after all.

She held up a necklace, delicate and shining, with a ring hanging from the chain. It was a carved gold circle, three strands of gold—sort of rose colored, and yellow, and white—all braided into a wreath.

Ethan! I love it.

475

She kissed me about a hundred times, and I started talking, even while she was kissing me. Because I felt like I had to tell her, before she put it on, before something happened. "It belonged to my mom. I got it out of her old jewelry box."

"Are you sure about this?" she asked.

I nodded. I couldn't pretend like it wasn't a big deal. Lena knew how I felt about my mom. It was a big deal, and I felt relieved that we both could admit it. "It's not rare or anything, like a diamond or whatever, but it's valuable to me. I think she'd be okay with me giving it to you because, you know."

What?

Ah.

"You're gonna make me spell it out?" My voice sounded weird, all shaky.

"I hate to break it to you, but you're not that great at spelling." She knew I was squirming, but she was going to make me say it. I preferred our silent mode of communication. It made talking, real talking, a lot easier for a guy like me. I brushed her hair off of the back of her neck, and attached the necklace at the clasp. It hung around her neck, sparkling in the light, right above the one she never took off. "Because you're really special to me."

How special?

I think you're wearing the answer around your neck.

I'm wearing a lot of things around my neck.

I touched her charm necklace. It all looked like junk, and most of it was—the most important junk in the world. And now it had become my junk, too. A flattened penny with a hole in it, from one of those machines at the food court across from the movie theater, where we had gone on our first date. A piece of yarn from the red sweater she had worn to go parking at the water tower, which had become an inside joke between us. The silver button I had given her for luck at the disciplinary meeting. My mom's little paper-clip star.

Then you should already know the answer.

She leaned in to kiss me again, a real kiss. This was the kind of kiss that couldn't really be called a kiss, the kind that involves arms and legs and necks and hair, the kind where the quilt finally slides down to the floor, and in this case, the windows unshatter themselves, the bureau rights itself, the clothes return to their hangers, and the freezing cold room is finally warm. A fire burst into flame in the small, cold fireplace in her room, which was nothing compared to the heat running through my body. I felt the electricity, stronger than what I'd become used to, and my heartbeat quickened.

I pulled back, out of breath. "Where's Ryan when you need her? We're really going to have to figure out what to do about that."

"Don't worry, she's downstairs." She pulled me back down, and the fire in the grate crackled even louder, threatening to overpower the chimney with smoke and flame.

Jewelry, I'm telling you. It's a thing. And love.

And maybe danger.

_____

"Coming, Uncle Macon!" Lena turned to me and sighed. "I guess we can't put it off any longer. We have to go down there and see my family." She stared at the door. The bolt unlocked itself. I rubbed her back, making a face. It was over.

The day had turned to dusk by the time we made it out of Lena's room. I had thought we'd have to sneak down to visit Kitchen, around lunchtime, but Lena simply closed her eyes and a room service cart rolled through the door and into the middle of her room. I guess even Kitchen was feeling sorry for her today. Either that, or Kitchen couldn't resist Lena's newfound powers any more than I could. I ate my weight in chocolate chip pancakes drenched in chocolate syrup, washed down with chocolate milk. Lena had a sandwich and an apple. Then everything dissolved back into kissing.

I think we both knew this could be the last time we lay around in her room like this. It seemed like there was nothing else we could do. The situation was what it was, and if today was all we had, then at least we would have this.

In reality, I was as terrified as I was exhilarated. But still, it wasn't even dinnertime, and it was already the best and worst day of my life.

I grabbed Lena's hand as we headed down the stairs. It was still warm, which was how I could tell Lena was in a better mood. The necklaces sparkled at her neck, and silver and gold candles hung in the air, as we walked through them and beneath them, down the stairs. I wasn't used to seeing Ravenwood looking so festive and full of light, which for a second made it feel almost like a real birthday, where the people celebrating are happy and light-hearted. For a second.

Then I saw Macon and Aunt Del. They were both holding candles, and behind them, Ravenwood was shrouded in shadows and darkness. There were other dark figures moving in the background, also holding candles. Worse, Macon and Del were dressed in long, dark robes, like acolytes of a strange order, or druid priests and priestesses. It just didn't seem like, well, a birthday party. More like a really creepy funeral.

Happy Sweet Sixteen. No wonder you didn't want to come out of your room.

Now you see what I was talking about.

When Lena reached the last stair she paused and looked back at me. She looked so out of place in her old jeans and my over-sized Jackson High hoodie. I doubted Lena had ever dressed like this in her whole life. I think she just wanted to keep a piece of me with her as long as she could.

Don't be scared. It's just the Binding, to keep me safe until Moonrise. The Claiming can't happen until the moon is high.

I'm not scared, L.

I know. I was talking to myself.

She let go of my hand and took the last step down from the landing. When her foot touched the polished black floor, she was transformed. The flowing dark robes of the Binding now hid the curves of her body. The black of her hair and the black of the robes blended into a shadow that covered her from head to toe, with the exception of her face, which was as pale and luminescent as the moon itself. She touched her throat, my mother's gold ring still hanging at her neck. I hoped it would help to remind her that I was there with her. Just as I hoped it was my mom who had been trying to help us all along.

What are they going to do to you? This isn't going to be some freaky pagan sex thing, is it?

Lena burst out laughing. Aunt Del looked over at her, horrified. Reece smoothed her robe primly with one hand, looking superior, while Ryan started to giggle.

"Compose yourself," Macon hissed. Larkin, somehow managing to look as cool in a black robe as he did in a leather jacket, snickered. Lena smothered the giggles down into the folds of her robe.

As their candles moved, I could see the faces nearest to me: Macon, Del, Lena, Larkin, Reece, Ryan, and Barclay. There were also faces that were less familiar. Arelia, Macon's mother, and an older face, wrinkled and tanned. But even from where I stood, or tried to stand, she looked enough like her granddaughter that I instantly knew who she was.

Lena saw her at the same time I did. "Gramma!"

"Happy birthday, sweetheart!" The circle broke, briefly, as Lena ran over to fling her arms around the white-haired woman.

"I didn't think you would come!"

"Of course I did. I wanted to surprise you. Barbados is an easy trip. I was here in the blink of an eye."

She means that literally, right? What is she? Another Traveler, an Incubus like Macon?

A Frequent Flyer, Ethan. On United.

I could feel what Lena was feeling, a brief moment of relief, even if I was only feeling stranger and stranger. Okay, so my dad was certifiable, and my mom was dead, sort of, and the woman who raised me knew a thing or two about voodoo. I was okay with all of that. It was just, standing there, surrounded by the actual card-carrying, candle-bearing, robe-wearing Casters, it felt like I needed to know about a lot more than living with Amma had prepared me for. Before they started in with all the Latin and the Casting.

Macon stepped forward in the circle. Too late. He held his candle high. *"Cur Luna hac Vinctum convenimus?"*

Aunt Del stepped up next to him. Her candle flickered as she raised it, translating. "Why on this Moon do we come together for the Binding?"

The circle responded, holding high their candles as they chanted. *"Sextusdecima Luna, Sextusdecimo Anno, Illa Capietur."*

Lena answered them in English. Her candle flared up until the flames almost seemed like they would burn her face. "On the Sixteenth Moon, the Sixteenth Year, She will be Claimed." Lena stood in the center of the circle, with her head high. The candlelight was cast across her face from all directions. Her own candle began to burn into a strange green flame.

What's going on, L?

Don't worry. This is just part of the Binding.

If this was just the Binding, I was pretty sure I wasn't ready for the Claiming.

Macon began the chant I remembered from Halloween. What had they called it?

"Sanguis sanguinis mei, tutela tua est.
Sanguis sanguinis mei, tutela tua est.
Sanguis sanguinis mei, tutela tua est.
Blood of my blood, protection is thine!"*

Lena went pale. A *Sanguinis* Circle. That was it. She held the candle high over her head, closing her eyes. The green flame erupted into a massive orange-red flame, exploding from her candle to every other candle in the circle, lighting them as well.

"Lena!" I shouted over the sound of the explosion, but she didn't answer. The flame sprayed up into the darkness overhead, so high I realized there couldn't be a roof, any ceiling at all in Ravenwood tonight. I threw my arm over my eyes as the fire turned hot and blinding. All I could think about was Halloween. What if it was happening all over again? I tried to remember what they were doing that night, to fight off Sarafine. What had they been chanting? What had Macon's mother called it?

The *Sanguinis*. But I couldn't remember the words, didn't know the Latin, and for once I wished I had joined the Classics Club.

I heard a pounding on the front door, and in an instant, the flames were gone. The robes, the fire, the candles, the darkness and the light were gone. It all just vanished. Without missing a beat, they became a regular family, standing around a regular birthday cake. Singing.

What the—?

"—Happy birthday to you!" The last few notes of the song ended, as the pounding on the front door continued. A massive birthday cake, three tiers of pink, white, and silver, sat on the coffee table in the center of the parlor, along with a formal tea service and white linens. Lena blew out the candles, waving the smoke away from her face, where seconds before there had been billowing flame. Her family burst into applause. Back in my Jackson High sweatshirt and jeans, she looked like any other sixteen-year-old.

"That's our girl!" Gramma put down her knitting and started to cut the cake, while Aunt Del scurried to pour the tea. Reece and Ryan carried in an enormous stack of presents while Macon sat in his Victorian wingback chair and poured himself and Barclay a scotch.

What's going on, L? What just happened?

Someone's at the door. They're just being careful.

I can't keep up with your family.

Have some cake. This is supposed to be a birthday party, remember?

The pounding on the door continued. Larkin looked up from his thick triangle of red velvet cake, Lena's favorite. "Isn't anyone goin' to get the door?"

Macon brushed a crumb from his cashmere jacket, looking calmly at Larkin. "By all means, see who it is, Larkin."

Macon looked at Lena and shook his head. She wouldn't be answering the door today. Lena nodded and leaned back into Gramma. Smiling over cake like the doting granddaughter she really was. She patted the cushion next to her. Great. It was my turn to meet Gramma.

Then I heard a familiar voice at the door, and I knew I would rather face anyone's gramma than what was waiting outside the door right now. Because it was Ridley and Link, Savannah and Emily and Eden and Charlotte, with the rest of their fan club, and the Jackson basketball team. None of them were wearing their daily uniform, Jackson Angels T-shirts. Then I remembered why. Emily had a smudge of dirt on her cheek. The Reenactment. I realized Lena and I had missed most of it already, and now we were going to fail history. By now, it was all over, except the evening campaign and the fireworks. Funny how an F would seem like a big deal on any other day.

"SURPRISE!"

Surprise didn't even begin to describe it. Once again, I had allowed chaos and danger to find its way to Ravenwood. Everyone crowded into the front hall. Gramma waved from the couch. Macon sipped his scotch, composed, as always. It was only if you knew him that you knew he was about to lose it.

Actually, come to think of it, why had Larkin even let them in?

This can't be happening.

The surprise party, I forgot all about it.

Emily pushed to the front of the group. "Where's the birthday girl?" She held her arms out expectantly, like she was planning to give Lena a big hug. Lena recoiled, but Emily wasn't that easily deterred.

Emily looped her arm through Lena's like they were long-lost friends. "We've been plannin' this party all week. We've got live music and Charlotte rented these outdoor lights so everyone can see, I mean the grounds of Ravenwood are *so* dark." Emily dropped her voice as if she were discussing selling contraband on the black market. "And we have some peach schnapps."

"You have to see it," Charlotte drawled, practically gasping for breath between words because her jeans were so tight. "There's a laser machine. It's a rave at Ravenwood, how cool is that? It's just like one a those college parties over in Summerville."

A rave? Ridley must have really pulled out all the stops for this one. Emily and Savannah throwing Lena a party and fawning over her like she was their Snow Queen? This must have been harder than getting them all to jump off a cliff.

"Now, let's go up to your room and get you ready, birthday girl!" Charlotte sounded even more like a cheerleader than she normally did, always overcompensating.

Lena looked green. Her room? Half the writing on her walls was probably about them.

"What are you talkin' about, Charlotte? She looks just *gorgeous*. Don't you think so, Savannah?" Emily gave Lena a little squeeze and looked at Charlotte disapprovingly, like maybe she should lay off the pie and put some effort into looking that gorgeous.

"Are you kiddin'? I would just die for this hair," Savannah said, winding a strand of Lena's hair around her finger. "It's so amazingly . . . black."

"My hair was black last year, at least underneath," Eden protested. Last year, Eden had dyed the underside of her hair black, leaving the top blond, in one of her misguided attempts to distinguish herself. Savannah and Emily had teased her mercilessly, until she dyed it back a whole day later.

"You looked like a skunk." Savannah smiled at Lena approvingly. "She looks like an Italian."

"Let's go. Everyone's waitin' on you," Emily said, grabbing Lena's arm. Lena shrugged them off.

This has to be some kind of trick.

It's a trick all right, but I don't think it's the kind you're imagining. It probably has more to do with a Siren and a lollipop.

Ridley. I should've known.

Lena looked at Aunt Del and Uncle Macon. They were horrified, as if all the Latin in the world hadn't prepared them for this one. Gramma smiled, unfamiliar with this particular brand of angel. "What's the rush? Would you children like to stay and have a cup of tea?"

"Hiya, Gramma!" Ridley called from the doorway, where she was hanging back on the veranda, sucking on her red lollipop

485

with an intensity that made me think if she stopped this whole thing might fall like a house of cards. She didn't have me to get her through the door this time. She was an inch away from Larkin, who looked amused but stood directly in front of her. Ridley was spilling out of a tightly laced vest that looked like a cross between lingerie and something a girl on the cover of *Hot Rod* magazine would wear, and a low-slung jean skirt.

Ridley leaned against the doorframe. "Surprise, surprise!"

Gramma put her teacup down. She picked up her knitting. "Ridley. What a pleasure to see you, dear! Your new look is very becoming, darling. I'm sure you'll have lots of gentlemen callers." Gramma flashed Ridley an innocent smile, though her eyes weren't smiling.

Ridley pouted, but continued sucking on her lollipop. I walked over to where she was standing. "How many licks does it take, Rid?"

"For what, Short Straw?"

"To get Savannah Snow and Emily Asher to throw a party for Lena?"

"More than you know, Boyfriend." She stuck out her tongue at me, and I could see it was streaked with red and purple. The sight was dizzying.

Larkin sighed and looked past me. "There're maybe a hundred kids out there, in the field. There's a stage and speakers, cars all along the road."

"Really?" Lena looked out the window. "There's a stage in the middle of the magnolia trees."

"My magnolia trees?" Macon was on his feet.

I knew the whole thing was a farce, that Ridley was bringing this party to life with every suggestive lick, and Lena knew it, too. But I could still see it in Lena's eyes. There was a part of her that wanted to go out there.

A surprise party, where everyone in school shows up. That must have been on Lena's regular-high-school-girl list too. She could deal with being a Caster. She was just tired of being an outcast.

Larkin looked at Macon. "You're never gonna get them to leave. Let's get this over with. I'll stay with her the whole time, me or Ethan."

Link pushed his way to the front of the crowd. "Dude, let's go. My band, the Holy Rollers, it's our Jackson High debut. It's gonna be awesome." Link was happier than I'd ever seen him before. I looked over at Ridley suspiciously. She shrugged, chewing on her lolly.

"We're not going anywhere. Not tonight." I couldn't believe Link was here. His mother would have a heart attack if she ever found out.

Larkin looked at Macon, who was irritated, and Aunt Del, who was panicked. This was the last night either one of them wanted to let Lena out of their sight. "No." Macon didn't even consider it.

Larkin tried again. "Five minutes."

"Absolutely not."

"When's the next time a bunch a people from her school are goin' to throw her a party?"

Macon didn't miss a beat. "Hopefully, never."

Lena's face fell. I was right. She wanted to be part of all this, even if it wasn't real. It was like the dance, or the basketball game. It was the reason she bothered to go to school in the first place, no matter how horribly they treated her. It was why she showed up, day after day, even if she ate on the bleachers and sat on the Good-Eye Side. She was sixteen, Caster or not. For one night, that was all she wanted to be.

There was only one other person as stubborn as Macon Ravenwood. If I knew Lena, her uncle didn't stand a chance, not tonight.

She walked over to Macon and looped her arm through his. "I know this sounds crazy, Uncle M, but can I go to the party, just for a little while? Just to hear Link's band?" I watched for her hair to curl, the telltale Caster breeze. It didn't move. This wasn't Caster magic she was working. It was another kind altogether. She couldn't charm her way out from under Macon's watch. She would have to resort to older magic, stronger magic, the kind that had worked best on Macon from the time she first moved to Ravenwood. Plain old love.

"Why would you want to go anywhere with these *people* after everything they've put you through?" I could hear him softening as he spoke.

"Nothing's changed. I don't want anything to do with those girls, but I still want to go."

"You're not making sense." Macon was frustrated.

"I know. And I know it's stupid, but I just want to know what it feels like to be normal. I want to go to a dance without practically destroying it. I want to go to a party I'm actually invited to. I mean, I know it's all Ridley, but is it wrong if I don't care?" She looked up at him, biting on her lip.

"I can't allow it, even if I wanted to. It's too dangerous."

They locked eyes. "Ethan and I never even got to dance, Uncle M. You said it yourself."

For a second, it seemed like Macon might relent, but only for a second. "Here's what I didn't say. Get used to it. I never got to spend a day in any school, or even walk through town on a Sunday afternoon. We all have disappointments."

Lena played her last card. "But it's my birthday. Anything could happen. This might be my last chance . . ." The rest of the sentence lingered in the air.

To dance with my boyfriend. To be myself. To be happy.

She didn't have to say it. We all knew.

"Lena, I understand how you feel, but it's my responsibility to keep you safe. Especially tonight, you have to remain here with me. The Mortals will only put you in harm's way, or bring you pain. You can't be normal. You weren't meant to be normal." Macon had never spoken to Lena like this. I wasn't sure if he was talking about the party, or me.

Lena's eyes shone, but she didn't cry. "Why not? What's so wrong with wanting what they have? Did you ever stop to think they might have gotten something right?"

"What if they have? What does it matter? You're a Natural. One day, you will go somewhere Ethan can never follow. And every minute you spend together now will only be a burden you will have to carry for the rest of your life."

"He's not a burden."

"Oh, yes he is. He makes you weak, which makes him dangerous."

"He makes me strong, which is only dangerous to you."

I stepped between them. "Mr. Ravenwood, come on. Don't do this tonight."

But Macon had already done it. Lena was furious. "And what would you know about that? You've never been *burdened* with a relationship in your life, not even a friend. You don't

489

understand anything. How could you? You sleep in your room all day and mope around in your library all night. You hate everyone, and you think you're better than everyone. If you've never really loved anyone, how could you possibly know how it feels to be me?"

She turned her back on Macon, on all of us, and ran up the staircase, with Boo trailing after her. Her bedroom door slammed, the sound echoing back down into the hall. Boo lay down in front of Lena's door.

Macon stared after her, even though she was gone. Slowly, he turned to me. "I couldn't allow it. I'm sure you understand." I knew this was possibly the most dangerous night of Lena's life, but I also knew it might be her last chance to be the girl we all loved. So I did understand. I just didn't want to be in the same room with him right now.

Link edged his way to the front of the crowd of kids still standing in the hall. "So is there gonna be a party or not?"

Larkin grabbed his coat. "It's already a party. Let's get out there. We'll celebrate for Lena."

Emily pushed her way next to Larkin, and everyone else trailed after them. Ridley was still standing in the doorway. She looked at me and shrugged. "I tried."

Link was waiting for me by the door. "Ethan, come on, man. Let's go."

I looked up the staircase.

Lena?

"I'm gonna stay here."

Gramma put down her knitting. "I don't know that she'll be coming down anytime soon, Ethan. Why don't you go with your friends and check in on her in a few minutes?" But I didn't want to leave. This might be the last night we spent together. Even if we were spending it in Lena's room, I still wanted to be with her.

"At least come out and hear my new song, man. Then you can come back and wait for her to come down." Link had his drumsticks in his hand.

"I think that would be best." Macon poured himself another scotch. "You can come back in a little while, but we have some things we need to discuss in the meantime." It was decided. He was kicking me out.

"One song. Then I'm going to wait out front." I looked at Macon. "For a little while."

The field behind Ravenwood was crammed with people. There was a makeshift stage at one end, with portable lights, the same kind they used for the night portion of the Battle of Honey Hill. There was music blasting from the speakers, but it was hard to hear over the cannon fire in the distance.

I followed Link to the stage, where the Holy Rollers were setting up. There were three of them and they looked about thirty. The guy adjusting his guitar amp had tattoos covering both arms and what looked like a bike chain around his neck. The bass player had spiky black hair that matched the black makeup around his eyes. The third guy had so many piercings it hurt just looking at him. Ridley hopped up, sat on the edge of the stage, and waved at Link.

"Wait till you hear us. We rock. I just wish Lena was here."

"Well, I wouldn't want to disappoint." Lena walked up behind us and wrapped her arms around my waist. Her eyes were red and teary, but in the dark, she looked just like everyone else.

"What happened? Did your uncle change his mind?"

"Not exactly. But what he doesn't know won't hurt him, and I don't care if it does. He's being so awful tonight." I didn't say anything. I would never understand the relationship between Lena and Macon, any more than she could understand the relationship between Amma and me. But I knew she was going to feel terrible when this was all over. She couldn't stand to hear anyone say anything bad about her uncle, not even me; for her to be the one saying it made it that much worse.

"Did you sneak out?"

"Yeah. Larkin helped me." Larkin walked toward us, carrying a plastic cup. "You only turn sixteen once, right?"

This isn't a good idea, L.

I just want one dance. Then we'll go back.

Link headed for the stage. "I wrote you a song for your birthday, Lena. You're gonna love it."

"What's it called?" I asked suspiciously.

"*Sixteen Moons*. Remember? That weird song you could never find on your iPod? It just popped into my head last week, all in one piece. Well, Rid helped a little." He grinned. "I guess you could say, I had a muse."

I was speechless. But Lena grabbed my hand, and Link grabbed the microphone, and there was no stopping him. He adjusted the microphone stand so that the mic was in front of his mouth. Well, to be honest, it was more like inside his mouth, and it was sort of gross. Link had watched a lot of MTV over at Earl's. You had to hand it to him, since he was about to get rolled off the stage, holy or not. He was pretty brave, all things considered.

He closed his eyes, sitting behind the drums, sticks poised in the air. "One, two, three."

The lead guitarist, the surly-looking guy wearing the bike chain, hit one note on his guitar. It sounded awful, and the amps began to whine on either side of the stage. I winced. This was not going to be pretty. And then he hit another note, and another.

"Ladies and Gentlemen, if there are any a either around." Link raised an eyebrow and a ripple of laughter moved through the crowd. "I'd like to say Happy Birthday, Lena. And now, put your hands together for the world premiere of my new band, the Holy Rollers."

Link winked at Ridley. The guy thought he was Mick Jagger. I felt bad for him, and grabbed Lena's hand. It felt like I had plunged my hand into the lake, in the winter, when the top of the water was warm from the sun and an inch below that was pure ice. I shivered, but I wouldn't let go. "I hope you're ready for this. He's going to go down in flames. We'll be back in your room in five minutes. Promise."

She stared up at him thoughtfully. "I'm not so sure about that."

Ridley sat at the edge of the stage, smiling and waving like a groupie. Her hair was twisting in the breeze, pink and blond strands beginning to loop around her shoulders.

Then I heard the familiar melody, and *Sixteen Moons* was blasting out of the amps. Only this time, it wasn't like one of the songs from Link's demo tapes. They were good, really good. And the crowd went wild, like Jackson High was finally getting to have a dance after all. Only we were in a meadow, in the middle of Ravenwood, the most infamous and feared plantation in Gatlin County. The energy was amazing, surging like a rave. Everyone was dancing and half the people were singing, which was crazy, since nobody had ever even heard the song before. Even Lena had to crack a smile, and we began to sway with the crowd, because you really just couldn't help it.

"They're playing our song." She found my hand.

"I was just thinking that."

"I know." She laced her fingers through mine, sending shivers through my body. "And they're pretty good," she said, shouting over the crowd.

"Good? They're great! As in, the greatest day of Link's life." I mean, it was crazy, the whole thing. The Holy Rollers, Link, the party. Ridley bobbing on the edge of the stage, sucking on her Ridleypop. Not the craziest thing I'd seen today, but still.

So later, when Lena and I were dancing and five minutes came and went, and then twenty-five, and then fifty-five, neither one of us even noticed or cared. We were stopping time—at least that's how it felt. We had one dance, but we had to make it last as long as we could, in case it was all we had.

Larkin was in no hurry. He was all tangled up with Emily, making out by the side of one of the bonfires someone had made out of old garbage cans. Emily was wearing Larkin's jacket and every now and then he'd pull down the shoulder and lick her neck or something gross. He really was a snake.

"Larkin! She's, like, sixteen," Lena called over toward the fire from where we were dancing. Larkin stuck out his tongue, which rolled further down toward the ground than any Mortal's could have.

Emily didn't seem to notice. She untangled herself from Larkin, motioning to Savannah, who was dancing in a group with

494

Charlotte and Eden behind her. "Come on, girls. Let's give Lena her present."

Savannah reached into her little silver bag and pulled out the little silver package that was sticking out of it, wrapped with silver ribbon. "It's just a little somethin'." Savannah held it out.

"Every girl should have one," Emily was slurring.

"Metallic goes with *everything*." Eden could barely stop herself from ripping off the paper herself.

"Just big enough for, like, your phone and your lip gloss." Charlotte pushed it toward Lena. "Go on. Open it."

Lena took the package in her hands, and smiled at them. "Savannah, Emily, Eden, Charlotte. You have absolutely *no idea* what this means to me." The sarcasm was lost on them. I knew exactly what it was, and exactly what it meant to her. *Stupid to the power of stupid.*

Lena couldn't look me in the eye, or we both would have burst out laughing. As we made our way back into the crowd of dancers, Lena tossed the little silver package into the bonfire. The orange and yellow flames ate their way through the wrapping, until the tiny metallic purse was nothing but smoke and ash.

The Holy Rollers took a break, and Link came over to bask in the glory of his musical debut. "I told ya we were good. Just one step away from a contract." Link elbowed me in the ribs like old times.

"You were right, man. You guys were great." I had to give him that, even if he did have the lollipop on his side.

Savannah Snow sauntered up, most likely to burst Link's bubble. "Hey, Link." She batted her eyes suggestively.

"Hey, Savannah."

"Do you think you could save me a dance?" It was unbelievable. She was standing there, staring at him like he was a real rock star.

"I just don't know what I'll do if I don't get one." She gave him another Snow Queen smile. I felt like I was trapped in one of Link's dreams, or Ridley's.

Speak of the devil. "Hands off, Prom Queen. This is my Hot Rod." Ridley draped her arm, and a few other key parts, around Link to make her point.

"Sorry, Savannah. Maybe next time." Link stuck his drumsticks in his back pocket and headed back onto the dance floor with Ridley and her R-rated dance moves. It must have been the greatest moment of his life. You would've thought it was his birthday.

After the song ended, he hopped back onto the stage. "We got one last song, written by a good friend a mine, for some very *special* people at Jackson High. You'll know who you are." The stage went dark. Link unzipped his hoodie, and the lights went up with the twang of the guitar. He was wearing a Jackson Angels T-shirt with the sleeves ripped off, looking as ridiculous on Link as he intended it to. If only his mother could see him now.

He leaned into the microphone and began to do a little Casting of his own.

> *"Fallin' angels all around me*
> *Misery spreads misery*
> *Your broken arrows are killin' me.*
> *Why can't you see?*
> *The thing you hate becomes your fate*
> *Your destiny, Fallen Angel."*

Lena's song, the one she wrote for Link.

As the music swelled, every card-carrying Angel swayed to the anthem targeted at them. Maybe it was all Ridley, and maybe it wasn't. The thing is, by the time the song was over, and Link had tossed his winged T-shirt into the bonfire, it felt like a few more things were going up in flames along with it. Everything that had seemed so hard, so insurmountable for so long, just sort of went up in smoke.

Long after the Holy Rollers had stopped playing, even when Ridley and Link were nowhere to be found, Savannah and Emily were still being nice to Lena, and the whole basketball team was suddenly speaking to me again, I looked for some small sign, a lollipop, anywhere. The lone, telltale thread that could come loose to unravel the whole sweater.

But there was nothing. Just the moon, the stars, the music, the lights, and the crowd. Lena and I weren't even dancing anymore, but were still clinging to each other. We swayed back and forth, the current of heat and cold and electricity and fear pulsing through my veins. As long as there was any music at all, we were in our own little bubble. We weren't alone in our cave under her covers anymore, but it was still perfect.

Lena pulled back gently, the way she did when something was on her mind, and stared up at me. Like she was looking at me for the first time.

"What's wrong?"

"Nothing. I—" She bit her lower lip nervously, and took a deep breath. "It's just, there's something I want to tell you."

I tried to read her thoughts, her face, anything. Because I was starting to feel like it was the week before Christmas break all over again, and we were standing in the hall at Jackson, instead of in the field at Greenbrier. My arms were still around her waist, and I had to resist the urge to hold her tighter, to make sure she couldn't get away.

"What is it? You can tell me anything."

She put her hands on my chest. "In case something happens tonight, I wanted you to know—"

She looked into my eyes, and I heard it as clearly as if she had whispered it in my ear, except it meant more than it ever could have if she had spoken the words aloud. She said them in the only way that had ever mattered between us. The way we had found each other from the beginning. The way we always found our way back.

I love you, Ethan.

For a second, I didn't know what to say, because "I love you" didn't seem like enough. It didn't say everything I wanted to say—that she had saved me from this town, from my life, my dad. From myself. How can three words say all that? They can't, but I said them anyway, because I meant them.

I love you, too, L. I think I always have.

She settled back into me, resting her head on my shoulder, and I felt her hair warm against my chin. And I felt something else. That part of her I thought I would never be able to reach, the part she kept closed off to the world. I felt it open up, just long enough to let me in. She was giving me a piece of herself, the only piece that was really hers. I wanted to remember this feeling, this moment, like a snapshot I could go back to whenever I wanted.

I wanted it to stay this way forever.

Which, it turns out, was exactly five more minutes.

⇥ 2.11 ⇤

Lollipop Girl

Lena and I were still swaying to the music when Link elbowed his way through the crowd. "Hey, man, I've been lookin' for you everywhere." Link bent over and put his hands on his knees for a second, trying to catch his breath.

"Where's the fire?"

Link looked worried, which was unusual for a guy who spent most of his time trying to figure out how to hook up and hide from his mom at the same time. "It's your dad. He's up on the balcony a the Fallen Soldiers, in his pajamas."

According to the *South Carolina Visitor's Guide*, the Fallen Soldiers was a Civil War Museum. But really it was just Gaylon Evans' old house, which was full of his Civil War memorabilia. Gaylon left his house and his collection to his daughter, Vera, who was so desperate to become a member of the DAR she let

Mrs. Lincoln and her cronies restore the house and turn it into Gatlin's one and only museum.

"Great." Embarrassing me in our house wasn't enough. Now my dad had decided to venture out. Link looked confused. He probably expected me to be surprised that my dad was wandering around in his pajamas. He had no idea this was an everyday occurrence. I realized how little Link actually knew about my life these days, considering he was my best friend— my only friend.

"Ethan, he's out on the balcony, like he's gonna jump."

I couldn't move. I heard what he was saying, but I couldn't react. Lately, I was ashamed of my dad. But I still loved him, crazy or not, and I couldn't lose him. He was the only parent I had left.

Ethan, are you okay?

I looked at Lena, at those big green eyes full of concern. Tonight I could lose her, too. I could lose them both.

"Ethan, did you hear me?"

Ethan, you have to go. It's going to be okay.

"Come on, man!" Link was pulling me. The rock star was gone. Now he was just my best friend, trying to save me from myself. But I couldn't leave Lena.

I'm not going to leave you here. Not by yourself.

Out of the corner of my eye, I noticed Larkin coming toward us. He had untangled himself from Emily for a minute. "Larkin!"

"Yeah, what's up?" He seemed to sense something was going on, and actually looked concerned, for a guy whose general expression was disinterest.

"I need you to take Lena back to the house."

"Why?"

"Just promise you'll take her back to the house."

"Ethan, I'll be fine. Just go!" Lena was pushing me toward Link. She looked as scared as I felt. But I didn't move.

"Yeah, man. I'll take her back right now."

Link gave me a final jerk, and we were tearing through the crowd. Because we both knew I might be a few minutes away from being a guy with two dead parents.

We ran through the overgrown fields of Ravenwood, toward the road and the Fallen Soldiers. The air was already thick with smoke from the mortar, compliments of the Battle of Honey Hill, and every few seconds you could hear a round of rifle fire. The evening campaign was in full force. We were getting close to the edge of Ravenwood Plantation, where Ravenwood ended and Greenbrier began. I could see the yellow ropes that marked the Safe Zone, glowing in the darkness.

What if we were too late?

The Fallen Soldiers was dark. Link and I took the steps two at a time, trying to get up the four flights as quickly as possible. When we got to the third landing, instinctively, I stopped. Link sensed it, the same way he sensed when I was going to pass him the ball when I was trying to run out the clock, and stopped alongside me. "He's up here."

But I couldn't move. Link read my face. He knew what I was afraid of. He had stood next to me at my mom's funeral, passing out all those white carnations for folks to put on her coffin, while my dad and I stared at the grave like we were dead, too.

"What if . . . what if he's already jumped?"

"No way. I left Rid with him. She'd never let that happen." The floor felt like it dropped out from under me.

If she used her power on you, and she told you to jump off a cliff—you'd jump.

I pushed past Link, up the stairs, and scanned the hallway. All the doors were shut, except one. Moonlight spilled onto the perfectly stained pine floorboards.

"He's in there," Link said, but I already knew that.

When I entered the room, it was like going back in time. The DAR had really done their job in here. There was a huge stone fireplace at one end, with a long wooden mantel, lined with tapered wax candles, dripping as they burned. The eyes of fallen Confederates stared back from the sepia portraits hanging on the wall, and across from the fireplace was an antique four-poster bed. But something was out of place, disrupting the authenticity. It was a smell, musky and sweet. Too sweet. A mix of danger and innocence, even though Ridley was anything but innocent.

Ridley was standing next to the open balcony doors, her blond hair twisting in the wind. The doors were thrown open, and the dusty, billowy drapes were blowing into the room, like they had been forced inside by a rush of air. Like he had already jumped.

"I found him," Link called to Ridley, catching his breath again.

"I can see that. How's it goin', Short Straw?" Ridley smiled her sickly sweet smile. It made me want to simultaneously smile back and throw up.

I walked over to the doors slowly, afraid he might not be out there. But he was. Standing on the narrow ledge, on the wrong side of the railing, in his flannel pajamas and bare feet. "Dad! Don't move."

Ducks. There were mallard ducks on his pajamas, which seemed out of place, considering he might be about to jump off of a building.

"Don't come any closer, Ethan. Or I'll jump." He sounded lucid, determined, and clearer than he had in months. He almost sounded like my dad again. That's how I knew it wasn't really him talking, at least, not on his own. This was all Ridley, the Power of Persuasion in overdrive.

"Dad, you don't want to do that. Let me help you." I took a few steps toward him.

"Stop right there!" he shouted, holding his hand out in front of him to make his point.

"You don't want his help, do you, Mitchell? You just want some peace. You just want to see Lila again." Ridley was leaning against the wall, her lollipop poised and ready.

"Don't you say my mother's name, witch!"

"Rid, what are you doin'?" Link was standing in the doorway.

"Stay out of this, Shrinky Dink. You're way out of your league here."

I stepped in front of Ridley, putting myself between her and my dad as if my body could somehow deflect her power. "Ridley, why are you doing this? He has nothing to do with Lena or me. If you want to hurt me, hurt me. Just leave my dad out of it."

She threw her head back and laughed, a sultry and wicked sound. "I could care less about hurting you, Short Straw. I'm just doing my job. It's nothing personal."

My blood ran cold.

Her job.

"You're doing this for Sarafine."

503

"Come on, Short Straw, what did you expect? You saw how my uncle treats me. The whole family thing, not really an option for me right now."

"Rid, what are you talkin' about? Who's Sarafine?" Link walked toward her. She looked at him. For a second, I thought I saw something pass across Ridley's face, just a flicker, but something real. Something that looked almost like genuine emotion.

But Ridley shook it off, and as quickly as it came, it was gone. "I think you want to go back to the party, don't you, Shrinky Dink? The band is warming up for the second set. Remember, we're recording this show for your new demo. I'm going to take it around to some of the labels in New York myself," she purred, staring intently at him. Link looked uncertain, like maybe he did want to go back to the party, but he wasn't sure.

"Dad, listen to me. You don't want to do this. She's controlling you. She can influence people, it's what she does. Mom would never want you to do this." I watched for some sign that my words were registering, that he was listening. But there was nothing. He just stared into the darkness. You could hear the sound of bayonets clashing and the battle cries of middle-aged men in the distance.

"Mitchell, you have nothing to live for anymore. You've lost your wife, you can't write anymore, and Ethan will be going to college in a few years. Why don't you ask him about the shoebox full of college brochures under his bed? You'll be all alone."

"Shut up!"

Ridley turned to face me, unwrapping a cherry lollipop. "I'm sorry about this, Short Straw. I really am. But everyone has a part to play, and this is mine. Your dad is going to have a little *accident* tonight. Just like your mom did."

"What did you say?" I knew Link was talking, but I couldn't hear his voice. I couldn't hear anything but what she had just said, replaying over and over in my head.

Just like your mom did.

"Did you kill my mother?" I started advancing. I didn't care what kind of powers she had. If she killed my mother . . .

"Settle down, big boy. It wasn't me. That was a little before my time."

"Ethan, what the hell's goin' on?" Link was beside me.

"She's not what she seems, man. She's . . ." I didn't know how to explain it so Link would understand. "She's a Siren. It's like a witch. And she's been controlling you just like she's controlling my dad right now."

Link started to laugh. "A witch. You're losin' it, man."

I didn't take my eyes off Ridley. She smiled and ran her fingers through Link's hair. "Come on baby, you know you love a bad girl."

I had no idea what she was capable of, but after her little demonstration at Ravenwood, I knew she could kill any one of us. I should never have treated her like she was just some harmless party girl. I was in over my head. I was only just beginning to realize how far.

Link looked from her to me. He didn't know what to believe.

"I'm not kidding, Link. I should have told you sooner, but I swear I'm telling the truth. Why else would she be trying to kill my father?"

Link started to pace. He didn't believe me. He probably thought I was going crazy. It sounded crazy to me, even as I was saying it. "Ridley, is that true? Have you been usin' some kinda power on me this whole time?"

"If you want to split hairs."

My dad let go of the railing with one hand. He extended his arm like he was trying to balance on a tightrope.

"Dad, don't do it!"

"Rid, don't do this." Link was walking toward her, slowly. I could hear the chain from his wallet jingling.

"Didn't you hear what your friend said? I'm a witch. A bad one." She took off her shades, revealing those golden feline eyes. I could hear Link's breath catch in his throat, as if he was really seeing her for the first time. But only for a second.

"Maybe you are, but you aren't all bad. I know that. We've spent time together. We've *shared* things."

"That was part of the plan, Hot Rod. I needed an in, so I could stay close to Lena."

Link's face dropped. Whatever Ridley had done to him, whatever she had Cast, his feelings for her were bigger than that. "So it was all crap? I don't believe you."

"Believe what you want, it's the truth. As close to the truth as I'm capable of, anyway."

I watched my dad shift his weight, his free arm still stretched outward, swaying up and down. It seemed like he was trying to test his wings, to see if he could fly. A few feet away, an artillery shell hit the ground outside and a spray of dirt burst into the air.

"What about everything you told me about you and Lena growin' up together? How you two were like sisters? Why would you want to hurt her?" Something passed across her face. I wasn't sure, but it almost looked like regret. Was that possible?

"It's not up to me. I'm not the one calling the shots. Like I said, this is my job. Get Ethan away from Lena. I've got nothing against this old guy, but his mind is weak. You know, one biscuit short of a picnic." She licked her lollipop. "He was just an easy target."

Get Ethan away from Lena.

This whole thing was a diversion to separate us. I could hear Arelia's voice as clearly as if she was still kneeling over me.

It's not the house that protects her. No Caster can come between them.

How could I have been so stupid? It wasn't a question of whether or not I had some kind of power. It was never about me. It was about us.

The power was what was between us, what had always been between us. Finding each other on Route 9 in the rain. Turning the same way at the fork in the road. It didn't take a Binding Cast to keep us together. Now that they had managed to separate us, I was powerless. And Lena was alone, on the night she needed me with her the most.

I couldn't think clearly. I was out of time, and I wasn't going to lose one more person I loved. I ran toward my dad, and even though it was just a few feet, it felt like I was running through quicksand. I saw Ridley step forward, her hair twisting in the wind like Medusa's whole head of snakes.

I saw Link step forward and grab her shoulder. "Rid, don't do it."

For a split second, I had no idea what was going to happen. I saw everything in slow motion.

My dad turned to look back at me.

I saw him start to let go of the railing.

I saw Ridley's pink and blond strands twisting.

And I saw Link standing in front of her, staring into those golden eyes, whispering something I couldn't hear. She looked at Link, and without another word, her lollipop went sailing over the railing. I watched it arc down to the ground below, exploding like shrapnel. It was over.

As quickly as my father had turned away from the railing, he turned back toward it, toward me. I grabbed his shoulders and pulled him forward, over the railing and onto the balcony floor. He fell in a crumpled heap, and lay there looking up at me like a frightened child.

"Thank you, Ridley. I mean, whatever that was. Thanks."

"I don't want your thanks," she sneered, pulling away from Link and adjusting the strap of her top. "I didn't do either of you a favor. I just didn't feel like killing him. *Today*."

She tried to sound menacing, but she ended up just sounding childish. She twirled a pink strand of hair. "Though that's not gonna make some people too happy." She didn't have to say who, but I could see the fear in her eyes. For a second, I could see how much of her persona was just an act. Smoke and mirrors.

Despite everything, even now, as I tried to pull my father to his feet, I felt sort of sorry for her. Ridley could have any guy on the planet, and yet all I could see was how alone she was. She wasn't nearly as strong as Lena was, not inside.

Lena.

Lena, are you okay?

I'm fine. What's wrong?

I looked at my father. He couldn't keep his eyes open, and he was having trouble standing.

Nothing. Are you with Larkin?

Yes, we're headed back to Ravenwood. Is your dad okay?

He's fine. I'll explain when I get there.

I slid my arm under my dad's shoulder, while Link grabbed his other side.

Stay with Larkin, and get back inside with your family. You're not safe alone.

Before we could even take a step, Ridley sauntered by us, back through the open balcony doors, those ten-mile legs stepping across the threshold. "Sorry, boys. I gotta jet, maybe head back to New York for a while, lay low. It's cool." She shrugged.

Even though she was a monster, Link couldn't help but watch her go. "Hey, Rid?"

She stopped and turned to look at him, almost ruefully. Like she couldn't help what she was any more than a shark could help being a shark, but if she could . . .

"Yeah, Shrinky Dink?"

"You're not all bad."

She looked right at him and almost smiled. "You know what they say. Maybe I'm just drawn that way."

Family Reunion

Once my dad was safely in the hands of the reenactment medics, I couldn't get back to the party fast enough. I pushed past the girls from Jackson, who had ditched jackets, and were looking skanky in their tank tops and baby tees, gyrating to the music of the Holy Rollers. Minus Link who, to his credit, was right on my heels. It was loud. Live band loud. Live ammo loud. So loud that I almost didn't hear Larkin's voice calling me.

"Ethan, over here!" Larkin was standing in the trees just past the reflective yellow rope that separated the Safe Zone from the You-Could-Get-Your-Butt-Shot-Off-If-You-Cross-This-Line Zone. What was he doing in the woods, past the Safe Zone? Why wasn't he back at the house? I waved to him and he motioned me over, disappearing behind the rise. Usually jumping that rope would've been a tough choice, but not today. I had no choice but to follow him. Link was right behind me, stumbling, but still somehow keeping up with me, just the way it used to be.

"Hey, Ethan."

"Yeah?"

"About Rid, I should've listened."

"It's okay, man. You couldn't help it. I should've told you everything."

"Don't sweat it. I wouldn't have believed you."

The sound of gunfire echoed over our heads. We both ducked, instinctively.

"Hope those are blanks," Link said nervously. "Wouldn't it be crazy if my own dad shot me out here?"

"With my luck lately, it wouldn't surprise me if he shot us both."

We reached the top of the rise. I could see the thicket of brush, the oaks, and the smoke of the artillery field beyond us.

"We're over here!" Larkin called, from the other side of the thicket. By the "we," I could only assume he meant him and Lena, so I ran faster. Like Lena's life depended on it, because for all I knew maybe it did.

Then I realized where we were. There was the archway to the garden at Greenbrier. Larkin and Lena were standing in the clearing, just beyond the garden, in the same place where we had dug up Genevieve's grave a few weeks ago. A few feet behind them, a figure stepped out of the shadows and into the moonlight. It was dark, but the full moon was right over us.

I blinked. It was— It was—

"Mom, what the heck are you doin' out here?" Link was confused.

Because his mom was standing in front of us, Mrs. Lincoln,

my worst nightmare, or at least in my top ten. She looked strangely in—or out of—place, depending on how you looked at it. She was wearing ridiculous volumes of petticoats and the stupid calico dress that cinched her waist way too tightly. And she was standing right at Genevieve's grave. "Now, now. You know how I feel about profanity, young man."

Link rubbed his head. This made no sense at all, not to him, and not to me.

Lena, what's happening?

Lena?

There was no response. Something was wrong.

"Mrs. Lincoln, are you okay?"

"Delightful, Ethan. Isn't it a wonderful battle? And Lena's birthday, too, she tells me. We've been waiting for you, at least, one of you."

Link stepped closer. "Well, I'm here now, Mom. I'll take you home. You shouldn't be out past the Safe Zone. You're gonna get your head blown off. You know what a bad shot Dad is."

I grabbed Link's arm, holding him back. There was something wrong, something about the way she was smiling at us. Something about the panicked look on Lena's face.

What's going on? Lena!

Why wasn't she answering me? I watched as Lena pulled my mom's ring out of her sweatshirt and grabbed it by the chain in her hand. I could see her lips move in the darkness. I could barely hear something, only a whisper, in the far corner of my mind.

Ethan, get out of here! Get Uncle Macon! Run!

But I couldn't move. I couldn't leave her.

"Link, Angel, you are such a thoughtful boy."

512

Link? It wasn't Mrs. Lincoln standing in front of us. It couldn't be.

Mrs. Lincoln would no more call Wesley Jefferson Lincoln "Link" than she would streak through the streets naked. "Why you would use that ridiculous nickname when you have such a dignified name, I cannot imagine," she'd say every time one of us accidentally called her house and asked for Link.

Link felt my hand on his arm and stopped. It was starting to register with him, too; I could see it on his face. "Mom?"

"Ethan, get out of here! Larkin, Link, somebody, go get Uncle Macon!" Lena was screaming. She couldn't stop. She looked more frightened than I'd ever seen her. I ran toward her.

I could hear the sound of a shell being released from a cannon. Then a sudden flurry of gunfire.

My back slammed into something, hard. I felt my head crack and everything sort of went out of focus for a second.

"Ethan!" I could hear Lena's voice, but I couldn't move. I'd been shot. I was sure of it. I fought to stay conscious.

After a few seconds, my eyes came back into focus. I was on the ground, my back against a massive oak. The gunshot must have thrown me backward into the tree. I felt around to see where I'd been hit, but there was no blood. I couldn't find the bullet's point of entry. Link was a few feet away, propped awkwardly against another tree. He looked just as out of it as I felt. I got to my feet, stumbling forward toward Lena, but my face slammed right into something and I ended up back on the ground. It felt just like the time I had walked into a sliding glass door at the Sisters' house.

I hadn't been shot; this was something else. I'd been hit by a different kind of weapon.

"Ethan!" Lena was screaming.

I got up again and stepped forward slowly. There was a sliding glass door there all right, except this one was some kind of invisible wall encircling the tree and me. I banged on it and my fist smacked against it but it didn't make a sound. I slammed my palms against it over and over. What else could I do? That's when I noticed Link banging on his own invisible cage.

Mrs. Lincoln smiled at me, with a smile more wicked than anything Ridley could muster on her best day.

"Let them go!" Lena shrieked.

Out of nowhere, the sky opened up and rain literally poured out of the clouds, like it was being dumped from a bucket. Lena. Her hair was waving wildly. The rain turned to sleet and fell sideways, attacking Mrs. Lincoln from every direction. In a matter of seconds, we were all soaked to the bone.

Mrs. Lincoln, or whoever she was, smiled. There was something about her smile. She looked almost proud. "I'm not going to hurt them. I just want to give us some time to talk." Thunder rumbled in the sky over her head. "I was hoping I would get a chance to see some of your talents. How I've regretted I wasn't there to help you hone your gifts."

"Shut up, witch." Lena was grim. I had never seen her green eyes like this, the steely way they were set on Mrs. Lincoln. Flint hard. Resolute. Full of hate and anger. She looked like she wanted to rip Mrs. Lincoln's head off, and she looked like she could do it.

I finally understood what Lena had been so worried about all year. She had the power to destroy. I had only seen the power to love. When you discovered you had both, who could figure out what to do with that?

Mrs. Lincoln turned to Lena. "Wait until you realize what you can really do. How you can manipulate the elements. It's the true gift of a Natural, something we have in common."

Something they had in common.

Mrs. Lincoln looked up at the sky, the rain running down beside her as if she was holding an umbrella. "Right now you're making rain showers, but soon you'll learn to control fire as well. Let me show you. How I do like playing with fire."

Rain showers? Was she kidding? We were in the middle of a monsoon.

Mrs. Lincoln held up her palm and lightning sliced through the clouds, electrifying the sky. She held up three fingers. Lightning erupted, with the flick of every manicured nail. Once. Lightning struck the ground, kicking up the dirt, two feet away from where Link was trapped. Twice. Lightning burned through the oak behind me, cleaving the trunk neatly in half. A third time. Lightning struck Lena, who simply held up her own outstretched hand. The flash of electricity ricocheted off her, landing instead at Mrs. Lincoln's feet. The grass around her started to smolder and burn.

Mrs. Lincoln laughed and waved her hand. The fires in the grass died out. She looked at Lena with a glint of pride. "Not bad. I'm happy to see the apple doesn't fall far from the tree."

It couldn't be.

Lena glared at her and turned up both palms, a protective stance. "Yeah? What do they say about the bad apple?"

"Nothing. No one has ever lived to say it." Then Mrs. Lincoln turned to Link and me in her calico dress and miles of petticoats, with her hair braided down her back. She looked right at us, her golden eyes blazing. "I'm so sorry, Ethan. I hoped our first meeting would be under *different* circumstances. It's not every day that you meet your daughter's first boyfriend."

She turned to Lena. "Or your daughter."

I was right. I knew who she was, and what we were dealing with.

Sarafine.

A moment later, Mrs. Lincoln's face, her dress, her whole body literally started to split down the middle. You could see the skin on either side pulling away like the crumpled wrapper of a candy bar. As her body split down the center, it started to fall like a coat being shrugged from someone's shoulders. Underneath was someone else.

"I don't have a mother," Lena shouted.

Sarafine winced, as if she was trying to look hurt because she was Lena's mother. It was an undeniable genetic truth. She had the same long, black, curly hair as Lena. Except, where Lena was frighteningly beautiful, Sarafine was simply frightening. Like Lena, Sarafine had long, elegant features, but instead of Lena's beautiful green eyes, she had the same glowing yellow eyes as Ridley and Genevieve. And the eyes made all the difference.

Sarafine was wearing a dark green corseted velvet dress, kind of modern and Gothic and turn-of-the-century, all at the same time, and tall black motorcycle boots. She literally stepped out of Mrs. Lincoln's body, which fused back together within seconds, as if someone had sewn up the seam. Leaving the real Mrs. Lincoln collapsed in the grass with her hoopskirt flipped up, revealing her knee-high support hose and her petticoats.

Link was in shock.

Sarafine straightened, shaking free of the weight, shuddering. "*Mortals.* That body was just insufferable, so awkward and uncomfortable. Stuffing its face every five minutes. Disgusting creatures."

"Mom! Mom, wake up!" Link pounded his fists against what was obviously some kind of force field. No matter what a dragon she was, Mrs. Lincoln was Link's dragon, and it must have been hard to see her tossed aside like a piece of inconsequential human trash.

Sarafine waved her hand. Link's mouth was still moving, but he wasn't making a sound. "That's better. You're lucky I didn't have to spend *all* my time in your mother's body over the last few months. If I had, you'd be dead by now. I can't tell you the number of times I nearly killed you out of boredom at the dinner table, droning on about your stupid band."

It all made sense now. The crusade against Lena, the Jackson Disciplinary Committee meeting, the lies about Lena's school records, even the weird brownies on Halloween. How long had Sarafine been masquerading as Mrs. Lincoln?

In Mrs. Lincoln.

I had never really understood what we were up against until now. *The Darkest Caster living today.* Ridley seemed so harmless in comparison. No wonder Lena had been dreading this day for so long.

Sarafine looked back at Lena. "You may think you don't have a mother, Lena, but if that's true, it's only because your grandmother and your uncle took you from me. I've always loved you." It was disconcerting how Sarafine could move so easily from one set of emotions to another, from sincerity and regret to disgust and contempt, each emotion as hollow as the next.

Lena's eyes were bitter. "Is that why you've been trying to kill me, *Mother*?"

,Sarafine tried to look concerned, or maybe surprised. It was hard to tell because her expression looked so unnatural, so forced. "Is that what they told you? I was simply trying to make contact—to talk to you. If it hadn't been for all their Bindings, my attempts would never have put you in any danger, a fact they knew. Of course, I understand their concern. I am a Dark Caster, a Cataclyst. But Lena, you know as well as anyone, I had no choice in that matter. It was decided for me. It doesn't change the way I feel about you, about my only daughter."

"I don't believe you!" Lena spat. But she looked unsure of herself, even as she said it, like she wasn't sure what to believe.

I checked my cell phone. 9:59. Two hours until midnight.

Link slumped against the tree, his head in his hands. I couldn't look away from Mrs. Lincoln, lifeless in the grass. Lena was looking at her, too.

"She's not, you know. Is she?" I had to know, for Link's sake.

Sarafine tried to look sympathetic. But I could tell she was losing interest in Link and me, which wasn't good for either of us. "She'll return to her previously unappealing state soon. Nauseating woman. I'm not interested in her or the boy. I was only trying to show my daughter the true nature of Mortals. How easily they can be influenced, how vindictive they are." She turned to Lena. "Just a few words from Mrs. Lincoln and look how easily this whole town turned on you. You don't belong in their world. You belong with me."

Sarafine turned to Larkin. "Speaking of unappealing states, Larkin, why don't you show us those baby blues, I mean yellows?"

Larkin smiled and squeezed his eyes shut, reaching his arms over his head like he was stretching after a long nap. But when he opened his eyes again, something was different. He blinked wildly, and with each blink his eyes began to change. You could almost see the molecules rearranging. Larkin transformed, and there standing in his place was a pile of snakes. The snakes began to coil and climb onto each other, until Larkin emerged once again from the twisting heap. He held out his two rattlesnake arms that hissed and crawled back into his leather jacket until they became his hands. Then he opened his eyes. But instead of the green eyes I was used to seeing, Larkin stared back at us with the same golden eyes as Sarafine and Ridley. "Green never was my color. One of the perks of bein' an Illusionist."

"Larkin?" My heart sank. He was one of them, a Dark Caster. Things were worse than I thought.

"Larkin, what are you?" Lena looked confused, but only for a second. "Why?"

But the answer was staring right at us, in Larkin's golden eyes. "Why not?"

"Why not? Oh, I don't know, how about a little family loyalty?"

Larkin swiveled his head, as the thick gold chain around his neck writhed into a snake, tongue flickering against his cheek. "Loyalty's not really my thing."

"You betrayed everyone, your own mother. How can you live with yourself?"

He stuck out his tongue. The snake crawled into his mouth and disappeared. He swallowed. "It's a whole lot more fun being Dark than Light, cousin. You'll see. We are what we are. This is what I was destined to be. There's no reason to fight it." His tongue flickered, now forked, like the snake inside of him.

"I don't know why you're so worked up about it. Look at Ridley. She's havin' a great time."

"You're a traitor!" Lena was losing control. Thunder rumbled over her head, and the rain intensified again.

"He's not the only traitor, Lena." Sarafine took a few steps toward Lena.

"What are you talking about?"

"Your beloved Uncle Macon." Her voice was bitter and I could tell it wasn't lost on Sarafine that Macon had all but stolen her daughter from her.

"You're lying."

"He's the one who has been lying to you all this time. He let you believe your fate was predetermined—that you didn't have a choice. That tonight, on your sixteenth birthday, you will be Claimed Light or Dark."

Lena shook her head stubbornly. She raised her palms. Thunder rumbled, and the rain began to pour, in thick sheets and torrents. She shouted to be heard. "That's what happens. It happened to Ridley and Reece and Larkin."

"You're right, but you're different. Tonight, you will not be Claimed. You will have to Claim yourself."

The words hung in the air. *Claim yourself.* Like the words themselves had the power to stop time.

Lena's face was ashen. For a second, I thought she was going to pass out. "What did you say?" she whispered.

"You have a choice. I'm sure your uncle didn't tell you that."

"That's impossible." I could barely hear Lena's voice in the shrieking wind.

"A choice afforded to you because you are my daughter,

the second Natural born into the Duchannes family. I may be a Cataclyst now, but I was the first Natural born into our family."

Sarafine paused, then repeated a verse:

"'The First will be Black

But the Second may choose to turn back.'"

"I don't understand." Lena's legs gave out from under her and she fell to her knees in the mud and tall grass, her long black hair dripping around her.

"You've always had a choice. Your uncle has always known that."

"I don't believe you!" Lena threw up her arms. Clumps of earth ripped up from the ground between them, swirling into the storm. I shielded my eyes as bits of dirt and rock flew at us from every direction.

I tried to shout over the storm, but Lena could barely hear me. "Lena, don't listen to her. She's Dark. She doesn't care about anyone. You told me that yourself."

"Why would Uncle Macon hide the truth from me?" Lena looked directly at me, as if I was the only one who would know the answer. But I didn't know. There was nothing I could say.

Lena slammed her foot against the ground in front of her. The ground began to tremble, then roll beneath my feet. For the first time ever, an earthquake had hit Gatlin County. Sarafine smiled. She knew Lena was losing control, and she was winning. The electrical storm in the sky flashed over our heads.

"That's enough, Sarafine!" Macon's voice echoed across the field. He appeared out of nowhere. "Leave my niece alone."

Tonight, in the moonlight, he looked different. Less like a man and more like what he was. Something else. His face looked younger, leaner. Ready for a fight. "Are you referring to my daughter? The daughter you stole from me?" Sarafine straightened and began to twist her fingers, like a soldier checking his arsenal before a battle.

"As if she ever meant anything to you," Macon said calmly. He smoothed his jacket, impeccable as usual. Boo burst out of the bushes behind him, as if he'd been running to catch up. Tonight, Boo looked exactly like what he was—an enormous wolf.

"Macon. I feel honored, except I hear I missed the party. My own daughter's sixteenth birthday. But that's all right. There's always the Claiming tonight. We've a couple hours yet, and I wouldn't miss that for the world."

"Then I suppose you will be disappointed, as you're not invited."

"Pity. Since I've invited someone myself, and he's dying to see you." She smiled and fluttered her fingers. As quickly as Macon had materialized, another man appeared, leaning against a willow trunk, where no one had been standing a moment before.

"Hunting? Where did she dig you up?"

He looked like Macon, but taller and a little younger, with slick jet-black hair and the same pallid skin. But where Macon resembled a Southern gentleman from another time, this man looked fiercely stylish. Dressed in all black, a turtleneck, jeans, and a leather bomber, he looked more like a movie star you'd see on the cover of a tabloid rag than Macon's Cary Grant. But one thing was obvious. He was an Incubus, too, and not—if there was such a thing—the good kind. Whatever Macon was, Hunting was something else.

Hunting cracked what must have passed for a smile, to his kind. He began to circle Macon. "Brother. It's been a long time."

Macon didn't return the smile. "Not long enough. I'm not surprised you'd take up with someone like her."

Hunting laughed, raunchy and loud. "Who else would you expect me to take up with? A pack of Light Casters, like you did? It's ridiculous. The idea that you can just walk away from what you are. From our family legacy."

"I made a choice, Hunting."

"A choice? Is that what you call it?" Hunting laughed again, circling closer to Macon. "More like a fantasy. You don't get to choose what you are, *Brother*. You're an Incubus. And whether you choose to feed on blood or not, you are still a Dark Creature."

"Uncle Macon, is what she said true?" Lena wasn't interested in Macon and Hunting's little reunion.

Sarafine laughed, shrilly. "For once in your life, Macon, tell the girl the truth."

Macon looked at her, stubbornly. "Lena, it's not that simple."

"But is it true? Do I have a choice?" Her hair was dripping, tangled in wet ringlets. Of course, Macon and Hunting were dry. Hunting smiled and lit a cigarette. He was enjoying this.

"Uncle Macon. Is it true?" Lena pleaded.

Macon looked at Lena, exasperated, and looked away. "You do have a choice, Lena, a complicated choice. A choice with grave consequences."

All at once, the rain stopped completely. The air was perfectly still. If this was a hurricane, we were in the eye. Lena's emotions churned. I knew what she was feeling, even without hearing her voice in my head. Happiness, because she had finally gotten the one thing she had always wanted, the choice to decide her own fate. Anger, because she had lost the one person she had always trusted.

Lena stared at Macon as if through new eyes. I could see the darkness creeping into her face. "Why didn't you tell me? I've spent my whole life terrified I was going to go Dark." There was another crash of thunder and the patter of rain began to fall again, like tears. But Lena wasn't crying, she was angry.

"You do have a choice, Lena. But there are consequences. Consequences you could not understand, as a child. You can't really begin to understand them now. Yet I have spent every day of my life pondering them, since before you were born. And as your *dear mother* knows, the conditions of this bargain were determined long ago."

"What kind of consequences?" Lena looked at Sarafine skeptically. Cautiously. As if her mind was opening to new possibilities. I knew what she was thinking. If she couldn't trust Macon—if he had been keeping this kind of secret all this time—maybe her mother was telling the truth.

I had to make her hear me.

Don't listen to her! Lena! You can't trust her—

But there was nothing. Our connection was broken in the presence of Sarafine. It was like she had cut the phone line between us.

"Lena, you can't possibly understand the choice you are being pressured to make. What is at stake."

The rain turned from a patter of tears to a screaming downpour.

"As if you could trust him. After a thousand lies." Sarafine glared at Macon and turned to Lena. "I wish we had more time to talk, Lena. But you have to make the Choice, and I am Bound to explain the stakes. There are consequences; your uncle wasn't lying about that." She paused. "If you choose to go Dark, all the Light Casters in our family will die."

Lena went pale. "Why would I ever agree to do that?"

"Because if you choose to go Light, all the Dark Casters and Lilum in our family will die." Sarafine turned and looked at Macon. "And I do mean, all. Your uncle, the man who has been like a father to you, will cease to exist. You will destroy him."

Macon disappeared and materialized in front of Lena, not even a second later. "Lena, listen to me. I am willing to make the sacrifice. That's why I didn't tell you. I didn't want you to feel guilty about letting me go. I have always known what you would choose. Make the Choice. Let me go."

Lena was reeling. Could she really destroy Macon if what Sarafine said was true? But if it was true, what other choice did she have? Macon was only one person, even though she loved him.

"There is something else I can offer," Sarafine added.

"What could you possibly have to offer that would make me want to kill Gramma, Aunt Del, Reece, Ryan?"

Sarafine tentatively took a few steps toward Lena. "Ethan. We have a way the two of you can be together."

"What are you talking about? We're already together." Sarafine cocked her head slightly and her eyes narrowed. Something passed across her golden eyes. Recognition.

"You don't know. Do you?" Sarafine turned to Macon and laughed. "You didn't tell her. Well, that's not playing fair."

"Know what?" Lena snapped.

"That you and Ethan can never be together, not physically. Casters and Lilum cannot be with Mortals." She smiled, relishing the moment. "At least not without killing them."

The Claiming

C*asters cannot be with Mortals without killing them.*

It all made sense now. The elemental connection between us. The electricity, the shortness of breath whenever we kissed, the heart attack that had almost killed me—we couldn't be together physically.

I knew it was true. I remembered what Macon had said, that night in the swamp with Amma, and in my room.

A future between the two of them is impossible.

There are things you don't see right now—things that are beyond any of our control.

Lena was shaking. She knew it was true, too. "What did you say?" she whispered.

"That you and Ethan can never really be together. You can never marry, never have children. You can never have a future, at least not a real future. I can't believe they never told you. They certainly kept you and Ridley sheltered."

Lena turned to Macon. "Why didn't you tell me? You know I love him."

"You had never had a boyfriend before, let alone a Mortal one. None of us ever dreamed it would be an issue. We didn't realize how strong your connection with Ethan was until it was too late."

I could hear their voices, but I wasn't listening. We could never be together. I'd never be able to be that close to her.

The wind began to pick up, whipping the rain through the air like glass. Lightning tore across the sky. Thunder crashed so loud the ground shook. Clearly we were no longer in the eye of the storm. I knew Lena couldn't control herself much longer.

"When were you going to tell me?" she screamed over the wind.

"After you Claimed yourself."

Sarafine saw her opportunity and took it. "But don't you see, Lena? We have a way. A way you and Ethan can spend the rest of your lives together, marry, have children. Whatever you want."

"She'd never allow that, Lena," Macon snapped. "Even if it were possible, Dark Casters despise Mortals. They would never allow their bloodlines to be diluted with Mortal blood. It's one of our greatest divides."

"True, but in this case, Lena, we would be willing to make an exception, considering our alternative. And we have found a way to make it possible." She shrugged. "It's better than dying."

Macon looked at Lena, and countered, "Could you kill everyone in your family just to be with Ethan? Aunt Del? Reece? Ryan? Your own grandmother?"

Sarafine spread her powerful hands wide, luxuriously, flexing her powers. "Once you Turn, you won't even care about those people. And you'll have me, your mother, your uncle, and Ethan. Isn't he the most important person in your life?"

Lena's eyes clouded over. Rain and fog swirled around her. It was so loud that it almost drowned out the sound of the shells at Honey Hill. I had forgotten we could get killed, by either of the two battles being waged here tonight.

Macon grabbed Lena by both arms. "She's right. If you agree to this, you won't feel remorse, because you won't be yourself. The person you are now will be dead. What she's not telling you is that you won't remember your feelings for Ethan. Within a few months, your heart will be so Dark, he won't mean anything to you. The Claiming has an incredibly powerful effect on a Natural. You may even kill him by your own hand—you will be capable of that kind of evil. Isn't that right, Sarafine? Tell Lena what happened to her father, since you are such a proponent of the truth."

"Your father stole you from me, Lena. What happened was *unfortunate*, an accident." Lena looked stricken. It was one thing to hear that her mother had murdered her father from crazy Mrs. Lincoln at the Disciplinary Committee meeting. It was something else to find out it was true.

Macon tried to turn the odds back in his favor. "Tell her, Sarafine. Explain to her how her father burned to death in his own house, by a fire you set. We all know how you *love* to play with fire."

Sarafine's eyes were fierce. "You know, you've interfered for sixteen years. I think you should sit the rest of this one out."

Out of nowhere, Hunting appeared just inches from Macon. Now he looked less like a man and more like what he was. A Demon. His slick black hair stood up like the hair on a wolf's back before it attacks, his ears sharpened to points, and when his mouth opened, it was the mouth of an animal. Then he just disappeared, dematerialized.

Hunting reappeared in a flash, on top of Macon, so quickly I wasn't even sure I had really seen it happen. Macon grabbed Hunting by the jacket and tossed him into a tree. I had never realized how strong Macon really was. Hunting went flying, but where he should have slammed against the tree, he barreled right through it, rolling to the ground on the other side. In the same moment, Macon disappeared and reappeared on top of him. Macon threw Hunting's body to the ground, the force cracking the earth open beneath them. Hunting lay on the ground, defeated. Macon turned back to look at Lena. As he turned, Hunting rose up behind him with a smile. I yelled, trying to warn Macon, but no one could hear me over the hurricane building above us. Hunting growled viciously, sinking his teeth into the back of Macon's neck like a dog in a fight.

Macon screamed, a deep guttural sound, and disappeared. He was gone. But Hunting must have hung on because he disappeared with Macon, and when they reappeared at the edge of the clearing, Hunting was still locked onto Macon's neck.

What was he doing? Was he feeding? I didn't know enough to know how or if it was even possible. But whatever Hunting was taking, it seemed to be draining Macon. Lena screamed, ragged, bloodcurdling screams.

Hunting pushed away from Macon's body. Macon lay slumped over in the mud, rain battering down on him. Another round of canisters rang out. I flinched, rattled from the proximity of live ammo. The Reenactment was moving toward us, in the direction of Greenbrier. The Confederates were making their final stand.

The noise from the rounds muffled the growling, an altogether different, but familiar sound. Boo Radley. He howled and leapt into the air toward Hunting, bent on defending his master. Just as the dog sprang toward Hunting, Larkin's body began to twist, spiraling into a pile of vipers in front of Boo. The vipers hissed, slithering over each other.

Boo didn't realize the snakes were an illusion, that he could run right through them. He backed away, barking, his attention on the writhing snakes, which was the opportunity Hunting needed. Hunting dematerialized and appeared behind Boo, choking the dog with his supernatural strength. Boo's body jerked as he tried to fight against Hunting, but it was futile. Hunting was too strong. He tossed the dog's limp body aside, next to Macon's. Boo was still.

The dog and his master lay side by side in the mud. Motionless.

"Uncle Macon!" Lena screamed.

Hunting ran his hands through his slick hair and shook his head, invigorated. Larkin wound back through his leather jacket, into his familiar human form. Between them, they looked like two drug addicts after a fix.

Larkin looked up at the moon, and then his watch. "Half past. Midnight's comin'."

Sarafine stretched her arms up as if she was embracing the sky. "The Sixteenth Moon, the Sixteenth Year."

Hunting grinned at Lena, blood and mud on his face. "Welcome to the family."

Lena had no intention of joining this family. I could see that now. She pulled herself to her feet, soaking wet, covered with mud from her own torrential downpour. Her black hair whipped around her. She could barely stand against the wind, and leaned into it, as if at any moment her feet would leave the ground and she would disappear into the black sky. Maybe she could. At this point, nothing would have surprised me.

Larkin and Hunting moved silently in the shadows until they were flanking Sarafine, facing Lena. Sarafine moved closer.

Lena raised a single palm. "Stop. Now."

Sarafine didn't stop. Lena closed her hand. A fire line shot up through the tall grass. The flames roared, separating mother and daughter. Sarafine froze in her tracks. She hadn't expected Lena to be capable of much more than what she probably considered a little wind and rain. Lena had taken her by surprise. "I'll never hide anything from you, like everyone else in our family has. I've explained your options, and I've told you the truth. You may hate me, but I'm still your mother. And I can offer you the one thing they cannot. A future with the Mortal."

The flames shot higher. The fire spread like it had a will of its own until the flames surrounded Sarafine, Larkin, and Hunting. Lena laughed. A dark laugh, like her mother's. Even from across the clearing, it made me shiver. "You don't have to pretend you care about me. We all know what a bitch you are, *Mother*. It's the one thing I think we can all agree on."

Sarafine pursed her lips and blew, as if she was blowing a kiss. Only the fire blew with her, shifting its direction, racing through the weeds to surround Lena. "Say it like you mean it, *darling*. Put some teeth into it."

Lena smiled. "Burning a witch? That's so cliché."

"If I wanted you to burn, Lena, you'd already be dead. Remember, you're not the only Natural."

Slowly, Lena reached forward and thrust one hand into the flames. She didn't wince, but remained completely expressionless. Then she stuck her other hand into the blaze. She lifted her hands above her head and held the fire as if it were a ball. Then she threw the flames as hard as she could. Right at me.

Fire smashed into the oak behind me, igniting the spray of branches faster than dry kindling. The flames raced down the trunk. I stumbled forward, trying to get out of the way. I kept moving until I reached the wall of my invisible prison. But this time, it wasn't there. I dragged my legs through the inches of mud, across the field. I looked over and saw Link falling alongside me. The oak behind him was burning even brighter than my own. The flames reached into the dark sky and began to spread to the surrounding field. I raced toward Lena. I couldn't think of anything else. Link stumbled over toward his mom. Only Lena and the fire line stood between Sarafine and us. For the moment, it seemed to be enough.

I touched Lena's shoulder. In the darkness, she should have jumped, but she knew it was me. She didn't even look at me.

I love you, L.

Don't say anything, Ethan. She can hear everything. I'm not sure, but I think she always could.

I looked across the field, but I couldn't see Sarafine, Hunting, or Larkin beyond the flames. I knew they were there, and I knew they were probably going to try to kill us all. But I was with Lena, and for just one second, it was all that mattered.

"Ethan! Go get Ryan. Uncle Macon needs help. I can't hold her much longer." I took off running before Lena could say another word. Whatever Sarafine had done to sever the connection between us, it no longer mattered. Lena was back in my heart and my head. As I ran through the uneven fields, that was all I cared about.

Except for the fact that it was almost midnight. I ran faster.

I love you, too. Hurry—

I looked at my cell. 11:25. I banged again on the door of Ravenwood and pushed frantically on the crescent moon above the lintel. Nothing happened. Larkin must have done something to seal off the threshold, not that I had any idea how.

"Ryan! Aunt Del! Gramma!" I had to find Ryan. Macon was hurt. Lena could be next. I couldn't predict what Sarafine would do when Lena refused her. Link stumbled onto the doorstep behind me.

"Ryan's not here."

"Is Ryan a doctor? We gotta help my mom."

"No. She's—I'll explain later."

Link was pacing on the veranda. "Was any a that real?"

Think. I had to think. I was in this alone. Ravenwood was a virtual fortress tonight. No one could break in, at least no Mortal, and I couldn't let Lena down.

I dialed the only person I could think of who would have no problem tangling with two Dark Casters and a Blood Incubus, in the middle of a supernatural hurricane. A person who was a sort of supernatural hurricane herself. Amma.

I listened to the phone ring on the other end. "No answer. Amma's probably still with my dad."

11:30. There was only one other person who could help me, and it was a long shot. I dialed the Gatlin County Library. "Marian's not there either. She'd know what to do. What the hell? She never leaves that library, even after hours."

Link was pacing frantically. "Nothin's open. It's a freakin' holiday. It's the Battle of Honey Hill, remember? Maybe we should just go down to the Safe Zone and look for the paramedics."

I stared at him as if a bolt of lightning had just come out of his mouth and hit me in the head. "It's a holiday. Nothing's open," I repeated back to him.

"Yeah. I just said that. So what do we do?" He looked miserable.

"Link, you're a genius. You're a freaking genius."

"I know, man, but what does that have to with anything?"

"You got the Beater?" He nodded.

"We gotta get outta here."

Link started the engine. It spluttered, but caught, like it always did. The Holy Rollers blasted out of the speakers, and for the record, this time they sucked. Ridley, she must seriously rock the whole Siren gig.

Link ripped down the gravel drive, and then looked over at me sideways. "Where are we goin' again?"

"The library."

"Thought you said it was closed."

"The other library." Link nodded like he understood, which he didn't. But he went along with it anyway, just like old times. The Beater shredded down the gravel drive like it was Monday morning and we were late to first period. Only it wasn't.

It was 11:40.

When we skidded to a stop in front of the Historical Society, Link didn't even try to understand. I was out of the car before he could even turn off the Holy Rollers. He caught up with me as I rounded the corner into the darkness behind the second-oldest building in Gatlin. "This isn't the library."

"Right."

"It's the DAR."

"Right."

"Which you hate."

"Right."

"My mom comes here like, every day."

"Right."

"Dude. What are we doin' here?"

I stepped up to the grating and pushed my hand through. It sliced through the metal, at least what looked like metal, leaving my arm looking like it was amputated at the wrist.

Link grabbed me. "Man, Ridley must've put somethin' into my Mountain Dew. Because I swear, your arm, I just saw your arm—forget it, I'm hallucinatin'."

I pulled my arm back out and wiggled my fingers in front of

his face. "Seriously, man. After all the things you've seen to-night, *now* you think you're hallucinating? Now?"

I checked my cell. 11:45.

"I don't have time to explain, but it's only going to get weirder from here on out. We're going down to the library, but it's not, like, a library. And you are going to be freaking, most of the time. So if you want to go wait in the car, that's cool." Link was trying to absorb what I was saying as quickly as I was saying it, which was rough.

"Are you in, or not?"

Link looked at the grating. Without saying another word, he stuck his hand through. It disappeared.

He was in.

I ducked through the doorway and started down the old stone stairs. "Come on. We gotta book."

Link laughed nervously as he stumbled after me. "Get it? Book? Library?"

The torches lit themselves as we scrambled down into the darkness. I grabbed one out of its metal crescent holder and tossed it to Link. I grabbed another and jumped the last stairs to the crypt room. One by one, the wall torches ignited as we stepped into the center of the chamber. The columns emerged, along with their shadows, in the flickering light from the mounted torches. The words DOMUS LUNAE LIBRI reappeared in shadow on the entranceway, where I had last seen them.

"Aunt Marian! Are you here?" She tapped my shoulder from behind. I almost jumped out of my skin, bumping into Link.

Link screamed, dropping his torch. I stomped on the flames with my feet. "Jeez, Dr. Ashcroft. You about scared the pants offa me."

"Sorry, Wesley—and Ethan, *have you lost your mind*? Do you have any recollection who this poor boy's *mother* is?"

"Mrs. Lincoln's unconscious. Lena's in trouble. Macon's been hurt. I need to get into Ravenwood, I can't find Amma, and I can't find a way inside. I need to go through the Tunnels." I was a little boy again, and it all just came tumbling out. Talking to Marian was like talking to my mom, or at least like talking to someone who knew what it was like to talk to my mom.

"I can't do anything. I can't help you. One way or another, the Claiming comes at midnight. I can't stop the clock. I can't save Macon, or Wesley's mother, or anyone. I can't get involved." She looked at Link. "And I am sorry about your mother, Wesley. I mean no disrespect."

"Ma'am." Link looked defeated.

I shook my head and handed Marian the nearest torch from the wall. "You don't understand. I don't want you to do anything, other than what the Caster librarian does."

"What?"

I looked at her meaningfully. "I need to deliver a book to Ravenwood." I bent down and reached into the nearest stack, and randomly pulled out a book, singeing the tips of my fingers. *"The Complete Guide to Poisonous Herbiage and Verbiage."*

Marian was skeptical. "Tonight?"

"Yes, tonight. Right away. Macon asked me to bring it to him personally. Before midnight."

"A Caster librarian is the only Mortal who knows where to access the *Lunae Libri* Tunnels." Marian looked at me

537

shrewdly and took the book from my hands. "Good thing I happen to be one."

———&———

Link and I followed Marian through the twisting tunnels of the *Lunae Libri*. At one point I counted the oaken doors we passed through, but I stopped after we got to sixteen. The Tunnels were like a maze, and each one was different. There were low-ceilinged passageways where Link and I had to duck to walk through, and high-ceilinged hallways where there seemed to be no roof over our heads at all. It was literally another world. Some passages were rustic, adorned with nothing but their modest masonry, while others were more like the hallways in a castle or museum, with tapestries, framed antique maps, and oil paintings hanging from the walls. Under different circumstances, I would've stopped to read the tiny brass plaques under the portraits. Maybe they were famous Casters, who knew. The one thing the passageways had in common was the smell of earth and time, and the number of times Marian found herself fumbling for her *lunae* crescent key, the iron circle she wore at her waist.

After what seemed like forever, we arrived at the door. Our torches were nearly out, and I had to hold mine up so that I could read *Rayvenwoode Manor* carved into the vertical planks. Marian twisted the crescent key through the final iron keyhole and the door swung open. Carved steps led up into the house and I could tell from the glimpse of ceiling above that we were on the main floor.

I turned to Marian. "Thanks, Aunt Marian." I held out my hand for the book. "I'll give this to Macon."

"Not so fast. I've yet to see a library card issued in your name, EW." She winked at me. "I'll deliver this book myself."

I looked at my cell. 11:45 again. That was impossible. "How can it be the same time that it was when we arrived at the *Lunae Libri*?"

"Lunar time. You kids never listen. Things aren't always as they seem, down below."

Link and Marian followed me up the stairs and into the front hall. Ravenwood was just as we had left it, down to the cake left out on plates, to the tea set, and the stack of unopened birthday presents.

"Aunt Del! Reece! Gramma! Hello? Where is everybody?" I called out, and they came out of the woodwork. Del was positioned by the stairs, holding a lamp over her head as if she was going to whack Marian over the head with it in another second. Gramma was standing in the doorway, shielding Ryan with her arm. Reece was hiding under the stairs, brandishing a cake knife.

They all started to talk at once. "Marian! Ethan! We were so worried. Lena has disappeared, and when we heard the bell from the Tunnels, we thought it was—"

"Have you seen *Her*? Is she out there?"

"Have you seen Lena? When Macon didn't come back, we began to worry."

"And Larkin. She didn't hurt Larkin, did she?"

I looked at them in disbelief, taking the lamp out of Aunt Del's hands, and handing it to Link. "A lamp? You really thought a lamp was gonna save you?"

Aunt Del shrugged. "Barclay went up to the attic to Shift some weapons out of curtain rods and old Solstice decorations. It's all I could find."

I knelt down in front of Ryan. There wasn't much time, about fourteen minutes to be exact. "Ryan. Do you remember when I was hurt, and you helped me? I need you to come do that right now, over at Greenbrier. Uncle Macon fell down, and he and Boo are hurt."

Ryan looked like she was going to cry. "Boo's hurt, too?"

Link cleared his throat in the back of the room. "And my mom. I mean, I know she's been a pain and everything, but could she—could she help my mom?"

"And Link's mom."

Gramma pushed Ryan back behind her, patting her on the cheek. She adjusted her sweater and smoothed her skirt. "Come, then. Del and I will go. Reece, stay here with your sister. Tell your father where we've gone."

"Gramma, I need Ryan."

"For tonight, I am Ryan, Ethan." She picked up her bag.

"I'm not leaving here without Ryan." I held my ground. There was too much at stake.

"We can't take an Unclaimed child out there, not on the Sixteenth Moon. She could be killed." Reece looked at me like I was an idiot. I was out of the Caster loop again.

Del took my arm reassuringly. "My mother is an Empath. She is very sensitive to the powers of others and she can borrow those powers for a time. Right now, she has borrowed Ryan's. It won't last for very long, but for now she is capable of anything Ryan can do. And Gramma was Claimed, obviously quite some time ago. So we'll go with you."

I looked at my cell. 11:49.

"What if we don't make it in time?"

Marian smiled and held up the book. "I haven't made a delivery to Greenbrier, well, ever. Del, do you think you could find the way?"

Aunt Del nodded, putting on her glasses. "Palimpsests can always find ancient lost doors. It's just brand new ones we have a little trouble with." She disappeared back down into the Tunnels, followed by Marian and Gramma. Link and I scrambled to keep up with them.

"For a bunch a old ladies," Link panted, "they really know how to move."

This time, the passageway was small and crumbling, with speckled black and green moss growing in sprays across the walls and ceiling. Probably the floors, too, but I couldn't see them in the shadows. We were five bobbing torches in otherwise total darkness. Since Link and I were at the back of the pack, the smoke was wafting into my eyes, making them tear and sting.

As we got closer to Greenbrier, I could tell we were there by the smoke that started seeping down into the Tunnels, not from our torches, but from hidden openings leading to the world outside.

"This is it." Aunt Del coughed, feeling her way around the edges of a rectangular cut in the stone walls. Marian scraped off the moss, revealing a door. The *lunae* key fit perfectly, as if it had opened just days ago, rather than hundreds of thousands of days ago. The door wasn't oak, but stone. I couldn't believe Aunt Del had the strength to push it open.

Aunt Del paused on the stairwell and motioned to me to pass. She knew we were nearly out of time. I ducked my head under the hanging moss and smelled the dank air as I made my way up the stone steps. I climbed out of the tunnel, but when I got to the top, I froze. I could see the crypt's stone table, where *The Book of Moons* had lain for so many years.

And I knew it was the same table, because the Book was lying on it now.

The same book that was missing from my closet shelf this morning. I had no idea how it had gotten there, but there was no time to ask. I could hear the fire before I saw it.

Fire is loud, full of rage and chaos and destruction. And fire was all around me. The smoke in the air was so thick, I was choking on it. The heat was singeing the hair right off my arms. It was like a vision from the locket, or worse, like the last of my nightmares—the one where Lena was consumed by fire.

The feeling that I was losing her. It was happening.

Lena, where are you?

Help Uncle Macon.

Her voice was dimming. I waved the smoke away so I could see my cell.

11:53. Seven minutes to midnight. We were out of time.

Gramma grabbed my hand. "Don't just stand there. We need Macon."

Gramma and I ran, hand in hand, out into the fire. The long row of willows that framed the archway leading into the graveyard and the gardens was burning. The brush, the scrub oaks, the palmettos, the rosemary, the lemon trees—everything was on fire. I could hear the last few canisters in the distance. Honey Hill was wrapping up, and I knew the reenactors would be on to the fireworks soon, as if the fireworks in the Safe Zone could in any way compare to the fireworks going on out here. The whole garden as well as the clearing was burning, surrounding the crypt.

Gramma and I stumbled through the smoke until we neared the burning oaks, and I found Macon lying where we had left him. Gramma leaned over him and touched his cheek with her hand. "He's weak, but he'll be all right." At the same moment, Boo Radley rolled over and jumped up onto all fours. He slunk over and lay down on his belly next to his master.

Macon struggled to turn his head toward Gramma. His voice was barely a whisper. "Where's Lena?"

"Ethan's going to find her. You rest. I'm going to help Mrs. Lincoln."

Link was by his mom's side and Gramma hustled in their direction without another word. I stood up, scanning the fires for Lena. I couldn't see any of them, anywhere. Not Hunting, Larkin, Sarafine—anyone.

I'm up here. On top of the crypt. But I think I'm stuck.

Hold on, L. I'm coming.

I made my way back through the flames, trying to stick to the pathways I remembered from being in Greenbrier with Lena. The closer I got to the crypt, the hotter the flames were. My skin felt like it was peeling off, but I knew it was actually burning.

I climbed on top of an unmarked gravestone, found a foothold in the crumbling stone wall, and pulled myself up as far as I could. On top of the crypt was a statue, some kind of angel, with part of her body broken off. I grabbed onto its—I don't know what, it felt something like an ankle—and pulled myself over the edge.

Hurry, Ethan! I need you.

That's when I found myself face to face with Sarafine.

Who plunged a knife into my stomach.

A real knife, into my real stomach.

The end of the dream we had never been allowed to see. Only this part wasn't a dream. I know, because it was my stomach, and I felt every inch of the blade.

Surprised, Ethan? You think Lena's the only Caster on this channel?

Sarafine's voice began to fade.

Let her try to stay Light now.

As I drifted away, all I could think was if you stuck me in a Confederate uniform, I'd be Ethan Carter Wate. Even down to the same stomach wound, with the same locket in my pocket. Even if all I had ever deserted was the Jackson High basketball team, rather than Lee's army.

Dreaming about a Caster girl I would always love. Just like the other Ethan.

Ethan! No!

No! No! No!

One minute I was screaming, the next, the sound was stuck in my throat.

I remember Ethan falling. I remember my mother smiling. The glint of the knife, and the blood.

Ethan's blood.

This couldn't be happening.

Nothing moved, nothing. Everything was frozen perfectly in place, like a scene in a wax museum. The billows of smoke remained billows. They were fluffy and gray, but they went nowhere, neither up nor down. They just hung in the air as if they were made of cardboard, part of a backdrop in a play. The tongues of flame were still transparent, still hot, but they consumed nothing and made no sound. Even the air didn't move. Everything was exactly as it had been a second before.

Gramma was hunched over Mrs. Lincoln, about to touch her cheek, her hand hanging in the air. Link was holding his mother's hand, kneeling in the mud like a scared little boy. Aunt Del and Marian were crouched on the lower steps of the crypt passageway, shielding their faces from the smoke.

Uncle Macon lay on the ground, Boo crouching next to him. Hunting was leaning against a tree a few feet away, admiring his handiwork. Larkin's leather coat was on fire and he was facing the wrong direction, halfway down the road toward Ravenwood. Predictably running from, rather than toward, the action.

And Sarafine. My mother held a carved dagger, an ancient Dark thing, high above her head. Her face was feverish with fury and fire and hate. The blade still dripped blood over Ethan's lifeless body. Even the drops of blood were frozen in the air.

Ethan's arm was stretched out, over the edge of the crypt roof. It hung, dangling, down toward the graveyard below.

Like our dream, but in reverse.

I hadn't fallen through his arms. He was ripped from mine.

Below the crypt, I reached up, pushing aside flame and smoke, until my fingers interlocked with Ethan's. I was standing on my toes, but I could barely reach him.

Ethan, I love you. Don't leave me. I can't do this without you.

If there was moonlight, I could have seen his face. But there was no moon, not now, and the only light came from the fire, still frozen, surrounding me on every side. The sky was empty, absolutely black. There was nothing. I had lost everything tonight.

I sobbed until I couldn't breathe and my fingers slipped through his, knowing I would never feel those fingers in my hair again.

Ethan.

I wanted to scream out his name even though no one would hear me, but I didn't have a scream left in me. I had nothing left, except those words. I remembered the words from the visions. I remembered every one of them.

Blood of my heart.

Life of my life.

Body of my body.

Soul of my soul.

"Don't do this, Lena Duchannes. Don't you mess with that Book a Moons and start this darkness all over *again." I opened my eyes. Amma stood next to me, in the fire. The world around us was still frozen.*

I looked at Amma. "Did the Greats do this?"

"No, child. This is your doin'. The Greats just helped me come along."

"How could I have done this?"

She sat down next to me, in the dirt. "You still don't know what you're capable of, do you? Melchizedek was right about that, at least."

"Amma, what are you talking about?"

"I always told Ethan he might pick a hole in the sky one day. But I reckon you're the one who did that."

I tried to wipe the tears off my face, but more just kept coming. When they reached my lips, I could taste the soot in my mouth. "Am I—Am I Dark?"

"Not yet, not now."

"Am I Light?"

"No. Can't say you're that, either."

I looked up in the sky. The smoke covered every-thing—the trees, the sky, and where there should have been a moon and stars, there was only a thick black blanket of nothing. Ash and fire and smoke and nothing.

"Amma."

"Yes?"

"Where's the moon?"

"Well if you don't know, child, I sure don't. One minute I was lookin' up at your Sixteenth Moon. And you were standin' under it, starin' up at the stars like only God in Heaven could help you, palms raised like you was holdin' up the sky. Then, nothin'. Just this."

"What about the Claiming?"

She paused, considering. "Well, I don't know what happens when there's no Moon on your birthday on the Sixteenth Year, at midnight. It's never happened before, far as I know. Seems to me there can't be a Claimin', if there's no Sixteenth Moon."

I should have felt relief, joy, confusion. But all I could feel was pain. "Is it over, then?"

"Don't know." She held out her hand and pulled me up, until we were both standing. Her hand was warm and strong, and I felt clear-headed. Like we both knew what I was going to do. Just as, I suspect, Ivy had known what Genevieve would do, on this spot, more than a hundred years ago.

As we opened the cracked cover of the Book, I knew immediately which page to turn to, as if I had known all along.

"You know it's not natural. And you know there's bound to be consequences."

"I know."

"And you know there's no guarantee it'll work. It didn't turn out so well the last time. But I can tell you this: I've got my great-great-aunt Ivy downtown with the Greats, and they'll help us if they can."

"Amma. Please. I don't have a choice."

She looked into my eyes. Finally, she nodded. "I know there's nothin' I can say that'll keep you from doin' it. Because you love my boy. And because I love my boy, I'm goin' to help you."

I looked at her and I understood. "Which is why you brought The Book of Moons *here tonight."*

Amma nodded, slowly. She reached toward my neck with her hand, and pulled the necklace holding the ring out from inside Ethan's Jackson High sweatshirt, which I still was wearing. "This was Lila's ring. He had to love you somethin' fierce to give it to you."

Ethan, I love you.

"Love is a powerful thing, Lena Duchannes. A mother's love, that's not somethin' to be trifled with. Seems to me, Lila's been tryin' to help out, as best she could."

She ripped the ring off my neck. Where the chain broke, I could feel a mark, cutting into my skin. She slipped the ring on my middle finger. "Lila would've liked you. You have the one thing Genevieve never had when she used the Book. The love a two families."

I closed my eyes, feeling the cool metal against my skin. "I hope you're right."

"Wait." Amma reached down and pulled Genevieve's locket, still wrapped in her family handkerchief, out of Ethan's pocket. "Just to remind everyone that you've already got the curse." She sighed uneasily. "Don't want to be tried twice for the same crime."

She laid the locket on the Book. "This time we make it right."

Then she took the well-worn charm off her own neck, and laid it on the Book, next to the locket. The small gold disc looked almost like a coin, the image faded with wear and time. "To remind everyone, if they're messin' with my boy, they're messin' with me."

She closed her eyes. I closed mine. I touched the pages with my hands, and began to chant—at first slowly, then louder and louder.

"CRUOR PECTORIS MEI, TUTELA TUA EST.

VITA VITAE MEAE, CORRIPIENS TUAM, CORRIPIENS
   MEAM."

I spoke the words with confidence. A certain confidence that only comes from truly not caring whether you live or die.

"CORPUS CORPORIS MEI, MEDULLA MENSQUE,

ANIMA ANIMAE MEAE, ANIMAM NOSTRAM CONECTE."

I called out the words to the frozen landscape, though there was nobody but Amma to hear them.

"CRUOR PECTORIS MEI, LUNA MEA, AESTUS MEUS.

CRUOR PECTORIS MEI. FATUM MEUM, MEA SALUS."

Amma reached for me, taking my trembling hands in her strong ones, and we spoke the Cast again, together. This time we spoke in the language of Ethan and his mother, Lila, of Uncle Macon and Aunt Del and Amma and Link and little Ryan and everyone who loved Ethan, and who loved us. This time, what we spoke became a song.

A love song—to Ethan Lawson Wate, from the two people who loved him most. And would miss him the most, if we failed.

BLOOD OF MY HEART, PROTECTION IS THINE.

LIFE OF MY LIFE, TAKING YOURS, TAKING MINE.

BODY OF MY BODY, MARROW AND MIND,

SOUL OF MY SOUL, TO OUR SPIRIT BIND.

BLOOD OF MY HEART, MY TIDES, MY MOON.

BLOOD OF MY HEART. MY SALVATION, MY DOOM.

Lightning struck me, the Book, the crypt, and Amma. At least, that's what I thought had happened. But then, I remember it feeling that way to Genevieve, too, in the visions. Amma was thrown back against the wall of the crypt, her head knocking against the stone.

I felt the electricity course through my body and relaxed into it, accepting the fact that if I died, at least I would be with Ethan. I felt him, how near he was to me, how much I loved him. I felt the ring, burning on my finger, how much he loved me.

I felt my eyes burning, and everywhere I looked, I saw a haze of golden light, as if it were coming from me somehow.

I heard Amma whisper. "My boy."

I turned toward Ethan. He was bathed in gold light, just like everything else. He was still motionless. I looked at Amma in panic. "It didn't work."

She leaned against the stone altar, closing her eyes.

I screamed, "It didn't work!"

I stumbled away from the Book, into the mud. I looked up. The moon was there again. I raised my arms above my head, toward the heavens. Heat burned through my veins where there should have been blood. The anger welled inside me, with nowhere to go. I could feel it eating away at me. I knew if I didn't find a way to release it, it would destroy me.

Hunting. Larkin. Sarafine.

The predator, the coward, and my murderous mother, who lived to destroy her own child. The gnarled branches of my Caster family tree.

How could I Claim myself when they had already claimed the only thing that mattered to me? The heat surged up through my hands, as if it had a will of its own. Lightning streaked across the sky. I knew where it was going even before it hit.

Three points on a compass, with no North to guide me.

The lightning exploded into flame, striking its three targets simultaneously—the ones who had taken everything from me tonight. I should have wanted to look away, but I didn't. The statue that had been my mother a moment before was strangely beautiful, engulfed in flame, in the moonlight.

I lowered my arms, wiping the dirt and ash and grief from my eyes, but when I looked back she was gone.

They were all gone.

The rain began to fall, and my blurred vision sharpened until I could see the sheets of rain hitting the smoking oaks, the fields, the thickets. I could see clearly for the first time in a long time, maybe ever. I made my way back toward the crypt, toward Ethan.

But Ethan was gone.

Where Ethan's body had been lying moments before, now there was someone else. Uncle Macon.

I didn't understand. I turned to Amma for answers. Her eyes were enormous, frightened. "Amma, where's Ethan? What happened?"

But she didn't answer me. For the first time ever, Amma was speechless. She was staring at Uncle Macon's body, dazed. "Never thought it would end like this, Melchizedek. After all those years, holdin' the weight a the world on our shoulders together." She was talking to him as if he could hear her, even though her voice was tinier than I had ever heard it. "How am I gonna hold it up on my own?"

I grabbed her shoulders, her sharp bones digging into my palms. "Amma, what's going on?"

She raised her eyes to meet mine, her voice barely a whisper. "You can't get somethin' from the Book, without givin' somethin' in return." A tear rolled down her wrinkled cheek.

It couldn't be true. I knelt next to Uncle Macon and slowly reached out to touch his perfectly shaven face. Usually, I would find the misleading warmth associated with a human being, fueled by the energy of the hopes and dreams of Mortals, but not today. Today, his skin was ice cold. Like Ridley's. Like the dead.

Without giving something in return.

"No . . . please no." I had killed Uncle Macon. And I hadn't even Claimed myself. I hadn't even chosen to go Light, and I had still killed him.

The rage began to well up inside me again, the wind whipping up around us, swirling and churning like my emotions. It was beginning to feel familiar, like an old friend. The Book had made some kind of horrible trade, one I didn't ask for. Then I realized.

A trade.

If Uncle Macon was here, where Ethan had been lying dead, could that mean that maybe Ethan was out there alive?

I was on my feet, running toward the crypt. The frozen landscape tinted in that golden light. I could see Ethan, lying in the grass in the distance next to Boo, where Uncle Macon had been just moments ago. I made my way over to him. I reached for Ethan's hand, but it was cold. Ethan was still dead and now Uncle Macon was gone, too.

What had I done? I had lost them both. Kneeling in the mud, I buried my head in Ethan's chest and wept. I held his hand against my cheek. I thought of all the times he had refused to accept my fate, refused to give up, to say good-bye.

Now it was my turn. "I won't say good-bye. I won't say it." It had come to this, just a whisper in a field of smoldering weeds.

Then I felt it. Ethan's fingers began to curl and uncurl, searching for mine.

L?

I could barely hear him. I smiled as I cried, and kissed the palm of his hand.

Are you there, Lena Beana?

I laced my fingers through his, and swore I would

never let them go. I held up my face and let the rain fall upon it, washing away the soot.

I'm here.

Don't go.

I'm not going anywhere. And neither are you.

⊰ 2.12 ⊱

Silver Lining

I looked at my cell. It was broken.

The time still read 11:59.

But I knew it was well after midnight, because the fireworks finale had started, even though it was raining. The Battle of Honey Hill was over for another year.

I lay in the middle of the muddy field, letting the rain wash over me. As I watched the small-time fireworks attempt to explode in the still drizzling night sky, everything was cloudy. My mind just couldn't focus. I had fallen, hit my head and a few other places, too. My stomach, my hip, my whole left side ached. Amma was going to kill me when I came home, banged up like this.

All I remembered was, one second I was holding onto that stupid angel statue, and the next second I was lying flat on my back in the mud, here. I thought a piece of that statue broke off when I was trying to climb to the top of the crypt, but I wasn't really sure. Link must have carried me out here after I knocked myself out like an idiot. Aside from that, it was like my mind had been wiped clean.

I guess that's why I didn't understand why Marian, Gramma, and Aunt Del were huddled near the crypt, crying. Nothing could have prepared me for what I saw when I finally stumbled over there.

Macon Ravenwood. Dead.

Maybe he had always been dead, I didn't know, but now he was gone. I knew that much. Lena threw herself onto his body, the rain drenching both of them.

Macon, wet from the raindrops for the first time.

The next morning, I pieced together a few things about the night of Lena's birthday. Macon was the only casualty. Apparently, Hunting had overpowered him after I lost consciousness. Gramma explained that feeding on dreams was much less substantial than feeding on blood. I guess he had never really stood a chance against Hunting. Still, it hadn't stopped him from trying.

Macon always said he would do anything for Lena. In the end, he was a man of his word.

Everyone else seemed to be all right, at least physically. Aunt Del, Gramma, and Marian had dragged themselves back to Ravenwood, with Boo trailing behind them, whimpering like a lost pup. Aunt Del couldn't understand what had happened to Larkin. Nobody knew how to break the news to her that she had not one but two bad seeds in her family, so no one said a thing.

Mrs. Lincoln didn't remember anything, and Link had a hard time explaining what she was doing in the middle of the battlefield in her petticoat and pantyhose. She had been appalled to find herself in the company of Macon Ravenwood's family, but had been civil as Link helped her to the Beater. Link had a lot of questions, but I figured it could wait until Algebra II. It would give us both something to do when things returned to normal, whenever that would be.

And Sarafine.

Sarafine, Hunting, and Larkin were gone. I knew that because when I came to, they had disappeared, and Lena was there, leaning against me as we walked back toward Ravenwood. I was fuzzy on the details, like everything else right now, but it appeared that Lena, Macon, all of us had underestimated Lena's powers as a Natural. She had somehow managed to block out the moon and save herself from being Claimed after all. Without the Claiming, it looked like Sarafine, Hunting, and Larkin had fled, at least for now.

Lena still wasn't talking about it. She still wasn't talking much at all.

I had fallen asleep on the floor of her bedroom, next to her, our hands still intertwined. When I woke up, she was gone and I was alone. Her bedroom walls, the same ones that had been so covered with writing you couldn't see an inch of the white walls underneath all the black, were now completely blank. Except for one, the wall that faced the windows was covered from floor to ceiling with words, only the writing no longer looked like Lena's. The girly script was gone. I touched the wall as if I could feel the words, and I knew she had been up all night, writing.

macon ethan

i lay my head down on his chest and cried because he
had lived
because he had died
a dry ocean, a desert of emotion
happysad darklight sorrowjoy swept over me, under me
i could hear the sound but i could not understand the
words
and then i realized the sound was me, breaking
in one moment i was feeling everything and i was feeling nothing
i was shattered, i was saved, i lost everything, i was
given
everything else
something in me died, something in me was born, i only
knew
the girl was gone
whoever i was now, i would never be her again this is
the way
the world ends not with a bang but a whimper
claim yourself claim yourself claim yourself claim
gratitude fury love despair hope hate
first green is gold but nothing green can stay
don't
try
nothing
green
can
stay

T. S. Eliot. Robert Frost. Bukowski. I recognized some of the poets from her shelf and her walls. Except for the Frost, Lena got it backward, which wasn't like her. Nothing gold can stay, that's how the poem goes.

Not green.

Maybe it all looked the same to her now.

I stumbled down into the kitchen, where Aunt Del and Gramma were talking in low tones about arrangements. I remembered the low tones and the arrangements when my mom died. I hated them both. I remembered how much it hurt for life to go on, for aunts and grandmothers to be making plans, calling relatives, sweeping up the pieces when all you wanted to do was crawl into the coffin, too. Or maybe plant a lemon tree, fry some tomatoes, build a monument with your bare hands.

"Where's Lena?" My tone was not low, and I startled Aunt Del. Nothing could startle Gramma.

"Isn't she in her room?" Aunt Del was flustered.

Gramma calmly poured herself another cup of tea. "I believe you know where she is, Ethan."

I did.

───൭

Lena was lying on the crypt, right where we had found Macon. She was staring up at the gray morning sky, muddy and wet in her clothes from the night before. I didn't know where they had taken his body, but I understood her impulse to be here. To be with him, even without him.

She didn't look at me, though she knew I was there. "Those hateful things I said, I'll never get to take them back. He never knew how much I loved him."

I lay down next to her in the mud, my sore body groaning. I looked over at her, her black hair curling, and her dirty wet cheeks. The tears ran down her face, but she didn't try to wipe them away. Neither did I.

"He died because of me." She stared up at the gray sky, unblinking. I wished there was something I could say to make her feel better, but I knew better than anyone that words like that didn't really exist. So I didn't say them. Instead, I kissed all the fingers on Lena's hand. I stopped when my mouth tasted metal, and I saw it. She was wearing my mom's ring on her right hand.

I held up her hand.

"I didn't want to lose it. The necklace broke last night."

Dark clouds were blowing in and out. We hadn't seen the last of the storm, I knew that much. I wrapped my hand around hers. "I never loved you any more than I do, right this second. And I'll never love you any less than I do, right this second."

The gray expanse was just a moment of sunless calm, in between the storm that had changed our lives forever, and the one still to come.

"Is that a promise?"

I squeezed her hand.

Don't let go.

Never.

Our hands twisted into one. She turned her head, and when I looked into her eyes, I noticed for the first time that one was green, and one was hazel—actually, more like gold.

It was almost noon by the time I started the long walk home. The blue skies were streaked with dark gray and gold. The pressure was building, but it seemed a few hours from breaking. I think Lena was still in shock. But I was ready for the storm. And when it came, it would make Gatlin's hurricane season look like a spring shower.

Aunt Del had offered to drive me home, but I wanted to walk. Though every bone in my body ached, I needed to clear my head. I jammed my hands in my jeans pockets and felt the familiar lump. The locket. Lena and I would have to find a way to give it back to the other Ethan Wate, the one lying in his grave, just as Genevieve had wanted us to. Maybe it would give Ethan Carter Wate some peace. We owed them both that much.

I came down the steep road leading up to Ravenwood and found myself once again at the fork in the road, the one that had seemed so frightening before I knew Lena. Before I knew where I was going. Before I knew what real fear felt like, and real love.

I walked past the fields and down Route 9, thinking of that first drive, that first night in the storm. I thought about everything, how I had almost lost my dad and Lena. How I had opened my eyes to see her staring at me, and all I could think was how lucky I was. Before I realized we had lost Macon.

I thought about Macon, his books tied with string and paper, his perfectly pressed shirts, and his even more perfect composure. I thought about how hard things were going to be for Lena, missing him, wishing she could hear his voice one more time. But I would be there for her, the way I wished someone had been there for me when I lost my mom. And after the past few months, after my mom sent us that message, I didn't think Macon was really gone, either. Maybe he was still out there somewhere, looking out for us. He had sacrificed himself for Lena, I was sure of that.

The right thing and the easy thing are never the same. No one knew that better than Macon.

I looked up at the sky. The swirls of gray were seeping across the flat blue, as blue as the paint on my bedroom ceiling. I wondered if that one shade of blue really kept the carpenter bees from nesting. I wondered if those bees really believed it was the sky.

It's crazy what you see if you aren't really looking.

I pulled my iPod out of my pocket and turned it on. There was a new song on the playlist.

I stared at it for a long time.

Seventeen Moons.

I clicked on it.

_____&

Seventeen moons, seventeen years,
Eyes where Dark or Light appears,
Gold for yes and green for no,
Seventeen the last to know.

Acknowledgments

IT ONLY TOOK THREE MONTHS to write the first draft of *Beautiful Creatures*. Turns out, the writing was the easy part. The getting it right part was harder, and took the help of a lot more people. Here is the *Beautiful Creatures* family tree:

RAPHAEL SIMON & HILARY REYL

Who saw it before there was anything to see

SARAH BURNES, OF THE GERNERT COMPANY,

AGENT EXTRAORDINAIRE

Who read it & got it from the start

COURTNEY GATEWOOD,

OF THE GERNERT COMPANY, AGENT 007

Who got it across the pond & beyond

JENNIFER HUNT & JULIE SCHEINA

LITTLE, BROWN'S MERCILESSLY GENIUS EDITORIAL TEAM

Who made us sweat & cry until we got it right

DAVE CAPLAN, OUR TALENTED AND PSYCHIC DESIGNER

Who created the road to Ravenwood just as we imagined it

MATTHEW CHUPACK

Who translated our Pig Latin into actual Latin

ALEX HOERNER, PHOTOGRAPHER TO THE STARS (AND US)

Who made us look good without any Casting

Our North Carolina Relatives, especially
Haywood Ainsley Early, Genealogist
Who helped us plant our family trees
& Anna Gatlin Harmon,
our favorite Daughter of the Confederacy
Who lent us her maiden name & kept us talkin' right

And Our Readers:
Hannah, Alex C, Tori, Yvette, Samantha, Martine, Joyce,
Oscar, David, Ash, Virginia, Jean x 2, Kerri, Dave,
Madeline, Phillip, Derek, Erin, Ruby,
Amanda, & Marcos
Whose wanting to know what happened next
changed what happened next
Ashly, aka Teenage Vampire Queen
Susan & John, Robert & Celeste, Burton & Mare
Who listened & cheered us on, as they have our whole lives
May & Emma
Who stayed home from school twice to edit out the cheese,
& who figured out the missing bit of the end,
as only a 13 & a 15 year old could
Kate P and Nick & Stella G
Who fell asleep every night to the sound of a laptop clicking

& of course,
Alex & Lewis
Who found all the holes
& made sure the universe didn't fall through them,
who put up with all of the above
and then some.

About the Authors

Like Amma, KAMI GARCIA is very superstitious, and like any self-respecting girl with Southern roots, she makes her biscuits by hand and her pies from scratch. She has relatives in the Daughters of the American Revolution, but has yet to participate in a reenactment herself. Kami attended George Washington University and has an MA in education. She is a teacher and reading specialist, and leads book groups for children and teenagers.

Like Lena, writing has gotten MARGARET STOHL in and out of trouble since she was fifteen. She has written and designed many popular video games, which is why her two bad beagles are named Zelda and Kirby. Margaret fell in love with American literature at Amherst and Yale, earned an MA in English from Stanford, and studied creative writing under poet George MacBeth at the University of East Anglia, Norwich.

KAMI AND MARGARET both live in Los Angeles, California, with their families. *Beautiful Creatures* is their debut novel. Kami and Margaret invite you to visit them online at www.kamigarciamargaretstohl.com.

SOME SECRETS ARE LIFE-ALTERING....
OTHERS ARE LIFE-ENDING.

Turn the page for a sneak peek at *Beautiful Darkness*,
the gripping sequel to *Beautiful Creatures*,
coming October 12, 2010.

↠ BEFORE ↞

Caster Girl

I used to think our town, buried in the South Carolina back-woods, stuck in the muddy bottom of the Santee River valley, was the middle of nowhere. A place where nothing ever happened and nothing would ever change. Just like yesterday, the unblinking sun would rise and set over the town of Gatlin without bothering to kick up so much as a breeze. Tomorrow my neighbors would be rocking on their porches, heat and gossip and familiarity melting like ice cubes into their sweet tea, as they had for more than a hundred years. Around here, our traditions were so traditional it was hard to put a finger on them. They were woven into everything we did or, more often, didn't do. You could be born or married or buried, and the Methodists kept right on singing.

Sundays were for church, Mondays for doing the marketing at the Stop & Shop, the only grocery store in town. The rest of the week involved a whole lot of nothing and a little more pie, if you were lucky enough to live with someone like my family's housekeeper, Amma, who won the bake-off at the county fair every year. Old four-fingered Miss Monroe still taught cotillion, one empty finger of her white-gloved hand flapping as she sashayed down the dance floor with the debutantes. Maybelline Sutter was still cutting hair at the Snip 'n' Curl, though she had lost most of her eyesight around the same time she turned seventy, and now she forgot to put the guard down on the clippers half the time, shearing a skunk stripe up the back of your head. Carlton Eaton never failed, rain or shine, to open your mail before he delivered it. If the news was bad, he would break it to you himself. Better to hear it from one of your own.

This town owned us, that was the good and the bad of it. It knew every inch of us, every sin, every secret, every scab. Which was why most people never bothered to leave, and why the ones who did never came back. Before I met Lena that would have been me, five minutes after I graduated from Jackson High. Gone.

Then I fell in love with a Caster girl.

She showed me there was another world within the cracks of our uneven sidewalks. One that had been there all along, hidden in plain sight. Lena's Gatlin was a place where things happened — impossible, supernatural, life-altering things.

Sometimes life-ending.

While regular folks were busy cutting back their rosebushes or picking past worm-eaten peaches at the roadside stand, Light and Dark Casters with unique and powerful gifts were locked in an eternal struggle — a supernatural civil war without any hope of a white flag waving. Lena's Gatlin was home to Demons and danger and a curse that had marked her family for more than a hundred years. And the closer I got to Lena, the closer her Gatlin came to mine.

A few months ago, I believed nothing would ever change in this town. Now I knew better, and I only wished it was true.

Because the second I fell in love with a Caster girl, no one I loved was safe. Lena thought she was the only one cursed, but she was wrong.

It was our curse now.

Perpetual Peace

The rain dripping off the brim of Amma's best black hat. Lena's bare knees hitting the thick mud in front of the grave. The pinpricks on the back of my neck that came from standing too close to so many of Macon's kind. Incubuses—demons who fed off the memories and dreams of Mortals, like me, as we slept. The sound they made, unlike anything else in the universe, when they ripped open the last bit of dark sky and disappeared just before dawn. As if they were a pack of black crows, taking off from a power line in perfect unison.

That was Macon's funeral.

I could remember the details as if it had happened yesterday, even though it was hard to believe some of it had happened at all. Funerals were tricky like that. And life, I guess. The important parts you blocked out altogether, but the random, slanted moments haunted you, replaying over and over in your mind.

What I could remember: Amma waking me up in the dark to get to His Garden of Perpetual Peace before dawn. Lena frozen and shattered, wanting to freeze and shatter everything around her. Darkness in the sky and in half the people standing around the grave, the ones who weren't people at all.

But behind all that, there was something I couldn't remember. It was there, lingering in the back of my mind. I had been trying to think of it since Lena's birthday, her Sixteenth Moon, the night Macon died.

The only thing I knew was that it was something I needed to remember.

—⟲

The morning of the funeral it was pitch-black outside, but patches of moonlight were shining through the clouds into my open window. My room was freezing, and I didn't care. I had left my window open the last two nights since Macon died, like he might just show up in my room and sit down in my swivel chair and stay awhile.

I remembered the night I saw him standing by my window, in the dark. That's when I found out what he was. Not a vampire or some mythological creature from a book, as I had suspected, but a real Demon. One who could have chosen to feed on blood, but chose my dreams instead.

Macon Melchizedek Ravenwood. To the folks around here, he was Old Man Ravenwood, the town recluse. He was also Lena's uncle, and the only father she had ever known.

I was getting dressed in the dark when I felt the warm pull from inside that meant Lena was there.

L?

Lena spoke up from the depths of my mind, as close as anyone could be and about as far away. Kelting, our unspoken form of communication. The whispering language Casters like her had shared long before my bedroom had been declared south of the Mason-Dixon Line. It was the secret language of intimacy and necessity, born in a time when being different could get you burned at the stake. It was a language we shouldn't have been able to share, because I was a Mortal. But for some inexplicable reason we could, and it was the language we used to speak the unspoken and the unspeakable.

I can't do this. I'm not going.

I gave up on my tie and sat back down on my bed, the ancient mattress springs crying out beneath me.

You have to go. You won't forgive yourself if you don't.

For a second, she didn't respond.

You don't know how it feels.

I do.

I remembered when I was the one sitting on my bed afraid to get up, afraid to put on my suit and join the prayer circle and sing *Abide With Me* and ride in the grim parade of headlights through town to the cemetery to bury my mother. I was afraid it would make it real. I couldn't stand to think about it, but I opened my mind and showed Lena....

You can't go, but you don't have a choice, because Amma puts her hand on your arm and leads you into the car, into the pew, into the pity parade. Even though it hurts to move, like your whole body aches from some kind of fever. Your eyes stop on the mumbling faces in front of you, but you can't actually hear what anyone is saying. Not over the screaming in your head. So you let them put their hand on your arm, you get in

the car, and it happens. Because you can make it through this if
someone says you can.

I put my head in my hands.

Ethan—

I'm saying you can, L.

I shoved my fists into my eyes, and they were wet. I flipped on
my light and stared at the bare bulb, refusing to blink until I
seared away the tears.

Ethan, I'm scared.

I'm right here. I'm not going anywhere.

There weren't any more words as I went back to fumbling
with my tie, but I could feel Lena there, as if she was sitting in
the corner of my room. The house seemed empty with my father
gone, and I heard Amma in the hall. A second later, she was
standing quietly in the doorway clutching her good purse. Her
dark eyes searched mine, and her tiny frame seemed tall, though
she didn't even reach my shoulder. She was the grandmother I
never had, and the only mother I had left now.

I stared at the empty chair next to my window, where she
had laid out my good suit a little less than a year ago, then back
into the bare lightbulb of my bedside lamp.

Amma held out her hand, and I handed her my tie. Sometimes
it felt like Lena wasn't the only one who could read my mind.

———— ⌒ঌ ————

I offered Amma my arm as we made our way up the muddy hill
to His Garden of Perpetual Peace. The sky was dark, and the
rain started before we reached the top of the rise. Amma was in
her most respectable funeral dress, with a wide hat that shielded
most of her face from the rain, except for the bit of white lace

collar escaping beneath the brim. It was fastened at the neck with her best cameo, a sign of respect. I had seen it all last April, just as I had felt her good gloves on my arm, supporting me up this hill once before. This time I couldn't tell which one of us was doing the supporting.

I still wasn't sure why Macon wanted to be buried in the Gatlin cemetery, considering the way folks in this town felt about him. But according to Gramma, Lena's grandmother, Macon left strict instructions specifically requesting to be buried here. He purchased the plot himself, years ago. Lena's family hadn't seemed happy about it, but Gramma had put her foot down. They were going to respect his wishes, like any good Southern family.

Lena? I'm here.

I know.

I could feel my voice calming her, as if I had wrapped my arms around her. I looked up the hill, where the awning for the graveside service would be. It would look the same as any other Gatlin funeral, which was ironic, considering it was Macon's.

It wasn't yet daylight, and I could barely make out a few shapes in the distance. They were all crooked, all different. The ancient, uneven rows of tiny headstones standing at the graves of children, the overgrown family crypts, the crumbling white obelisks honoring fallen Confederate soldiers, marked with small brass crosses. Even General Jubal A. Early, whose statue watched over the General's Green in the center of town, was buried here. We made our way around the family plot of a few lesser-known Moultries, which had been there for so long the smooth magnolia trunk at the edge of the plot had grown into the side of the tallest stone marker, making them indistinguishable.

And sacred. They were all sacred, which meant we had reached the oldest part of the graveyard. I knew from my mother, the first word carved into any old headstone in Gatlin was *Sacred.* But as we got closer and my eyes adjusted to the darkness, I knew where the muddy gravel path was leading. I remembered where it passed the stone memorial bench at the grassy slope, dotted with magnolias. I remembered my father sitting on that bench, unable to speak or move.

My feet wouldn't go any farther, because they had figured out the same thing I had. Macon's Garden of Perpetual Peace was only a magnolia away from my mother's.

The twisting roads run straight between us.

It was a sappy line from an even sappier poem I had written Lena for Valentine's Day. But here in the graveyard, it was true. Who would have thought our parents, or the closest thing Lena had to one, would be neighbors in the grave?

Amma took my hand, leading me to Macon's massive plot. "Steady now."

We stepped inside the waist-high black railing around his gravesite, which in Gatlin was reserved for the perimeters of only the best plots, like a white picket fence for the dead. Sometimes it actually was a white picket fence. This one was wrought iron, the crooked door shoved open into the overgrown grass. Macon's plot seemed to carry with it an atmosphere of its own, like Macon himself.

Inside the railing stood Lena's family: Gramma, Aunt Del, Uncle Barclay, Reece, Ryan, and Macon's mother, Arelia, under the black canopy on one side of the carved black casket. On the other side, a group of men and a woman in a long black coat kept their distance from both the casket and the canopy, standing shoulder to shoulder in the rain. They were all bone-dry. It was like a church wedding split by an aisle down the middle, where the relatives of the bride line up opposite the relatives of the groom like two warring clans. There was an old man at one end of the casket, standing next to Lena. Amma and I stood at the other end, just inside the canopy.

Amma's grip on my arm tightened, and she pulled the gold charm she always wore out from underneath her blouse and rubbed it between her fingers. Amma was more than superstitious. She was a Seer, from generations of women who read tarot cards and communed with spirits, and Amma had a charm or a doll for everything. This one was for protection. I stared at the Incubuses in front of us, the rain running off their shoulders without leaving a trace. I hoped they were the kind that only fed on dreams.

I tried to look away, but it wasn't easy. There was something about an Incubus that drew you in like a spider's web, like any good predator. In the dark, you couldn't see their black eyes, and they almost looked like a bunch of regular guys. A few of them were dressed the way Macon always had, dark suits and expensive-looking overcoats. One or two looked more like construction workers on their way to get a beer after work, in jeans and work boots, their hands shoved in the pockets of their jackets. The woman was probably a Succubus. I had read about them, mostly in comics, and I thought they were just old wives' tales, like werewolves. But I knew I was wrong because she was standing in the rain, dry as the rest of them.

The Incubuses were a sharp contrast to Lena's family, cloaked in iridescent black fabric that caught what little light there was and refracted it, as if they were the source themselves. I had never seen them like this before. It was a strange sight, especially considering the strict dress code for women at Southern funerals.

In the center of it all was Lena. The way she looked was the opposite of magical. She stood in front of the casket with her fingers quietly resting upon it, as if Macon was somehow holding her hand. She was dressed in the same shimmering material as the rest of her family, but it hung on her like a shadow. Her black hair was twisted into a tight knot, not a trademark curl in sight. She looked broken and out of place, like she was standing on the wrong side of the aisle.

Like she belonged with Macon's other family, standing in the rain.

Lena?

She lifted her head, and her eyes met mine. Since her birthday, when one of her eyes had turned a shade of gold while the other remained deep green, the colors had combined to create a shade unlike anything I'd ever seen. Almost hazel at times, and unnaturally golden at others. Now they looked more hazel, dull and pained. I couldn't stand it. I wanted to pick her up and carry her away.

I can get the Volvo, and we can drive down the coast all the way to Savannah. We can hide out at my Aunt Caroline's.

I took another step closer to her. Her family was crowded around the casket, and I couldn't get to Lena without walking past the line of Incubuses, but I didn't care.

Ethan, stop! It's not safe—

A tall Incubus with a scar running down the length of his face, like the mark of a savage animal attack, turned his head to look at me. The air seemed to ripple through the space between us, like I had chucked a stone into a lake. It hit me, knocking the wind out of my lungs as if I'd been punched, but I couldn't react because I felt paralyzed—my limbs numb and useless.

Ethan!

Amma's eyes narrowed, but before she could take a step the Succubus put her hand on Scarface's shoulder and squeezed it, almost imperceptibly. Instantly, I was released from his hold, and the blood rushed back into my limbs. Amma gave her a grateful nod, but the woman with the long hair and the longer coat ignored her, disappearing back into line with the rest of them.

The Incubus with the brutal scar turned and winked at me. I got the message, even without the words. *See you in your dreams.*

I was still holding my breath when a white-haired gentleman, in an old-fashioned suit and string tie, stepped up to the coffin. His eyes were a dark contrast to his hair, which made him seem like some creepy character from an old black and white movie.

"The Gravecaster," Amma whispered. He looked more like the gravedigger.

He touched the smooth black wood, and a carved crest on the top of the coffin began to glow with a golden light. It looked like some old coat of arms, the kind of thing you saw at a museum or in a castle. I saw a tree with great spreading boughs, and a bird. Beneath it there was a carved sun, and a crescent moon.

"Macon Ravenwood of the House of Ravenwood, of Raven and Oak, Air and Earth. Darkness and Light." He took his hand from the coffin, and the light followed, leaving the casket dark again.

"Is that Macon?" I whispered to Amma.

"The light's symbolic. There's nothin' in that box. Wasn't anythin' left to bury. That's the way with Macon's kind—ashes to ashes and dust to dust, like us. Just a whole lot quicker."

The Gravecaster's voice rose up again. "Who consecrates this soul into the Otherworld?"

Lena's family stepped forward. "We do," they said in unison, everyone except Lena. She stood there staring down at the dirt.

"As do we." The Incubuses moved closer to the casket.

"Then let him be Cast to the world beyond. *Invado pacis, revert out Atrum Incendia.*" The Gravecaster held the light high over his head, and it flared brighter. "Go in peace, back to the Dark Fire from where you came." He threw the light into the air, and sparks showered down onto the coffin, searing into the wood where they fell. As if on cue, Lena's family and the Incubuses threw their hands into the air, releasing tiny silver objects not much bigger than quarters, which rained down onto Macon's coffin amidst the gold flames. The sky was starting to change color, from the black of night to the blue before the sunrise. I strained to see what the objects were, but it was too dark.

"*Per illa lacina, sit reus.* With these words, he is free."

An almost blinding white light emanated from the casket. I could barely see the Gravecaster a few feet in front of me, as if his voice was transporting us and we were no longer standing over a gravesite in Gatlin.

Uncle Macon! No!

The light flashed, like lightning striking, and died out. We were all back in the circle, looking at a mound of dirt and flowers. The burial was over. The coffin was gone. Aunt Del put her arms protectively around Reece and Ryan.

Macon was gone.

Lena fell forward onto her knees in the muddy grass.

The gate around Macon's plot slammed shut behind her, without so much as a finger touching it. This wasn't over for her. No one was going anywhere.

Lena?

The rain started to pick up almost immediately, the weather still tethered to her powers as a Natural, the ultimate elemental in the Caster world. She pulled herself to her feet.

Lena! This isn't going to change anything!

The air filled with hundreds of cheap white carnations and plastic flowers and palmetto fronds and flags from every grave visited in the last month, all flying loose in the air, tumbling airborne down the hill. Fifty years from now, folks in town would still be talking about the day the wind almost blew down every magnolia in His Garden of Perpetual Peace. The gale came on so fierce and fast, it was a slap in the face to everyone there, a hit so hard you had to stagger to stay on your feet. Only Lena stood straight and tall, holding fast to the stone marker next to her. Her hair had unraveled from its awkward knot and whipped in the air around her. She was no longer all darkness and shadow. She was the opposite — the one bright spot in the storm, as if the yellowish-gold lightning splitting the sky above us was emanating from her body. Boo Radley, Macon's dog, whimpered and flattened his ears at Lena's feet.

He wouldn't want this, L.

Lena put her face in her hands, and a sudden gust blew the

canopy out from where it was staked in the wet earth, sending it tumbling backward down the hill.

Gramma stepped in front of Lena, closed her eyes, and touched a single finger to her granddaughter's cheek. The moment she touched Lena, everything stopped, and I knew Gramma had used her abilities as an Empath to absorb Lena's powers temporarily. But she couldn't absorb Lena's anger. None of us were strong enough to do that.

The wind died down, and the rain slowed to a drizzle. Gramma pulled her hand away from Lena and opened her eyes.

The Succubus, looking unsusually disheveled, stared up at the sky. "It's almost sunrise." The sun was beginning to burn its way up through the clouds and over the horizon, scattering odd splinters of light and life across the uneven rows of headstones. Nothing else had to be said. The Incubuses started to dematerialize, the sound of suction filling the air. Ripping was how I thought of it, the way they pulled open the sky and disappeared.

I started to walk toward Lena, but Amma yanked my arm. "What? They're gone."

"Not all a them. Look—"

She was right. At the edge of the plot, there was only one Incubus remaining, leaning against a weathered headstone adorned with a weeping angel. He looked older than I was, maybe nineteen, with short, black hair and the same pale skin as the rest of his kind. But unlike the other Incubuses, he hadn't disappeared before the dawn. As I watched him, he moved out from under the shadow of the oak directly into the bright morning light, with his eyes closed and his face tilted toward the sun, as if it was only shining for him.

Amma was wrong. He couldn't be one of them. He stood there basking in the sunlight, an impossibility for an Incubus.

What was he? And what was he doing here?

He moved closer and caught my eye, as if he could feel me watching him. That's when I saw his eyes. They weren't the black eyes of an Incubus.

They were Caster green.

He stopped in front of Lena, jamming his hands in his pockets, tipping his head slightly. Not a bow, but an awkward show of deference, which somehow seemed more honest. He had crossed the invisible aisle, and in a moment of real Southern gentility, he could have been the son of Macon Ravenwood himself. Which made me hate him.

"I'm sorry for your loss."

He opened her hand and placed a small silver object in it, like the ones everyone had thrown onto Macon's casket. Her fingers closed around it. Before I could move a muscle, the unmistakable ripping sound tore through the air, and he was gone.

Ethan?

I saw her legs begin to buckle under the weight of the morning—the loss, the storm, even the final rip in the sky. By the time I made it to her side and slid my arm under her, she was gone, too. I carried her down the sloping hill, away from Macon and the cemetery.

She slept curled in my bed, on and off, for a night and a day. She had a few stray twigs matted in her hair, and her face was still flecked with mud, but she wouldn't go home to Ravenwood, and no one asked her to. I had given her my oldest, softest sweatshirt and wrapped her in our thickest patchwork quilt, but she never stopped shivering, even in her sleep. Boo lay at her feet, and Amma appeared in the doorway every now and then. I sat in the chair by the window, the one I never sat in, and stared out at the sky. I couldn't open it because a storm was still brewing.

As Lena was sleeping, her fingers uncurled. In them was a tiny bird made of silver, a sparrow. A gift from the stranger at Macon's funeral. I tried to take it from her hand just as her fingers tightened around it.

Two months later, and I still couldn't look at a bird without hearing the sound of the sky ripping open.